DEAF ROW

A

MYSTERY

BY

RON FRANSCELL

WILDBLUE
PRESS

WildBluePress.com

DEAF ROW published by:
WILDBLUE PRESS
P.O. Box 102440
Denver, Colorado 80250

WILDBLUE PRESS is registered at the U.S. Patent and Trademark Offices.

ISBN 978-1-957288-55-0 Hardcover
ISBN 978-1-957288-54-3 Trade Paperback
ISBN 978-1-957288-53-6 eBook

Interior Formatting by Elijah Toten
www.totencreative.com
Book Cover Design by Tatiana Villa
www.viladesign.net

DEAF ROW

To all old folks who feel overlooked, underestimated, invisible, and one good fart away from the Big Sleep.

"We're growing old. It's getting late."
—Ben Folds

"The tragedy of life is not death ...
but what we let die inside of us while we live."
—Norman Cousins

CHAPTER 1

WOODROW BELL CHECKED his watch, although he had no place special to be. Nursing homes just made him feel that time was passing unusually fast.

The big man damn-near filled the cramped visitors' foyer as he surveyed the dreary day room of the Old Miners Home. The sun was going down. It was Sunday, and the two nurses were elsewhere. Pale September twilight swathed the cheerless room as white-haired shadows silently drifted in for dinner, like dust that hadn't yet been blown away.

Now past seventy, Bell knew he, too, was closer to the end than the beginning. It haunted him.

It wasn't just the drabness of the Old Miners Home, with its dog-eared furniture, folding dinner tables, or the giant craft-paper calendar on the bulletin board that was utterly empty. It was the stiff knees … the hard mornings … the shrinking social circle … caring less and less about more and more … not remembering if it was the first time or the last time … getting up twice a night to pee a thimbleful … the AARP junk mail … the unreliable pecker … the fear you can't finish the Sunday crosswords because you must have Alzheimer's … the daughter who never calls … the mystery of why you ever voted for Democrats … already knowing which suit you'll be buried in ... and being invisible to the rest of the world.

It all pissed him off most days.

And today was one of those days. After months of making excuses, he'd been tricked by his closest friend, Father Bert Clancy, into visiting the Old Miners Home. It wasn't because a *priest* lied, not even because a *friend* lied, but because Bell didn't immediately realize he was being played. He especially hated that.

In truth, the St. Barnabas Senior Center hadn't been the Old Miners Home since the Nixon Administration, but everybody in the trifling mountain village of Midnight, Colorado, still called it the Old Miners Home. Good or bad, small towns seldom quit on a memory.

Ironically, there was more life in the Old Miners Home than the rest of Midnight.

But Bell still hated the place—or maybe the metaphor of the place—no matter what they called it. It made his prostate clench because of all the ways he might die, he most feared cancer down there.

The reason for Father Bert's subterfuge was George Tomer, once one of the regulars from the coffee shop, now confined to a wheelchair with Lou Gehrig's disease. He was only sixty-eight, only a few years younger than Bell. He was near the end.

Orphaned by a house fire as a teenager, the town had never expected much from George. He was liked well enough, or rather not disliked. He inspired no strong feelings either way. Neither academically nor athletically gifted, nobody noticed that he wasn't there with his twenty-nine classmates to collect his diploma.

That summer, he took a job as a mortuary apprentice at Richter's Funeral Home, sleeping in the dank basement with the occasional corpses and his boyhood rock collection (the only thing to survive the fire that killed his parents and sister). Every day, he had turned paler in appearance and spirit until he had lapsed into forlorn invisibility.

So when George Tomer unexpectedly announced his engagement to a beautiful out-of-town girl, his upcoming nuptials made him visible again. He rose, phoenix-like, from the ashes. This pallid orphan boy was no longer the pitiable night undertaker, but now a man in full, with prospects. He reveled in the attention.

For months, he glowed when he spoke about his beloved, a music major—or was she an art major?—at the University of Colorado. She grew more splendid with each retelling. The townsfolk of Midnight grew keen to meet this siren, but she never visited. Exams, you know, and European vacations to study the masters. Oh, and summers in the city.

Finally, the blue-haired ladies of the Sanitary Aid Society decided to throw an engagement party for young George and his bride-to-be. They set the date with a unanimous voice vote and dispatched a delegation to inform George, who was rendered literally speechless by the news.

On the day George's beloved was to be introduced to Midnight, tragedy struck. The girl was killed in a car crash. When the girl's obituary appeared in the next week's Midnight Sun, the town grieved as much for her as it might for any favorite daughter. Poor George had endured another unspeakable loss, and still so young. The community tried to express sympathy to the young lady's family, but the cards and bouquets all came back as undeliverable.

It wasn't long before they discovered the girl had never existed. She had been a figment of young George Tomer's desperation. And because he was a mortician, he lost his license for reporting a fake obituary.

George never married, and he never left Midnight. He went back to being pitiable and transparent. He burrowed into his lonely life selling polished river rocks to tourists. Sometimes, he'd disappear for days into the endless mountains and gulches around Midnight, collecting stones that he'd bring home to the constantly churning tumblers in the dirt-floor basement of a weather-beaten, clapboard bungalow that was crumbling around him.

And every morning in his later years, when he thought maybe everyone had forgotten about his make-believe bride, he wandered down to Tommyknockers Café to listen to the old men who told their bullshit stories, argued about nonsense, relived glory days that were never as glorious as the retelling, solved all the problems of the world, and called themselves—only partly in jest—Deaf Row.

Small towns have long memories, and Midnight was no different. And none of the codgers of Deaf Row had forgotten George's imaginary girlfriend. They merely needed all the friends they could get. And besides, this quiet, mild-mannered rock hound whose life was marred by one little fantasy was no more wicked than any of them. Who among them had never lied about a woman?

Then George got Lou Gehrig's and within a few years, he needed more care than he could give himself. He'd lived at St. Barnabas for three years now. Thanks to Father Bert, the church covered the costs of his care, but George was more forgotten than ever. Only the old men of Deaf Row, George's last and only friends, came around to see him anymore.

Backing through the balky door from the home's residential wing, Father Bert wheeled George into the dayroom. He parked his friend at his favorite spot beside a cracked window that on warmer evenings would open onto Sunrise Street, a narrow alley that ran past the east end of the two-story brick building. Likewise, at the western end of the building was Sunset Street. How appropriate, Bell thought, that a nursing home would be built precisely between Sunrise and Sunset. It couldn't have been a coincidence, Bell thought. He simply didn't believe in coincidence.

"Good to see you, George," Bell said, dragging a folding chair close while Father Bert fastened the top button on George's brown cardigan. Bell recognized it as one of Father Bert's old sweaters.

The crooked silhouette of a smile fell across George's thin, cracked lips, then was gone. Most of his nervous system was dead or dying, although his senses of smell, sight, taste, hearing and touch were apparently intact. His muscles were decaying, writhing uncontrollably under his parchment-thin skin. His breathing was tortured and shallow, and getting worse. Unable to swallow, his dinner flowed through a tube … and his doctors knew he was completely aware of his own slow death.

"Looking good, you ol' coot," Bell said. "Got a new girlfriend yet?"

Father Bert shot a disapproving scowl. George's imaginary girlfriend never really died, but instead lived on in the merciless teasing he endured placidly for years on Deaf Row, as if maybe he knew he deserved it. But for Bell and the others, the jibes were a sign of affection among brothers.

George's right index finger twitched.

"That means 'no,'" Father Bert interpreted. In truth, it also meant "yes," "hello," and anything else George wanted to say but couldn't. His finger flutters were always open to interpretation.

Death was Bell's life work. He'd poked his fingers in it as a Denver homicide detective, caused it as a combat grunt, questioned it as a son. Even if he hadn't come to a certain détente with death, he recognized all its cruel colors. He had to admit he liked its infallibility: death is, after all, statistically and historically more certain than life. Once it exists, every living thing struggles desperately to stay alive, yet being dead requires no effort whatsoever. Simple.

Living was more mysterious to him. Especially toward the end. Dying was messier, less comfortable and—to him— stunk worse than actually being dead. Bell didn't want to die, to be sure, but he especially didn't relish the dying.

Bell shifted in the rickety little folding chair. At six-four, two hundred and fifty pounds, he wasn't fat, just mountainous. And that's what his gunny started calling him back in 'Nam: Mountain Bell. The nickname stuck through thirty-four years as a Denver cop and followed him into retirement in Midnight.

"The guys keep your chair open down at Tommyknockers. Just for you," he said. "We're minus one butt."

Tears seeped into George's blue eyes, but he could say nothing. He was locked inside there somewhere, unable to speak and barely able to cry about it.

George struggled to lift his quaking right arm, which hadn't yet shriveled into a curled claw like his left. He stretched his clenched hand toward Bell.

"He has something for you, Mountain," Father Bert said, "even though you're an ass who doesn't deserve it."

"Such language for a priest ... especially an ass of a priest," Bell said as he clasped George's hand and felt something fall into his palm from the trembling fingers.

It was a small but heavy black stone, impossibly shiny. Its mirror-smooth finish was not silver but almost metallic. A pebble in Mountain Bell's callused bearpaw of a hand.

"Why, that's really something, George," he said, holding it up between his thick thumb and index finger. "It's ..."

"Hematite," Father Bert said. "Bloodstone. Legend says it's only found on ancient battlefields. The petrified blood of warriors. Some folks think it inspires optimism, but they don't know you like I do."

Bell turned the stone in his thick fingers.

"You found this, George? You polished it?"

Again, a smile surfaced for a fleeting moment then sunk back into the impenetrable, diseased shell that encased George.

"He knew you were coming," Father Bert said, "and he wanted you to have it. It was in a little box he marked PROFANITY PEAK. He wouldn't leave his room today without it. For you."

Bell wasn't good at being soft. It seldom came out right. Even when he might have saved his marriage so long ago, when the right words eluded him. Even when it might repair the frayed connection with his daughter Sarah. Even when his own father was dying. Now, it was too late to try.

"This rock is … damn special," Bell said, managing his best rumpled smile. "I'll keep it for good luck. Maybe put it in a … I dunno … a belt buckle or something. Thanks."

Suddenly, George erupted in a massive coughing jag. Two nurses rushed to his side as Father Bert and Bell stood by helplessly.

"He'll be fine," the nursing supervisor spoke in a calming voice as she loosened George's collar. "Only saliva in his lungs. Happens a lot, bless his heart. His throat just doesn't work right. But we need to take him back to his room to settle him down and help clear it out."

The priest and Bell watched as they wheeled George back through the heavy old oak doors to his little room in the hallway on the other side. The nurse turned to them and forced a smile.

"It means a lot that you came," she said. "He'll be fine …well, you know what I mean. But please don't stop coming."

OUTSIDE THE OLD Miners Home, Bell paced the buckled sidewalk of Main Street as he fingered the black stone in the pocket of his leather jacket.

A car passing on Main Street flipped on its headlights. The twilight sky was high, and the first stars were out. Except for its warm glow on the highest peaks around Midnight, the sun had set and the air was turning cold. Somewhere, someone had laid a fire and the slightest whiff of burning pine made Mountain Bell hope for a long autumn and a short winter. Winters, though, seemed to be getting longer.

He also hoped, for George's sake, that the dying would be short. If not painless, then as merciful and swift as possible. He didn't want to come back, ever.

The lowering light cast a pall over Midnight. The first snow wouldn't be long.

The dinner hour came earlier in September. The sidewalks rolled up at dark, except for the places that still served beer. As Bell loitered there waiting for Father Bert, Duke Kelleher passed in his old primer-gray pickup, lifting two fingers from the steering wheel in a tepid wave. Bell nodded back at the retired mechanic, an unrepentant drunk who likely hadn't worked on an engine since "Little Deuce Coupe" was a Top 40 hit.

Bell felt right at home.

Nine years ago, when he finally put in his papers at the Denver Police Department, his pension bought more than his tidy, century-old Victorian with bad pipes and peeling gingerbread. It bought solitude. Space. Freedom.

He'd waited on a lot of cold sidewalks in his life. There were some things people simply didn't understand about cops, and he got tired of explaining himself. Toward the end, every time he'd tell a story, it came out like an apology. Bell wasn't good at apologies, even the ones he should have made. So he stopped explaining.

"Are the visiting hours over?" The man's voice startled Bell, who was rarely caught off-guard.

Bell turned to see an elderly man, maybe in his nineties, standing a breath's distance away. Unruly wisps of white hair sprouted haphazardly from his veiny scalp. His neatly pressed Oxford shirt was buttoned all the way to the loose-fitting collar around his withered neck, but he wore no tie. One wingtip was untied. He wore no coat but held a single artificial daisy in his palsied hand. He smelled vaguely of ointment stains and old mattresses. Bell knew almost everyone in town, at least by sight, but this old man was a stranger.

"No," Bell said. "I think they're just serving dinner."

"Are you a doctor?"

Bell smirked.

"Not hardly."

"You should be. You look like a doctor, you know."

After a lifetime of making snap decisions about people, Bell was amused. He'd played many outsized roles in his undercover days—bouncers, carnies, bikers, even a slicked-back televangelist who had a thing for little boys—but never a doctor.

"Maybe I coulda been a doctor," Bell said, "but my ex-wife always said I was too quick to lose my patience."

It took a few seconds, but the old guy finally got it. He laughed delicately, as if a full-blown guffaw might rupture something.

"Oh, that's rich! 'Lose patience,'" the old man said, so delicately patting the upper arm of Bell's leather jacket that he barely felt it. "I get it! Very funny, you know."

A streetlight hummed to life in the dying light. Father Bert was still inside. Bell checked his watch.

"Visiting somebody?" the talkative old guy asked.

"A friend. You?"

"My wife. She's waiting inside. I come every week."

His ex-wife always said Bell's smile looked like an unmade bed, flat and mussed up. He was no better at smiling than he was at being soft, two flaws which, when he thought about it, could be related.

"The flower is for her?"

"Oh yes," the old man said. "A daisy. That's her name, you know. Daisy Nelson. Today's her birthday, you know. I can't bake a cake, but I can bring her flowers, you know."

"I'm sure she'll like that."

"Nelson."

"Sorry …?" Bell said.

"Luther Nelson. That's me, you know. The boys call me Nellie."

The old man extended his bony right hand, which felt like it might turn to powder in Bell's big paw. The handshake was airy.

"Happy to meet you, Nellie. I'm Woodrow Bell. Um, the boys call me Mountain."

The old man did a double-take. His frayed smile revealed his toothless, gray gums.

"Oh. Mountain Bell, eh? Catchy. I get it! The phone company. Very funny, you know."

Yeah, funny, Bell thought. He chafed about the nickname at first, but it grew on him. It used to draw a few smiles, but since the phone company known as Mountain Bell was swallowed up in corporate mergers more than thirty years before, few people under forty understood the reference.

"Not from around here, are you, Nellie?"

"Oh my, no. Got a place up the road in Wisdom Gulch."

Bell had never met anyone from Wisdom Gulch, an abandoned company town that was corroding high up in the mountains. The ruins were accessible only by foolhardy rubes who routinely risked their lives and trucks on a treacherously narrow, white-knuckle switchback the locals called O'MyGawd Road.

"I thought Wisdom Gulch was a ghost town," Bell said. "I never saw anybody up there."

"Oh no," the old man said. "Just gotta know where to look, you know. Lots of folks up in there. My mother and father have a place just down the road from me."

Bell cocked his good ear toward the old man.

"Pardon me," he said. "Who lives down the road from you?"

"My mother and father."

Bell saw no trace of insincerity in Luther Nelson's shrunken face. He knew the contours of deceit, the little tells that even the best liars and grifters couldn't mask. Luther Nelson hadn't misspoken, and he wasn't lying, but this shriveled little man couldn't possibly have living parents.

"Your mother and father are alive?" Bell asked.

"Of course!" Nellie replied. "They're waiting for us. Got a big venison roast in the oven, just like the old days, you know. I told them you were coming. They'll be so glad to see you! So much has happened while you were overseas. Oh, and bring all your medals!"

The evening air turned cold. Bell took off his jacket and draped it around Luther Nelson's bony shoulders.

"Let's go inside, Nellie," Bell said softly. "Daisy must be worried about you."

The old man smiled as Bell guided him back toward the Old Miners Home.

"Are you a doctor?" he asked Bell. "You look like a doctor, you know."

Bell patted the gnarled hand that had looped around his big forearm for support as they shuffled toward the front door.

"No, Nellie," he said. "I'm just an old cop."

Luther Nelson stopped stone-cold in his scanty tracks.

"Oh my, then you found her killer?"

Bell fumbled for a coherent answer to an incoherent question, but he only had another question.

"Whose killer?"

"Cherish. My little girl. A sin, what they done to her."

"Cherish?"

"That's her name. Have you seen her?"

Bell took a deep breath and looked into Nellie's rheumy, faded green eyes.

"Nellie, did someone kill Cherish?"

The old man stopped and stared off toward the darkening mountains. His lips quivered. Tears welled in his eyes. A keening like a wounded rabbit rose in him. Without a word, Nellie lifted a trembling hand toward his face and jabbed his gnarled index finger into his right ear.

Again.

And again.

Before Bell could calm him, Nellie's ragged, yellowed fingernail had pierced the fragile skin of his ear. As gently as he could, Bell restrained the old man's hand as a thin red line of blood trickled down Nellie's neck and stained his collar.

Father Bert, looking concerned, stepped out of the home's main door, and saw them. He hurried to help Bell with the agitated old man.

"My God, Nellie," the priest said, "you had us worried. Let's get back inside where it's warm and take a look at you."

Nellie didn't resist as Bell and Father Bert led him back into the warmth of the nursing home. Once safely inside, Bell stood in the doorway, partly to block another escape but mostly to avoid stepping even two paces farther into that sorry wasteland.

As Father Bert delivered Nellie to the relieved nurses, the old man turned to Bell. His eyes were sad, beseeching.

"I want to go home, doctor," he begged as they led him back through the dayroom, among the colorless ghosts who were no more tethered to their present than Luther Nelson. Nobody looked up. They were sheltered in their own worlds, which cast hopeless shadows across their sallow faces. And it seemed poor Luther Nelson's last, best memory was one best forgotten.

"Please let me go home, doctor! Tell them!" Nellie cried to Bell as they led him away toward a calming chemical fog. Their eyes locked for a split second before Nellie and his keepers disappeared behind those distant doors on the sunset side. "Tell them, please. My daughter is waiting at home for me!"

Bell had seen enough. Dying shouldn't be so hard, he thought.

He stared at the floor, helpless and a little angry.

On the cold tile lay Nellie's plastic daisy, bloodied.

CHAPTER 2

A SIGN IN the window read, "Tommyknockers Diner … Wireless Since 1899."

As usual, Bell arrived late on that chilly Monday morning, a freckle past seven. He'd stayed awake late, haunted by Luther Nelson and the unsettling scene at the Old Miners Home. Now, he craved steak and eggs—and answers.

"You're late, Woodrow," said Cotton Minahan, the old fire chief. "Day's damn near done. We're all morning people here."

Bell growled as he sloughed off his heavy leather coat and draped it over his usual chair beside Father Bert.

"Yeah, well, I hate morning people," Bell grumbled. "And mornings. And people."

The morning began, as it did any day Father Bert was there, with a blessing. Frankly, it always pushed the limits of priestly propriety. Most Catholics believe a prayer is a direct and intimate conversation with God, and the person praying—particularly if he's a priest—must show the appropriate respect for the Almighty. Humor is taboo. But Father Bert Clancy, who had a history of nonconformity that the Archbishop privately might have called "blurry blasphemy," tended to include his secular friends and their foibles in his conversations. The Pope wouldn't approve, but the Pope didn't live in Midnight.

So, the old priest crossed himself and bowed his head:

"God, please grant us the senility to forget the people who never liked us, the good fortune to run into the ones who did, and the eyesight to tell the difference. Through Christ our Lord. Amen."

Deaf Row's non-Catholics waved their fingers wildly across their chests like spastics. Some of the guys had been there since Fancy O'Neil, the waitress, put the first pot of coffee on at six a.m. Hell, they competed fiercely to be the first one at the door when it was unlocked. To a bunch of old guys who no longer noticed they were no longer noticed, being first at anything was a monumental triumph. Old men settle for small victories.

They called themselves Deaf Row. They were an irregular crew of old men who held fast to the little-boy tradition of naming their club, which, in this case, was just a small-town coffee klatsch.

On any given morning (except Sunday) seven or eight old guys gathered at a table in Tommyknockers' front window to fabulate, debate and cuss about all the things that occupy old men: death, politics, colonoscopies, guns, women, cars, sex, loss, the senselessness of designer coffee, mortality, how time moves more quickly now, Viagra, missed opportunities in life, prostates, the diverse flavors of Metamucil, and fishing. Or something really deep and important, such as the relative stamina of car batteries, which might be a metaphor for what keeps old men alive when they don't really want to talk about what keeps old men alive.

These were the kind of guys who never once wore cufflinks. Most struggled with the pervasive notion that nobody in a small town ever did much worth doing. Their little lives in their little town left little mark.

So when Bell arrived, the regular crew, minus Doc William Frederick Ely, was there. "Bones"—as everyone called him—was a retired GP who'd doctored Midnight for more than fifty years and bragged about circumcising every mayor since 1979. The table was already steaming through its regular fourth pot and arguing its regular nonsense. Today, that happened to be an argument over the fragility of mountains.

"Them are real mountains," said Minahan, who "retired" shortly after he was ticketed for drunk fire-truck racing. He pointed at an Alaska 1998 calendar that had never been taken down from Tommyknockers' cluttered wall for more than twenty years. But when he wasn't being a smartass, he was a dumbass.

"They look all sharp and wild," Minahan insisted. "Not like these pussy mountains in Colorado. People have wore 'em down."

Dan Coogan snorted. He was the retired editor of the town's weekly newspaper, the semi-conscious *Midnight Sun,* where he still wrote a local history column every week. He also had only one vocal cord and sounded a lot like Andy Devine when he talked.

"People don't wear down mountains!"

The obstinate Cotton Minahan dug in.

"Well, in the old days they did!"

"Minahan, you're the most unnecessary genius in the world," Coogan squeaked back. "You're the Einstein of total unnecessariness. It's high time the world celebrated you."

Minahan didn't miss a beat. He was indeed a preternatural genius: He had an instinctive knowledge of people, which he used to push their buttons.

"Hey, Coog, do you recall that one time when I asked for your opinion?"

The balding old newspaperman pondered it for a second.

"No."

"Me neither."

Bell and the rest of Deaf Row laughed. Even Fancy, a one-time hippie chick who got snowed-in at Midnight for the hard winter of '69 and never left. She was long past her sell-by date. But she'd waited on the old guys for damn near twenty years now. She knew everything they'd forgotten. Now, she whisked in to refill empty cups, her subtle way of changing the subject.

For every birthday, she'd bring out a cinnamon roll with a single candle, and she'd hector each one of them until they bought tins of caramel popcorn and Christmas nuts for her granddaughter's school fund-raisers. She held her own with these guys because she'd long ago learned these lions were toothless, and even though she was hurtling toward the end of her middle age, being their "young gal" gave her enormous power over them.

Plus, she loved each one more than she'd ever admit. She always cried when one died.

And many had died. On a high shelf above the daily specials were seventeen upside-down coffee mugs, one for every Deaf Row inmate who'd passed. And every Fourth of July morning, the living raised their cups to the dead. More recently, it had become a tradition for somebody to mark that solemn moment with a deliberate belch.

To everyone else, they were only relics in a museum. Tommyknockers Diner, which smelled like bacon, coffee and toast even after it closed every night, occupied the first floor of the old opera house built a couple years before the turn of the last century. Now, it was owned by a bank that couldn't sell it; its upper floors were empty, and Tommyknockers had been its only tenant for thirty years.

The cafe was named for the grizzled, trickster gnomes that haunted the mines. Mostly invisible, tommyknockers were said to be the ghosts of dead miners whose underground tappings were either a sign of good luck or a warning of an impending cave-in. One could never be sure. But despite the lack of clarity, a miner risked eternal misery if he doubted the tommyknockers' power.

The mahogany walls—original to the eatery's opera-house days—were festooned with dozens of old hardhats, each one bearing the name of countless area mines and the name of the miner who wore it. Some dating back to the 1800s weren't hardhats at all, merely shellac-brimmed derbies with carbide lamps. Seven different calendars from seven random years adorned the place. And slapped across the front of the old-fashioned cash register was a bright red bumper sticker:

We're all here because
we're not all there

But Tommyknockers was otherwise a perfectly cheap hometown diner where itinerant cooks worked only until they afford to blow town. Where vintage Formica tables and vinyl-padded chairs teetered on the uneven wood floors. Where lunch was served on a ragged assortment of plates, mostly survivors of four decades of careless waitresses. And most of whose thick ceramic coffee mugs, white as Sunday, bore battle scars.

"All right, listen up, fellow codgers. I got an announcement," said Ollie Fuhrman as he stood to address this society of old farts and a couple of leaf-peepers who stopped for breakfast.

One of the regulars, Ollie was in his 80s, a former Korean War Seabee who came home after the war and started a rock-hauling business. Not a quarry, just a service to haul boulders that routinely fell on county roads, construction sites, and the occasional house. He sold most of these monstrous stones as landscape décor for the flatlanders' McMansions down in the Denver suburbs. Now his son ran the place.

"I'm gonna run for county commission," Ollie said with great flourish.

"Whatever for?" asked Roxy Snipes as he dumped a third teaspoonful of sugar into his cup.

The annoyingly analytical Roxy was like a dog who chases cars: Once he got what he was after, he rarely knew what to do with it. As the former bookkeeper for the Cibola Mine, the last big operation to close in Flatiron County, his main preoccupation since his wife Eunice died ten years ago was a running game of Solitaire he played on his thirty-year-old Tandy computer (which he bought used). That's all he did on his crappy little machine, only Solitaire. Nobody really knew how many games he'd played, or how much imaginary money he lost, but he kept track of it all. Meticulously. Obsessively.

But the methodical Roxy fervently believed he'd discovered "the secret math" of Solitaire—plus, he wanted his imaginary money back. Roxy's magical key was seven. That's all. Just seven.

But when his confidence wavered, he believed it might be eight.

Or six. And lately, he'd begun to suspect the intentions of the jacks.

Still, Ollie was insulted.

"Why do you play Solitaire, you finicky old dipstick?"

It was a question that had never occurred to the soft-spoken bookkeeper, who tucked his weak chin in the collar of his starched button-down shirt and stared silently at his lap.

"Because you're bored, Snipes, ferchrissakes," Ollie continued. "You're bored. I'm bored. We're all just bored old men, goddammit. At least I'm doing *something* before my pecker dries up and falls completely off. Sorry, Father Bert, for sayin' pecker and all that other stuff."

Father Bert smiled and raised his hand as if to bless his irreverent friend. The cussing was mere background noise to Father Bert. He'd been a combat chaplain in Vietnam and hadn't celebrated a Mass at St. Barnabas since he retired ten years back. He was no stranger to profanity. He even used it to great advantage, not always gracefully.

At seventy-five, Father Bert Clancy wasn't Deaf Row's oldest member but was the most senior, having outlived all those before him. He was also its most reliable. Even though he volunteered generously at the Old Miner's Home he had once helped to keep open, he seldom missed a morning with his buddies. His presence reassured them, and he knew that.

And Bell … well, he liked the way a good cuss word rolled around in his mouth, too.

"That's very good news, Ollie," Bell said. "Let me be the first to say I'm voting for you, dammit."

"Why, thank you, Woodrow. Your endorsement means a lot to this old bastard."

Bell shrugged as he cut into his breakfast steak, medium rare.

"It's just that I hate politicians and I reckon there's no way you'll live long enough to finish your first term," he said as he dipped a hunk of steak in his over-easy egg yolk. "In my eyes, that pretty much makes you a perfect politician."

Deaf Row again erupted in laughter. Even Fancy smiled broadly, although deep down inside she hoped none of them, even Ollie Fuhrman, would die anytime soon.

"I'm afraid I might be lactose intolerant," Elroy Richter interjected, apropos of nothing. Elroy's father inherited and ran Richter Funeral Home for fifty years. His greatest hope in life was that no customer would suddenly wake up in his embalming room. His second greatest hope was that his son Elroy would take over the family business someday.

He didn't.

A father hopes his son will love what he loves, but Elroy didn't share any of his father's hopes. He started his working life as a summer-vacation mortician's apprentice. The most practical professional advice his father offered was to always fill the hearse's gas tank the afternoon before Midnight High School's junior prom because it was a drunker-driving night than New Year's Eve.

One day, a young man's decapitated corpse was delivered from a horrifying one-car crash on the O'MyGawd Road. Elroy tended to the boy's mangled, headless torso until a deputy delivered the head. Elroy recognized him as a boy from school. Head here and body there, he walked out of the embalming room and never went back. Not even when his father's arthritis made embalming impossible, forcing Elroy's dad to sell the family mortuary.

They didn't ever have much of a relationship after that. Elroy eventually went off to college and became a teacher. He came home to Midnight to instill a passion for chemistry and physics in hormonal high school kids who only cared about the chemistry and physics of making out in the backseat.

Today, Elroy worried the cream in his coffee was killing him—the same cream he'd been drinking most mornings for at least fifteen years.

"You're crazy, Elroy," Minahan sneered.

"Go to hell, Cotton," Elroy snapped back. "I'd just hate to wake up in the future and find I'm not there."

But dying was about the only thing Midnight could count on.

With fewer than nine hundred taxpaying souls, Midnight was wedged deep in the crotch of a high-mountain canyon. It was barely a half-mile, limit to limit. Nobody came here anymore, so between the kids who lit out for Denver at first chance and the ones who died, this small town just kept dwindling.

Once, more than a hundred years ago, it was known as "the richest square mile in the world" because the plentiful gold seemed inexhaustible. Thousands of dreamers came. Overnight, a small city boomed, populated by dreamers who clawed, carved and cracked open the mountain's belly for the ore inside.

Fortunes were won and lost. Midnight thrived as hotels, saloons, gambling halls, and whorehouses sprung up like weeds. There was even a grand opera house where Oscar Wilde and Buffalo Bill himself performed among the celebrities of the day. Midnight, not Denver, might have become the capital of Colorado but for the lack of a single vote when it came time to choose.

But when the gold played out, Midnight dried up as quickly as it had blossomed. The faintest hearts left, but the real dreamers hung on, fanning out into the treacherous mountains to seek gold and silver on tiny claims that honeycombed countless gullies, ravines, and talus slopes. In time they, too, abandoned their dreams, leaving punctured, wounded mountains that would never completely heal. To hike in those mountains around Midnight today was to risk falling into claustrophobic shafts where nobody would ever find you, so deep your screams would die before they reached fresh air.

Crumbling Colorado 58 and glacial Lame Johnny Creek no longer delivered riches, except for the sun-burned, pothead snowboarders heading back down the mountain at the ass-end of winter weekends. They spilled down the mountains from higher up in Vail or Breckenridge, all passersby.

The whole town used to work for a living, but now most didn't care much. Main Street had no shoe store, no car wash, no A&W (which closed for vacation five years ago and never re-opened), no mechanic and no dry goods— but four saloons and a brew pub, a pizza place, a part-time Chamber of Commerce, a nursing home, a bank, and Tommyknockers Diner.

Midnight's town hall was housed in a former grand hotel that was now a building inspector's nightmare; the four-man police department filled the kitchen and its lone jail cell had once been the territory's first walk-in freezer (according to a weathered bronze historical plaque on the front steps). The most hopeful structures in town were the two schools where enrollment ebbed, and an old Carnegie library that functioned more as an Internet café than a book lender.

The post office was built in 1959 and was still the newest building in town.

At the far end of town was the unfortunately named Bar F restaurant and motel, whose gas station rented skis to the flatlanders in winter. Its incandescent yellow-and-red livery diverted a passerby's attention, however briefly, from thin-shingled cottages stripped of all traces of paint by weather and time, boarded-up storefronts that long ago quit seeking tenants, cockeyed chain-link fences, and the snow and ice that lay like a stubborn glacier on the south side of Main Street, in the perpetual shadow of mostly empty, red brick buildings.

More than a hundred years of history had come and gone. Midnight's moment had passed. Most everybody in town was merely waiting, with varying degrees of patience, to die. The only mystery was how the end would come.

But a different mystery possessed Elroy Richter, now an octogenarian who sold his family's mortuary in the Nineties, but still filled in when the lone embalmer took vacation or was hungover.

He was sniffing his index finger intently.

"Smell this," he said, holding his knobby, discolored finger under Cotton Minahan's suddenly unwilling nose. "That smell right to you?"

Minahan shoved his hand away.

"Jesus Christ Almighty, Elroy," he snarled. "I don't even want to think where that goddamned birdy claw has been — sorry, Father Bert, but some people exceed the limits of my medication."

BY NINE A.M., most of Deaf Row had scattered back to whatever occupied them for the rest of their days. Only Bell, Father Bert and the old newspaperman Coogan remained.

They nursed their last lukewarm cups while Fancy scribbled the lunch specials on a green chalkboard behind the counter and the dishwasher made a racket in back.

"You know, Bert, that was a chickenshit thing you did yesterday," Bell said.

The priest feigned ignorance.

"You gotta be more specific, big man."

"You set me up."

"I set you up?" the priest asked in his calmest pastoral voice. "I took you to visit an old friend who is lonely and all locked up in himself. You made a dying man's day a little brighter. Yeah, I can see why you're pissed."

"Yeah, I'm pissed. First, I hate that place," Bell snapped. "And second, you know it."

"You did a good thing, Woodrow. What's good isn't always easy," Father Bert said. "A cop oughta know that."

"Yeah, well, if you do it again, this cop oughta shoot you," Bell chided. The words still hung in the air as he wondered if it were a sin to threaten to shoot a priest.

The three old men sat in uncharacteristic silence for a moment. Coogan scratched his pure white mop of perpetually uncombed hair and Father Bert swirled his creamy coffee as if he hadn't swirled it twenty times already. Through Tommyknockers' plate glass window, Bell could see the mid-morning sun barely peeking into the upper floors of the buildings across Main Street. Another morning drifted by.

"Tell me about the old fella on the sidewalk," Bell said. "Luther Nelson."

"Sad story," Father Bert said, staring down into his cup. "Born and raised up in Wisdom Gulch. His dad was a hard-rock miner in the good ol' days and so was Luther until the Oro played out. Brother killed in Guadalcanal or Iwo Jima. His wife Daisy died—when, Coogan? Maybe ten, fifteen years ago? Luther lived alone in his little shack up in Wisdom Gulch, same house where he grew up, until the dementia started ten years ago. So I brought him down the mountain to the Old Miner's Home."

Bell grimaced.

"So he's … confused?"

Father Bert pursed his thin lips.

"Some days are better than others," he said. "Funny thing about Alzheimer's, the memories are lost in reverse order, so he can remember good moments with his daughter, but not his own age. The good moments are coming in shorter bursts these days. But he's safe and warm and gets three hots."

"He said he had a little girl. Cherish. What happened?"

"Murdered. Back in the late Sixties, I think. Terrible thing. He and his wife never got over it. Some days, like yesterday, it all washes over him again like it happened yesterday. Other days, she's alive and coming to visit. It's a cruel disease, Woodrow. It sometimes takes all the good memories and leaves only the bad."

Coogan, a walking encyclopedia of local history, piped up.

"You know, I read all the stories in the *Sun*'s morgue about it," the old editor said, taking off his thick glasses. "Happened right before I got here. One of those freaky things, real grisly. Back in those days, reporters avoided being too graphic, so the Sun's stories kind of danced around the gruesome stuff. People were scared to death. But those same folks who complain about lurid crap in a 'family' newspaper were gleefully gossiping about every gory detail."

"What do you mean 'freaky'?"

Father Bert shook his head.

"Oh, I heard horrible things. I came to St. Barnabas after the war, but people were still talking about it. Worst thing that ever happened around here."

Coogan nodded.

"People said she was raped and a big spike was hammered through her brain. Somebody told me her eyes were sewn shut. Maybe just rumors. I was just a kid, first job as a reporter, and I'd never heard such things. To this day, I don't know how much was true. You know how a story grows in a small town."

Bell was intrigued.

"Did they ever catch the killer?"

"Never did," Coogan said. "Local folks blamed Satan worshippers from Denver. Or a wandering biker gang from California. Or hopped-up hippies. A hundred stupid theories but no answers. I don't think the local cops ever had a clue."

Bell leaned back in his chair and crossed his thick arms over his head as he stared at the elaborate pressed-tin ceiling, another relic of the old building's past.

"There's always a clue," he said. "Coog, is there any way I could get copies of those stories?"

THE DAY WARMED up, and Bell spent most of it in his shed with his cursed weathervane.

Some old men only get older. Some get obsessions. Roxy Snipes had his solitaire. Father Bert had the Old Miners Home. Dan Coogan had his weekly newspaper column. Ollie Fuhrman had whatever kept his pecker from drying up. And Bell had his weathervane.

Not long after Bell bought his old prairie Victorian house in Midnight—a sturdy brick Carpenter Gothic originally built by one of Midnight's turn-of-the-century mine bosses—he dreamed of a big wind. Because he didn't believe dreams were anything but a brain scrambling to make sense of random synaptic sparks, he didn't even attempt to give it meaning. But in his dream, he saw a peculiar weathervane spinning wildly at the highest point of his steeply pitched roof. Its ornament was a black iron rabbit, but unlike the directionals whirling beneath it, it didn't spin in the storm. The rabbit's butt remained steadfastly pointed into the wind, backasswards.

Only Bell knew the significance of the rabbit. Over the next few months, he scavenged what he needed to build it— angle iron from a broken bed frame, a front-wheel spindle from a wrecked car, a smooth sheet of steel from an old truck hood, rusty rods from an abandoned mine headframe in the mountains, and some lost hubcaps from weeds along the highway. He'd grown up on a farm, so he knew the basics of cutting torches and welders.

Problem was, Bell could never balance his weathervane perfectly. He could never make his rabbit properly face *into* the wind. If it moved at all, it always pointed downwind. It simply didn't work. He'd weighed his parts meticulously, shaved off fractions of fractions of ounces, positioned every piece with NASA precision. It still didn't work.

So Bell's frustrating weathervane was mothballed for months at a time, coming out only on those days (and nights) when his mind and his hands were unsettled. Today was one of those days.

Bell filed down a weld as Dan Coogan appeared in the doorway, sun at his back. He had a fat manila envelope in his hand.

"I knocked but you didn't answer," Coogan said. "I figured you might be out here."

Bell glanced at his watch. Four o'clock.

"Christ, Coog, time flies. I get lost down here."

"Might help if you had a cell phone, Woodrow. Or any kind of phone, for that matter."

How odd, Bell thought, that Coogan's damaged voice sounded like his half-round file rasping against iron.

"Nobody calls and I don't call anybody," Bell said. "I don't need to send pictures of my private parts to anybody. My damn thumbs are too big to type on those tiny little keyboards. And whatever I'm doing, I don't want to be interrupted."

"Charlie never calls?"

"Nope."

"Why?"

Bell didn't miss a beat.

"Because I don't have a phone."

A bemused Coogan tossed his envelope on Bell's workbench.

"Yeah, well, there's everything you ever wanted to know about Cherish Nelson's murder and a little that you didn't. There's a few pictures in there and some old notes, but mostly just copies of stories. Fresh from the *Sun*'s morgue, where stories go to die."

Bell slid an inch-thick sheaf of photocopies from the envelope.

"Thanks, Coog," he said. "Gimme the short version."

"December 1969. Seventeen-year-old girl's mutilated body was found in the mines' old dynamite bunker up on Powderhouse Road that even squatters abandoned back in the '50s. No witnesses, no suspects, no arrests. Seems like the whole town turned out for the girl's funeral at St. Barnabas. She's buried up in that little Wisdom Gulch cemetery."

"Cause of death?"

"Stories just said 'head trauma.' Could be a lot of things, I s'pose. Nothing in there about a rape or autopsy or spikes or anything else. Family paper, small town and modest times, you know. Not like now."

"Who worked the case?"

"Midnight PD. Joe Harper was the lead detective ... well, the *only* detective. Little banty-rooster guy, kinda cranky like you, but he was a good cop, too. Retired years ago and left town. Don't know much more."

Bell scribbled Harper's name and town on the envelope with a pencil nub.

"Why the Midnight cops?" Bell asked. "Why not the sheriff?"

"She disappeared down here," Coogan said. "The sheriff's office wasn't much smarter. Just a missing kid, probably just run away. Small potatoes. When they found her body, I hear Joe Harper moved heaven and earth to keep the case."

"Never anything else like it, before or since?" Bell asked.

Coogan shook his head.

"Not here. And not in the county. The paper followed it pretty close at first, then published occasional updates in the first year. After that, not much."

"Old news, huh?"

"The world was changing pretty fast back then, Woodrow," Coogan said. "Folks didn't forget. You know how it goes. Life just went on."

Bell swept his big, callused hand across the dusty workbench, wiping a swath of dust and filings away. Life was a convenient excuse for forgetting the dead, he thought.

"Coog, I owe you," he said.

"You thinking about opening it back up, Woodrow?"

"Hell, you know I'm retired, Coog."

Coogan smiled as he turned toward home.

"Ain't we all," he said in his hoarse little voice. "Ain't we all."

AFTER THE OLD newspaperman left, Bell poured himself a stiff bourbon and spread the old clippings across his workbench. Over the next couple hours and a couple more bourbons, a few new details came into focus.

Several schoolmates saw Cherish Nelson on the sidewalk outside Midnight High. She'd planned to meet some of her girlfriends at Spinks Drug, which doubled as a malt shop where the kids liked to go. But she never got there. A frantic Luther Nelson alerted the Midnight cops later that night. She was described as five-foot-eight—tall for a girl—

with shoulder-length, dishwater blond hair pulled back into a little ponytail, wearing black-rimmed glasses, a maroon pullover sweater, parka, and bell-bottom jeans.

About two weeks later—the day after Christmas—a weekend prospector found her maimed corpse in the empty, decaying caretaker's house at the dead end of Powderhouse Road, which led to the isolated stone bunkers where the mines had once stowed enough blasting powder to level Midnight. So they were built at a safe distance, with only one brave (or desperate) soul to keep watch. But after World War II, the mines no longer needed the crumbling bunkers, and they were left to squatters, teenage partiers, and other varmints.

At her funeral, Cherish Nelson was remembered as a sweet girl from a good, hard-working family. She sang along to her 45s by The Supremes, had a crush on that dreamy Paul McCartney, and cried for a day when JFK was killed, although she wasn't entirely certain why. Her dreams were every small-town girl's dreams: To someday marry a boy who'd take her away to the big city.

Then they buried her forever.

As a former homicide detective seeking answers, Bell longed to know what the stories omitted:

Who was the last to see Cherish Nelson alive?

What made her a potential victim?

Was there a boyfriend her parents didn't know about?

Did the people closest to her have alibis?

What was the murder weapon?

What did the autopsy reveal?

What evidence remained secret?

What happened to the physical evidence?

Most of all, Bell had a hunch the caretaker's shack was significant. Too often, he'd seen cops look right past a crime scene, as if it were a random spot where something bad happened. They seldom asked, "Why here?" Was it the seclusion of the place? Or was it something deeper and more sinister?

If Bell had a phone, he might have also had a phone book, but he had neither. So he jotted himself a quick note in the margin of Cherish Nelson's obituary: *Find Harper.*

The dead girl's eyes met his. He remembered Sarah at seventeen. He didn't allow himself to imagine his pain if he'd lost her back then. The armor he wore was impenetrable. Maybe if he'd been softer, he wouldn't have lost her later … anyway, it was too late now, and it occurred to him that Sarah was turning forty soon and he hadn't heard from her in, oh, a long time. He scribbled another note to himself: *Find Sarah.*

It was dark now, well past the dinner hour. Bell flicked off his desk lamp. Through the window, he saw a halo around the stuttering bulb in the old streetlamp across the street.

Snow's coming, he thought.

CHAPTER 3

FALLING OUT OF a dream always troubled Bell.

Last night, he dreamed about ticks conspiring in the septic tank. Although he put no special stock in dreams—especially the nonsensical ones—he hated not knowing how they ended. He didn't believe in coincidence, so even absurdity needed an explanation. His restless mind wanted tidy answers, even when the questions were stupid.

Bell lay in bed longer than usual. It wasn't last night's bourbon. It wasn't even the ticks in the pipes. Instead, he knew from the edgy air in his bedroom and the dull light seeping under the blackout drapes that it had snowed. And he wasn't sure he wanted this day to begin.

As always, his morning pee took a while to get going. He buzzed his antique Norelco shaver over his stubbly face, mostly because he didn't care to wait for the warm water to find its way up from the balky tank in his basement for his razor.

The hard face in his mirror sagged. It was only vaguely familiar because Bell never spent much time examining himself. He knew how to smile but he preferred not to get people's hopes up by doing it too much. He managed his crumpled little smirk and shook his head. The smile couldn't hold, and the mirror knew there was no going back.

He hadn't chased a ghost in nine years, and he really didn't want to start now. He saw his victims like that, ghosts. He didn't believe in the boogy-boogy kind of ghosts, but it was better than visualizing the dead the way he last saw them, faces gone, fingers curled in deathly talons, guts spilled, splashed on the walls or bedsheets or car upholstery, eyeballs devoured by maggots, stinking and rotting, drained of blood and life. It was easier to think of them as reasonably whole but ethereal, not catchable but ... there.

On the other hand, Bell sometimes looked at living people and saw corpses. Yeah, it was weird, but to be fair, he didn't imagine them all as homicides. Some were just pale and past caring.

Maybe Luther Nelson was lucky, Bell thought: He didn't know the difference.

Bell needed coffee, but some impatient ghosts were waiting.

THE OLD MEN of Deaf Row were already jousting when Bell came in a little before eight that morning, after clomping the skiff of snow from his boots on the "You Are Here" welcome mat outside the front door.

"As of today," Cotton Minahan announced to everyone, "I haven't had any booze for thirty days."

A couple of the guys raised their coffee mugs in tribute, although none of them truly believed that Minahan, a notorious fan of Wild Turkey, had gone on the wagon.

"Really?" squeaked Coogan, the skeptical old newspaperman who barely tolerated Minahan anyway. "A whole thirty days?"

Minahan rolled his eyes.

"Well, hell," he said, exasperated, "not all in a row!"

The whole table groaned, even Father Bert. He saw no sin in drinking—he was fond of saying that whenever four priests gather together, there shall be a fifth—but he worried about the old fire chief's pride in his excesses. And maybe his liver.

"C'mon," Minahan pleaded. "That was funny!"

Bell said nothing, just shook his head. He could see that the normally acerbic Ollie Fuhrman—the newest candidate for the Flatiron County commission—was choking back a caustic (and likely hilarious) comment.

"Hey, at least I can joke about my problem," Minahan continued, clearly miffed. "You never hear Roxy joking about his Solitaire addiction."

That was too much for Ollie, politics be damned.

"You want sympathy, Cotton? Well, you can find it in the dictionary somewhere between 'shit' and 'syphilis.'"

Deaf Row roared as the out-maneuvered Minahan sulked. Fancy refilled everybody's cup, and gave Ollie an affectionate peck on his mottled, bald head. It made him blush because he secretly carried a torch for Fancy.

Everybody settled back into their side conversations about grandkids and other old-man stuff. Bell stirred his coffee, absorbed in something else.

"Get a chance to look at those old stories?" Coogan asked.

"Yeah. Thanks."

"What do you think?"

Bell didn't want to admit he was, in fact, intrigued by the mystery of Cherish Nelson.

"A lot I don't know."

"Well, that's all I got," Coogan said. "Maybe the cops still have the files. It's been a while, but don't they have to keep open cases around?"

Bell shrugged.

"Small town cops. Who knows?"

"How about Joe Harper, the detective? He'd know," Coogan said. "He never got over it, I hear."

Bell knew how that was. He'd had a few of those unsolved cases that jammed in his craw. Out of self-preservation, he'd moved on, but he never forgot. Some nights when he couldn't sleep, he retrieved his copies of the files from old evidence boxes in the basement and searched for missed clues.

"Ollie, you seen Joe Harper lately?" Coogan croaked down the table.

Fuhrman thought about it. "Yeah, up in Bitter Creek, I think. Saw him a couple weeks back, in the co-op. Wife's gone now—damn Alzheimer's—so Joe's daughter moved in with him. Gotta be in his late eighties, and he ain't doin' too good. Got one of them air-tanks he wheels around everywhere, with a tube in his nose."

Father Bert tossed a sugar packet on the table, as if he were upping the ante.

"So let's go," he said.

"Go where?" Bell asked.

"Bitter Creek."

"I ain't goin' up O'MyGawd in the snow. No way. I've ridden with you. You might have friends in high places, but if we slide off that road, we'll pass all your saints on the way *down!*"

"Relax. I've got four-wheel-drive."

"Some other time, padre." Bell gulped his coffee and crossed his big arms across his chest. "Riding with you on flat land is scary enough. Besides, I got other stuff to do."

Father Bert smiled.

"There is no other time, Woodrow," the priest said, more serious now. "And you haven't had another thing to do since before global warming. And there's something I want to show you on the way. Let's go."

Bell dug in. He wasn't afraid of much, but sliding off the edge of a mountain ranked pretty high.

"Some other time."

"You're a ghost driving a meat-covered skeleton that's made of stardust," Father Bert said. "What have you got to be afraid of?"

"You're fff…" Bell caught himself, mid-eff. It was a favorite word, a juicy word that got people's attention, but he always balked at blurting it to a priest. "…*friggin'* crazy."

"Yeah? And you're a big fff … friggin' chicken," Father Bert mocked him. "Now let's get out of here so we can beat the avalanches before they sweep us off that mountain."

At that moment, Fancy thumped two large go-cups of hot coffee in front of him. She knew, even before Bell himself knew, that he was going on a weird field trip with the persistent priest.

"You're like some big ol' rock on the beach," she told Bell, "and he's the ocean. It might take a while, but everybody knows he's gonna wear you down. The ocean don't quit."

Bell cursed under his breath.

THE O'MYGAWD ROAD was half goat path, half tightrope.

It zig-zagged up one side of a sheer mountain and down the other, topping out at over ten thousand feet. On a clear day, they say you can see Kansas, but nobody stops to look.

To be fair, it was built at a time when wagons, not cars, hauled supplies to the thin-air mining camps like Wisdom Gulch and Sometimes Creek. But now it was merely the shortest route between Midnight and Bitter Creek, twelve petrifying miles *over* the top of a mountain instead of seventy mundane miles on proper highways *around* the mountain. Nobody in Midnight had the time or treadwear for such nonsense.

But the trade-off was no small thing. O'MyGawd was so narrow that drivers unconsciously leaned away from the ledge, apparently using their own body weight to keep the odds in their favor.

Avalanches and rockslides frequently scraped the gravel two-track clean off the slope. In winter, the road was one long black-diamond run. In spring, big rains carved jagged ravines that could swallow a pickup whole. Even dry times were perilous. Go too fast and its washboard surface might bounce you right over the edge; go too slow and you risked meeting somebody coming the other way, which always forced the uphill driver to back up to the nearest wide spot so the two cars could inch past each other in a hair-raising slow-dance along the precipice.

Even locals stayed away on windy or foggy days. Cell phones didn't work up there. Smart GPS devices pretended it wasn't even an option. And the road was too narrow for tow trucks, so county crews simply pushed stalled vehicles over the edge into the hungry abyss.

In short, if you couldn't overcome the basic human instinct to stay away from precarious places, you probably didn't belong on the O'MyGawd Road.

And Woodrow Bell didn't belong. It wasn't a fear of heights, really. It was more a fear of falling a helluva a long way and dying in a messy pulp.

To make matters worse, he was a terrible passenger.

And to make matters the absolute worst, Father Bert was a crappy driver.

Normally, he only fired up his tubercular, twenty-year-old Ford Bronco, as wide and lumbering as a tuna boat, to haul groceries to the rectory and the Old Miners Home, or chauffeur an astonished nun to a surprise birthday dinner. God's work. He avoided driving it down the mountain to Denver because it drank gas like Cotton Minahan drank Wild Turkey. His pension couldn't support a priest and a rummy truck, too.

So the very fact that Father Bert contrived this road trip made Bell think the priest had God's work in mind. And Bell hated being dragged into God's work.

"So where are we headed?" Bell asked as he pulled himself into the Bronco's well-worn passenger seat and turned the heater all the way up. "What the hell kind of sacred mission have you come up with?"

"It's not a secret mission," Father Bert replied.

"*Sacred*, not secret," Bell said. "Where are we going?"

"Sorry. My hearing is going and this loud old engine doesn't help."

"It's long gone."

"Hong Kong?"

"What?"

"What?"

Bell growled. Father Bert's deafness sometimes annoyed him, but he understood. This wasn't a vain old man too proud to wear hearing aids.

Straight out of seminary, Bert Clancy went to Vietnam as a Marine chaplain. Rather than stay safe behind the lines, he ignored the rules that kept God out of battle. He went into the jungle, villages, rice paddies, and hot LZs with his boys—most of them kids younger than him. He carried the wounded to safety and watched some of them die. He gave first aid to the living and last rites to the dying. He delivered sermons in knee-deep monsoon mud and baptized his god-forsaken flock in the Mekong River. He still missed them all, the living and the dead.

But ironically, it was in the comparative safety of the command post at Dong Ha, where his boys had built a little chapel from the garbage of war, that Father Bert himself nearly died. While hearing confessions one morning, an artillery shell exploded outside his makeshift church. The blast hurled him forty feet into God's hands. A corpsman carried him to D Med, where the doctors got his heart started again, but his wrecked eardrums would never be the same.

Bell and Father Bert shared that war, and the scars it left. Same combat, different battles. They didn't talk much about it, for their own reasons, but they knew without saying.

They became fast friends when Bell came to town, even though the retired detective wanted nothing to do with God. The priest didn't push it. He was droll, faithful, honest to a fault, and quirky in his habits; he hunted, drank, gambled (a little) and cussed (more than he should). And he called Bell on his grumpy shit regularly, at least when he could hear him.

But most of all, Father Bert looked for good in people, where Bell looked for motives. The priest believed he had a purpose, where Bell had forgotten what his purpose was. They were two halves of the same whole. Different but the same.

They needed each other.

"So you haven't asked where we're going," Father Bert said as they rolled down Main Street, then turned left at the Bar F toward the mountain. The skiff of snow was already melting.

Bell cocked his head in his exasperated way. "Where are we going?"

"You asked about Joe Harper up in Bitter Creek," he said, "but I thought you should see something first. Two birds."

"What's that?" Bell asked, cupping his big, rough hands around a dribble of heat from the vent.

"Something for your investigation."

Bell huffed.

"I don't have an investigation."

The priest smiled, his eyes on a mangy dog darting across the road ahead.

"Then it's God's work, and you're along for the ride."

God's work. Like the trick at the nursing home yesterday, or a dozen other sleights of hand the old priest concocted to keep Bell's old heart from shriveling entirely. Father Bert was misguided, Bell knew. His heart had dried up long ago.

The pavement ended and the old Bronco gulped into a lower gear as they started up O'MyGawd.

Bell reflexively groped for his seatbelt. Father Bert noticed.

"You don't need that," he said.

"Why's that?" Bell asked. "God's watching over us? Jesus is our insurance policy?"

"Nope. If we go off this road, that wussy seatbelt isn't gonna save you anyway."

Bell scooted down in his seat and snugged the belt tighter. Snow remained on the dirt road, especially in the shaded stretches, just enough to make Father Bert's worn tires to spin a little on the steepening grade. The engine strained as if it was pulling against the mountain itself.

"Got it in four-wheel-drive?"

Father Bert glanced through his steering wheel at the dash. "Yeah, a half tank."

"No, do you have … nevermind."

Up they went, the wheezing Bronco slipping toward the summit, its back axle skidding sideways on the snow. Bell's legs stiffened against the wet floorboard.

"Sometimes I wonder if I have already felt every feeling I'll ever have," the priest said out of nowhere. "You ever feel like that?"

Bell thought about it for a moment. Not because he didn't have those thoughts, but because he never talked about them out loud. Besides, the threat of a fatal plunge at every hairpin wasn't conducive to casual conversation.

"I have a feeling right now," he said, "that I'd like you to keep your eyes on the road. But honestly, I've had that feeling a lot, so no."

"I'm serious, Woodrow. Do you think there's more to this life, or are we just waiting? Do you think you simply dissolve into the sky? Just go behind a cloud for eternity?"

The Bronco's back tires spun slightly as they rounded another sharp turn. From where Bell sat, it looked like they were only inches from a certain plummeting death. Maybe fiery. Screaming all the way. That'd certainly be a new feeling.

Out of habit, Bell grabbed the oh-shit handle over his window. This wasn't exactly the moment he'd choose to philosophize about eternity.

"Look, padre, I spent a lifetime trying not to feel anything. I probably didn't feel it the first time, and I ain't likely to start now. Feelings fff... flub up your heart. But I have really good feelings about four-wheel-drive. Just so you know."

Father Bert shifted down and the Bronco lurched as all four of its wheels got traction.

"Oh, that's much better," he said. "You should have mentioned it earlier."

WISDOM GULCH LAY in the cold fold of two mountains, below the timberline a couple miles downslope from where the O'MyGawd Road crested as it dropped into the next valley beyond. A narrow two-track cut through the pines, crabbed across a couple rocky hills, and ended amid a dozen weather-beaten structures, all that was left of the once-thriving metropolis of Wisdom Gulch.

Father Bert rolled the old Bronco up to a ramshackle cabin on the far edge of the little ghost town. Its roof had caved in, its windows long shattered. The front door was gone, maybe for firewood. The clapboard siding sloughed in gray heaps all around, like dead skin it had shed. A crumpled tin flue dangled precariously inside, disconnected from the missing woodstove that some flatlander might have taken to sell on eBay.

"Dreams die," Bell brooded as they walked around the sad ruin. "And they leave ugly corpses."

"Remember Luther Nelson from yesterday?" Father Bert asked.

Bell nodded.

"This was his place. He grew up in this house."

Bell couldn't believe it. From every angle, he could see completely through the place. It was a weathered wooden skeleton, shot up in places. All of its flesh, warmth, connective tissues—all of its life—were gone.

"You said he lived here up til a year or so ago?" Bell asked.

"The mountain doesn't waste time taking it back. But Luther didn't really understand how bad it had gotten. He was already ... you know. He desperately needed care, but he couldn't leave his possessions. He kept everything he ever owned in those old steel dynamite crates, so one day I took Luther to the home and stored all his stuff in the church's garage."

"Poor guy."

Father Bert pulled up his coat collar and turned away, toward the remains of Wisdom Gulch.

"Once upon a time, this was the center of Colorado's gold rush," he said. "They had a church, hospital, school, and all the usual industrial works. Right over there"—he pointed toward a meadow of yellow grass—"there are some old railroad tracks, for Pete's sake."

Father Bert continued his story as they walked along a path past a two-story stone building. The granite block over its front door read, "I.O.O.F."

"Luther's dad was a miner named Andrew Nelson, out of Pennsylvania. He married, raised two sons, and worked his whole life in the mountain's belly. His kin back East thought he was a lunatic for living in these mountains. But it turned out Andrew wasn't a lunatic. He just couldn't give up easy. Luther probably inherited that from him."

The few inches of snow were firm, not frozen. It creaked under their boots. Up here, winter arrives like a long, early sigh. It moves down the mountain, maybe a hundred feet a day, till it hits the valley. After a season, the spring pushes back. Even in June, some of this October snow will still be there.

After some distance, the path split into two. One way had shrubs and vegetation, all dormant for the coming winter. The other was bleaker.

Another fifty yards along that dismal trail, at the edge of the bony, bare aspens, was a broken-down cemetery. Its wrought-iron fencing had been mostly scavenged, but a few wooden and stone markers remained clustered within the imaginary border. The graveyard's main entrance was a rusted ranch gate, upon which hung an equally rusty sign: Odd Fellows Cemetery, Wisdom Gulch.

Bell stood still. How many times had he done this? A hundred? A thousand? Once upon a time, it mattered. Part of the contract he had with the dead. Now it only felt empty. Now he hated cemeteries as much as he hated goddamned nursing homes.

And he never knew where to stand. It felt wrong somehow to step on a grave, but he didn't know why. Here, where markers were haphazard and missing, it was hard to know where someone might lie.

"So in 1942, a government telegram arrived," Father Bert continued. "Andrew's son James had been killed on an island whose name he couldn't pronounce. The grief started small, but grew too big. Andrew built his own coffin, dug his own grave in the Wisdom Gulch cemetery, got drunk on his own moonshine, and shot himself right there in the hole one night in the fall of 1943. His wife and Luther shoveled dirt on top of him and left for Denver. This gray rock here? This is Andrew."

Bell squatted and touched the stone. No name, no dates, no epitaph. Just a big chunk of raw, worthless granite, probably from the mine tailings. Permanent waste.

"They probably had no reason to stay. What happened to them?"

The priest shrugged.

"The widow, I don't know, but Luther came back. He worked at the mine, too. Eventually he married Daisy, another miner's daughter. They had their own daughter, Cherish, whom they raised in that old company bungalow you just saw, where he grew up. He hauled this rock here himself."

"It'd last longer than an old wooden cross, I guess," Bell said. "The mines couldn't spring for a real headstone, eh?"

"Well, they didn't care. They eventually abandoned everything back in the late '50s, and went elsewhere. A few hardy misfits like Luther stayed on and scratched out a living as small-time prospectors and mountain men. Luther continued to hunt for gold and do odd jobs in town, but he never found enough to feed his family, only enough to feed his gold fever. He filled the larder with wild meat, traded gold flakes for clothing, fuel, and other staples. Tough life."

"Especially for a kid."

"When the time came, he sent Cherish down the mountain to live with cousins, so she could attend a proper school."

Bell looked around. His internal radar jolted awake.

"That's her over there, next to her mom, Daisy," Father Bert said, pointing to the thick grass nearby.

An overgrown patch concealed another big rock and a simple, modern headstone a few feet away, a deliberate thing that didn't belong in this place of rust, rot, and weeds. Maybe like Cherish herself.

Bell swept back the tall, dead mountain grass, and brushed a frosting of snow from the cold stone.

CHERISH NELSON
June 30, 1952-December 9, 1969

"Who put up the headstone?" Bell asked.

"The church," Father Bert said.

"So, you did it?"

Father Bert shrugged. "I wanted people to say her name. Maybe just some hunter who stumbles on this place and pauses here. Doesn't matter if he knew her. As long as somebody speaks her name, she's remembered."

Bell remembered the names of each victim who had a name. Some didn't. Like Baby Grace.

"Isn't there something in the Bible about knowing the number of your days?" Bell asked as he touched Cherish Nelson's engraved dates.

"'Teach us to number our days, that we may gain a heart of wisdom,'" the priest recited from memory. "It's Psalm 90:12."

"English, padre. What does it mean?"

Father Bert looked up into the low clouds, in no rush to answer.

"Live to the end," he said after a moment or two.

"Chr ... criminy. Why's it always a mystery with you guys?"

Father Bert smiled.

"It's never a mystery for you?"

Bell suppressed the urge to flip off the priest. He wasn't especially religious, and it wasn't about offending God, but he didn't want to take any chances. Anyway, Father Bert seemed to understand his disapproving look.

"You see, it's not the ability to count how many days we've already lived or to calculate how many days we have left," the priest said. "It just means you should understand how brief life can be. When you know that we only have so many days on this earth, you make your days count."

Math was never Bell's best subject, but he knew seventeen was too young. How many days was that? His brain fumbled with the numbers and got all tangled up. Maybe it didn't matter at all. Endings always came too fast.

"Five thousand, two hundred and thirty-two," Father Bert said.

"How the hell ...?"

"Nuns."

Bell stood and surveyed the lonely patch. His short breaths came out in little clouds of frozen vapor.

"My hands are cold," he said.

But Father Bert wasn't finished. Whatever deal he wanted to make hadn't yet been sealed.

"When a man loses his wife he is a widower," he said. "A wife can become a widow, and a child might be orphaned. But think about this: We don't have a word for the parent who loses a child. Why's that, you think?"

Bell hitched his fleecy coat collar up around his ears, only partly for warmth. Bell didn't care about the words anymore.

"I don't have a clue. Didn't your nuns know?"

Father Bert shrugged and said nothing.

"Maybe it doesn't matter," Bell said.

"Woodrow, we all want to feel that our existence mattered," the priest said, his hands shoved deep in his pockets. "We want to know we will be missed when we are gone."

If Bell was a fool, then he wanted to be his own fool, not somebody else's. Part of him resented that his friend—a priest no less—would play such a game.

"Look, I get it," he said. "You want it all laid out, nice and neat. But it's never nice and neat. And it's never easy. I'm too old for this shit. Sorry, but this case is fifty years cold, dammit. The kid's dead, her killer's probably dead, mom's dead, and dad's a whackadoodle. What good comes of all this? It's a waste of time."

Father Bert got that peaceful look Bell never had.

"God doesn't waste pain."

Before Bell could protest, the priest continued, measuring his words carefully.

"This story isn't finished," he said. "All of us hope there'll be someone to write our missing ending. We just want justice to be done. But if our lives are reduced, in the end, to a pile of bleached bones in a clandestine grave or a coroner's box, who will care? Who will remember?"

Bell tried to warm his hands by blowing into them.

"So you think Cherish Nelson needs me, eh?"

Then Father Bert said what Woodrow Bell had secretly known—and desperately tried to deny—since the night before.

"No, Gunny," he said softly, invoking their shared past and mutual ghosts. "I think you need her."

BITTER CREEK WASN'T far, only a few miles as the crow flies. But crows weren't forced to four-wheel back to the main road, slalom uphill to the crest of O'MyGawd Road, then burn up their brakes weaving down a thirty-degree grade for another half-hour. On ice.

It was lunchtime when they rolled into the tiny village, which was smaller and nearer to death than Midnight. Father Bert craved a sandwich. Bell craved a beer. The mercantile was also a bait shop and a tavern (still advertising Schlitz beer in the front window), so they wheeled into the gravel parking lot and went inside.

While Father Bert snatched a couple microwave burritos from the cooler, Bell ordered two Coors at the bar and asked about Joe Harper.

The old detective's log cabin was exactly where the bartender said it'd be: two car lengths past the service station, turn right off the highway at the "Keep Out" sign and follow the road to the end, back in the trees. It hadn't seen new paint in a long time and the metal roof was starting to rust. A hopelessly decaying International pickup sat in the weeds beside the house, two tires flat. A newer model Oldsmobile—not new by any means, but newer than the museum-piece pickup—was parked behind it. Bell reckoned it belonged to Harper's daughter.

Inside the cabin, a yappy little dog barked like a little semi-automatic pop gun. Bell instinctively patted his breast pocket for his badge and ID, but before they could knock, a middle-aged woman, barely five feet tall, answered the door. She wore a stained gray sweatshirt and shapeless black denims, and she wasn't exactly welcoming.

"Yeah?"

"Ma'am, my name's Woodrow Bell and this is Father Bert Clancy. We're looking for Joe Harper."

The woman stared at them while the little dog continued to bark its fool head off.

"Is this the right place?" Bell asked.

"Whaddya want?"

"We want to ask Joe about an old case he worked a long time ago."

"Cops?"

"No, ma'am. Not exactly."

"Not exactly? Then what *exactly*?"

Bell wasn't in the mood. He leaned closer, his bulky frame casting a shadow over the woman's scowling face.

"Ma'am, we're not from the government, the Mormon Church, the homeowners association, Game and Fish, or the Interwebs. We're not here to seize your guns, or steal your identity, or confiscate your garden gnomes. I'm a retired Denver homicide detective and this guy is a damn priest. Look at him. We only want to see if Joe Harper can help us solve a little girl's murder. Now, would it be too much to ask: Is this the right place?"

The dog shut its yap and ran, but the feisty woman at the door stood her ground.

"Let 'em in, June." The man's voice was thin, more permission than command.

The woman stepped back and opened the big pine door wide, never saying a word or beckoning them inside. Bell edged past her into a cramped living room that reeked of mothballs, antiseptic, dirty underwear, and piss. Like the nursing home, only stronger. Bell associated it with impending death.

A tiny, wizened man sat dead-center on a threadbare sofa, tethered to an oxygen tank by clear plastic tubing. His eyes were sunken, and his too-big pajamas hung on him the way a sheet hangs on a clothesline. His bald head and face were scabbed with angry red sores, and Band-Aids patched a half-dozen needle jabs in his cadaverous arms.

"Are you Joe?" Bell asked as Father Bert stood in the doorway.

"Who's asking?" The man barely had enough breath to speak.

"My name is Woodrow Bell, and this is my friend Father Bert Clancy. We're from over in Midnight and we think you might be able to help us."

"Father ... Hoo-Hah What's-it ... gonna give me ... last rites? I don't need ... no priest."

Bell knew where June got her manners.

"It's okay," Bell reassured him. "He's not here for you."

"So what's ... your story?"

Bell looked for a chair where he could sit, to be at eye-level with the old man. There were none, and none were offered.

"I'm retired Denver homicide. Father Bert here has been telling me about a case you worked a long time ago. Cherish Nelson."

The old man's gray face brightened. His lip quivered as he looked past Bell and pointed his bony finger at the mantel over the fireplace. It was crowded with family photos, some fading away entirely in the slanted light of the dirty window.

But among the faces was a familiar one in a silver frame. A little girl, maybe a middle-schooler in the picture, with dishwater blond hair, smiling shyly for the camera. Bell had seen her face before. On her obituary.

"This is her?" Bell asked, reaching for the photo.

The old man nodded and started to wheeze. Bell studied her face. Kodacolor rendered her more innocent, more vulnerable, than the newspaper's little black-and-white image of the older Cherish.

"Couldn't ... recognize her ... after," he rasped as he turned his face away from that particular memory.

"Was there any motive?" Bell asked.

Harper answered with his own question.

"You got ... the monster ... who done it?"

Bell shook his head. "No. I'm just taking a fresh look. Probably nothing new, but I wanted to ask if you..."

Harper's rheumy eyes turned angry.

"I was ... a good ... cop. I didn't ... fuck up."

"No, no. You didn't. I just want to keep the case alive. You want to keep it alive, don't you?"

"Shoot ... him."

"We have to find him first. Then we'll shoot him. Can you help us?"

"Ask ... me."

"Did you have any good suspects at the time?"

Harper shook his head weakly, almost imperceptibly.

"None," he said.

"Motive?"

Harper's crusty lips oozed his answer.

"Freak ... sex fiend."

"Was she raped?"

Harper nodded. "Tied up ... for days ... and worse."

Harper said nothing but ran his bony finger like a blade from his crotch to his collarbone.

"Mutilation?"

"Gutted her ... like a deer ... heart gone."

Mucking around in daily perversity had numbed Bell. He seldom knew where polite society drew the line. In his former life, his ex-wife would elbow him discreetly when a simple cocktail-party question decayed into vivid descriptions of hungry maggots, shot-gunned skulls, rotten babies, and all the assorted fuckery that men do.

But he glanced at the doorway. Father Bert was looking at his shoes and June held her hand over her mouth. This wasn't work for the squeamish.

"Is that how she died?" he asked.

Harper shook his head. "Post … mort."

"Then how'd she die?"

The desiccated old detective wormed a gnarled finger into his left ear.

"Spike."

Bell remembered Luther Nelson on the nursing home sidewalk, jabbing his finger into his bloody ear. Harper must have told him.

"Was there anything you never told anyone?" Bell asked, one cop to another.

Harper looked suspiciously at Father Bert.

"He's okay," Bell reassured him. "He has to keep our secrets. God's rules."

Harper again raised his contorted fingers to his face.

"Sewed … her eyes … closed. Alive."

Then silence. Father Bert looked pale.

Something twisted in Bell's gut. Dismemberment, a missing heart, eyes sewn shut, a spike through the brain. This wasn't teenagers playing Satanic games, or even an ordinary pedophile with a sadistic streak.

"You didn't forget her," Bell said. "You're one of the good guys."

Harper just hung his head.

"Dreams … come," he murmured.

Bell understood what he meant.

"Do you have any of your old files here?" Bell asked.

Harper shook his head. The light was going out.

"See … Midnight PD."

"Anything else that's popped into your mind in the past fifty years we should look at?"

The old detective swiped a knotty hand at the air, wiping it all away in one painful stroke. Whatever little energy he had for ghosts had dissipated.

Bell turned to June, the photo of Cherish Nelson still in his hand.

"May I take this and make a copy? It might be the only photo anybody has. I promise I'll keep it safe and send it right back."

June was softer now.

"Jesus, keep it," she said. "Let him start to forget. I never knew who that girl was and Papa never talked about her before today. Never knew why some strange girl's picture was up there anyhow."

Bell knew.

Lesser men never want to remember their failures. Good men never want to forget.

Maybe Bell didn't know Joe Harper, but he knew now he was a good man and a good cop. He knew Harper did the best he could. Bell knew about nightmares.

And Bell feared that he might have missed his chance, too. A hundred chances.

As they left, Father Bert paused on the porch and prayed silently for the haunted old detective before making the sign of the cross at the front door.

Too late, Bell thought. The demons were already inside.

ALL THE WAY back home over the demonic O'MyGawd Road, Cherish Nelson's life and ghastly death preoccupied Bell. Not its foulness, but its enigma. It all meant something, but what? Small towns have a thousand eyes. How could such a twisted psycho live unnoticed among the reasonably normal citizens of Midnight … or move among them without arousing suspicion?

And where did he go? Even without the case file, this didn't feel like a one-off thrill killing by a frenzied amateur.

But neither was it clean and controlled. The killer didn't just kill the only witness to an abduction and rape; he blended sex and agony in a staggering butchery. At the slaughter's climax, he—and the killer was almost certainly male—couldn't control himself.

Beyond that ... nothing. Bell couldn't even be sure that Joe Harper's memories were accurate, or what he had forgotten. The old case file should contain a timeline and victimology that would reveal more. It might even contain some evidence, but after fifty years, Bell wasn't expecting much. Stuff tended to get lost.

"What now?" Father Bert asked.

"Shift down," he said. "Your brakes are burning up."

The priest geared into second and the Bronco growled like a crouching cougar. An *elderly* cougar.

"I watched you with Joe Harper. You looked like you'd seen a ghost."

Bell shifted uncomfortably in his seat.

"Yeah, he was the ghost of the future me, if I make it another twenty years. At least he had somebody to take care of him."

Father Bert smiled big. "Shall I reserve a room at the Old Miners Home in your name?"

"Fff ... forget you," Bell grumbled.

At the next turnout, Father Bert pulled over to let the brakes cool. Just a few feet from the bumper, the road dropped off into infinity. On a tree nearby, some wag had nailed a hand-painted sign:

"It is Forbidden to kill yourself here."

It would be a good place for a long-drop suicide. Through the mud-flecked windshield, they could see a hundred miles east, past Denver, maybe to Kansas. They sat quietly there, staring even farther, past Kansas.

"When I was in second grade, I bought a big balsa glider with my milk money, and my dad helped me build it," Bell said, uncharacteristically wistful. "Damn thing must have had a wingspan of at least five feet. We tested the glider in the backyard and it flew like a dream.

"But then Dad had one of his big ideas—but he warned we could only do it once. So I agreed, and we drove up to a spot just like this in the mountains. Dad notched the glider to this big-ass rubber band and pulled the model way, way back and let it go. We watched that glider sail on and on and on until it was just a speck and then"—Bell's big hands blossomed open like a magician's—"it was gone.

"In my mind," he said, "it's still flying."

Father Bert imagined his friend's model airplane spiraling endlessly in the updrafts or swooping between raindrops. The priest tended to make everything about hope or faith, of course, but Woodrow never talked like that. Right now, he might be talking about immortality … or musing about all the other dumb things he did in his life. One could never tell with him.

"Maybe it is," Father Bert said after a long, quiet moment. It had been an emotional day and he wanted to ask more, but Bell hated to be quizzed about his feelings. He called it "interrogation," and he almost always lawyered up. He certainly never confessed.

This time, though, was different.

"Cases like this kill cops," Bell said, the plains unfurling almost two miles below. "Joe Harper's been dead for a long time."

"So you're bailing out?"

"I didn't say that."

"You'll look into it?"

"I didn't say that either."

"What did you say, then?"

"We might waste time we don't have. We might not find all the answers we want."

Father Bert shrugged.

"Welcome to my world, Gunny."

Bell opened the glovebox and rummaged around.

"Still got that holy water in here someplace?"

"Under your seat."

Bell fished around the wet floorboards and came up with a pint of Jameson's, a good Irish Catholic whiskey. The priest favored it over Bushmill's, which was distilled by the damn Protestants in the North. It was cheap stuff, just about perfect for stowing under the seat of a beater truck, so he called it his "survival kit." In these mountains, it never hurt to be prepared for the worst.

Bell belted one back and passed the bottle to Father Bert, who was more delicate with whiskey. They both grimaced as it trickled down. Good stuff.

"The kids always get to me," Bell said, his belly warmed.

"As it should be," Father Bert said.

Bell knew he could be a hard-headed asshole. He didn't apologize for that. Being the tough guy in any situation made it hard for him to admit his own mistakes and flaws, but it was the armor that protected him.

Inside, though, was a secret core of softer stuff. He didn't show it much. Almost never. But when he did, Father Bert was the only one who could hear.

"I had a case a long time ago," Bell said, staring off the mountain. "Fisherman found an ice chest floating in a city reservoir. When he opened it up, there was a little rotten body inside, a kid about two years old. Decomposing bad. She'd been dead for at least three months. Medical examiner said her skull was crushed into a hundred pieces, and most of her bones were either broken or had been broken in the past."

"Saints preserve us," Father Bert whispered, crossing himself.

"Problem was, we had no missing kids. Her skull was so destroyed that we couldn't do an artist's sketch. DNA wasn't a thing yet. No eyewitnesses. No clues in the ice chest, except a bloody pink ribbon in her hair. So we had nothing. Not a damn thing."

Bell took another swig of the whiskey.

"We put it in the national database, put out flyers, got some media. I even gave her a name: Baby Grace. I looked damn hard at her parents, but I couldn't make the case before they disappeared completely. I spent a lot of weekends and late nights spinning my wheels, but after a while, other cases came in and it just slipped to the bottom of the pile. A year later, I still had nothing."

The old detective wasn't haunted by Baby Grace in that supernatural way he called the ghostly "wooo-hooo" sense. She was merely a metaphor for something ... defeat, or unfairness, or unkept promises, or how a name can be forgotten forever, or the fraud he secretly felt he was ... basically every damned thing that twisted his gut.

"Not every mystery can be solved, Woodrow," the priest said.

"Bullshit. Just bullshit."

"You tried. I know you. If you couldn't solve it, nobody could."

"I didn't. But in the process, I lost a good woman, a good life, a good boat ... and Sarah. She was seventeen, you know."

"You still have Sarah."

Bell had nothing to say about that. He didn't feel like he still had Sarah. His daughter had been collateral damage in the divorce. He lost himself after that, for a while, and then he lost her, too. She became a woman when he wasn't looking.

Now, they only talked—really talked—a couple times a year. On those rare occasions when he got down to Denver, he always asked her to dinner, but she was always too busy. It was complicated. But he knew he had nobody else to blame. He wouldn't admit it, even to Father Bert, but he'd broken his own heart.

"It still pisses me off," Bell continued. "Somebody killed Baby Grace and got away with it."

"For now."

"I don't trust your afterlife, padre. Eternity takes too long."

"Maybe this is your chance to make it right, in a way."

Didn't work that way, Bell thought. Even if he was intrigued by Cherish's case, the thought of wading around again in that swamp chilled him. Another unsolved child murder might kill him. He took another swallow of whiskey.

"It's too late for making things right. And this won't be easy. I'm not a cop anymore. I don't have all that cool stuff. I don't even have a damn phone. And all I have to show for it are some nightmares, sore knees, and a bad attitude."

"We act on nightmares, not daydreams, Woodrow," Father Bert said. "I saw you with Joe Harper today, and you were like a bloodhound who'd picked up a scent. You can walk away from this, and nobody would blame you. But sleep on it. Talk to Charlie. Get drunk. Or work on your cursed weathervane. Just don't walk away too quick."

Bell screwed the cap back on the whiskey bottle and shoved it back under the seat.

"Let's go home," he said.

Most decisions were never this hard for Bell. The puzzle drew him, but time had erected obstacles for him, for Joe Harper, and for Cherish Nelson. Father Bert fired up the old Bronco and eased it back onto the O'MyGawd Road.

"But first," the priest said, "one more stop."

NOBODY WENT OUT Powderhouse Road anymore except horny teenagers and tweakers. It snaked more than a mile through the dense forest along Lame Johnny Creek. It was totally inaccessible in winter, and only barely accessible after the season's first snow, even in a hulking four-wheel-drive Bronco. The county graded it occasionally, probably just to spend whatever road-grading budget was left at the end of the fiscal year.

The old stone powderhouse itself, more than a hundred years old and long abandoned by caretakers and squatters, was falling in on itself. Its sturdy, native-granite walls—built to blunt any eruption of the mine's explosives inside—thwarted the elements, but the roof's thick wooden rafters had collapsed long ago.

This was where a prospector found Cherish Nelson's profanely desecrated corpse.

With some difficulty, Bell and Father Bert circled the rubble, stepping carefully around debris half-hidden by the melting snow to peek through empty casements at the jumbled mess inside.

Windows were long gone, gables caved in, jambs taken for firewood. The last recognizable bit of architecture was an impregnable wooden basement door. It was jammed cock-eyed on its hinges by the shifting walls, at the bottom of a sunken stairwell obscured by decades of weeds out back. The place was being reclaimed by the earth, occupied only by vermin.

For the priest it was a haunted place. For the old detective, a crime scene.

"I only see a ruin. What do you see here?" Father Bert asked as Bell stopped to pick up a shard of rusty iron.

"It's isolated. The killer probably knew it existed before he brought her here, so he has some local connection. If there was a lot of noise, nobody would hear, especially inside those stone walls. He knew he wasn't likely to be interrupted."

"So he planned it carefully?"

"Or the place was important to him in another way. I don't know."

"Important how?"

"Symbolic. Nostalgic. Remote. Maybe something that makes no sense at all. Psychopaths don't think like us. That's why we're always so puzzled by them."

"I don't understand," the priest said.

"A serial killer—and that's what we might have here—views everything through the warped prism of his desired reality, what he *wants* to be true. The crime scene, the weapon, the victim herself are all just extensions of his delusions. So place is important. It's not accidental."

The mention of a serial killer—just those two inherently deviant words—chilled the priest.

"*Serial killer*? Are you serious?"

Bell was dead serious.

"If Harper's memory is reliable, this wasn't a slash-and-dash murder. He kept her alive for a while, tortured her, sewed her eyes shut, drove a spike through her brain, and disemboweled her. Nobody does that once. He's a fff... friggin' deviant freak. He's acting out. That doesn't go away. But there's still a lot we don't know."

The priest stepped back, as if the stone walls might reach out and grab him.

"Do you think there's still any evidence in there?"

Bell knew the decaying structure's secrets might now be beyond his reach, buried irretrievably under its own rot.

"No fingerprints or DNA, certainly. If there was blood spatter, it's long gone. I gotta believe Harper picked up all the physical evidence at the time. No fff ... flipping way those dicks in town would bring cadaver dogs up here, even if they had 'em. But the place itself tells us something."

After a long moment, the priest had one last question.

"Do you think he killed her here?"

That answer, too, was in Joe Harper's case file, wherever it might be.

And Bell still didn't know if he wanted to look.

WHENEVER BELL FELT the urge for secret conversation he went to Lucille.

She understood him. No ordinary woman ever truly understood Bell, and on those rare times when he was honest with himself about soft stuff, Bell had to admit he never truly understood them either.

But not Lucille. He knew every square inch of her, inside and out. She was curvy and loud, but she required less attention than any woman Bell ever knew, except maybe Fancy. And she listened. After each time he'd been with her, his mind was calmer.

And although Bell wasn't her first, he was her last. That's all that mattered to him.

Bell unlocked the old wooden shed behind his house and swung the double doors wide open. Cobwebs and dust floated into autumn's low-slung sunlight. Gingerly, he peeled back an oiled war-surplus tarp and Lucille's chrome front fender-tip glistened in the sun.

Lucille was a 1959 Harley-Davidson Panhead. She'd been a gift he didn't deserve, but for more than fifty years, when he'd lost a wife, a daughter and almost every other important thing in his life, Lucille had always been there.

Bell threw the heavy tarp across his workbench, careful not to let it touch the dirty concrete floor. He gently wiped a thin layer of mountain dust from Lucille's black gas tank and leather seat with an old T-shirt. Except for a few replacement parts and some minor cosmetic work, she was as authentic and beautiful as the day he first saw her.

Rabbit would have wanted her that way.

It was Rabbit who loved her first, who dreamed of her, who named her. And it was Rabbit who first understood Lucille's power over men.

Percival Sumner Rising— nicknamed "Rabbit" by his Marine buddies because of his big ears and slight overbite— was a smiling, sandy-haired enigma wrapped in a deep-fried Texas conundrum. His mother taught Latin at a little high school in Comfort, Texas, where his father was chairman of the draft board. Percival was a Hill Country renaissance kid, a tinkerer fascinated with machines, an All-Texas halfback, and a National Merit Scholar.

When he graduated in 1965, he went to college in Austin. He strayed through three majors in two years, ashamed to admit to his parents that he was more fascinated by photography than studying business or law or whatever they imagined for him. And even though nobody would know it to look into his serene blue eyes, he began to grow uneasy about the war and the odd passions it spawned on campus.

By the fall of 1967, Percival was drifting sideways. He scraped together some cash from a part-time job at a camera store and bought a used motorcycle from a professor who'd developed a new interest in LSD. He began spending his weekends on long rides out into West Texas, where he could be alone with his thoughts, and whatever other god-forsaken creatures were out there. He didn't want anyone to see the turmoil in his heart.

On one soul-searching jaunt into the emptiness, Percival arrived at a surprising conclusion: He was going to war. Two of his high school friends, both sent to the front lines by Percival's own father, had already been killed. Consumed by a kind of survivor guilt, Percival gave up the safety of his scholarship and college deferment, and enlisted in the Marine Corps.

On that last weekend before Christmas, before returning home to say goodbye, and before boarding the bus to Parris Island, Percival went to the old Paramount Theater in Austin, where he saw the new Paul Newman movie, *Cool Hand Luke*. In one scene, a sweaty Southern chain gang is aroused in a collective wet dream as a buxom blonde in impossibly short cutoffs performs an erotic car wash—inspiring a Cajun con played by George Kennedy to spurt: "Anything built like that just gotta be named *Lucille*."

That night, Percival popped a Lone Star and christened his faithful bike Lucille.

A few days later, he parked her in the work shed out back of the little house in Comfort where he grew up, and covered her with an old blanket. Then he kissed his crying mother goodbye because she couldn't bear to see him off at the bus terminal, where his father shook his hand and waved goodbye.

Parris Island is where Percival Sumner Rising became "Rabbit," where Woodrow Francis Bell became "Mountain," and where the two became fast friends. Even though the brawny, brooding kid from Genoa, Colorado, and the bright, profoundly imperturbable Texas college boy were equally overwhelmed by the rigors of Marine basic training at Parris Island, they helped each other. A bond formed. These only sons of different mothers became brothers.

By spring of '68, they were in Indian Country, a couple riflemen in Tango Company, Third Battalion of the Ninth Marines, or just the 3/9, which occupied uncertain ground in Quang Tri Province. By summer, Rabbit and Mountain had already drawn blood, and they quarreled playfully over who was the most accurate or the fastest shot. Brothers.

Rabbit was seldom without his old Nikon camera, which his mother mailed to him shortly after they got in-country. Sometimes, he humped it into the boonies, where he captured some gritty images of life at war, even when he was knee-deep in the yellow-red mud of the rice paddies. He was often focusing on Mountain, his favorite subject, maybe because Bell's stony scowl made him look like a genuine warrior.

There was no dark side to Rabbit. The deeper the shit, the more he smiled. He trusted that his life could never be worse than this, that he'd never bleed. Where Bell was dark and silent, Rabbit was sunny and gregarious. He talked constantly about life after the war, finding someone to love, having children and grandchildren … and riding his beloved Lucille, who had come to represent freedom—not the patriotic kind but the kind where fear didn't make all your choices. He didn't grasp mortality, not like Bell.

To Rabbit, Lucille was not a motorcycle. She was immortality itself.

Thanks to his flirtation with college, Rabbit was promoted to lance corporal ahead of Mountain, who paid little attention to the chain of command anyway. Rabbit was still Rabbit.

And Lance Corporal Woodrow "Mountain" Bell was already the "old man" in their platoon when he turned twenty-one on 5 April 1969, just sixteen days "short" of going home.

That day, the captain assigned their platoon to a deep recon mission from a remote LZ into the boonies, where triple-canopy jungle, a fortnight of fog, and prolonged monsoon rains choked every human movement down to a slow-mo shadow-dance. The VC still moved freely through the Ashau Valley at night on trails and roads camouflaged with potted trees and shrubs so they couldn't be seen from the air. Rabbit and Bell's platoon was sent to sniff them out.

At the edge of the LZ, they huddled in the razor grass in the shadow of the dark, stinking jungle. Lance Corporal Percival "Rabbit" Rising spoke softly to his men, half of them on their first recon. He deployed his men in a standard array, and put himself on point.

Bell bristled.

Bell always walked point. Walking yards ahead of the others, a point man's life expectancy in Indian Country was short, maybe ten days. He was the easiest target, the most likely to trip a booby trap.

But the best ones trusted nobody else, and Bell was one of the best. His eyes were sharp and his steps were soft. He heard what the others didn't. He could smell the enemy, especially at night. It was a point of pride that nobody ever got hit while Mountain Bell was walking point.

Besides, he felt more exposed when some fucking new guy was on point, diddy-bopping through the boonies so loud Hanoi could hear them coming.

"Happy birthday, bro," Rabbit said.

"Bullshit," Bell said. "I'm point."

Rabbit was serious, even if he was smiling.

"I ain't losing you on your birthday, big guy. And you're short. You shouldn't even be here."

"Fuck that. You're short, too. Same as me."

"You ain't walking point," Rabbit half-whispered. "That's an order, goddammit."

Back at the firebase, in the hooch, on liberty, they were equals. Not here. Even so, Rabbit rarely pulled rank, and Bell never showed him up in front of the other guys. But he was still pissed.

"Aye aye," he said, then whispered so nobody but Rabbit could hear, "motherfucker."

Rabbit just smiled bigger.

"Oooh.… rah," he said in his long, slow Texas drawl.

Twenty minutes later, Lance Corporal Percival Sumner "Rabbit" Rising was dead.

Killed by a VC sniper.

A head shot.

Nothing John Wayne about it. Just dropped him in his tracks, shearing off half his face. The platoon poured a shitstorm of lead into the jungle, but they were shooting at ghosts.

Bell himself retrieved the body, which he carried over his shoulder back to the LZ. He wouldn't let anyone else do it. While he waited for the dust-off, he turned the undefiled half of Rabbit's face away and cried for the last time in his life.

Up to that moment, Bell was like every other grunt, at war with a thirteen-month calendar. Now, sixteen days and he could go home, which he had desperately wanted to do … yesterday. Up to that moment, he had counted the days down as if he were in prison, not caring as much about winning or losing the goddamned war, but just wanting to escape it.

Up to that moment.

Bell re-upped for another tour, then another and another, always taking combat assignments. He didn't want to die, but he just wasn't ready for The World. Vietnam hadn't yet given him back what it had taken from him.

It never did. He finally rotated back Stateside in the hot summer of 1971, older than his years but alive. Assigned to the Philadelphia Naval Yard, he volunteered to escort the corpses of dead Marines to their hometowns, little burgs and big cities that he knew he wasn't seeing on their best days.

Rabbit came to him a lot, maybe every day. It wasn't a memory, but a ghost he'd never exorcised. Then, almost a year after he'd come home, while returning a private first-class who was killed on his sixth day in-country to be buried in a small country cemetery in Blanco, Texas, he wrestled with his ghost in a desperate little motel room. And lost.

Comfort was only forty miles away, down a dusty, farm-to-market road.

Rabbit was there.

He found the sad little house where the Risings lived. An American flag draped limp from its pole on the porch. The lawn was a week past mowing, but a thick bank of rose bushes thrived. A tree swing still hung from the live oak in the front yard.

Rabbit's parents, Ray and Donna, invited him in for sweet tea, and he sat with them for a long time. The front room was filled with pictures of their son. His casket's folded flag sat in a glass case on the mantel. There were no photos of grandkids because Rabbit had been their only son. But it didn't feel like a sad room to Bell. Life had gone on.

The conversation meandered. Donna was still teaching, but Ray had quit the draft board after Rabbit was killed and never looked for another job. No, they never knew Percival had a nickname, but it pleased them to think he had endeared himself to his men.

They knew Bell from letters and pictures, but if they wondered why he'd never called or written to them after Rabbit died, they were too kind to say so. They were proud of their lost boy, and they felt his presence more than his absence. And they hoped—no prayed—that Bell would come back again.

In those few surprisingly happy hours, Bell realized Rabbit's smile had come from Donna, his big ears from Ray, and his spirit from both.

After lunch, they took Bell to the cemetery to see Percival's grave, where Donna brought new roses from her garden every week and laid them on standard-issue white marble stone. Sweating under the Texas sun, Bell imagined Rabbit down there, whole again and cool under the Texas dirt, smiling. As he left, he saluted his old friend.

They went back to the house and said their goodbyes. Ray admired Bell's rental car: a shiny new Ford LTD that didn't have even a thousand miles on it yet.

"The Marines do it right," he said.

Bell wasn't sure how the next thought tumbled into his mind from nowhere.

"Whatever became of Lucille?" he asked.

A surprised glance flew between the Risings. Without a word, Ray beckoned Bell to follow him to the little garage that sat at the end of the gravel drive.

In that garage, tender threads of summer's high sunlight fell upon the debris of three tangled lifetimes, put away where it wouldn't be seen or cause any more pain. Rusty Tonka trucks, a dried-out baseball glove hanging from a nail, outgrown bicycles, and other playthings huddled in the musty shadows.

But there, in a dark corner under an old parachute silk, was Lucille. She was as beautiful as he'd imagined. Bell's jaw clenched. He had no words.

"Hasn't been out since he put 'er there," Rabbit's father said. "I reckon we just never knew what to do. Mama couldn't ride her, and I couldn't sell her. So … well, there she is. Good ol' bike. It's a shame."

Bell traced his finger through the caliche dust on the sleek fender.

"He loved this bike," Bell said. "All the time. Other guys were jabbering about the girls they left behind, and here's Rabbit – sorry, Percival – mooning about his motorcycle. By God, he only wanted to be … home-free."

A long silence fell. In the live oaks outside, Bell heard a mourning dove's low lament.

"Would you take her?" Ray asked.

"What?"

"Lucille. Would you take her? Please?"

The question sideswiped Bell. He pushed back, but he was off-balance.

"I … couldn't," he stammered. "Hell, I never rode a cycle. I don't have a way to get it back to Philly. And I just don't have the money. Sorry, I …"

Ray smiled wide, and Bell saw Rabbit in him.

"I'll teach you what you need to know in two minutes. She's easy as pie. You ride her back to the East Coast and we'll turn in your rental in San Antone. I'll even throw in the helmet. And I ain't selling it to you. Rabbit would have wanted you to have her … to take care of her. It's his gift. Whaddya say?"

Bell's brain instantly sifted through a thousand reasons this was a bad idea. Only one couldn't be argued: *Rabbit would have wanted you to have her*.

They shook on it there in the dusty garage. Bell got to know Lucille on that long trip back to the coast, to the Marines, to a life interrupted. They talked out there—or Bell talked and Lucille listened—and for the first time in a long time, Bell was at peace.

Now, again, here in Midnight, a thousand miles and years away, he wasn't at peace. He hadn't been for a long time, but at this moment, it was worse. He caressed Lucille's glossy tank. He needed her to say something. Anything.

He might as well ask the dust.

Bell was a gunnery sergeant when he left the Corps in 1977. He moved to Denver and got work as a city cop. Intuitive and tough, Bell was a natural leader with a daunting physical presence, so he quickly moved up through the ranks, getting his homicide shield after only six years on the force.

He treated 'Nam like a shameful secret, rarely talking about it. In fact, he hid from it. He spent a lot of time trying to shake its stench. He couldn't get clean.

He crammed his Purple Heart and all his other medals into a greasy old toolbox. Even now, Bell thought about certain guys. He couldn't always remember their names, but he wondered whatever happened to them. Like one guy, a Montana kid who had both his arms and legs blown off. Bell and two other guys were soaked in his blood as they threw him on the dust-off. Bell still wondered if he made it—and if he did, if he was angry at them for not letting him die.

Later, Bell married a pretty Nebraska girl who waited tables in his favorite diner, and they had a daughter, Sarah. At times, they were less like a family and more like a Marine platoon. A Sunday in the park was more like troop movements. A trip to the grocery store felt like a recon mission. Family vacations were planned better than D-Day. Bell wasn't abusive or mean. He just detested chaos.

Not surprisingly, the marriage ended in divorce after twelve years. Sarah went with her mother back to Nebraska, where she grew up and then moved to a new life of her own in California. She never married and had no kids. Years ago, she came home to Denver to run a big hotel downtown, but from Bell she was politely estranged.

Only a few women passed through his life after the divorce. Bell had been alone for most of it, and that was fine with him. He wasn't happy alone, but he reckoned he was neither a prize catch nor a fit partner. And a lot of the women he dated in those days were tedious, spiritless, flavorless women who liked to watch game shows.

It mildly impressed the guys on Deaf Row that Bell had been a Marine gunnery sergeant. It fascinated them that he had been a homicide detective in the big city. But it flat gave them a simultaneous stiffy to think about Bell dating Charlie. (But then, Bell thought, those guys would be dazzled by a fella who'd trained his beagle to roll over.)

At any rate, he insisted his perfect woman didn't exist: She'd be a savior as well as needing saving, a believer, a mirror, a sidekick, a therapist, a devil's advocate, a catalyst, maybe a forbidden fruit—or at least someone just beyond Bell's grasp.

That was Charlie. She was twenty years younger than Bell, but she was an old soul. Their relationship was built on cynicism about relationships. He didn't care that she was roughly his daughter's age, but he knew other people did.

The first time they met, at Midnight's annual car show in the park, neither was looking for anyone. Both were, in a way, damaged. She was pretty in a Colorado way, and he was more manly than most guys her age.

Charlie—she hadn't been Charlotte since kindergarten—ran her own company, which she'd inherited from her father, who had inherited it from his father. The Maloney family motto at Atlas Disposal was "Three Generations Gone to Waste." Charlie actually drove one of her three garbage trucks. A carelessly cultivated sunflower blonde, she preferred soiled gray sweatshirts and jeans too loose for her slim hips. On dates.

But for a garbage truck driver, Charlie was complex, spunky and sensual. She wasn't a sucker for romance and fluff. She harbored no illusions about their entanglement. She kept it real. In fact, she could get along perfectly well without Bell, and they both knew it. It's not simple being complex.

She could also be stubborn and impossible. She won in life by not giving in. In a test of wills, she'd outlast Bell ... and maybe that had already happened.

They weren't married, nor headed for it. It wasn't worth the risk to either of them. Neither one could easily say "I love you" out loud, but they occasionally thought about each other when they were apart, which was most of the time. They had their own lives.

At night, Charlie was quietly tapping out a novel on her fancy computer, although she never showed it to Bell. She didn't want to be that naked. He didn't even know what it was about, except that she once told him she hoped some fourteen-year-old girl would carry it to school every day until she found a boy who liked to dance.

So it was complicated. In many ways, she was Bell's doppelganger: tough, smart, witty, and capable of sparring with a cynical, sarcastic, intelligent partner. In each other, they saw reflections of their own strengths and weaknesses—and vulnerabilities. Plus, Charlie liked Bell's liquor.

Bell's biggest gripe about Charlie was that she sometimes reached out to hold his hand in the hardware store, a taboo in man spaces. He always pulled away and quietly growled. That's why she did it.

And that's all anybody needed to know about Charlie Maloney.

FOR MOST OF his cop days, Bell carried the same semi-auto Colt .45 handgun he carried in Vietnam. It wasn't standard issue, but it comforted him.

After he retired, he wrapped the holstered Colt in an old T-shirt and put it in a shoebox on the top shelf of his closet, out of sight. He never saved things to pass on to Sarah, who didn't care about his stuff, but he damn sure wasn't going to let it go. It was only a gun, but it'd feel to Bell like a betrayal to sell it or give it away. He'd carried it the day Rabbit died, and Bell was morbidly certain the gun had been spattered with his friend's blood.

Then he traded up. Not for comfort or sentimental reasons but for raw, beastly firepower. He wanted a gun as big as he was. He wanted noise, and he wanted the biggest, baddest legal gun on the market.

Smith & Wesson's 500 Magnum was, indeed, the most powerful handgun in the world, more powerful than Dirty Harry's. Bell didn't hunt anymore because it had become entangled in his conflicts about death. But this fifty-caliber double-action hand-cannon could blow a hole clean through a foot-thick tree trunk. He knew because he did it.

One didn't merely pick up a 500, one hefted it. Its cartridges alone weighed a full ounce and cost three bucks each. It had an intimidating ten-inch barrel, weighing more than four pounds, and was too loud to shoot indoors (he did that, too).

It didn't matter to Bell that it only held five cartridges. He told the gun-store salesman if he needed more than five shots, then he was in the kind of trouble one gun wasn't going to get him out of.

He wore it on a holster harness favored by chopper pilots in Vietnam. It looped over his shoulders, hugging the monster handgun against his chest, where it was easier to draw and didn't throw him off-balance when he walked.

Today, he really wanted to shoot something. Not trees, targets, or innocent animals, just squeeze off a box of those big shells into an unmissable hillside, on the off-chance that the deafening boom would drown out all the other noises in his head.

So he strapped on the shoulder holster and grabbed some ear plugs from the junk drawer. Then he went out to the shed and stripped the canvas tarp off Lucille, with whom his relationship was not complicated at all. He never wore a helmet because he reckoned, at his age, it wouldn't take much damage to the rest of his worn-out body to kill him anyway.

He wasn't sure where they'd go. They'd just go. Maybe down the mountain, maybe up. Maybe a hundred miles, maybe not. Didn't matter. He and Lucille only needed to get away from all these people and find an obliging hill that didn't mind being shot twenty times.

THAT NIGHT, DINNER was bourbon and microwave popcorn. Bell dined alone on his front porch, wrapped in his big coat. The cold braced him; the early darkness hid his unsocial drinking.

As he usually did, he turned in before nine o'clock, no drunker than the night before. Or the night before that.

It didn't matter. Charlie never stayed, he never slept through the night—even sober ones—without needing to pee, and his dreams never made sense.

CHAPTER 4

THE MIDNIGHT POLICE Department was closed.

Bell rattled the locked door, where a handwritten sign pronounced, "We eat lunch too."

Chief Willie May, better known as "Buckshot," never took this cop stuff seriously. Most holidays, he didn't even have a uniform in town. He only hired badge-heavy security guards, flashlight-wielding town marshals, and C students from community college criminal justice programs. They were all giddy about the real guns they'd always dreamed of wearing, but probably shouldn't. Joe Harper, a good cop by all accounts, was a relic of another time.

But Buckshot was a good ol' boy, even if he was barely forty years old. Nobody else wanted the job and the mayor didn't want to pay for a real professional. Out in the real world—which is what Bell called the spaces beyond Midnight's town limits—Buckshot couldn't get a job sucking the farts out of junked squad-car seats.

Nine years ago, when word got around that an honest-to-God Denver homicide detective had retired in Midnight, Chief May hunted Bell down. He wanted to talk cop, but he didn't really know the language. He kept nervously hitching up his striped trousers, which were weighted down by his gun belt and his prodigious gut. Pretty quickly, Bell tagged him as being a nose hair above rent-a-cop.

Right about now, Bell knew Buckshot would be down at the Bar F interrogating a chicken-fried steak.

So Bell crossed the street and walked a block to the diner, where he found the chief alone in his usual booth with his usual plateful of country gravy.

"Hey there, Chief," Bell said, sliding into the booth across from Buckshot. "Jesus, that stuff'll kill you. Don't you ever eat salad?"

"Hey, Bell," the butt-sprung chief said. "Salad's for rabbits. Want some of this man food?"

"Nah. But I need something else from you. About a cold case from way back, 1969, before you were chief."

"Oh, hell, if my memory was any worse," Buckshot said, "I could plan my own surprise party."

"Do you think I could take a look at your file on Cherish Nelson? Joe Harper worked it."

"Good man, they say. Quit when I came on." The chief seemed peeved about it, as if Harper's resignation had something to do with him—which it probably did. "Lost track of him. Probably dead."

"Nope. He's alive up in Bitter Creek. Bad off, but still kickin'. He told me you still had his case file on the murder."

Buckshot shrugged his fat shoulders.

"Shit, Bell, 1969? Fifty-some years? Chances are, no way. But you make me laugh. We got one file cabinet and nobody knows how to operate it. None of my guys was even alive back then. The bad guy is probably dead or older than you. And I never heard of this ... this ..."

"Cherish Nelson. A murdered high-school girl in *your* town."

"I got nothin'. What's your interest?

Bell shrugged.

"Old guy stuff."

"Oh, okay, so farting and dying, eh?"

The chief laughed at his own joke and shoveled another bucket of gravy-slathered cube steak into his mouth. Under the table, Bell wadded up a paper napkin, reminding himself to keep cool.

"But you'll take a look, right? Just in case?"

"What's the big deal?" the chief answered, not laughing now. "Ain't you retired? Walmart's not hiring?"

Bell hated that word "retired." It was a fancy word for "elderly," and he wasn't elderly. Yet.

"Let's just say I'm waiting for a management position," Bell said, but the soft-sell clearly wasn't working. "So maybe I drop by this afternoon to take a look at your files? Professional courtesy?"

Chief May turned serious.

"Let me save you a trip, big guy. We got nothin', *comprende*? No cold case, no detective, no file cabinet, no folders, no evidence locker, no professional courtesy, nobody to chase your wild goose, and no fuckin' interest in helping some old fart jack off. None."

Bell stared at Chief Willie "Buckshot" May the way he once stared at mouthy Denver punks, then he chucked his crumpled napkin across the worn Formica table as he stood to leave.

"You got some gravy on your chin, kid."

BELL SPENT THE rest of the chilly afternoon in his shed, wrestling with the enigma of weathervanes and everything else.

It wasn't only about steadiness in a storm, but about balance, too. He built it to withstand a hurricane-force white-out and be there in the morning, but the balance still confounded him.

How hard could it be? he asked himself when he first started welding it together almost eight years ago. In the middle of the project, he said, "This is harder than I thought." Now, he just said "shit" a lot.

"Shit," he said when one of the windcups fell off in his hand, unwelded. In that moment, he thought seriously about gathering up all this junk and hurling it into Charlie's garbage truck. But in the next moment, this heap of scrap was only another unsolved case he couldn't shake. He had those, yes, but he never really walked away from them voluntarily, as much as he sometimes wanted to.

The weathervane had always taken his mind off the inconsequential dust that drifted through his day. Not this time. Not even a loosened part of it.

In the past two days, he'd seen two rotten buildings, a slaughtered child's grave, an empty file cabinet, and a dead man who still breathed, barely. They were all tangled up. It didn't help that he'd been stiff-armed by a fat Barney Fife.

The shadow of Cherish Nelson plucked some chord deep down where he didn't think he could ever be touched again, much less by a shadow. Suddenly and secretly, his life was thrown out of balance, like a loose load sliding sideways in the back of a pickup. Not merely an unsolved child-killing, but hard evidence that the decorated Detective Sgt. Woodrow "Mountain" Bell was just another small-town geezer preoccupied, like all small-town geezers, with local history.

Bell seesawed between his young and unhappy and his old and unhappy. This was the first time he'd been old. It just happened. There'd been signs, but he thought it would pass. Charlie should have made him feel young, and she tried mightily, but she actually made him feel old.

Now ... this. He could walk away from Cherish Nelson. If he didn't, she might become one more goddamned unsolved case, like Baby Grace. But she needed to know how her forgotten story ends. In return, she might help Bell believe he hadn't become completely invisible either.

It was all about risk.

"It's five o'clock somewhere, big boy. Can I buy you a drink?"

Charlie smacked him on the ass. Bell wasn't surprised. He'd heard her walking across the rutted dirt he called a driveway. He knew her by the pace of her steps—she was always in a hurry.

"You oughta step lighter," he said. "Heard you coming a block away."

"Bullshit. You just don't know anybody else who shows up at the end of the day with a bottle of Jack Daniel's. Well, except Father Bert maybe, but he doesn't slap your butt ... does he?"

Charlie looked at life as a kind of ritual, so an evening whiskey was an act of devotion.

"You're not gonna laugh?" she asked. "Oh God, maybe it's true!"

Bell smiled.

"Nah. Everything is just funnier when you're quiet."

They went inside, grabbed two glasses, and sat together on Bell's worn sofa. After toasting to a good garbage day, Charlie spoke while Bell was in mid-sip.

"So," she said, "you gonna do it?"

The question surprised Bell but he didn't feign ignorance.

"Who the hell told you?"

"A little birdie."

"Yeah, a Catholic birdie, I bet. What the hell ever happened to the sanctity of the confessional?"

"Number One, big guy, you weren't in the confessional," she said. "Number Two ... are you gonna do it or not?"

Bell nursed his whiskey for a moment.

"I don't know."

"Pussy."

"What?"

"You're a pussy," Charlie scolded. "Lost your fire in the belly ... your balls?"

"My balls are fine, missy," he said. "Almost as big as yours. Anyway, why do you give a shit?"

Then Charlie took one of her hard lefts, as she often did when deflecting his interrogation.

"I like that sunrise is a color," she said. "And every day is a new color."

"What the hell ...?"

Charlie sipped her whiskey and nonchalantly scratched a stain on her jeans.

"Good days and good lives are two different things," she said.

"Now you're just saying airy-fairy shit."

"We're all just drifting on the backs of dead sailors."

"Goddammit."

She continued without a hitch.

"Don't wake up one morning and realize you've lost the moon while you were counting the stars."

Bell stopped protesting altogether.

"If you've never stared off into the distance, it's a shame," she continued.

"Oh, ferchrissakes," Bell said, exasperated. "I have no fucking clue what you're talking about and neither do you. This is your way of annoying me until I do whatever you want. Which is ... what?"

Charlie turned to Bell and looked him straight in the eye.

"Get off your ass. You're burning daylight, Gunny. All this brooding and self-doubt isn't helping Luther Nelson learn what happened to his little girl. You owe it to him. And to her. And maybe to yourself. If you don't do it, nobody does. You were put on this earth for this one thing. Think about that. Everything you've done up til now was for this *one* thing ..."

She didn't miss a breath.

"I don't say this too much and I'll deny it if anybody asks, but I love you. And I don't want to watch you fade out like this. Plus, if you don't do it"—Charlie cupped her breasts together—"no more of this."

Bell sat there, speechless for a moment. Then he noticed that certain impish glint in her eye.

"The goddamned priest put you up to this, didn't he?"

Charlie smiled.

"Well, not the part about boobies."

THE NEXT MORNING, Charlie rose before sunrise and walked home. Bell showered and walked to Tommyknockers.

He stomped his wet boots as Father Bert began his blessing over Deaf Row.

"Lord, so far today, we've done all right. We haven't gossiped, haven't lost our tempers, haven't been greedy, grumpy, selfish, or gluttonous. But in a few minutes, God, we're going to have our first cups of coffee and then we're probably going to need a lot more help. Through Christ our Lord. Amen."

Bell draped his big coat over his chair back and sat down. Before his butt hit the chair, Fancy had a cup of hot, black coffee in front of him. Cream and sugar weren't his thing.

He didn't waste time.

"Any of you guys besides the Holy Man know Luther Nelson back in the day?"

Ollie Fuhrman, the quarry man, spoke up first. For maybe the first time ever, nobody else said anything.

"I did. He drove a rock hauler for me sometimes when he needed cash. He'd go over the O'MyGawd like it was nobody's business. Didn't scare him at all," Fuhrman said. "Never brought a lunch so I'd bring him an apple or peach every day, then he'd disappear for a couple months until he needed money again. He'd do anything. Good man."

"Before or after his daughter died?" Bell asked.

"Both. It changed him."

"How's that?"

"I dunno. Like somebody let the air out," Fuhrman said. "He just sorta collapsed in on himself. Funny thing: He never got right until years later when he started gettin' confused. The moment his daughter and his wife were alive again his head, he was the old Luther. Sad stuff."

Bell stirred the ghostly cream in his coffee.

"Why do you ask?" Doc Ely said. He knew Luther, too. "Is it about his girl? Such a shame."

"Both, I guess," Bell admitted.

"Well, Luther never came down the mountain to see me unless he busted a big bone or needed a lot of stitches," Bones said. "Sometimes not even then. A couple times, I saw where Daisy had sewn him up herself with needle and thread. Anyway, they didn't have a pot to piss in, so I never charged him anything. But he'd always come back a few days later with some venison or elk meat. He didn't want handouts."

"And his girl?"

"Never saw her before ... you know ... before she was murdered," the old doctor replied. "Daisy gave birth in her own bed up in that god-awful little cabin. If the girl— *Cherish, was it?*—if she ever got sick, Luther and Daisy cared for her themselves."

"Do you think she was abused?" Bell asked.

Doc Ely paused an uncomfortable moment.

"No, I don't think so," he said. "But who knows what goes on behind closed doors?"

Ollie Fuhrman jumped in. "No way," he said emphatically. "Luther wasn't the kind. Daisy either."

People were almost never what they seemed, Bell knew. And most murders are committed by friends and relatives, usually in a convulsion of blind rage. He had to ask. But rape, torture, and ritualistic butchery weren't ordinary family violence. Sewing a young girl's eyes shut, driving a spike through her brain, and gutting her like an animal was something beyond split-second, irrational impulse.

"You saw her after she was found?" Bell asked the white-haired doctor.

"Joe Harper asked me to do a kind of autopsy. Elroy's dad ran the mortuary back then. The closest thing we had to a hospital, imagine that. So they brought her to the embalming room. I saw her for the first time on that stainless-steel table there. I'll never forget. I was only in my thirties back then, a young doctor a few years out of med school. I'd seen a little human mess but not like that."

Minahan, Snipes, and the rest were transfixed. This wasn't their usual playful banter.

"Doc, what do you remember?" Bell knew it wasn't breakfast-table conversation, but the only photographs of that horrible examination existed in Bones's head. And he wanted to know. Now.

"Jesus, Bell. Here?"

Bell looked around the table. Everybody seemed more curious than sickened, as if they were getting a glimpse behind a grim curtain. Some of them had been in war, some were hunters. He nodded at Bones.

"It was horrible. This teenage girl, naked on that steel table. Unrecognizable. Whoever opened her up and cut out her heart wasn't a surgeon. He was careless and probably used a hunting knife, not a scalpel. Her other internal organs were nicked and sliced, too. It all looked post-mortem, thank God. The rest ... you really want to know this crap?"

Bell nodded as Father Bert looked away and shifted nervously in his chair.

"She was alive for the rest. The rape, the sewed-up eyelids, then finally that spike in her ear ... "

"How ..." Bell looked around and changed his words. "Do you recall what ear?"

Doc Ely closed his eyes and tipped his head back, trying to visualize what he never wanted to see again. Then he stuck his right index finger in his right ear.

"What happened to it, the spike?"

Bones shrugged. "Joe Harper probably took it. Big, rusty mother. A railroad type spike. About this long"—he held two fingers eight or nine inches apart—"and it pierced her brain stem. She died instantly."

"Anything else?"

"Isn't that enough?"

"Sorry, Bones," Bell said. "I just need to know."

"Her hands and fingers were badly damaged, so she must have put up a helluva fight. A searcher found her bloody clothes, shoes, and a broken necklace in the powderhouse and brought them to the mortuary. I recall she had some white powder in her hair. In fact, her whole body was abraded. She smelled like an abrasive cleanser. Every inch of her skin had been scraped clean with sandpaper or steel wool or something after she died. That's it. I left the room, and when I had a chance to think about what I'd just seen, I puked."

The whole table sat uncharacteristically silent.

"The clothes," Bell asked. "What happened to them?"

Bones Ely didn't know. "We didn't have DNA or computer databases back then, so her bloody dress and underwear weren't the kind of evidence they'd be today, especially in a podunk police department like ours that didn't have fancy forensics. Somebody just stapled them in an ordinary paper grocery bag and probably gave them to Joe Harper. He might have kept them for a while, then threw 'em out or gave them back to Luther. I don't know. Different times back then."

Nobody said anything. Fancy, normally imperturbable, stood there stock-still with a coffee pot in her hand and tears in her eyes.

For a few seconds, Bell was deep in thought and Father Bert was deep in prayer.

Then they looked at each other.

MOMENTS LATER, ON the sidewalk outside Tommyknockers, they hastily pulled on their coats and spoke in a language only close friends could translate.

"Where ...?"

"Church attic ..."

"Was there ...?"

"Don't know. Would they ...?"

"I don't know. If they ..."

"C'mon. Short way ..."

"A church has ..."

"An attic? Yep. And basement, too ..."

Bell and Father Bert were too creaky to sprint, but they walked as fast as their arthritic knees would allow. Across Main Street, down an alley behind the Old Miner's Home, up the narrow slot between the one-time brothel and the former nunnery, through the half-acre town park to St. Barnabas. In truth, it was less than a city block, but they were both wheezing when they arrived at the church's unlocked back door.

"Unlocked? Really?" the old cop asked.

"We don't care how they come in," the old priest said as he pushed the door open.

This was no small thing. Bell hadn't been in church for an unseemly long time, even a church attic. He always thought he'd lost faith when Rabbit died, but maybe it was longer. No matter. He didn't miss it or regret it.

They hurried through a little mud room behind the sacristy to a narrow staircase that "Mountain" Bell could barely navigate. At the top of the stairs, Father Bert tugged a string, and a single bulb lit up an ungodly mess. Water-stained boxes, helter-skelter piles of broken furniture, vestments tossed around, tarnished candlesticks and other unidentifiable religious metal, broken stained glass, statues of the saints, stacks of coverless, spineless Bibles that couldn't possibly be taken to the county dump without risking eternal damnation, all blanketed in dust and mouse turds. To Bell, it looked a lot like the priest's little rectory next door.

"Nobody has used this attic since I left," Father Bert said. "Rather than clean out this rat hole, the new guys rented the old whorehouse's garage. It always gave them a sinful thrill to say they were going to the bordello for a little box. Now let's see ... St. Anthony, pray for us."

Father Bert dived in. Stooped in the faltering light of the ancient bulb, he rummaged through the clutter, tossing boxes and church ornaments around like a blasphemous whirlwind. He raised a cloud of dust but knew exactly what he was looking for: a war-surplus footlocker with rusty latches and a busted lock.

Bell could only see the priest's ecclesiastical ass in the darkest corner of the attic when the dust parted.

"Jesus, Mary, Joseph and the donkey! Here it is!" Father Bert suddenly barked. "Make yourself useful and give me a hand."

Pushed up under the eave was a World War II-era barracks footlocker, Army green. "Pvt. Luther Nelson-Midnight Colo" was stenciled across the lid. It wasn't in great shape, but it did its job, still protecting his gear after more than seventy-five years.

Not without risking simultaneous cardiac arrest, Bell and Father Bert dragged the heavy case out into the light.

"Jesus Chr ... " Bell caught himself too late, in a church of all places. "How the hell did you get it up here?"

Father Bert smirked. "God helped me more than you did."

The stubborn latches required a wallop with a heavy metal cup Bell found on the floor.

"That was a communion chalice," the priest said.

Bell rubbed it against his coat sleeve. "Sorry," he said.

The trunk's lid growled as Father Bert lifted it. Bell caught a musty whiff of the mysterious stuff inside. Whatever it was, it filled the footlocker. Junk? A life maybe?

If this was Luther Nelson's life, he thought, it wasn't much of a life.

Father Bert started a gentle kind of archaeological excavation. Beneath two empty trays, the top layer was folded wool shirts and trousers. They came from a time long past and were impossibly flattened by time and the unregulated temperatures of a mountain attic.

Next, snugged between layers of clothing, a few small personal items too valuable to abandon but value-less to anyone but Luther: fading family photographs, a pocket watch even older than Luther himself (likely his father's), a few coins and military ribbons, a pocketknife, a Bible, some letters from his parents postmarked during the war, and some small, cheap pieces of women's costume jewelry.

As gently as he could, Father Bert set them aside on a stack of obsolete hymnals. Bell picked up a few of Luther's trifling treasures, hoping they might speak to him. They didn't.

"No rings," Bell said. It was an observation, not a question.

"Luther is wearing his," the priest said. "Daisy was buried with hers."

The third layer was Daisy and Cherish's clothing, more colorful than the lives they led in that sorry little cabin, and more fragile than they were. His wife and daughter were long gone when Father Bert rescued Luther and packed up his things. Luther had kept them, so Father Bert kept them, too.

"He told me once, back when he was still living mostly in this real world, that he liked to smell them and imagine his girls alive again," Father Bert said.

Now, the priest buried his face in the dresses and blouses and inhaled. He tried to imagine Daisy and Cherish alive on Earth again, but he smelled nothing of them now. However, he also trusted they were very much alive somewhere else.

"All these years," Bell said. "Why did you keep this stuff?"

The priest ran his hand along the riveted edge of the footlocker.

"I had a parishioner once who had a dog," Father Bert said. "He loved this dog more than life itself. One day, the dog got sick and kept getting sicker, so the man took him to the veterinarian.

"The vet said it'd cost nine hundred dollars to treat the dog. My guy wasn't made of money. He was just a widower teacher. But he emptied every last dime from his savings to save his dog. He told me later he never missed all that money."

"I bet the dog was happy he did," said the always sardonic Bell.

"No," said the occasionally sardonic Father Bert. "The dog died that same day. But it was worth every penny to my friend to *try* to save him."

Bell had nothing to say.

"That's why I kept this stuff. My heart ached for Luther and I never once missed the space."

Father Bert laid the dresses aside on a pile of old vestments and turned back to the trunk.

The next layer was a ragged wool Army blanket, not worth much except for padding.

And beneath it, at the bottom, were a man's dried-up leather Oxfords and an unmarked paper bag full of ... something.

As Father Bert reached for it, Bell grabbed his arm.

"Don't touch it!" he said. "If it's what I think it is, it's evidence."

Bell looked around for something to lift out the bag, which had likely grown brittle over the decades. He pulled an ornate scoop from a pile of tangled junk.

"That's a reliquary," Father Bert said.

"Now it's a spatula," Bell said. "If this junk was sacred, you wouldn't have dumped it in the attic, for God's sake."

He slid the fancy flat end carefully under the brown paper and gently jiggled it loose. He lifted it slowly, careful not to touch it with his bare hands. Old habit. He knew no fingerprints or touch DNA would have survived past Christmas that year, but he didn't want to risk contaminating its contents if the sack ripped.

"Get me that mixing bowl over there," Bell said as he balanced the brittle bag on his makeshift pancake-turner.

"That's a baptismal font."

"Oh, then in that case, fetch the baptismal lid, too."

Bell gingerly lowered the bag into the misshapen bowl—it must have been knocked over by a flailing baby—and slapped the cover over it.

"Close up the trunk real tight and push it way back in there where nobody will mess with it," Bell said. "If this bag is the crime-scene evidence, we don't know what else might be hidden in there."

Father Bert shoved the footlocker back into its hiding place under the eaves and hid it behind piles of boxes. Nobody came up here anymore, but unexpected things happened in churches.

"Now let's take a look inside," Bell said, moving toward the stairs. "I have some rubber gloves back at the house."

They were, in fact, kitchen cleaning gloves he kept under the sink for noxious jobs. They'd been there a while. Maybe years. But they were still sealed in their wrapper. Sterile. More or less.

BELL COULDN'T FIND his scissors, so he put a fresh blade in his box cutter. Ever so carefully, he slit the side of the bag into two wide flaps so he could remove its contents with minimal damage to the paper—which might provide its own evidence.

Inside, folded neatly, was a pair of ripped jeans, a thin maroon sweater, some plain panties—all stiff with massive brown blood stains. No shoes. A blood-encrusted silver chain and heart-shaped locket were entangled in a pair of broken cat-eye glasses that were out of style by 1969. The Nelsons simply couldn't afford a more fashionable pair to please the editors of *Seventeen* magazine.

To Bell, it was evidence of a crime. To Father Bert, these were artifacts of a life stopped horribly and too soon. Today, he calculated Cherish Nelson would be around seventy. The priest imagined her life might have been a good one if a random path had led her north instead of south. One way, a long, natural life; the other way, an unnatural ending drawn out too long. He said a silent prayer for her soul.

Bell slipped every bloody thing back into the grocery bag, then sealed it all in a plastic trash bag.

He wasn't sure where to go from here. He wasn't a cop anymore; he had none of the sophisticated forensic scientists, computers, crime-scene analysts, profilers, or even a dozen rookie cops to boss around. He didn't even have a damn phone. He was just an old fogey with an old gun.

He and Father Bert didn't say anything for a while. It had been a sacred moment for both of them, in different ways. It was barely lunch time, but Bell grabbed Charlie's bottle of Jack Daniel's and two glasses, and the priest followed him out to the front porch.

"You've done this a lot," Father Bert said. "I haven't."

Bell sipped slowly.

"It's what I do," he said. "Or did."

"Do you ever get used to it?"

"I wish I could say 'no,' but maybe yeah. It was easier to keep it at arm's length when I was young. I could only afford to worry about the case. Now, I'm old, and I have felt some of the things those people have felt."

"What do you do?" Father Bert asked him.

"There's a room in your heart and head where you dump all this bad shit and lock the door. A long time ago, I wanted to feel something, but I couldn't without losing some of the spark I needed to catch the bad guys. I always told myself there'd be time to cry later."

"Did you ever cry?"

Bell gulped his whiskey and poured a new one.

"Hell, I told myself for so long to 'cry later' that 'later' never came."

They sat a long time without saying anything.

"You saw shit in 'Nam. You've seen shit since then, too," Bell said. "How do *you* deal with it?"

The priest bowed his head, not in prayer but contemplation, Bell went on.

"If somebody hasn't held a dead baby that's still warm, then they can't understand," he said. "I mean, people die every day, right? But when you're grieving, ordinary people in ordinary places don't talk about it. So I began to seek out places where they spoke that same language, like the squad or the cop bars. Eventually, I just stopped speaking that language, too."

He didn't actually have to say it. Father Bert knew.

"I once did a funeral for a baby only fifty-one days old," the priest said, softer than before. "He died of a heart defect so grievous that doctors predicted he would only live one or two days. So for his whole life he exceeded expectations. He was never weighed down with regrets. He never sinned. He dreamed. He was loved by everyone who touched him. And he had no bad memories ..."

Father Bert watched the muscle in Bell's jaw tighten. "And I held him when he died. So ... I know."

They sat in silence a while longer and passed the bottle. Bell had built an impermeable shell around himself, and he was uncomfortable when he exposed the soft stuff inside. Now he was done.

But not Father Bert.

"So what's happening with Cherish Nelson?"

Bell paused a long time.

"No promises," he said, taking another sip of his whiskey. "It's only a favor to you, okay? I'll look, but I'm not gonna waste a lot of time on it. Then will you shut up?"

Father Bert thought about Luther Nelson, who needed this more than either of them.

"At times like this, I wonder why God lets this stuff happen, but I don't have any answers. People think priests know everything. But I must remind myself that Heaven remains above and the earth below. You say you'll cry later, and I guess I'd say I'll *know* later."

"You're more patient than I am," Bell said. "And for the record, I don't think you know anything."

"Well, big guy, if I'm wrong about God, then I wasted my life," Father Bert said. "But if you're wrong about God, then you've wasted your eternity."

Bell huffed.

"Maybe that's why I don't pray, padre," he said. "I can't wait that long."

DENVER WAS A hundred miles down the mountain and a hundred years ahead of Midnight.

Bell's 1991 Crown Victoria was an unmarked, unlocked tuna boat he kept parked in the alley. Back in its glory years, then-Detective Bell had driven it to crime scenes and coffee shops until he and the sedan both mustered out twenty years later. Rather than send it to auction, the department sold it to him cheap. Now it just sat most of the time, petulantly refusing to start on some winter mornings. The only time he locked it was zucchini season, when "prowlers" would leave sacks of surplus squash on the front seat. As with Charlie, Sarah, and everybody else, his relationship with the Crown Vic was complicated.

Not today. All night, Bell thought about the bloody bag, Cherish Nelson, and his conversation with Father Bert. He needed hard answers and real evidence, but he had only theories and gut feelings. He carefully placed the trash bag containing Cherish's personal effects on the Crown Vic's broad backseat where it wouldn't slide around and headed through town toward the main highway into the city.

Bell usually tuned his obsolete radio to an oldies station out of Denver, but as he descended his mountain, it fuzzed out. When a new signal crackled back in, some rapper rapped about ... honestly, he didn't understand one single damn word. He'd crossed some line of vapor where the sky's invisible currents had changed direction, where what he knew for sure became unknowable. He switched it off.

He wasn't exactly sure what day of the week it was—in retirement, every day was the same—but it was a workday, the traffic was a nightmare, and Bell's old district straddled a special ring of Hell. It encompassed Denver's highest crime areas. He never had a chance to sit around, shooting the shit and making espresso like the suburb guys and their Lexus crimes.

Jazz—that is, Detective Sgt. Jasmine Jackson—was still on the job. When she got her shield, Bell was her first partner. A cynical, middle-aged, white former Marine gunnery sergeant paired with a black girl who escaped her rough upbringing in the old Five Points neighborhood to major in psychology at Colorado State. She'd been recruited by a progressive chief of the painfully white DPD to add the best people of color it could find.

Their partnership didn't start well, and Bell had been pretty sure it wouldn't end well, either.

But he was wrong.

Jazz busted her ass. She sat across the desk from him in the bullpen and listened to every word. She heard what a real cop sounded like. She learned fast. She was an incalculable asset in the worst neighborhoods, where she knew the street instinctively, spoke the language, and was trusted only slightly more than the white guy. She trusted Bell with her life. And she was a consistently better shot than Bell, who openly groused about it in the squad room but was secretly comforted.

She came to call him "Big Man," not "Mountain." Way back then, she was a single mother, and her four-year-old son was "Little Man."

Now Jazz had earned her bones. "Little Man" graduated from Annapolis and became a career Marine officer. Jazz grew up alongside him, and now she was one of the decorated veteran detectives who bitched about rookies and the brass, and who caught all the tough cases. She was fast approaching sixty, her hair had a dusting of gray, and her own retirement was around the corner. She'd seen all the same awfulness Bell saw and grown her own protective shell. She and Bell had evolved into different sides of the same coin.

"Big Man!" Jazz hollered when she saw Bell enter the noisy squad room carrying a black plastic trash bag. "Comin' back to apologize for all the donuts you stole?"

She met him halfway across the room and hugged him in a way she never would have in the old days. Some partners went further, but Jazz and Bell kept it real.

They hadn't talked in a few years, not since Bell came down from his mountain and cajoled her into seeing a ballgame with him. In fact, he'd bought the ticket for his daughter Sarah, who backed out at the last minute.

"It's really good to see you, Jazz," he said as they embraced. "I mean it."

"At my age—and especially at *your* age—it's good to be seen," she replied, brushing aside sentimentality. "Say, did you ever learn to shoot straight?"

Jazz always made Bell smile.

"It was never me," he said. "It was the damn gun."

Bell caught a few of the fresh-faced youngster detectives smiling. He recognized none of them.

"Coffee?" she asked.

"Not this pig piss," he said. "Some place private we could talk?"

"Sure. Room One is open. You remember the way, old man?"

"Hell, I spent more time in there than with my wife ... which is probably why I ain't married anymore. Back then, we called it 'interrogation.' Now you call it what, an 'interview'?"

"Put down your rubber hose, Sipowicz," she teased him. "Now we just make 'em drink the coffee. It's so bad they'll confess to shit they never did."

Inside the old interrogation room, Jazz closed the door and Bell took the seat usually reserved for the cop.

"Oh, that's cruel, Big Man," she said. "Leave me the asshole chair."

"And your point is...?

They laughed, but Jazz cut to the chase.

"Okay, you don't come down to the big town for shits and giggles," she said. "What's up?"

"What, no foreplay?"

"I forget ... what's foreplay again?" Jazz asked, only half joking. "Seriously, what's up?"

"I need a favor."

Jazz rolled her eyes.

"No offense but the last time you asked me for a favor, I had to cavity-search an eighty-six-year-old lady."

Bell feigned shock.

"Yeah, but it was the biggest drug bust of your career!"

Jazz flipped him off.

"Okay, this favor," she said. "What is it this time? Undercover tranny?"

"You've got the look," Bell said, "but no. I'm looking into a really cold case—for a friend."

"Right, a friend. Gimme the big picture."

"Fifty-something years old. Young girl. Possible serial. No autopsy. No case file. No witnesses. No forensics. No leads. No evidence," Bell said. "Except this."

He tugged the loose end of the black plastic trash bag beside his chair.

"No way," Jazz said, pushing back the air between them.

"No way what?" Bell didn't do innocent.

"No way *in hell*. Unh-unh. Negative. Nope. Not no how. Let me be clearer: Are you fucking nuts?"

"I haven't even asked yet."

"I know you better than you think," Jazz said. "And you know the regs: Only DPD stuff. Even if I wanted to run your outside stuff through the crime lab—and I don't—no way I'm gonna get a colonoscopy from Internal Affairs. Not for you. No way."

"Technically, 'middle age' is around forty ... " Bell interjected, risking bodily injury.

"And technically I can shoot your ass right now."

Bell persisted.

"C'mon, Jazz. You can call it a DPD cold case and nobody would know."

"No."

"Quick DNA testing?"

"No."

"Blood spatter?"

"No."

"Prints?"

"No."

"Cadaver dog?"

"No."

"Carbon dating? Quantum physics? Nuclear fission?"

"No, no, and no. Zip. Love you, Big Man, but ... no."

"I can see you're on the fence," Bell said. "Want to think about it overnight?"

"No."

The unstoppable force had met the immovable object. The immovable object won.

"Sorry, Jazz," a suddenly serious Bell said. "I didn't mean to jam you up. I just wanted to give this little girl's father some closure. Maybe some justice. I retired, but I guess I never stopped wanting to help the people who were powerless to help themselves. Maybe it's just a mortality thing. One last good deed. You'll get it ... someday."

"That sappy shit's not gonna work either," said Jazz, who did indeed know Bell better than he thought. "Go peddle your BS somewhere else. And did I mention? No."

Discouraged and outmaneuvered, Bell shrugged and extended his big paw. "I gave it my best shot. No hard feelings, partner. Next time I'm in the city, dinner? I wanna hear everything about Little Man. Semper fi."

Detective Sgt. Jasmine Jackson reached across the table and shook her old partner's hand. A hug didn't seem right. "Sure, Big Man. Stay safe out there."

Bell seemed to slump as he waved sadly from the door. He left Jazz sitting alone in the interrogation room and soon disappeared from the squad room where he'd literally spent the best part of his life. He now seemed smaller than Jazz remembered. She hated to disappoint her mentor, but he taught her to always go by the book. And it caused a little hitch deep down to think it might be the last time she ever saw the Big Man.

But Jazz had other work to do. As she rose to walk around the table, she nearly stumbled over the black plastic trash bag Bell left beside his chair.

"You son of a bitch," she muttered louder than she should.

Outmaneuvered.

As a detective, Bell had spent a lot of nights on Denver's East Colfax Avenue. Once dubbed the "longest, wickedest street in America," locals knew it was the place to find the city's guiltiest pleasures: hookers, drug dealers, junkies, homeless panhandlers, and dollar-an-hour motels. East Colfax alone generated half of Bell's cases.

The hookers, junkies, and homeless were still there, but the avenue had undergone a kind of urban renewal since Bell retired. There were now legal marijuana dispensaries like Rocky Mountain High and Electric Lettuce at every intersection, attracting as many suburban tokers as a burgeoning influx of California slackers.

And on every other corner was one of those trendy coffee boutiques, where the Mercedes crowd and hipsters paid green-haired baristas six bucks for burned caffeine and free Wi-Fi. The coffee at Tommyknockers was better and cheaper, but Bell needed something else.

It was mid-afternoon, but the place was crowded. Almost everybody in the place had their faces in a laptop, were texting or talking on their phones, or bopping to music streaming through little earbuds. All of them sipped fancy coffees that were mostly not coffee. Nobody talked to anybody else.

Who the hell drinks coffee at this time of day? Bell wondered. He waited as patiently as he ever could in a long line while people ordered their vented skinny iced frapple whatever. The beach-blond, thirty-something California lady waiting ahead of him was dressed like a cold-blooded Eskimo and texting furiously until it was her turn.

"I'd like a vanilla coconut-milk cappuccino, no foam but whipped cream, steamed exactly to one-twenty-four degrees," she said. "Tall. No, vente."

Then she whispered something in the order-taker's ear and went down the line to wait for her ... whatever the hell.

Bell stepped up.

"Black. Hot. No cream or sugar. In a cup."

The girl with a lip-ring behind the counter started to say something but she knew it was a fool's errand to try to explain good coffee to old folks. As he held out his one-dollar bill, Lip-Ring Girl told him the California Eskimo had already paid for his coffee.

So Bell walked up to the Eskimo lady.

"That was very nice of you," he said. "Thank you."

"You're welcome," she said, nuzzling deeper into her stylish fake-furry coat. "I know how you senior citizens, like, don't have much money. It's just my way of like saying 'thank you' for Pearl Harbor and stuff."

Bell started to say something, but he knew it was a fool's errand to try to explain history to young folks. Instead, he had a question.

"Those were the days, ma'am. Hey, my phone cord wouldn't stretch all the way down here. Do you think I might borrow yours? A Medicare emergency."

"Bummer," she said, holding out her phone. "Here."

"Sorry, ma'am," he said. "Old-man fingers. Could you dial for me? 303-555-0112."

She punched in the number and handed her iPhone to Bell, who wasn't exactly sure where the sound would come from. As it rang, he found the sweet spot and held it close to his ear. Then it clicked, and his daughter answered.

"Hello, this is Sarah ..."

"Hey, Sarah. Dad here. Long time no ..."

"Leave a message after the beep and I'll get back to you as soon as I can. Have a great day!"

He waited for the beep.

"Hey, Sarah. Dad here," he said. "I'm down in the city today. I know you're probably at work but I'm wondering if I could take you to dinner tonight. My treat. Wherever you want. It'd be great to see you. It'd be nice to catch up. Just let me know ..."

All at once, he realized she had no way of calling him back, even if she wanted to. For a long time, she'd never called back anyway. *Maybe I should get a phone*, he thought. But it was too late for today, maybe ever.

He handed the Eskimo Lady her phone, collected his boring coffee, and headed back up his mountain.

CHAPTER 5

IF DEAF ROW fined its tardy members a thousand dollars, Bell would still be late.

He hated looking so needy that he'd sit there alone—before sun-up on winter mornings—eagerly awaiting the company of codgers.

So the morning's blessing was already under way, as it usually was, when he came through the front door.

"Lord, help us to live without coffee," Father Bert prayed, "and to ignore our aches and pains, to never complain, to resist correcting each other, to always tell the truth, to relax without whiskey, to love unconditionally, and to tolerate those who sin differently than us ... so that we may be at least as worthy of Heaven as our dogs. Through Christ our Lord. Amen."

Except for the cheap line about dogs, Bell knew Father Bert was praying for his defective soul.

Both Bell and the prayer had interrupted a fascinating conversation about the cosmic implications of Solitaire.

"Not every game is winnable," said Roxy Snipes. He'd know: He kept obsessive records of his gaming, including the number of games, percentage of wins and losses, and every possible combination of suits. Because he never knew exactly how to relate to people, every so often he reported his dizzying stats to his Deaf Row buddies, who were merciless.

"Here's the thing: In every game there are certain cards available to the player, and certain cards not available," Roxy explained—again. "Available cards are the seven that are face up on the table, and every third card through the remaining deck, another eight. Twenty-one cards face down on the table plus sixteen in the deck, are unavailable. So, fifteen cards are available, thirty-seven are unavailable. The odds of winning are only one in fourteen. No aces appear in one of every twenty-seven games. There's no move on the deal for every seventeen games. And in one of two-hundred seventy-one games, the cards on the table are all black or all red. Personally, I think the number seven is statistically important but that's just me."

Cotton Minahan was the most cutthroat, although it must be said that he was an equal-opportunity sniper. His superpower was zeroing-in on every man's soft spot.

"I don't know what you just said," Minahan scoffed, "but I'm sure the ladies love it when you whisper your Solitaire math in their ear. Oh, wait, you wouldn't play Solitaire if you had a lady."

Deaf Row erupted in a simultaneous snort.

"Laugh all you want," Roxy said, and he was serious. "There are many unsolvable situations, so there are games that can only last a certain number of moves before they are guaranteed to end badly."

"Personally, I just cheat," Dan Coogan squeaked.

"Who loses if you cheat?" Roxy sniped. "And what do you win if you cheat? You beat yourself and get nothing for it."

"But I get nothing if I *win*," Coog pointed out. "Either way, when I'm done, I got nothin' and I just deal another hand."

"Roxy, how many games you think you've played?" Minahan asked.

"Not that many."

"Bullshit. How many? Thousand, two thousand, five thousand? Give us a number."

Snipes didn't need to guess. His stats catalogued ten years of playing almost every night and filled three big notebooks on the breakfast table where he never ate breakfast.

"Four hundred thirty-eight thousand, one hundred sixty-seven."

The whole table went quiet. Even the unflappable Bell was startled by the number.

"But I've won thirty-six thousand, five hundred and thirteen, Mister ... Mister ..." Roxy wasn't good at comebacks.

Father Bert rescued him.

"Rox, what would you say is the secret to winning?"

Roxy Snipes shrugged.

"You gotta be observant," he said. "You gotta focus your perception and act deliberately. You can't rush it. You can't win if you don't watch closely. It's all about patterns."

"That's all? Patterns?" the priest asked.

"Well, that ... and luck."

Perception, patience, patterns ... and luck. For once, Bell followed the old guy's mathematical gibberish.

"And one more thing," Snipes added. "The whole point of Solitaire is counting down to one."

Bell got it.

It wasn't only Solitaire.

The whole point is counting down to one.

THE REST OF the week, Woodrow "Mountain" Bell confined himself to his shed and his rabbit weathervane.

He welded the defective windcup and dismembered every moving part. He then measured every square millimeter and placed them on the most sensitive scale he could find out in The World. He filed lightly here and there until every part balanced down to a gnat's ass.

The sun was sinking when Bell painstakingly reassembled every piece, as he had ten or twenty times a year for a painfully long time. And for the hundredth time, maybe thousandth, he carried it to the alley, clamped it to a sawhorse, checked the plumb and level, and waited for a stiff-enough mountain breeze to turn it.

It didn't take long. A stiff draft came down the slope of the mountain and funneled through the alley like a wind tunnel. The arms twirled listlessly on their axis ... but the rabbit on top spun around, but never pointed into the wind. *Shit.*

Bell felt like punting the whole mess into the next county when Elroy Richter shuffled into the alley on his nightly walk.

"Hey, Woodrow," Elroy said. "How's that homemade anemometer coming?"

"Homemade what?"

"Wind gauge, weathercock, weathervane, what have you," the physics teacher and amateur weather buff said. "A little meteorological humor."

Apparently, meteorology isn't that funny, Bell thought but didn't say.

"Yeah, well, it's bigger than me, I'm afraid, and that's saying something. I can't make it work. Pisses me off. I've checked it dozens of times or more. It just won't spin right. Everything is perfectly in balance."

"That's your problem," Elroy said.

"What do you mean?" Bell was more than a little annoyed that yet another Midnight knucklehead would have a solution to a puzzle he couldn't solve. Their solutions were all wacky and never worked.

"It's all about balance."

"It's perfectly balanced, goddammit."

"And that's your problem," Elroy insisted again.

"Educate me." Bell stepped back and dared Elroy Richter to take a closer look. *Couldn't be worse than everybody else's cockamamie advice*, he thought.

"Your weathervane must be *out* of balance to work right," the old teacher said.

Bell cocked his head like the RCA dog. Elroy grasped the metal rabbit between his thumb and forefinger.

"You've heard of somebody taking the path of least resistance, right? People are lazy. They'll do the thing that requires the least energy, right? For example, your perps—is that the right word, perps? It's easier for your perps to steal somebody else's money than to earn it themselves. Everything—not just people—takes the path of least resistance: Lightning, a river, a pop fly coming down ..."

Bell felt this conversation veering off into jibber-jabber, but Elroy continued.

"Both sides of your rabbit must have equal *mass*, but the *area* of the front and back of the rabbit must be unequal. The rear end is bigger, so more resistant. That makes the front end the point of least resistance and thus the point of least resistance will face *into* the wind."

Bell fogged up. He knew less about mass, area, and resistance than what women want, about which he knew nothing. He couldn't fathom how something—*anything*—must be imperfect to work perfectly.

But Elroy must have felt young again. He continued his lesson with vigor.

"Now if you consider aerodynamics, turbulence, and friction, then ..."

"Whoa," Bell stopped Elroy mid-lecture. "Let's just leave it at "the rabbit's ass must be bigger than its ears.""

When Elroy eventually continued his evening stroll, Bell and his grinder shaved the edges of his rabbit's head, torso, and ears. He remounted it on the sawhorse in the alley and waited for the wind to come up again. It soon did.

And the big-assed rabbit turned into the breeze, not away.

Mounting it on the roof became an urgent impulse, but it was turning dark and the old Victorian's roof was too steep for such an old man, even in daylight. He hated to ask for help with anything, but he was forced to make this one exception. Maybe tomorrow. Maybe spring.

In the black air of his room later that night, Bell floated in the netherworld that exists between awake and asleep, on the threshold of unconsciousness where the mind is free to drift. He saw a rabbit with half a face drinking wind while thunder clapped. Luther Nelson walked behind the trees and went into a dark building, where ... Bell startled awake with a jerk. He looked at his digital alarm clock, and only twenty minutes had passed since he crawled into bed.

Bell put no special stock in dreams but if he had a phone, he'd call Charlie, to know she was there. Or he'd call Sarah, to know she was safe. Or he'd call the damn priest, to know if he might want a glass of bourbon.

Instead, he lay there alone in the deathly silence and dark a long time, unable to sleep.

WHEN BELL ARRIVED at Tommyknockers the next morning, he needed coffee quicker than usual.

Fancy knew that look and had a cup of hot, black at the table before he could sit.

"Steak and eggs, over medium, sausage, no toast?" she asked. If Bell ate, that was always his order.

"Not this morning," he replied. "Thanks."

Doc Ely was telling a story about how one of the Winkelmanns—he wasn't sure which one—died in his bed years ago.

"They didn't find him for eighteen months," Doc said. "When they did, he was a skeleton, picked clean by his two cats, who then starved to death and were picked clean by rats."

"Jeez, Bones," Minahan piped up. "Breakfast here."

"Sorry. I just wonder how somebody could die in Midnight and not be found for eighteen months. How awful to not be missed here, of all places. If one of you guys didn't show up for a couple weeks, I'd ..."

"Assume my chihuahua ate my face?" Minahan quipped. Father Bert broke in.

"Fellas, this might be a perfect time to seek some grace. Ollie, take off your hat, please."

"Sorry," Ollie smirked. "I thought that was only for the National Anthem."

Father Bert scowled at him before the blessing.

"Lord, as we go through our day, please keep your arm around our shoulders and your hand over Ollie's mouth. Through Christ our Lord. Amen."

Bell couldn't wait for absolution, or a second cup of coffee. He excused himself and found Fancy behind the counter.

"Can I use your phone?" he asked her.

"Sure, hon," she said. She stuck her hand down her apron and handed him her smartphone.

"No, a real phone," he said.

"Flip phone?"

"What the ...? No, before that ... I think."

"You mean, connected to the wall? With a little roundy-round thingy? A curly leash that looks like a pig tail?" Fancy teased. "Yeah, we ain't had one of those since the last century."

"Goddammit. Okay, do you know where there's a pay phone?"

"Sure, hon," Fancy said, pointing the way. "Go right on Main Street, past the hardware store. Take a left at the bank and you'll be smack-dab in the 1990s. Look for the Macarena and Tickle Me Elmo. Can't miss 'em."

Bell stared at her like ... a homicide detective.

"Try this," Fancy said, again holding out her smartphone. "You're gonna love the 21st century. Phone sex alone is worth the trip."

"Phone sex? You have sex with your phone?" Bell handed her phone back to her as if he held a dead mouse.

"Nevermind." Fancy rolled her eyes. "Whaddya need there, Marconi?"

"I need you to dial ... er, punch or whatever ... a number for me." He fished a business card from his wallet. "303-555-8799."

The waitress's thumbs flew, and she handed her phone back to Bell.

"Where's the ear hole on this thing?"

She turned it right-side up.

It rang a few times before a woman answered.

"This is Detective Jackson. Who's this?"

"It's me. Woodrow. Big Man."

"You come up as Fancy Something."

"What do you mean?"

"You using Fancy Something's phone?"

"How the hell did you know that?" The DPD's phone-tracing equipment must have gotten much faster, Bell thought.

"Jesus Christ." Jazz sounded truly exasperated. "Look, let's skip the belated tech lesson. You calling about that little package you accidentally forgot on purpose last week?"

"I wondered where that went! I must be getting' old. I keep forgetting where I put things. Glad you found it for me. You're a life-saver, June."

"Jazz."

Bell winked mischievously at Fancy.

"See? I'm getting Old-timer's Disease. Anyhow, I figure maybe you could use whatever I forgot down there, Jane. Is that how you say it?"

"It's pronounced 'go to hell,'" she shot back. "No, I don't need a big bag of your crap. And, no, I don't need the shit storm I'm gonna be in."

That was all Bell needed to know, and it warmed him. He knew he could count on his old partner. She could never walk away either.

"I can come down to the city to get it any time, Janet," he said. "Just call Fancy at the Tommyknockers Diner at ..."

"I got her number right here," Jazz interrupted.

"How the hell ...?"

"Oh, fercrissakes. Look, put the phone down before you launch missiles in North Korea or some damn place. If I need to get hold of you, I'll call Fancy Something. I'm sure she'll know where you are, because you never go anywhere. Don't call me again, Big Man. Understand? I'll call you. Maybe soon."

Bell breathed easier.

"Sure enough," he said in the general direction of Fancy's phone. "Don't call you, you'll call me. Got it. And, hey, stay safe out there, Judy."

He heard a faint electronic "fuck you" as he handed the phone back to Fancy Something.

All at once, he knew the next big obstacle in his "case," if he could call it that yet. In fact, it was the obstacle he confronted in almost all of his big cases for more than thirty years.

Patience.

PATIENCE SUCKED.

It was unnatural. Bell was more patient when he was an impatient teenager. The closer he got to his end, the less waiting seemed like a good idea. The whole world around him moved faster and faster every day, while he moved slower and slower. Standing-by now felt like living in reverse. And now Fancy Something was his only connection to Jazz and whatever the DPD crime lab might learn from his macabre package.

The coming week felt like two. That's possibly because the fellas of Deaf Row seemed to be thinking slower than normal humans.

Once a sharp reporter, Dan Coogan reported that on Tuesday he went to Georgetown and ordered a hamburger from a bank ATM.

Roxy Snipes showed up on Wednesday wearing two mismatched socks, blue and brown. So he went home to change—and came back wearing their mates, brown and blue.

On Friday, Ollie Fuhrman talked about the Great Depression, when his dad and mom were so poor they could barely make hens' meat, which to him must have been the cheapest meat possible. Cotton Minahan (of course) corrected him with great delight because the fruit didn't always hang so low.

Charlie took Bell for a walk in the Midnight cemetery on Saturday, only because it was quiet before winter. He knew she had her way of praying. She liked being there. He didn't, but he liked being where she went.

Charlie was even prettier in the afternoon light. He seldom saw her at that time of day. Her skin was smoother, her hair lighter. She stopped every so often to pull a weed or pick a wildflower. Bell was captivated by her natural grace and the ironic humor of her finding beauty in a graveyard.

She didn't talk much there among the headstones, but she told him, out of nowhere, that there had been three men she loved for sure, and four she might have loved, and one she didn't love quite enough. She never said if Bell was any of them.

And on Sunday night, after a day of prayers, Father Bert knocked on Bell's front door with a fifth of Jameson, which tended to make time pass even slower.

"Isn't it a sin for a priest to drink on Sunday?" Bell asked as he opened his door wide for his best friend.

"Nope," Father Bert replied, "and we can smoke cigarettes and get tattoos, too. Otherwise, it's an unbearably spartan life. The Pope only allows us to be human on days ending in 'y.'"

"You know where the glasses are, party boy," Bell needled the priest.

Father Bert hollered from the kitchen.

"All you've got in here are plastic football cups."

"Is that a problem?"

The priest came back with two shots of whiskey, straight up, in giant game-day beer cups.

"These are priceless collectibles, Woodrow," he said. "Craig Morton hasn't been the Broncos quarterback for forty years."

"Make me an offer."

Father Bert settled into Bell's worn-out leather recliner that no longer reclined.

"Charlie and me took a walk in the Midnight cemetery yesterday," Bell said as he sniffed his plastic whiskey. "Did you know there's a sign on the front gate that says, 'Come back soon'?"

The priest shrugged. "Good advertising. But don't worry, you're too cranky even for the Devil. If God passes on you, too, you're going to be the first human in the history of humans to live forever."

"Not if I keep drinking whiskey from fff ... friggin' forty-ounce cups," Bell said.

Father Bert badly wanted to say something priestly about how death is just living ashes to ashes, dust to dust, or about how a good life isn't necessarily a long life but a life without regrets, or how the universe was messy and crowded, but without coincidence. It was hard to resist a little soul-saving, but he already knew Bell's soul was a tough nut to crack.

"Wanna watch some fff ... football?" he said instead.

"No cable."

"Play some gin?"

"You cheat."

"Go for a drive?"

"Jesus doesn't love me enough to let me get into a car with you," Bell said.

"Don't say that!" Father Bert barked. "Jesus loves you, you son of a bitch!"

Nothing shocked Bell anymore, except Father Bert's loose definition of godliness.

"Can a priest cuss like that?"

"Only around asshats. I'll give it up for Lent," the occasionally sarcastic Father Bert promised. "So ... Cherish Nelson? Anything?"

"There it is. You've been beating around that burning bush since you got here."

"And you haven't said a word about it all week. What's up?"

People didn't get it about homicide detectives. They had no more answers than priests and professors. Sometimes, they didn't want to say anything about anything. Sometimes they were as impatient for *something* as anybody else.

And cops like Bell knew better than anyone else that sometimes the hero loses.

He explained how he took their bloody parcel to his old partner at Denver PD, how he hoped she would secretly run it through the crime lab against the rules, and how he hoped they'd find some microscopic clue that survived fifty years in a paper sack. And he further explained how it all might go sideways.

"One thing bugs me," Bell said. "Well, a lot of things bug me, but this one thing is big: Do you think Luther Nelson will even know if we break this case? Will he remember anything about Cherish and what happened? Wouldn't it a blessing if he has forgotten all of it?"

Father Bert, who didn't understand everything, understood this.

"He'll know," the priest said. "I don't think you can ever forget someone who was once the reason you smiled."

EARLY MONDAY MORNING, the boys on Deaf Row descended into one of those conversations that only old men can have. Or want to.

"I got up and peed at two a.m.," Cotton Minahan said.

"I got up and peed twice at three and four," Ollie Fuhrman said, as if a deuce beat an ace.

"I got up and peed three times between midnight and five a.m.," said Dan Coogan, not to be outdone.

"I peed at eight," Roxy Snipes deadpanned, "and I got up at nine."

Even Father Bert laughed.

At that moment, a hundred-year gust of icy north wind swept Bell through the front door, the perfect cue for the priest's daily blessing.

"Lord, we thank You for the thrill of life. As our knees begin to ache, our fingers lose their dexterity, and our midnight trips to the john increase, we ask that You watch over us, especially in the dark. Through Christ our Lord. Amen."

Something wasn't right. Bell's usual cup of hot, black coffee didn't wait at Bell's place on Deaf Row, and on this cold morning, it was especially missed. He dropped into his chair and looked for Fancy, who must have been back in the kitchen.

After a few minutes, when she finally came through the swinging kitchen door, she ... wasn't Fancy.

"What the hell?" a suddenly agitated Bell said to nobody in particular. "Where's Fancy? Where in the goddamned hell is Fancy?"

The little blue-haired lady who wasn't Fancy paid no attention (or didn't hear). She looked too old for this short-order shit. She shambled among Tommyknockers' few occupied tables at the speed of stop, cranking herself over a bad hip. She was so old that if she dated any of the Deaf Row guys, they'd call her a cougar. She didn't seem to know anybody, and nobody seemed to know her—not like Fancy. Everybody knew Fancy, *so where the hell was she?*

"Down boy," Coogan said. "She's gone."

"Gone?" Bell demanded. "Gone-gone or just gone?"

"I think gone, but maybe gone-gone," the word guy replied. "But she could be gone-gone-gone. I dunno. One of those."

Fancy never took vacations or sick days. She didn't have a husband, boyfriend, or kids to delay her. She might take an afternoon off to get her lady parts checked, but never in the morning. She didn't go to morning Mass. She never overslept. She was never late. And sadly, Bell realized, none of them ever noticed. But today, of all days ...

"She musta been going down to Denver," Ollie Fuhrman guessed. "She was wearing her shiny shoes."

Bell swiveled toward Ollie. "You saw her?"

"Passed at the door," Ollie said. "She was goin' out, and I was comin' in."

"She didn't say anything?" Bell was starting to sound like an interrogator.

"'Good morning, Ollie' or somesuch. That's about it. Seemed like she was in a hurry."

"Did she seem angry? Happy? Sad?"

Ollie shrugged his bony shoulders.

"What's the big deal, big guy?" Roxy asked.

"Nothing," Bell said as he stood to leave. He wasn't happy. "If she shows up, somebody come and get me pronto."

Nobody except Father Bert knew what had irritated their oft-irritated friend this time, except that maybe the old lady didn't bring his coffee fast enough.

FANCY HAD, INDEED, gone to Denver.

With Charlie.

On their way down the mountain that morning, Fancy's cellphone chimed and a Denver number popped up.

"Is this Fancy, Big Man's, er, Woodrow's friend?"

"Yes," she said hesitantly. "Who's this?"

"Detective Jasmine Jackson at DPD. Call me Jazz. We talked last week sometime ... or Woodrow talked to me on your phone. Am I catching you at a bad time?"

"No," Fancy lied. She wasn't sure she should admit to a cop she was on her phone while she drove down a mountain road. "What's up?"

"Is Woodrow handy? I need to talk to that big lug. I keep telling him to get his own damn phone, but ... well, you know Woodrow."

"Well, detective, I'm heading to Denver right now," Fancy said. "I can find him for you when I get home later today, if that works."

There was a long pause.

"I've got a better idea," Jazz said. "Can I meet you someplace when you get to the city?"

Fancy sidestepped.

"I've got a thing this morning," she said. "Maybe after lunch?

"Perfect. Does one o'clock work? I'll text you where to go," the detective said. "No need to read it while you're driving."

Busted.

"Sure," Fancy said. "That'll work."

They exchanged goodbyes and hung up.

"Who was that?" Charlie asked.

"Woodrow's friend Jazz," she replied. "She wants to meet."

Charlie shook her head.

"Not me," she said emphatically. "I don't want her to tell Woodrow we were in the city. He'd want to know everything."

Fancy often got lost in Denver, and Charlie was no help. It wasn't the easiest place to navigate, and they were both intimidated by the sheer size and activity of the "big town." The morning rush-hour traffic frightened Fancy more than she already was. But with the help of her phone's GPS and Charlie's dead reckoning, she found the place they needed to be and surprising nobody more than herself, they weren't late. She took some silly pride in that.

After she dropped Charlie off, she killed a couple hours in Denver, then rewarded herself with a mani-pedi and lunch at a salad buffet in a Lakewood strip mall. While she sat, preoccupied, over her mixed greens, her cellphone pinged. It was a text from Detective Jackson.

It told Fancy to meet her at one p.m. at a warehouse in Park Hill, not Denver's worst neighborhood but certainly not the best, either. Jazz also texted a photo of herself—a professionally dressed, older black woman holding up what looked like a police badge—so Fancy would know the woman she was looking for wasn't a hacker rapist.

It all felt like a cool, scary spy movie to Fancy.

After lunch, her phone led her back to eastbound I-70. Eventually, she ducked off the interstate and crossed the railroad tracks into Park Hill's warehouse district. Her phone's map stair-stepped her through a maze of gigantic industrial buildings. Many had long loading docks for lumbering eighteen-wheelers that came and went on the narrow streets, passing her within inches. This might be the day, she thought, that she'd die in her little Fiesta.

Her destination was around the next corner, the voice in her smartphone told her. When Fancy pulled up, the place looked abandoned. There was a fenced-in storage yard but no activity and no obvious place to park. She pulled up beside the long line of loading bays and just waited for something. Jazz, a call, a sign from God ... something.

Then her phone pinged. It was another text from Jazz.

"Pull into the next alley straight ahead," is all it said.

Fancy rolled forward to a narrow, busted up asphalt strip between one warehouse and the next. There, an older black woman in a leather jacket and gloves leaned against her black sedan.

Fancy pulled up close and rolled down her window. Cold air rushed in. The black woman held up a gold shield as she walked toward the Fiesta.

"You Fancy Something?" she said.

"That's me. Are you Detective Jackson?"

Fancy saw a gun on her hip. She stiffened and relaxed at the same moment.

"Really, just Jazz," she said. "Sorry for all this cloak-and-dagger bullshit but they've got surveillance cameras in the precinct parking lot. I need to keep this under the radar."

Jazz handed Fancy a cellphone, one of those cheapies you could buy at any convenience store and toss in the trash when you were done.

"This is for Woodrow," Jazz said. "My home number is already programmed into it. Tell him to call me real late tonight. I really need to talk to him."

Fancy held the phone in her hand like it contained atomic secrets.

Jazz started to walk away but came back.

"And we need a secret password so he knows this shit is real. Let's see, what can it be? I know. You tell him Jazz said 'Fuck you, Big Man.'"

Fancy sat there for a minute or two after Jazz's black sedan disappeared around the corner. It was time to meet Charlie where they agreed and head home. She meandered through the maze of narrow warehouse streets back toward the interstate.

On the way back up the mountain, Charlie didn't say much, if anything, and Fancy didn't push it. So she had plenty of time—maybe too much time—to think. She wondered what strangeness Bell might be tangled up in. She wondered if Tommyknockers could install a salad bar ... even if it probably wouldn't go over well in meat-and-potatoes Midnight. She wondered when the classic rock station on her car radio would lose its signal.

But mostly she wondered when Charlie would feel the first side effects of her chemo.

CHARLIE SHOWERED IN Bell's upstairs bathroom before dinner while he marinated a couple steaks for grilling out back.

So he wasn't expecting Fancy at his front door. And definitely not still in her shiny shoes.

"Hey, girl, I was worried about you," he said, and he wasn't lying. "You okay?"

She slapped the cheap cell phone in his big paw.

"Jazz says to call her at home late tonight," Fancy recited from memory. "She said she really needs to talk to you. Her number is in the phone. And you owe me. I coulda been killed by the CIA or something."

"You saw Jazz? What the hell? Where?"

"Denver. She asked me to meet her," Fancy said. "Very Jason Bourne."

"What did she want?"

"I have no idea. She just gave me this phone for you. That's it."

Bell smiled in his rumpled way.

"I owe you and her, big time," he said. "She's my old partner. A stand-up cop. I'm not sure what she's up to, but it's something. And you helped. Come on inside where it's warm ..."

"Nah," Fancy said. "I need to get home."

"Love 'em and leave 'em," Bell said. "Story of my life."

"Aw, Woodrow, you know I'll only stop loving you when the mute guy tells the deaf guy that the blind guy saw the legless guy walk on water."

Bell huffed.

"Like I haven't heard that a million times" he said as Fancy walked back down his creaky porch steps.

"I'll see you tomorrow morning," she said, "when you're late for coffee."

After Fancy left, Bell studied the baffling device in his hand. He knew the tiny keyboard was for dialing or whatever. That was the extent of his cellphone knowledge. After a lifetime of feeling like he knew the important things in life and had seen things most people never would or should, he was suddenly dumber than a teenager about simple communications between humans.

After dinner, he'd ask Charlie to explain the mysteries of these gadgets.

THAT NIGHT, A little after eleven and still not sure what a Google was, Bell pushed the button Charlie showed him.

After a couple weird "rings," Jazz answered.

"Hey, Big Man."

"How the hell did you know it was me?"

"Don't you ...?" Jazz sounded irritated. "Jesus Christ, I don't have the time or the crayons to explain this to you. But I'm glad you got the phone. It was the fastest way for us to talk."

"About what?" Bell asked.

"If you say anything about this, I'll say you've got dementia and then I swear I'll shoot you."

"Okay, okay," an impatient Bell agreed. "Tell me, dammit."

"Against my better judgment, I ran your stuff through the crime lab," Jazz reported. "I told them an elderly homeless guy with projectile diarrhea and tapeworms dropped it off, and we weren't sure what it was. That's sorta true."

"Thanks a lot, *partner*."

"Anytime, *partner*," she cracked back, then continued. "So, they did their usual magic and they found out that all that biological material on all the clothing was too degraded to get a useful DNA sample. Fifty years in a paper bag in the attic, fluctuating temps, the body dumped outdoors, contamination ... the DNA is all broken down into nothingness. Sorry, Big Man. We got zilch on the clothes."

"Well, shit," Bell said. "I'm not surprised but ... shit."

"I know you're disappointed. Back then they just didn't preserve evidence like we do now. You know the drill. Even if they'd had DNA, the lab guys said these bloodstains and the stuff you thought was semen were useless after about six months, give or take."

Bell was defeated. He'd staked a lot of hope on the bloody clothing. Now ... nothing.

"Thanks, Jazz. I really mean it," he said. "I know you took some risks for me. All the bullshit aside, I loved you then and I love you now."

"You didn't let me finish, butthead," she responded.

"Sorry. It seems like 'no evidence' is kinda the last word."

"Well, it isn't," she said. "Remember that locket? It was all crusted over with dried blood. Sealed it up tight. The lab guy had work hard with a razor blade to get it open. It contained a couple pictures, probably dad and mom, judging by the age of the pictures and clothing. And something else."

"What?" Bell knew that tantalizing tone. Jazz liked a good cliffhanger.

"A single hair," she said. "A partial DNA profile came back. Turns out the hair had been trapped inside the locket by a kind of shell of dried blood. Follicle was still attached. All encased from the elements. No air and reasonably protected. Probably locked in there when the killer closed it. It wasn't in great shape, but it was useable."

"And what did they find? Anything?"

"It wasn't hers," Jazz said. "It was male."

"Maybe her dad's?"

"Nope."

"How do you know?" Bell asked. "You've got nothing to compare."

"We ran it through CODIS, and we got a hit. It wasn't her dad."

Another cliffhanger.

"Holy shit, woman," Bell blurted. "Who?"

"Tell me I'm a better shot than you."

"What ...?"

"Say, 'Jazz shoots way better than me.'"

"Are you shitting me?" Bell damn near bellowed. "You have a crucial piece of evidence in a murder and you're holding it hostage?"

Jazz was calm.

"This evidence waited fifty years," she said. "It can wait ten more seconds. Go ahead and say it."

Bell gritted his teeth and lowered his voice.

"You're a better shot than me ... but if you don't tell me right now, I'm gonna shoot you point blank."

Jazz giggled a rare giggle. She didn't giggle.

"You'd probably still miss, Big Man."

"Jazz, dammit ..."

Bell could hear papers rustling in the background.

"Your person-of-interest is a real sick dude with a fat file," she said. "Name is Erskine Midwinter. DOB 7/31/54. White. No birth certificate. Unknown birthplace. Unknown father. Not much of a paper trail. Only a sentencing memorandum his lawyers submitted to the judge."

"That would make him about fifteen in 1969," Bell said. "So he's a few years younger than me."

"Except you weren't dumped by your mom at Evergreen Home for the Deaf in 1960 at the age of six ..."

"Six?" Bell could hardly believe it.

"It gets worse," Jazz said. "Evergreen dumped him at the State School for the Retarded at age nine, then they dumped him at the old Schattenland Lunatic Asylum way the hell up in the mountains in '65 at the tender age of eleven ..."

"That's a lot of dumping."

"Back then, if parents didn't want a kid, they found any reason to pawn him off on somebody else," Jazz said. "Maybe he was deaf, but it's possible he didn't need to be institutionalized in the first place."

"How do we know all this?"

"He told the pre-sentence investigator everything," she said. "So maybe it's true or maybe it's bullshit. But it's all we got."

"What does he say happened to him at the asylum?" Bell asked.

"He escaped briefly when he was twelve, and a search posse found him a month later only a half-mile away, hiding in a cave or mine shaft up toward Profanity Peak. He was still wearing the white gown that the problem kids wore, eating whatever animals and bugs he could catch. They took him back to the asylum and at age thirteen, he fatally stabbed another mental patient in the neck with scissors and was chained up in solitary for eight months. Then the asylum closed."

"Closed?

"Yeah, bankrupt. 1969 or so. I Googled the place. It was a private business paid to take all the nut jobs the state didn't want anymore," Jazz explained. "The owners were embezzling the state money. Living conditions got horrifying. When it went under, they just opened the gate and let a hundred crazies, mostly kids like Midwinter, walk off. The owners ran away so fast they left everything there. The place was too remote to demolish, so it's still up there, all the shit inside, almost like it was fifty years ago. Little Man took me there on a hike once. Spooky old stone mansion like 'Dracula' or something."

"The dead patient," Bell asked. "What was his or her story?"

"Her. Sixteen. Admitted for 'fits,' presumably epilepsy. Probably shouldn't have been there at all."

"And our friend Erskine was a juvie and obviously insane, so no charges," Bell said.

"You got it," Jazz said. "Most of that stuff comes from the shrinks he saw in all those places. Then poof, a year after his asylum killing, he walks out the gate. Nobody knows where he goes or what he does until 1977 when he's charged with three counts each of kidnapping and first-degree aggravated assault. The DA couldn't make the attempted rapes. You'll want to read these god-awful reports but take my word, not over breakfast or before bed."

Bell asked for and got a sanitized synopsis. Three girls, different times, different Denver suburbs. Fourteen to seventeen. All snatched at knifepoint in broad daylight near different schools over a two-year period. All three escaped before he raped them. And all three identified a guy who talked like a deaf man and had a "dead eye." DPD's Major Crimes Unit got lucky and accidentally stumbled upon Midwinter living under the ramshackle bleachers at the abandoned Lakeside speedway.

"Turns out, he really had a weird eye," Jazz added. "Not the empty, evil kind of eyes we saw every day on gangbangers and killers. A jail doctor said Midwinter's right eye was permanently damaged, maybe blinded, by fertilizer or drain cleaner or some similar chemical when he was a kid. The doc described it as a 'foggy, bloodshot, wooden marble.'"

"Convicted?"

"Made a deal. He confessed to three agg-assault charges in exchange for dropping the kidnappings. The judge gave him three tens, consecutive—thirty years—and let's see ..." more pages rustling ... "paroled in 2003."

"So his DNA went into CODIS?" Bell asked.

"Eventually, she said. "Evidence in his 1977 cases was tested in 2016 to compare to similar cases after he was paroled, but there was no match. His DNA went to CODIS anyway, just in case others popped up. None did."

"His description?"

Jazz recited from Midwinter's 2003 face sheet.

"Forty-nine years old. Five-eight, 150 pounds. Gray hair. Damaged right eye. Mostly deaf. Speech impediment. Scorpion self-tattooed on his right arm. No known friendlies. Even the hard cases thought he was crazy and stayed away. Half his sentence was served in the box for unprovoked violence against other inmates. Periodic hallucinations, disorganized thinking, diagnosed as paranoid schizophrenic in prison but frequently resisted medication."

"Where is he now?"

"In the wind," Jazz said. "Visited his parole officer once and never went back. Disappeared into thin air. No warrants, no busts, no tracks. He's a goddamned ghost."

That vexed Bell. *Who just disappears when every cop is looking for you? When there's a surveillance camera on every corner? When every cop's computer knows your face and name?*

"His prison jacket says marshals talked to his mother around '04. Little Erskine was apparently her only child, but she had no knowledge of his whereabouts. She didn't even know he was paroled ... and didn't care. The marshal's notes say, 'Uncooperative.' Loving family, huh? Name was, let's see, Rosemary Midwinter."

"What else do we know about her?" Bell asked.

"Nothing yet," Jazz said. "I just started backgrounding her this morning. Last known address Purgatory."

"The town or the punishment?"

"The town, dumbass."

"This Erskine would be, what, in his seventies now?" Bell asked. "So mom would probably be in her nineties, if she's still around. Anything else?"

"That's all we got, Big Man," Jazz said.

"No Social Security? Medicare claims for 'dead eyes'? No new kidnapping or sex predator busts? Maybe he's dead. Have you checked Spacebook?"

"Jesus, I've only had this stuff for two days! I'm still working it when I can, but I've got real cases and I'm keeping this on the down low. You'll just have to be ... nevermind. That ain't gonna happen. Give me some time. And it's Facebook."

Bell didn't have much wiggle room with Jazz, but he had one more request.

"In your free time, would you check NCIC for any missing teenage girls in the Rocky Mountain region with any similar elements from 1969 to now, minus his stretch in prison?"

Jazz agreed too fast.

"Sure, Big Man. Just as soon as you get brother Denzel to tickle my ass with a feather."

CHAPTER 6

DEAF ROW WAS, as always, well into its second round of caffeine when Bell showed up.

Cotton Minahan was talking about religion.

"I've been born again," he said. "So, I believe in the traditional definition of marriage: One man and a series of women."

A collective groan rose from the table.

"What, like none of you guys has been to Racks!" Minahan responded defensively.

Racks was a strip club up in Vail that displayed trophy deer and elk heads on its walls, a perfect complement to the warm ambience of glitter and Motley Crue, and the inescapable fragrance of sweaty strawberries.

Father Bert sensed a blessing was now or never.

"Guys, guys, guys," he said. "Let's take a moment to pretend we believe more in a higher power than bare boobs."

"Can a priest say 'boobs'?" Roxy asked, completely serious.

Father Bert moved on quickly.

"Lord, You gave us childhoods. You gave us good hearts. And You gave these boys wives. Sorry to bother You on this glorious morning. I was simply reminding my friends. Through Christ our Lord. Amen."

The only times Bell had visited a stripper bar had been on the job. A lot of his "clients"—pushers, small-time mobsters, sex traffickers, porn peddlers, and more—hung out in such places, eliminating any erotic fascination for him. And truth be told, it aroused him more to watch the girls put their clothes back *on* than seeing them come off.

But today, he was interested in seeing something else.

"Boys, anybody know how to get up to the old Schattenland asylum?" he asked.

He knew by the look on each of their faces that they did.

"Local folks called it Mount Misery," Elroy said. "Those kids were treated awful. The guards starved them, made them work like slaves, and beat them. I hate to think what else happened in the dark."

"It was a popular place for teenagers back in the day," Coogan explained. "The girls got scared and the boys acted brave. Then, um, nature took over. But I'm not sure I could find my way up there anymore."

"I can," said Father Bert.

Given the spooky place's naughty history, Deaf Row was unanimously surprised. *A priest?* Maybe that's how he knew about boobs.

"Nobody watched or protected the patients," Father Bert said. "It would have been too expensive to hire real orderlies and guards. They were all locked in together— men, women, kids, adults. It didn't matter. Deplorable. They exploited and molested each other in the most abominable ways."

Bell listened intently, as everyone else did.

"Sometimes a patient died," Father Bert said. "And sometimes the girls—and I mean *young* girls—had their rapists' illegitimate babies. An asylum was an unfriendly environment for infants. Worse, their poor, troubled mothers were unprepared to take care of themselves, much less another living, breathing human. Many of the babies, maybe most, died."

The priest crossed himself before he continued.

"There's a little cemetery hidden in the woods up there. Hired men wrapped their little bodies in soiled sheets and took them out to this hidden cemetery, where they'd built a scaffold that"—Father Bert's voice faltered ever so slightly—"had a trap door rigged over a deep hole. It was so no single one of them had to throw a baby's corpse into a black hole. They were more concerned with their own souls than the babies'.

"So, they put the dead child on the trap door, sprinkled it with lime, and tripped the mechanism. The baby fell into that mass grave with all the other dead babies. No names, no blessing, no memories, no sign that they'd ever existed."

Bell looked away rather than let the fellas see that his eyes were moist. But so were theirs.

"Years later, I was a young, idealistic priest in a wealthy suburb of Denver," Father Bert went on. "A parishioner had been one of the asylum's hired men when he was young, and he confessed his sin to me. I went up there and found a deep depression in the earth right where he said it would be. By then, the sides of that unholy grave had collapsed and, mercifully, dirt and stones filled the hole.

"I rushed back to Denver and immediately asked the archbishop for permission to consecrate that spot, but he denied it. The babies were never baptized, he said, so the Vatican disapproved. I went higher up the chain, but nobody would buck the Pope. Nobody."

Bell smiled. He'd admired his friend's plain-spoken, rebellious devotion for a long time, but suddenly even more.

"So, I consecrated that spot on my own. The Pope might not have approved, but I gave a proper funeral for those little souls. And I placed a stone there so they wouldn't be forgotten."

But that wasn't the end of the priest's story.

"I paid for that stone with my career," he said. "The archbishop—God rest his soul—exiled me to a remote outpost, a declining little parish where priests went to die. It was punishment for my insubordination, but he didn't know

I'd never want to leave. And that, my friends, is how I got to St. Barnabas."

"Bless you, Father," Ollie Fuhrman said softly. The priest nodded and smiled.

"Woodrow, I can take you there," Father Bert said. "If you can swear you'll be a good passenger."

Bell shook his head.

"I'll be a good passenger, padre, when you become a good driver."

THE ROAD TO the asylum was unearthly. Over the past fifty years, the mountain had reclaimed the steep, bumpy two-track. It was now a barely visible, frozen crease through a narrow gap in the pines.

Father Bert's elderly Bronco lumbered along at a mile an hour, bouncing every loose thing inside. Even though he had geared into four-wheel-drive, his tires occasionally spun on the frosty surface. Winter came earlier at this altitude, so the Bronco's heater did its best to keep up, but sometimes the best is not enough.

"The asylum is still about a mile up," Father Bert said. "Should be there in, oh, thirty minutes, give or take."

Bell pulled up his coat collar. Conversation was difficult over the Ford's engine noise and overworked heater fan.

"You might have mentioned this part," Bell complained.

"But I didn't fart."

"Not *fart*," Bell growled. "Nevermind."

Father Bert spoke next as they bumped along.

"What do you expect to find here, Woodrow?"

"I don't know. It's like a wolf's tracks in the snow. You're not sure where the wolf is, but you can find where he's been."

Bell told the priest about Erskine Midwinter, the institutions, his brutalities. The monstrous boy had grown into a monstrous man. Bell hadn't yet connected the dots that led to Cherish Nelson, but Midwinter's dots led someplace evil. Where? Bell didn't know, but the Schattenland asylum is where it started.

"It might be a wild goose chase," he said.

Father Bert heard him just fine.

"In the end, we will be judged by the evil we did, for sure," the priest said, "but also by the good we left undone. You already know that, or we wouldn't be freezing our asses off right now."

"Can a priest say 'ass'?"

"Only in the presence of an actual ass," he said. "The Pope says it all the time."

The priest was silent for a while as they trundled through the trees, going higher.

"I've always wondered if we could go back to our childhoods and see that exact moment when we were committed to what we would become," Father Bert said.

Bell didn't think about it very long. It spilled out like an unburdening.

"I went home after the war. But it wasn't the same home. I couldn't be the same person who left. I had to make new mistakes," he said. "But in a lot of ways, I'd never really left that place. I always thought I was a fraud, that I'd forgotten something important, that I was not doing what I was supposed to do, and I was already late for ... whatever.

"I still feel that way, all the stuff I always hated, like dead bugs splattered against my windshield in the dark. But now I think we're all that way. Me, you, Charlie ... and my guy, this Erskine Midwinter. So maybe this is the place he can't leave."

Father Bert nodded. "Maybe so.

They crept farther into the trees. Their path narrowed until the pines were an arm's reach out of both side windows.

"That was a good thing you did," Bell said. "The babies and the blessing."

"Today is what?" Father Bert strained to hear above the din.

"Babies. Blessing," Bell thundered. "I don't know why I try, goddammit."

Father Bert grinned.

"This thing you're doing is a blessing, too," he said. "You could have walked away, and you nearly did. But you didn't."

Bell brushed off the sentiment.

"New mistakes," is all he said.

THE ABANDONED SCHATTENLAND Lunatic Asylum rose from the forest like a rotten tooth.

Bell and Father Bert had parked more than a half-mile away, blocked by the forest from going any farther. They hiked the rest of the way under a murky grey, impressionist sky, not dark and not light. The darkening canopy of pines increasingly deflected light, snow, and casual curiosity.

When they could finally see the asylum through the trees, Bell thought the Gothic derelict looked haunted on even the clearest mountain days. That they were easily twenty miles from the nearest town, damn near straight up a mountain, made it even creepier.

Father Bert told the story like a docent in a museum: Built during the Depression by an immigrant German psychiatrist named Schattenland, vagrants earned a dollar a day to collect large stones to build the asylum. Schattenland envisioned a progressive utopia where his patients might be healed by calm and refuge, so he chose a location as remote as he could find in the Colorado mountains.

Unfortunately, despite Schattenland's good intentions, the asylum quickly overflowed. And most of his patients were merely difficult children institutionalized by penniless parents.

During World War II, anybody named Schattenland would have been eyeballed as a likely Nazi collaborator, so he sold the asylum and fled America. The new management kept the name but had no scientific vision, no concern for the patients' wellbeing, and no reluctance to profit from unhealthy minds.

Overnight, Schattenland went from a place for healing to a horror show.

After the war, the State of Colorado paid per head to relieve overcrowding in its own mental hospitals, so the Schattenland asylum crammed as many unfortunates into its dank spaces as possible. Beatings, gang rapes, even murders went uninvestigated. Some big companies paid for ethically questionable experiments to be conducted on the inmates, enriching Schattenland's investors even more.

In 1969, an enterprising *Denver Post* reporter exposed Schattenland's horrors. The house of cards tumbled. State money dried up and the owners faced criminal charges, so they simply unlocked every door and gate, then vanished in the night. The mad inmates scattered to the winds, too.

And again overnight, Schattenland changed. This time, it went from horror show to haunted house.

"I'm not sure this place looked any less fearsome back in its heyday," Bell said. He was astounded by the asylum's size and history. Mount Misery was an apt sobriquet.

Bell and Father Bert pushed through the decaying front door, their portal into the outer rings of Hell.

The old asylum had been ravaged by time and trespassers. For decades, it had attracted high-altitude squatters, horny teenagers, hikers, and other adventuresome intruders who were fascinated with forgotten things.

The third floor, where patients were housed in one mammoth wing, now contained only dreadful stories and the debris of its past: sagging bed frames whose mattresses had been shredded by mice, indecipherable scratchings and sketches on the walls, a broken TV, one roller skate, antique fixtures that probably never worked very well, shattered lightbulbs still in their sockets, desks, busted toilets, even clothing. Windows were broken or falling in, doors—all bored with peepholes—tilted off their hinges, and rodents multiplied.

At the opposite end of a long, labyrinthine hallway, past a steel gate, were the administrative offices, with hulking oak desks, cracked leather chairs, and wrecked windows that must have thrown beautiful light once. The anteroom, probably the secretary's work area, housed a decaying desk, a rotary phone, a vintage typewriter, and a coat closet held shut with a banged-up Houdini padlock. Scattered papers littered the floor, their words long ago faded. Bygone sofas and the tarnished skeletons of Tiffany table lamps lent a kind of phantom elegance, a different world from the other wing of the wrecked asylum.

In the city, an abandoned building like this would be covered in graffiti, but this was too far and too inaccessible for urban taggers. It was too far and too steep for scavengers and looters to come for junk, or to haul their junk out. *The path of least resistance.*

The cop and the priest said almost nothing as they walked through the cold, drafty halls, picking up peculiar items such as medical instruments and old skeleton keys. How these artifacts had not already been carried off was inexplicable to Bell, except that not every wanderer who came here was a thief. Or they knew the place was cursed.

On the second floor, ten feet closer to perdition, they came upon the madhouse's empty kitchen, dining room, and abandoned upholstery and repair shop. Crippled wicker wheelchairs, three-legged benches, baby cribs, broken crutches, a damaged piano, and every other kind of cheap furniture imaginable, all draped in cobwebs, were piled in one corner. Forlorn spools of thick, black catgut used to stitch old shoes stood in ranks among antique cobbling benches. Only the smaller hand tools were missing, probably because they were more easily carried down the mountain in backpacks.

And in the windowless basement, down a narrow flight of shrieking wooden stairs, Bell and Father Bert entered the realm of the dead. They first peeked inside a dark roomful of suitcases piled up nearly to the ceiling and some clothing hanging in a closet. Next to it was a tiled slaughterhouse where the asylum's meat must have been butchered. Large hooks dangled from the ceiling.

And next to the butchery was the morgue.

"The hired man in my church told me they would store the bodies all winter because the ground was too frozen to dig a grave," Father Bert said. "This must be where they ..."

Besides the stairs back to the natural world above, the only other door out of the basement led from the morgue to the secluded cemetery in the trees behind the old asylum. Bell pulled the heavy knob and it came off in his hand. So, grabbing a rusty shovel, he pried the rotten wood open, loosing a blast of winter air that smacked them in the face.

Father Bert knew the way. In a tumbledown caretaker's shed back there, Bell and the priest found rusty axes, shovels and other digging implements ... and a couple dozen unpainted wooden crosses in a pile, waiting for names.

They trudged on through a few inches of snow to a nameless graveyard filled with nameless dead. It didn't look like a cemetery because no fence encircled it and all the handmade wooden crosses had had long since rotted away. But under a blanket of snow, Bell could make out rows of subtle mounds over a couple of dozen graves. Bell reckoned frozen ground or ancient roots had forbidden deeper holes. These were probably simple, shallow graves mounded with stones to keep predators away. He hated the thought of it.

And farther down the invisible path was the mass grave Father Bert had sanctified. Now, it was only an indistinct circle being swallowed up by the forest. The only way to know that an untold number of babies' bodies lay beneath the snow was a small granite marker left by a determined young priest a long time ago. It said, "To those who shall not be forgotten."

"Who padlocks a coat closet?" Bell asked out of nowhere.

"What?"

"Upstairs, in the secretary's office," Bell said. "There was a bolted door where the coat closet should be."

Father Bert squinted at Bell, incredulous.

"With every godforsaken piece of Hell we saw in there—the wheelchairs, the toys, the slaughterhouse, the morgue, for God's sake—you remember a *closet*?"

Bell started back, retracing their footsteps in the snow.

"Trust me," he said. "It's not a closet."

Bell grabbed a steel digging bar from the caretaker's shed as he barreled back down the snowy path toward the asylum's morgue door.

"What are you planning to do, Woodrow?" the priest asked, hustling close behind in the slippery snow.

"You'll see," he said.

"Wool *what*?"

Bell cursed under his breath and plowed ahead.

The day was long past when Bell could take two steps at a time, up or down. But what he lacked in the length of his steps, he made up for in forward momentum. Father Bert fell further behind as they climbed three flights of stairs to the little secretary's alcove. The closet door had been bolted for more than fifty years. Whatever it contained was important enough to lock up securely, but for some reason, the fleeing owners couldn't take it with them.

Bell could tell from the stout padlock's scars that he wasn't the first to try to break in, but he'd damn sure be the most determined. It looked like a lock from an Old West prison and might even have been the same kind that Schattenland's ward keepers used to lock in the patients every night.

He hacked at it a couple times, fruitlessly. He stepped back and swung the digging bar like a baseball bat, connecting squarely twice. The lock held.

Then with a forty-pound swing so powerful that even Babe Ruth would be impressed, Bell walloped the door itself, putting nothing more than a small dent in the thick hardwood. The wood must have been two inches thick and been further reinforced inside, like a safe. Then he tried to stab the bar into the hairline gap between the door and frame, to pry the whole damn thing out. No luck.

"Might this work?" Father Bert said.

He dangled an old skeleton key between his fingers.

"Where the hell ...?" Bell was astonished.

"It was hanging on a hook under the desk," the priest said. "Right where my grandmother hid the key to her hope chest, on a hook under her sewing table."

Bell slipped the key into the padlock and the unbreakable steel shank, frozen in place for almost as long as Bell had been alive, clicked but didn't open. With a couple more whacks, the rust surrendered, and it popped open.

Unshackling the padlock was the easy part.

The intractable door didn't budge. A buckled floor, a half ton of wood and god-knows-what reinforcement behind it, arthritic hinges ... the damn thing was wedged in its frame with no handle to pull. And Bell had no tools thin enough to shove into the narrow slot between the door and jamb that might lever it free.

"Try this," Father Bert said. He unfolded a pocketknife big enough to cut a steak.

"Can a priest carry a knife that big?" Bell asked. "Hhh ... heck, can he carry a knife at all?"

Father Bert smiled. "Self-defense against demons and confessions gone wrong."

The priest slid the blade into the tight groove that was thinner than a pencil lead. He ran it down the length of the door until it hit something metal on the other side. Then he slid it up until, again, it hit a metal obstruction.

"You got a knife, Woodrow?" he asked.

Bell fished in his pocket for his folding knife, which he was embarrassed to admit wasn't as long as his friend's.

"Slide yours in and go up until it stops," the priest instructed. "Then press it up hard."

Bell wondered if the priest had any idea what he just said. But he did as he was told while Father Bert slid his knife down until it thumped against the metal behind. Then he pushed down hard with both hands.

Something heavy clanked inside. The door cracked open.

"Are you shitting me?" Bell gusted, heaving the door open far enough to get inside. "Did your grandma have one of these in her pantry, too?"

"Nope," Father Bert said. "In the outhouse. Internal latches. Bears and Grandpa were a problem."

The space behind the door was filled with ... dark. They saw nothing but black.

"You don't have a flashlight in your magic pocket, do you?" Bell tried to pull the door wider, but it high-centered tight against the warped floor.

"As a matter of fact, I do," the priest said. He fished around his other pants pocket and pulled out a cellphone. He pressed a few buttons, and a bright light came on.

"I'll be damned," Bell said. "I didn't know you had one of those. There's a flashlight in it?"

"And a camera. And a clock. And a record player that plays whatever song you tell it."

Bell's eyebrows arched as Father Bert squeezed into the small gap and shined his light into the cubby behind the door. Bell tried but couldn't see around him.

"Okay, now that's interesting," the old priest said, peering into the darkness.

"What?" the impatient old cop demanded.

"There's stuff in here."

Bell raised his voice. "Goddammit, what?"

"Language, Woodrow."

"If you can say 'shit,' I can say 'goddammit,' dammit. Now, what the hell is in there?"

Father Bert leaned farther inside.

"Books."

Bell was befuddled. "You mean, like a library? Why would anybody lock up some old books?"

"Not that kind of books." Father Bert handed Bell his cellphone flashlight to peek inside for himself.

Inside, Bell saw three or four giant, leather-bound ledgers, the kind courthouse clerks used before computers. Hell, before ballpoint pens. As big and thick as a trunk lid, with old-fashioned hubbed spines, they lay stacked on a stout oak writing desk. That was all. The space was otherwise empty. Not even dust had intruded.

Bell took one step into the room and heard the floorboards groan painfully. He stepped back outside.

"Padre," he said. "You go."

"No way."

"C'mon, have faith," Bell encouraged. "You're half my size. You won't fall as fast or land as hard."

Father Bert shined his light on the floor, where a roof leak had stained and rotted the wood planks for decades. He scowled before taking a cautious step inside while Bell held his waistband. The floorboards creaked again, but not as sorely. He took another step, then another, until he reached the stack of ledgers.

"Now what?" he asked Bell.

"Look inside," he said. "What do you see?"

The priest opened the top volume's heavy cover and bent down for a closer look.

"The handwriting is too small, and too indecipherable in this light. There are a lot of columns and rows, filled with scribbling," he said, flipping through it. "Pages and pages."

Bell considered their options.

"Then let's get them out here," he said.

Father Bert shot him a querulous look. "And how will we do that? If I pick up one of these books, I'll be heavier than you. Then I'll fall faster and hit harder."

Bell looked around for something he could use as a kind of sled to pull the ledgers across the feeble flooring, one by one. He saw nothing.

"Wait here," he said, as if the priest had a choice.

Bell disappeared down the hall, toward the patients' wing on the far side of the building. In a few minutes he returned, pushing a rickety wicker wheelchair with a broken seat. But the wheels worked and that's all that mattered. He took off his belt and looped it around the rear handlebar then shoved it toward Father Bert.

"Put one of the books on this," he said, "and I'll pull it out."

The priest lifted one ledger—easily twenty-five pounds, maybe more—and laid it across the cracked wooden armrests, then Bell pulled it out. He removed the book and shoved the wheelchair back inside. Twice again, he reeled ledgers into the light.

When they finished, Bell reached inside to grip the priest's hand and guided him to the safety of stronger floors.

Bell glanced at a few pages in all of them. He couldn't decode the handwriting, except the left-most column appeared to be people's names. The sun had fallen behind the trees, a north wind had kicked up, and the air had quickly turned very cold. Their breath came out in frosty clouds.

"We can't stay here to translate all this," he said. "We need to take these back down the mountain."

"We're parked a half-mile away, Woodrow. With old man knees. In the snow. In the cold. Maybe in the dark, if we don't hurry," the good father said. "How the hell are we gonna do that?"

"Can a priest say 'hell'?" Bell asked. "Never mind. I suppose you're required to say it occasionally. Anyway, you take one and I'll take two. And we'll hurry."

Father Bert scoffed. "Neither of us 'hurries.' But if we're going, let's go."

He crossed himself and hoisted one of the big books. Bell hoisted the other two, knowing they weren't as heavy now as they'd be at the bottom of the hill.

They skidded and lurched down the slippery slope to the priest's cantankerous Bronco, where they turned the fussy heater on high and gulped the last of the priest's hidden pint of Jameson's to warm up. Then they bounced back to Midnight in the dark.

They weren't sure what they had in the back seat, much less whether the books would reveal anything about Erskine Midwinter, but they knew one thing for certain: Those ledgers had been better protected than the patients at Mount Misery.

BACK IN MIDNIGHT, they spread the fragile ledger books across Bell's dinner table. Bell put out a box of cookies, two slices of leftover pizza, and two beers, but their curiosity and better judgment outweighed their hunger.

Even under brighter light, row upon row, column upon column, the handwritten entries were too small and incomprehensible, except for the occasional familiar words and numbers that appeared. But they were too few and too far between to make much sense. The rest might have been code, technical abbreviations, or simply chicken-scratchings. They didn't know.

In each book, the script changed for a few pages, then again a few pages later, and again and again. All of it was cryptic. They agreed they could pee in the snow more legibly.

"You know what they say about doctors' handwriting," Father Bert said, only half-joking. "These must be doctors."

Every forty or fifty pages, a date would be jotted at the top of a page, allowing them to put these ledgers in order. On the first page of the first ledger, the date "April 17, 1942," and on the last page of entries in the last book, "October 29, 1969."

"So the entries start about the time ol' Doc Schattenland catches a boat back to Germany and the new owners take over," Bell surmised. "And they end about the time the swindlers bail out."

"And if the entries are made by doctors, they came and went frequently," Father Bert pointed out.

The old cop and the old priest pored over the pages for a couple hours, gleaning only the vague impression that these jottings documented interactions between the asylum's medical staff and Schattenland's patients. Beyond that, it made no sense to them.

"The only handwriting I've seen that's worse is Dan Coogan's," the priest said. "And sometimes he can't even read it."

Out of the blue, Bell had an idea.

Fifteen minutes later—near ten p.m.—they stood in the old newspaper editor's kitchen on Blossom Street with their big books. They'd interrupted him. He was writing this week's column for the *Midnight Sun*, about Midnight's first real celebrity: A 1920s prospector who died and was kept on ice for fifty years in a backyard storage shed, where curious gawkers would pay a dollar apiece to see his frosty carcass.

They had a more somber story. Coogan already knew the story of Mount Misery, but they told him about wandering through the abandoned asylum that afternoon, the cold patient lockups, colder morgue, cemetery, decaying offices—and the secret cubby.

"Sounds like a real fun day, fellas," Coog said, "but why the hell... sorry, Father ... why the heck are you both standing in my kitchen past my bedtime?"

Bell piped up.

"We need your help, Coog. You have a lot of experience reading bad handwriting. But you also have a lot of experience making sense of bad handwriting. And seeing how different things relate to each other. You know, what it all means."

Coogan was petulant.

"My handwriting isn't that bad," he said. "That's just gossip."

Bell persisted.

"Look, back when I was a real cop, we had experts in this kind of thing," he said. "Now I've only got you and the guys. You helped me before on this case. Now I'm looking for information about an inmate back in the Sixties named Erskine Midwinter, but we can't make out this gibberish. I don't know if there's anything about him in here, but it might help me help Luther Nelson. You've spent your whole career making sense of things that don't make sense. Just take a look, would you?"

Coogan's mouth had fallen open.

"God Almighty—sorry, Father—I mean goddammit, Woodrow, I don't think I've heard you say that much in one sitting for the past nine years. Impressive."

Being impressive, Bell sensed an opening.

"So could you look at these, Coog, and tell us what you see?"

Coogan surrendered.

"Hell, it isn't like I have other things to do like, oh, writing my future Pulitzer Prize-winning column every week," he said. "No promises. I'll see what I see unless I don't see anything, then I'll tell you what I saw."

"Fair enough," Bell said.

"Bless you, Coog," Father Bert said. "You're doing God's work here, you old fart."

Coogan cocked his head as they turned to leave.

"Hey, wait a minute. Can a priest say 'fart'?" he asked, but they were already halfway out the door.

THE NEXT MORNING, Dan Coogan stomped his feet in the cold outside of Tommyknockers.

All the other guys sat inside, drinking their second cups of coffee, as usual, when Bell came across the street toward the diner.

"Hey, Coog," he said. "You look like hell. Up late with that column?"

"No," he snipped. "I was up all night with your damn project."

Bell apologized out loud, but was secretly eager to hear what Coogan found.

"And it's a three-volume horror story, Woodrow," the old newspaperman said.

Bell was a little surprised. He reckoned Coog had seen worse in his career, but the task might be bigger than the old guy. Clearly, he was wrong.

"A lot of these inmates were kids, and they weren't insane at all," Coogan continued. "They had just been passed among various institutions because they had behavior problems, developmental disabilities, or had merely been abandoned by their families."

Strait jackets, beatings, lobotomies, electroconvulsive therapies, solitary confinement, powerful drugs—sometimes administered by non-medical staffers—were all preferred therapies at Schattenland.

"Your fella, Erskine Midwinter, shows up a few times in the ledgers," Coogan reported, glancing at a notebook he carried. "They tried everything on the poor kid. He was even considered a good candidate for a lobotomy in 1965 ..."

"Eleven years old," Bell said.

"But the doctor resigned before the surgery," Coogan continued. "So he got electroshocks every week in 1966 ..."

"Twelve."

"And finally an anti-psychotic zombie drug called Thorazine in 19579 ..."

"Thirteen."

And Bell knew that in 1969 Erskine Midwinter re-entered a world that never wanted him. He must have been more than angry. He must have wanted vengeance on ... anyone.

"There's a lot more, Woodrow," Coogan said.

A cold wind rushed down Main Street.

"Should we go inside where it's warm?" Bell asked.

"No," he said. "This is pretty bad stuff. I don't want the guys ... you know."

Bell nodded. "So, what else did you find?"

Coogan flipped a page in his reporter's notebook.

"Did your mom ever make Pilgrims Porridge for breakfast when you were a kid?"

"Sure," Bell said. "Didn't everybody's?"

"Yeah, well, back in the 1960s, Pilgrims Porridge wanted a bigger share of the breakfast cereal market. So they secretly funded an experiment at the Dallas Institute of Technology to prove Pilgrims Porridge was more nutritious than its competitors.

"The kids at Schattenland were their guinea pigs," Coogan said. "Starting in 1968, these so-called 'feeble-minded' children were fed big bowls of Pilgrims Porridge every day for two months, not knowing it was loaded with radioactive chemicals to help scientists trace the yummy stuff as it gurgled through their digestive system."

"Good god," Bell said.

"Those ledgers recorded it all. Pilgrims Porridge paid the asylum fifty bucks for every patient who participated. In the end, Schattenland sold out innocent children for about four thousand bucks. Pilgrims Porridge made millions, but nobody gave a good-goddam what it cost those poor kids."

At the risk of seeming callous about dozens of furtively poisoned children, Bell had to ask about one.

"Midwinter. Was he ...?"

"Yeah, he was one of them. But a year after this experiment, the asylum went belly up and those kids scattered. Your guy, too. Nobody ever knew what it did to them."

Again, Bell apologized.

"I didn't know, Coog."

Dan Coogan waved him off, as if it wasn't a big deal. But it was a big deal to the old newspaperman.

"You go find your guy, Woodrow," he said. "If you don't mind, I'd like to keep your big books for a while longer. I'll take care of them, and you'll always know where they are."

Coogan walked away toward Blossom Street. Maybe tomorrow he'd see the boys on Deaf Row, but right now he needed some time alone.

And Bell wondered how fast he could get to Purgatory.

PURGATORY (THE TOWN, not the punishment) nestled in a glacial valley near the Continental Divide, a different world high above the metro-cowboy swank of Denver.

Across the mountains to the north was Paradise Peak Ski Resort, a four-mountain snow spectacle where Hollywood celebrities and hedge-fund billionaires in their designer winterwear landed in their private jets to stay in their luxury ski-in chalets—and where *People* magazine maintained a winter bureau. Over the mountains to the south was Twilight Basin Ski Area, where déclassé ski-bums slid down the one mountain in scruffy parkas on last year's skis.

And right between Paradise and Twilight was Purgatory. Nobody settled there on purpose, although plenty of the locals wanted out as soon as possible.

A sign at the edge of town read, "Welcome to Purgatory—Slow the Hell Down." It didn't matter because only one road entered Purgatory, and the other end of it went nowhere. All but one of its "streets" were streets in name only, being unpaved. The only gas station had pumps but ran out of gas every couple of weeks. If ten computers signed onto the hamster-wheel Internet at the same time it crashed, but the good news was that there were only fifteen computers in town. The biggest nearby town was Eagle Fork (Pop. 849), but the good groceries and hardware stores were at least ninety miles farther down the other side of the mountain.

So most of Purgatory's citizens knew when Bell parked his Crown Vic in front of the town's only diner, Burgatory. A little bell tinkled as he entered. Inside, a year-old auto parts calendar was tacked up behind the register, a flyswatter hung beside the kitchen door, and three two-tops sat unbussed. In summer, there'd be flies.

A weary waitress, short and stout and well past her Midol years, refreshed a couple local codgers' coffee with her right hand and balanced three dirty plates in her left. She looked eighty, Bell guessed, older than all of them, but she carried herself like a thug.

"Excuse me, ma'am," Bell said over the counter, maybe a little louder than he should, in case she was hard of hearing.

"I'm looking for an old friend I knew a long time ago. Somebody told me his mom was living here in Purgatory. Name is Rosemary, I think. She was Rosemary Midwinter when I knew her son back in the day, but maybe she got married. Know her?"

The waitress wore a name tag that simply said, "Don't Even Ask." She sized Bell up.

"You ain't from around here, big fella," she said. The old guys got a kick out of it. "What'd you say your name was?"

Bell wasn't ready to reveal he was a curious cop, so he cupped his hand behind his left ear. "Say again? Deaf on one side."

"Your name?" she said louder.

"I'm not Wayne," he said.

Now the waitress hollered.

"Your name, goddammit!"

"So sorry, ma'am," he said, pointing to his "bad" ear. "I'm Woodrow Bell. Old friend of her boy's. Long time ago. She might not even remember me. Do you know Rosemary?"

Don't Even Ask wasn't done with Bell. She spoke loudly this time.

"What's your business, Wayne or Woodrow or whoever? Sellin' somethin'?"

Bell faked a big smile.

"Happily retired, ma'am," he said. "Forty years workin' for the City of Denver ... if you can call being a government employee 'workin,' am I right?"

Everybody laughed except Don't Even Ask, who smelled like cigarettes and Aqua Net hair spray. In some old ladies it was possible to see vestiges of the pretty girls they once were, but not her. Her tired eyes were set deep. They looked as if she smeared on blue eye shadow with her thumb and drew on her eyebrows with a Sharpie. A hard life was written all over her face, but she probably made other lives hard, too, Bell thought. Hers must not have amounted to much if she was waiting tables in an end-of-the-road greasy spoon when she should already be on her second walker.

"And you knew her how?" she asked Bell.

"Her cow?"

The waitress wasn't frustrated. She was pissed.

"You ... knew ... her ... HOW?" she thundered.

Bell shrugged and pointed to his ear again.

"Her son Erskine and I was in the deaf school together when we was just grade-school squirts. Little Ersy—that's what we called him—didn't talk real good but when he did, he talked about his mom. Homesick kid, you know? Now I'm tryin' to find him, and I thought maybe his mom might know where he got to, if she's still alive."

Don't Even Ask still looked suspicious.

"Deaf school, huh?"

Bell cocked his "good" ear toward her.

"Say again," he said, "death mule?"

The elderly waitress muttered something under her breath that sounded to both of Bell's good ears like "fuckin' deaf asshole." But he smiled wide like a half-deaf old fart she thought he was.

"Ain't seen her in a blue moon," Don't Even Ask said as she sprayed window cleaner on the countertop and wiped the sticky laminate from the last century. When she reached to the far side of the counter with her right hand, Bell spied a small but conspicuous prison tattoo, a wristwatch with no hands.

"So you know her?"

"Once."

"So do you know where I might find her?" Bell pressed.

Don't Even Ask turned away.

"Green and white trailer up Packer Road, maybe two miles," she said. "Can't miss it, but she won't be around 'til past dinner hour, maybe seven. But don't expect much. She don't remember a lot. Long time ago. Different days. Different life."

Bell pushed again, a tad too far.

"Does she ..."

She cut him off mid-question.

"Look, dumbass, if you're not eatin' then get the hell out," Don't Even Ask snarled. "This is a restaurant not a quiz show."

"This was a haunted disco?" Bell again pointed to his "bad" ear and acted surprised. "Bet them ghosts' favorite song is 'Stayin' Alive'!"

The waitress flipped him off. The old guys got a big kick out of that one. Bell just turned and walked out of Burgatory.

A LITTLE PAST seven in the winter darkness, Bell turned off the blacktop onto Packer Road, marked by a "Dead End" sign.

After the longest two miles he'd seen since Vietnam, he pulled up on the dirt patch in front of a green-and-white trailer. Peeling, gray plywood covered a few windows that must have broken a long time ago. A half-dozen old tires held down the tin roof. Privy out back. A propane tank perched on cinder blocks off to the side. Last summer's weeds stood tall, dead, and unmowed. No car, no gate, no dog, no neighbors, no signs of life in any direction. The old detective wondered if Don't Even Ask had directed him to the local meth lab.

Maybe so. The grungy mobile home sat far enough off the blacktop for him to wonder why a ninety-year-old woman would live this far out, unless she wanted to die and not be found for a week or two. A meth lab was more likely.

Bell wasn't carrying. But to be on the safe side while he checked out the place, he kept the engine running and slid his driver seat back slightly until most of his head was shielded by the exterior pillar between the front and back doors. It was an extra layer of security for patrol cops and gangbangers who feared ambushes in bad neighborhoods—and retired detectives in fluky spots.

Something else bugged him. Something ever-so-slightly unnatural, like a coffee cup handle turned to the left. It wasn't the old men in the diner, or the noxious waitress, or a trailer untethered from the rest of the world ... but all those things.

He had no strategy. He'd always been good at thinking on the fly when things went sideways, such as playing deaf with a hinky source to gain credibility.

So Bell shut off the engine, got out of his car, and knocked on the metal door.

Bell didn't smell the telltale cat-piss stench of a typical rural meth lab, and he didn't see any lights inside, but somebody was there. He stepped to one side of the door, as far as the rickety porch would allow.

A moribund bulb—*a porchlight at death's door*, Bell mused—flickered on.

The door opened slightly, and a gust of old-lady air rushed out. He thought he saw two familiar eyes—maybe it was the finger-painted blue mascara, maybe the weariness. Probably both.

Don't Even Ask.

"I knew you were a cop," she said as she opened the door wider, but still holding it like a shield. "Wayne or whoever."

"What gave it away?"

"Cop car. Cop eyes looking all around. Cop bullshit."

Don't Even Ask—Rosemary Midwinter—knew her cops, Bell had to admit. *Like son, like mother.* She was coarse and mean. Probably a hooker back in the day, maybe a junkie turned thief, or worse. She'd probably done hard time, too. That would explain the tattoo, her toxic attitude, why she lived in a decaying trailer, and had to paint herself up to serve bad coffee to bad tippers in a hash house in Purgatory. No pension.

"Yeah, well, I'm not a cop anymore," Bell said. "I'm really retired, like I said."

"So no gun and no balls," she sneered.

"Listen, Rosemary, I'm only here to talk. I got no beef with you."

"Fuck off," she said.

"It's about your son Erskine."

She peered suspiciously at Bell through the door's torn screen.

"Why the fuck do you care about him?"

Bell said nothing. Only a cop could see the flicker behind her garish eyes. He'd touched a nerve.

"I haven't seen that motherfucker in fifty years," she continued. "He bunked with me after he ran away from the loony bin. Feds told me a long time ago the fucker did a stretch for raping little girls or something. I hope he took it up the ass every morning. He was a motherfucker to the end."

For Bell, the greeting-card sweetness of that image was only eclipsed by the sound of an ex-con grandmother calling her son a motherfucker. But he wasn't done.

"Were you married or involved at the time?" he asked. "Was that guy the dad?"

That set Rosemary back for a second or two. She had no profane comeback or obscene suggestion. She just stared holes in him until she could speak again. Something changed. Bell didn't get it.

"I was raped."

Bell didn't see that coming, but in the next split-second he wasn't surprised. Her anger shined through whatever vulgar defenses she'd built around herself.

"I'm sorry, Rosemary," he said. "That shouldn't have happened to you. Shouldn't happen to anybody."

He'd been here before, but mostly as an observer, usually from another room. Jazz was always the one in whom rape victims confided. He learned by listening. He knew it wasn't about him, although he'd understand if Rosemary judged all men, including him. Maybe even her own son. Nevertheless, Bell consciously resisted crossing his arms or reaching out. Besides, she didn't seem like the touchy-feely type. But then, he wasn't either. It was a job, Bell reminded himself.

"Was the guy ever busted?" the old cop asked.

"Why the fuck do you care? That prick's been dead almost sixty years now. I hope they're rotting in Hell."

Now Bell knew Rosemary's rapist wasn't a stranger. Angry ex-boyfriend? Neighbor? A brother or cousin? Maybe a molesting father or uncle? Whoever it was, she knew his name. How else would she know—or care—that he died decades later?

And *they're*? Was she gang-raped?

As always, Bell had more questions than answers. It was the curse of good detectives. Like it or not, there was always one more thing to ask, one more thing to know.

"Who was it?" Bell asked.

"No way." Rosemary shook her head. "No way."

"Okay, but Erskine was his?"

"You figured that out on your own, Sherlock?" she snapped.

"Did you tell anybody? A friend? Your parents?"

Rosemary again fixed him in her glare. Another nerve.

"I was twelve fucking years old, dumbass. Who'd believe a twelve-year-old kid?"

Bell did the math. If Erskine Midwinter was born in 1954 to twelve-year-old Rosemary, she was born in '42. She was only in her late seventies, much younger than she looked.

"It's been a long time," he said, "but I could connect you with somebody if you want. Maybe somebody who could help. Or just listen."

Rosemary Midwinter blew him off.

"Pffft. I don't like you, I don't like cops, and I don't like shrinks. And I'm tired of shooting the shit with you, Wayne or whatever. My son was a black stain on everything. He reminded me every fucking day of ... oh, just get the fuck off my property and don't come back."

"Not a problem," Bell said. "Sorry about bringing up all these bad memories. I hope things work out for you."

"Never did before," she said. "I won't hold my breath."

Bell had one last request of Don't Even Ask.

"It's a long trip home. Can I use your facilities?"

For the first time all day, Rosemary Midwinter smiled as genuinely as she probably had since the Johnson Administration.

"The 'facilities'? You crack me up, Wayne. Yeah, out back. And don't get your cop piss on the seat."

And with that, she closed her door. Bell heard the deadbolt click, and the dusky porchlight went black.

In the dark, he walked carefully through the dried-up thistles around the trailer, where he could smell the outhouse before he saw it. Only a couple old screws held the wood door on its hinges, and it didn't close all the way. Not a huge privacy issue way out here.

Bell unspooled some toilet paper from a roll hanging on a rusty nail. He wiped the busted seat all the way around. Then he wrapped the soiled wad in a few feet of clean tissue, stuffed it in his jacket pocket, and left.

On the way back to Midnight, Bell had plenty of windshield time. Thoughts fermented. He wondered about a lot of things. What was Rosemary hiding? Does a butt even have DNA in it? Should he get a new jacket now? How'd she get home from the diner? And why would anyone sit in a muddy green truck at the side of a dead-end dirt road after dark, watching Rosemary Midwinter's trailer?

CHARLIE HAD BUILT a fire in Bell's perpetually cold house and waited for him to come home.

It wasn't his habit to stay out past bedtime, but she didn't worry much about him. He could take care of himself in the dark. But she also knew that if he stayed out late, something was on his mind, and he would need her to listen.

A little past eleven, Charlie saw headlights pan across the wall and heard the old Crown Vic crunch into the alley snow. Soon, she heard Bell stomping his big boots on the porch.

"Now this is a nice surprise," he said, coming through the back door in a cold swirl. "What's up?"

"I made you dinner," she said. "Well, I *bought* you dinner. Then I ate it. So I *made* you a new dinner. Then it got cold. Then I made a fire and looked for a book to read. Did you know you don't have any books?"

"I already read them all."

"Uh-huh. All the books? Ever written? In the world?"

"How many could there be?" he asked.

"Will you read mine?"

"If you ever finish, I will. Well, most of it. Will there be dirty bits?"

Charlie rolled her eyes. "You suck."

Bell hung his coat on the back of the basement door and grabbed a beer from the fridge. He hunkered down at his breakfast table while Charlie heated his cold chicken-fried steak slathered in congealed white gravy.

"What keeps you up so late tonight?" she asked.

"At the moment? You."

"You didn't say anything about going walkabout," she said. "That's not you."

Charlie was right. Bell spent most of his days in Midnight and when he didn't, Charlie always knew. Except this time.

"I left early to Purgatory," he said. "Sort of a spur-of-the-moment thing. An hour up the mountain and an hour down."

Bell had opened the door, and Charlie let him walk through.

"And then ...?"

He told her about the diner, Don't Even Ask, the tattoo, the deaf ruse, the dead-end road, the trailer, Rosemary Midwinter, the rape, her ghost-son Erskine, the fuck-you goodbye, the guy in the pickup, the long drive home, even the black ice over the pass ... but not the outhouse.

When she left the kitchen briefly, Bell delicately plucked the repulsive wad of toilet paper from his coat pocket, sealed it in a plastic sandwich bag, and quickly hid it in the never-used flour canister under the cabinet ... then washed his hands for longer than usual.

"So after all that, what are you thinking?" Charlie asked when she returned.

Bell said nothing for a while. The detective's body language gave him away. Fact is, he was thinking a lot, but none of it was coming together. A cop's life had convinced him the universe was crowded and full of coincidences. Now, he'd feel naked, like he was getting too old, to admit to Charlie there was something about the whole thing that he couldn't define.

"I just need to sleep on it," was all he said.

"I remember when my mother started losing all her memories," she said. Bell felt a non sequitur coming on. "There were the pictures she kept in her mind and the sound of our laughter in the hall and the song they played at her wedding ... and some clowns."

Bell was speechless. Charlie's mind didn't work like everybody else's, but this bordered on babble.

"Are you having a stroke?" he asked her.

"Mom always talked about her first circus and the clowns seemed magical to her," Charlie replied. "My point is this: The story only makes sense when you know about the clowns. When you find your clowns, it'll make perfect sense."

Bell was tired. So they went up to his dark bedroom and fell into bed. Charlie snuggled up close and he held her tight, but they didn't make love. He smelled apple shampoo in her hair and drifted into a twilight dream about flying to post-apocalyptic Denver because Sarah was getting married, and he intended to bring expired baked beans to her reception ... and some clowns.

But just before he slipped away to his ethereal supermarket, Charlie's head bolted up from his shoulder.

"I forgot to tell you," she said in the dark. "Doc Ely called me and said he needed to talk to you as soon as possible. Sorry."

Doc Ely had to wait.

The next morning, after Charlie showered and left to her garbage rounds, Bell drove all the way to Denver ask another favor of his old partner Jazz Jackson.

"You have dementia, Big Man," she told him, "whispering" in a way that everybody in the squad room could hear.

Bell had started the whole conversation by dropping his little plastic bag full of crumpled, slightly discolored toilet tissue on the detective's desk. She made it worse when she asked what it was. Then he made it even worse when he wondered if she might run his poopy TP through the crime lab. And that's where Jazz questioned Bell's mental health.

"You can't prove that," he challenged her loudly, then his tone became much softer and serious. "Look, I didn't ask you to smell it. Just see what it tells us."

"Did you have a search warrant?"

"No," he said, "but I'm not a cop. I don't need one. I'm just an innocent civilian poop collector who supports his underpaid local law enforcement."

"You're an insane son of a bitch, that's what you are," Jazz said. "You can't go around wiping people's butts in case they might poop out evidence in a murder case. That's just sick. You're sick. And if you hand it to us, then you're a poop-collecting *cop*."

"Well, to be fair, stealing her dentures was out of the question."

Jazz shook her head, exasperated by Bell. Again.

"What do you think this shit—literally—is gonna prove?" she asked. "That she is exactly who she claims to be, this pervert's mother? You seriously think some elderly woman might pretend to be his mom?"

"Yes, for one," he said. "For two, it might give us a connection to the guy who allegedly raped her if we can compare her and her bad-guy son. For three, her DNA profile might be better than a degraded, fifty-year-old hair sample. For four ... okay, there's only three but that's enough for us."

"Oh no, not 'us,' Big Man. This is your snipe hunt," Jazz said. "I shoulda shot you the last time, so don't piss me off. I got a lot of bullets."

Bell surrendered.

Truth be told, he didn't think it'd fly, but he had to try.

What the hell did he expect anyway? His only other option wasn't much of an option: He knew a guy at a private DNA lab that charged more money than his police pension paid, even if Bell got a deep discount.

And Jazz was right. He was a dog chasing a car ... he had no idea why he wanted it. Jazz's career shouldn't hang on an old man's gut feeling—*about what exactly?*

Jazz smiled her oblique smile that gave Bell hope she probably wouldn't shoot him.

"Look, I hope it works out and you can get some closure for your friend," she said. "And I want to help, Big Man, but I think you're heading down a rabbit hole here."

Bell had to concede she was right. It was a rabbit hole. Then she used his own words against him. He was right then, and she was right now.

"This is old-fashioned cop work, just like you taught me: knock on doors, talk to people, and use your head."

"I also told you that most of the time, it's not a long, complicated calculation that leads us to a single, undeniable fact ... it's a big pile of hunches and probabilities," he said, dispirited. "So, I'm sorry, Jazz. I shouldn't have put you in the middle. Grasping at straws, I guess."

"Do what you know better than anybody I've ever known: old school."

"Speaking of old school," he said. "Did you check the magic computer for any similar cases back in our guy's day?"

Jazz reached in her top desk drawer and slid a manila envelope across her desk toward Bell. He pulled it discreetly into his lap.

"Sorry I couldn't be more help, Big Man," she said. "You know the rules."

Jazz stood up, a signal for Bell to move along. She had her back to the few investigators still hanging around during the Friday lunch hour. So Bell got up to leave, too, his envelope shielded from view.

"Oh, one more thing," he said. "Rosemary Midwinter had a prison tat. I'm thinking she did time and probably has a long rap sheet. She'd have been born around '42, give or take. Could you ...?"

Jazz frowned and said nothing, Instead, she gripped Bell's elbow tightly as she escorted him toward the door.

"I saw what you did back there," she whispered in the doorway. "Fool me once, shame on you. Fool me twice ..."

Bell looked taken aback. Sort of.

"Dropping your butt bag in my open drawer," Jazz said. "Nope. Not this time."

Busted. Bell turned back toward Jazz's desk to retrieve his evidence, such as it was.

"Stand down, Big Man," Jazz said as she tugged on his elbow. "On your way out, just check your coat pocket."

Outmaneuvered.

ON THE WAY back up the mountain, Bell called Sarah on his burner phone. She didn't pick up—again—so he left a message. The rest of the way home, he hoped she'd call back, but the highway to Midnight was a gauntlet of dead zones, even if he'd never heard of dead zones.

Jazz's packet sat on his passenger seat, unopened. He could tell by the heft of it that it was more than a few pages but probably not a case-breaker. Just another piece of a complicated puzzle, another dot to be connected, and a shitload of other cop metaphors for more, not all.

Later that night, Bell settled into his big chair with a glass of bourbon and Jazz's envelope. She had collected more than fifty missing persons' reports about younger teenage girls abducted after school. They came from everywhere between Wyoming and New Mexico during Erskine Midwinter's presumably free years between 1969 and 1977, and since 2003. *Some* were likely runaways or parental abductions, but investigators at the time assumed *most* were. Missing teenagers weren't the highest priority in a big-city police department, especially back in the hippie days. At any rate, none of the girls were ever found. All of their cases had gone stone-cold a long time ago.

Most curious to Bell, Jazz included no unsolved murders that came close to matching Cherish Nelson's monstrous slaughter. It wasn't an oversight or petty distinction. Jazz would have looked for those first, not just regionally but nationally. They simply didn't exist.

Midwinter—or whatever psychopath he chased—had either stopped after Cherish Nelson, gone where he couldn't do it again, or evolved into a freak so perversely organized that none of his victims were ever found.

Bell wanted to believe Cherish was his last, but his gut told him she was more likely his first.

CHAPTER 7

THE NEXT MORNING, Bell arrived late at Tommyknockers, as was his habit.

Earlier, Ollie Fuhrman had dreamed up a game with simple rules: Each of them was required to look in his wallet to find one ordinary item that had extraordinary value in his life and to explain it out loud. Nobody wins, nobody loses. Everybody plays or nobody plays.

The boys of Deaf Row agreed, although Roxy Snipes was pretty sure his boring life had produced no such artifact. Father Bert sensed his trepidation and suggested a blessing might be appropriate before they began.

"Lord, the next time that any of us at this table think we are something," he prayed, "please remind us that so do the little dots on dice. Through Christ our Lord. Amen."

It was Ollie's idea, so he went first. He opened up his once-shiny, black leather wallet and searched all its secret pockets. Tucked inside one was a yellowed newspaper clipping, two paragraphs long and laminated to protect it against the inevitable creek-dunkings and machine-washings of a man's life. It was from the May 19, 1950, edition of the *Midnight Sun* and it told, in the terse vernacular of old-time journalism, about a high school junior named Alfred George Fuhrman who won the county spelling bee.

"I never won anything before that or since," he said. "So I carry this around to remind myself to smile the next time I win something."

"Maybe the county commission, eh?" Roxy said. All the boys raised their cups to Ollie.

Everybody agreed that the irksome Cotton must go next. He rummaged in his billfold for a long time before pulling out a dried-up condom whose sell-by date was in the last century.

"I carry this just in case Roxy ever gets a date," he smirked.

In reality, they all knew without him saying it, that condom symbolized an old man's undying hope. Or maybe how that part of their lives had leaked away as they grew old. Or maybe a keepsake from a missed opportunity. Or all those things.

Then Doc Ely volunteered to go. He knew exactly what and where he kept his favorite photograph of his late wife. In it, she was young and pretty, smiling at the prom camera, looking like a Hollywood princess. They'd all known Caroline, and they'd all known her to be beautiful inside and out, always the first at their doors, no matter what tragedy or triumph. They had no inkling of her sadness until her multiple sclerosis confined her to a wheelchair and she shot herself.

Nobody expected Bones to explain. They knew.

Dan Coogan came next. He displayed a fishing license that expired in 1972.

"I was carrying this the last time I fished with my brother David," Coogan said. "He knew he was dying of pancreatic cancer but didn't want to ruin a glorious day on the river by telling me. He caught the biggest rainbow I've seen before or since, and by God, he put it back in the river because he didn't think it should die, too."

The boys all knew how it felt. They'd all lost somebody. Nobody said anything for a while.

Roxy pulled a folded fifty-dollar bill from behind the plastic accordion of family photos.

"My father told me, when I was old enough, that a man should always carry fifty dollars in his wallet," he explained. "A lot of his customers had absolutely nothing and he always felt sorry for them to come to their end with nothing.

"I put my only granddaughter through college and grad school at Stanford, and now she's a big-time professor down in Boulder, but I never touched that fifty-dollar bill."

The other guys quickly checked to see what cash they carried.

"It was just good advice from my dad about having cash to cover whatever unexpected expenses might come up," Roxy said. "I'm pretty sure he didn't intend it to be a deep lesson about manhood. But to me, it was."

On the other hand, Elroy Richter carried only two pennies tucked deep inside his billfold.

"Before my father passed away in 1974, he told me that when you find a penny heads up, it is a loved one saying hello from the great beyond," he said. "So I would pick up every penny and put it in my wallet as a good luck charm.

"When my wife Helen got towards the end of her life, we talked about pennies. I asked her to find my dad and send me two pennies from the other side. After her funeral her sister and me went to dinner and she found two pennies on the floor, heads up. These are them."

Father Bert patted Elroy on the shoulder.

"I guess I'm up, eh?" the priest said. He showed his friends a picture of five smiling children in a department-store photo studio.

"Are those yours?" the impertinent Cotton asked.

Father Bert didn't take the bait.

"Yeah, in a way," he said. "You guys know I was a chaplain in Vietnam when I was barely out of seminary. I joined a Marine unit in Indian Country, and even though the Corps wanted its holy men to stay at the base camp, these were my guys, and I believed God intended that I should go out on reconnaissance patrols with my guys. That's where I would be needed most.

"It was one of those recons that a Cleveland kid named Harry Schirick—we called him Dutch—took the point. Well, we ran face-first into a VC ambush. An RPG hit between Dutch's legs and flayed both of his femoral arteries. He sprayed blood in every direction. Shrapnel peppered every inch of him. One piece of metal literally protruded from his right eye. I was soaked in his blood."

Some of the guys had served, some hadn't, but only Father Bert and Bell had been in combat. Stories of battlefield horrors were alien to the others, and they all wondered what they might do under fire.

"A corpsman tried furiously to plug all of Dutch's holes while I knelt over him, ready to administer his last rites, when he asked me if he was going to die. I told him he needed to stay with us, that he had babies to make."

Father Bert told them how the firefight lasted more than an hour before a medevac arrived and plucked Dutch Schirick and the other wounded Marines to safety, but not soon enough for some of them.

"So he died?" Coogan asked.

Father Bert grew pensive.

"I assumed he did," he said. "I didn't know for a long time. Then in 1985 a letter arrived right here at St. Barnabas with a Cleveland postmark. It contained this picture and a very short note from Dutch that said, 'You saved me so I could make them. Bless you.'"

The boys of Deaf Row needed a happy ending. They all wanted to believe in happy endings, preferably without all the pain that precedes them, but happy nevertheless. Leave it to the priest to tell a story that made them believe even the worst stories might end happily when the time came.

Bell swished his coffee in his cup. He hated Ollie's little navel-gazing idea. He'd rather cough up his pancreas than expose himself like those guys had. But he'd agreed, albeit reluctantly. Everybody or nobody. And he was the last everybody.

He bobbled around in his wallet long enough that nobody truly expected him to play. They knew him too well. And he knew too well what he pretended to look for.

But suddenly, he fixed his attention on Roxy.

"Rox, your granddaughter," he said. "You told me once what she did. You know, what does she teach?"

"Oh, hell, Woodrow, stuff I never understood. Genealogy or somesuch. Like those places where you spit in the tube, and they can tell if you came from Africa or South Nigerio or something. She trains those DNA outfits, and her kids get jobs at places like that."

"Genetics?" Bell asked. His mind was already ten steps ahead

"Yeah, that," Roxy said.

"How long has it been since you talked to your granddaughter, Roxy?"

"Been a while. Maybe last Christmas."

Bell stood up and motioned for "Pops Rox" to follow him outside.

"That's too long," Bell said. "You got a phone? Let's go call her right now. I bet she'd love to hear from her Pops."

Roxy Snipes fidgeted but he did as he was asked. The two of them walked out the door and headed as quickly as two senior citizens could down Main Street toward Roxy's house across the alley from the old JC Penney's.

They left so urgently that Bell left his wallet on the table, open to the only photo he carried. It showed a young blond girl, no more than six, sitting on her father's lap. The proud man's smile was as broad as his shoulders. None of the fellas on Deaf Row had ever seen Woodrow so young or so happy.

DR. JESSIE HUDSON'S day job was teaching genomics and forensic biology to mostly diligent grad students at University of Colorado. But she also founded and led CU's influential Institute of Human Genetics, which provided expert DNA testimony in court cases, researched genomic issues, and supported medical examiners and crime labs worldwide.

At forty, she was already recognized as one of America's foremost geneticists. Her recent paper on the legal and ethical ramifications of retail DNA testing not only sent a shudder through the at-home genealogy giants like Kindred. com and GenePool.com, but commanded the attention of both Congress and social media.

But the thing that most astonished Bell was that the dynamic Dr. Hudson was in her office when her grandfather called. And she happily took his call, not because his sacrifices made all this happen—she did that—but they made it easier. She was proud of her genes, and she knew good genes.

"Hello, Pops," she said. "I love hearing from you. You always brighten my day. What's happening up in your mountains today?"

"Same old mountain stuff, baby doll," he replied, leaning against his cluttered kitchen counter. He'd called her "baby doll" since she was born. "Not much changes in the mountains. But I have a friend who thinks you might be able to help us with something right up your alley."

"Anything for you, Pops. What can I do?"

"I'm gonna put you on the phone with him. His name is Woodrow Bell, and he is—or was—a detective in Denver. He's working on a case that's ... well, he can tell you. Hold on."

Roxy handed the receiver to Bell.

"I'm happy to 'meet' you, Dr. Hudson," he said. "Your grandfather couldn't be prouder, even though he's not real sure what you do. I suppose that's the beauty of it. He doesn't care what you do. He's proud no matter what."

"Thank you, Mr. Bell. And I'm proud of him, too. So, tell me about this case of yours."

Bell explained it all from the beginning. Cherish Nelson, the bloody clothes, the locket and hair, Erskine Midwinter, the cruelties at the asylum, Purgatory and the strange visit with Rosemary Midwinter, the cold cases ... and his foul business in the outhouse.

"And you want me to analyze the DNA on your toilet paper," Dr. Hudson said.

"You're as smart as your grandpa says you are," he said. "But yes, I do. I've run out of options downtown."

"What do you expect to learn from your, um, toilet paper that you don't already know?" she asked.

"I don't know."

"How might this woman's DNA—if it's there at all—help you solve your murder?"

"I don't know."

"Are you even on the right killer's trail?"

"I don't know."

Dr. Hudson exhaled on the other end of the line.

"Mr. Bell..."

"Woodrow. Please."

"Woodrow, I don't know where to start listing the obstacles and hazards," she said, "so I'll start at the end: I'm skeptical."

Bell had no immediate response. He was disappointed, to be sure, but he wouldn't let go.

"Okay, 'skeptical' isn't 'no.' What are your biggest obstacles and hazards?"

"They're *your* obstacles and hazards, not mine," the great geneticist responded coolly. "But Number One, you don't have the actual original DNA profile of your Mr. Midwinter, which might or might not be valid, and we'd need that for comparison.

Bell started to respond, but Dr. Hudson wasn't done.

"Number Two—no pun intended—your outhouse DNA is a very iffy proposition. There's probably more raccoon spit than human DNA on that nasty seat.

"Number Three, I have no idea what you expect to learn from this alleged fecal DNA, probably because you have no idea what this shit means—okay, that pun was intended.

"Number Four, I am uncomfortable with anybody secretly collecting DNA from anybody, even the Wicked Witch of Purgatory.

"Number Five, it's expensive, and neither of us has that kind of money," she said. "So, do you want to discuss Numbers Six through Fifty?"

Bell persisted, as was also his habit.

"So you'll think about it?"

Dr. Hudson responded in her most patient voice, normally reserved for freshmen.

"Woodrow, I like you," she said. "You're very cute. Under different circumstances, we might be lovers. But ... no."

"Really?" Bell replied. "Lovers?"

"No." She turned serious. "And regarding this case ... I can't."

Bell turned serious, too. He had one last, desperate shot, and he hoped it would hit home.

"A young girl is gone, and her father hasn't known why for a long, long time," he said. "Luther Nelson is losing his memories bit by bit, and it won't be long before he doesn't even know he had a little girl. It would give him peace—and it would give me peace— to know why she's gone before he can't remember why ever again. If you can't help us, it's over."

The other end of the line was silent when Roxy took the phone from Bell.

"Jessie, baby doll," he told his granddaughter. "You're my world. But I have this strange feeling that everything

I ever did in my life since I was a boy was supposed to bring you and me to this one moment right here. I don't know why God finagled it this way, but we have a chance to do something good and right and I don't want to miss it. Woodrow needs you, Luther needs you, and I need you—more than air, baby doll. Can you please help?"

With that, Roxy handed the receiver back to his friend and left the kitchen.

It took a few moments before either of them spoke. Bell went first.

"Well, I didn't see that coming."

"My grandfather and I have always had this kind of Vulcan mind-meld thing where he knows my unspoken thoughts," Dr. Hudson said. "I'm guessing your father planted a fruit seed that nobody thought would sprout, right? People made fun of him. He watered it every day in spring and summer. But it grew and eventually it bore fruit, surprising everyone but him. Am I right?"

She was. Bell's father's peach tree died a long time ago, when nobody was left to tend it where it shouldn't have grown anyway.

"That's amazing. How did you know?" Bell asked. "Is that about his genes?"

"No," she replied. "It's about his stubbornness. He grew a stubborn tree. And he grew you, too."

"A personal flaw, I know."

"I have a grad student who can help you," she said. "This is a limited-time offer. We will arrange the testing at an outside lab, which you'll pay for. We'll analyze the profile, which you'll pay for. You'll provide your suspect's original DNA profile, at your expense. You'll provide us with your icky toilet paper within the next twenty-four hours. And you'll pretend to always be fascinated by Pops's goofy Solitaire theories. You have ten seconds to agree or the deal is off. One ... two ..."

"Yes. Absolutely yes," Bell damn near yelled. "Thank you. I'll owe you one."

"You'll owe my grandfather one. This is for him."

BELL DIDN'T WASTE a minute.

He quick-stepped back to Tommyknockers for his wallet, then the short block to his house, where he snatched the plastic bag from his flour canister, and fired up the Crown Vic. He passed the town-limit sign before his balky heater stopped blowing cold.

On the way, he overcame his handicap of fat thumbs and techno-boobery, and managed to accidentally press the right buttons to reach Jazz.

"What's up, Big Man?" she answered.

"How the hell ...?"

"Are we gonna do this every time?"

"I just can't ..."

Through the phone, Bell felt Jazz slapping her forehead.

"What fresh Hell can I help you with today?" she asked.

"I need a favor."

"No shit."

"I need you to ask the crime lab to email the original Midwinter DNA profile to Dr. Jessie Hudson up at CU, stat," said. "She's a genetics expert who's gonna help us on this case."

"*You*, not *us*," she corrected him abruptly.

"You're so modest. That's what I like about you, Jazz. You never want to take the credit."

"Or the blame," she said. "But what am I supposed to tell the crime lab guys?"

"Make something up. They won't care. She's a rock star in forensic circles, and they'll piss themselves like groupies to help her out."

He slowly spelled out the private email address Dr. Hudson gave him.

"Copy that," Jazz said. "And I have something for you, too. Your Rosemary Midwinter has a long-ass rap sheet, going back to the '60s. A slew of prostitution and heroin busts, stolen property, fleeing police, resisting, assault and battery, criminal trespass, and larceny. A year in Jefferson County lockup for an attempted break-in at a pharmacy. Then a four-year stretch in the state pen on two counts of trafficking. She filed a federal lawsuit in 1982 against several male prison guards, alleging brutality, bribery, and sexual abuse, but it was thrown out. Paroled in '84, did her bit with her PO, then she fell off the radar completely. That's all I got."

"That explains her hostility about cops," Bell said. "I owe you one."

"You owe me ten, Big Man," she said, then hung up.

A CAMPUS COP pointed Bell to the BioSciences building. Dr. Hudson's offices were down a labyrinth of corridors, but he found them, and her. She shuffled through papers stacked in neat piles across her big desk like her grandfather's Solitaire cards.

Beyond that, there was no resemblance. She was pretty enough, even with her reading glasses perched on the end of her nose. She didn't notice the big man at her open door until he rapped on the jamb. Even then, she was too absorbed to look up.

"No office hours today," she announced, absorbed in some official-looking paper. "See your TA."

Bell smiled.

"The dog ate my homework, ma'am," he said.

The voice must have sounded too low and too old to be a student, even her oldest one. She looked up to see a big, unfamiliar man filling the frame of her office door.

"I'm sorry," she said. "Can I help you?"

"You said we might be lovers, so I wanted to check you out."

A flicker of recognition darted across her pleasant but very earnest face.

"Mr. Bell?"

"Who wants to know?" he joked.

"It's nice to put a face to the voice. I'm sorry about all that, but my students can be a nuisance. Please come in and have a seat."

Bell thanked her, but he wasn't staying long.

"We had a deal, so I brought you this with twenty hours to spare," he said, pulling a small, plastic bag from his coat pocket and placing it on Dr. Hudson's desk. She picked it up like a dead bug.

"I hope you'll be very gentle with it," he added. "It's got great sentimental value."

The professor looked anxiously for a place to put it and found none, so she just sat there with a poopy plastic bag dangling from her fingers.

Bell plucked a business card from a holder and scribbled his phone number—or his best guess anyway—on the back. Then he turned serious.

"This is a good thing you're doing, Dr. Hudson. If we've got any shot at closing this case, you might be it. So, I'll get out of your hair while you get this freak show on the road."

He turned to leave, but stopped in the doorway.

"And you should know," he said, "I've already got a girlfriend."

ON THE LONG way back to Midnight—more windshield time—Bell contemplated his faceless clowns, remembered that Doc Ely had something urgent to tell him, and thought about how he must pay more attention to Roxy Snipes's Solitaire.

To Charlie, too. He day-dreamed about dreaming of her, even if he didn't put much stock in dreams. Her private smell swirled in him. But for all the questions he'd ever asked and answered, one totally escaped him. It was about true love. He didn't know if he knew what it was or if he'd ever felt it. That's not to say that he didn't have a sincere affection for Charlie, because he did, but he'd never worn "I love you" like a second skin. It wasn't fair—*he* wasn't fair—to her.

At that imperceptible point in the mountains where his radio fuzzed back to the oldies station, he thought about how, a month ago, life was simpler. That he could sit on his porch and hear the crows cawing in the trees, watch jets streak across the blue, hear the children in the park, smell the pine smoke of autumn fires. That nothing in this world is ever still. That it wasn't that long ago he followed a routine which protected him from the feeling that his time had passed. That, right now, his life was defined by what he'd lost more than what he'd gained.

But by God, Bell couldn't remember the instant he broke with himself. Or with Sarah. Or she with him.

As the highway rose toward the divide, he walked the thin wire between his kinship with the Deaf Row boys and the profound relief of solitude. He tilted more and more toward aloneness, where he could live in his past, long before war and homicide, where time was endless, and death was a train station where nobody got off.

The boys on Deaf Row felt it, too. That very morning, when asked to find something of intimate value in their wallets, most had produced artifacts of loss—well, except for the ever-hopeful Father Bert, who wasn't afraid of whatever came next.

Bell knew his friends tended his same secret fears: That death might hurt, that it might be undignified, that there'd be something he left unsaid, that he might have pissed off everybody who would miss him.

When snow clouds shrouded the peak's head and fat snowflakes flurried across the road, here was Bell, an accidental knight hunting for clowns that might or might not exist. He had already sucked Dan Coogan, Elroy Richter, Doc Ely, and Roxy Snipes into his horror circus, too.

Just before the highway sloped down into Midnight, Bell turned onto the frozen dirt road that led to the Colorado A-frame Doc Ely and his wife Caroline had built forty years ago. They were healthy and happy back then. Today, smoke still rose from its chimney, but gravity was pushing it, inch by inch, down the hill.

Snow fell harder now. The radio guy said the season's first big blow was coming. All bundled up, the slow-moving Bones carried firewood—only two split logs at a time—through a layer of new snow to top off a tottering rick beside his front door.

"Let me help you with that, Doc," Bell said as he got out of the Crown Vic.

Bones Ely was too old to be up here alone, but he'd never leave. This was to be his and Caroline's forever home, their last best place. To him, it still was. He'd scattered her ashes among the pines out back, and he spoke to her every night. When the time came, that's where he wanted to be, too, because he wanted to be able to talk to her for eternity.

Bell loaded a half dozen seasoned pine logs into his big arms, and in no time, they'd refilled Doc's rack. Then they stomped the snow off their boots and went inside, where it didn't smell like a lonely old man, but of woodsmoke.

The place was an organized mess. Unwashed dinner plates, unfolded *Midnight Sun*s and *Denver Post*s, dirty socks, old books butterflied on chair arms, grocery bags of kindling, more coats, hats, and boots than Doc would ever wear hung by the door, furniture disarranged and marred. Down the hall, he could see Doc's unmade bed. But Bell got the feeling the chaos made sense to Doc, but only Doc.

Only Doc's desk appeared to have some almost sacred order. Papers were stacked neatly, exactly four pens lined up in a perfect rank, his antique lamp poised perfectly over the blotter, and his leather chair tucked neatly beneath. A medical book sat on one corner, perfectly squared up. It all looked like an island of sanctuary amid the tumult everywhere else.

"Sorry it took me so long, Doc," Bell said. "Charlie told me you needed to see me and, well, life happened. Anyway, here I am, late as always. What's up?"

Doc chided Bell. "You need a damned phone."

"So I've heard."

"And you left the diner this morning before I could grab you."

"Sorry. Something came up. Let's say I had a phone or you grabbed me after coffee. What was on your mind?"

Doc Ely slid open his desk's top drawer and pulled out two tissue-thin sheets of yellowing carbon paper.

"Ever since you asked about the Nelson girl, I been thinking about the whole mess," he said. "Then I started to think I must have written up some kind of report for Joe Harper. Look around. I don't throw anything away. So, I rummaged around here for a few days. Every box, drawer, file folder, every damned place where I might have stuck the carbons fifty years ago."

"And ...?"

"These are them," he said, handing the smudgy sheets to Bell, who quickly scanned them. The narrative was an unusual mix of medical lingo and plain English, what one might expect from a small-town family doctor doing his first forensic autopsy. But nothing leapt off the page for Bell.

"Anything we didn't already talk about?" Bell asked.

"Plenty," Doc said.

Bell looked up, more than a little curious. "Like what?"

"Her hands and feet had been bound, but no actual ligatures were found," Doc said. "Judging by the bruises and imprints, they were chains, about the size of tire chains, wrapped several times."

"Anything else?"

Doc cocked his neck to see the report from Bell's angle and put his finger on an abstruse paragraph that started, *"Lateral nontherapeutic sutures (approximately 00) of superior and inferior palpebra ..."*

"Doc, explain it to me like I'm a sixth grader," Bell said.

"Somebody who wasn't a doctor sewed the girl's eyelids together using a thick needle and cord," the doctor translated. "In this case, a string of catgut was probably stitched with an awl used by leatherworkers and cobblers."

"Jesus."

"Here's something else interesting," Bones continued. "The sutures started on the lower lid of the left eye and zig-zagged to the right. Same on the right eye: The stitching starts on the bottom lid and goes left to right."

"What's significant about that?" Bell asked.

"Your killer is probably left-handed. A right-hander would have reversed the direction."

Bell looked up at Doc Ely but said nothing.

"And there's more, Woodrow."

Bell exhaled, girding himself. He thought he'd seen and heard all the cruelties and savageries one human could visit upon another. He hadn't. But he learned a long time ago that it's better to seem outwardly indifferent than unnerved.

"I told you the spike was driven into her right ear canal directly into her brain stem. She died instantly," the doctor said. "But if we assume she was lying on her back and this lunatic wanted to watch her face at that awful moment and he didn't want to screw it up, then he probably held the hammer with his left hand. Of course, there are other ways he might have done it, but if I had to bet my own money, I'd bet he's a lefty."

"Can I keep this report for a while, Doc?" Bell asked. "I promise to take care of it."

Doc Ely waved as if he were swatting a fly.

"Keep it forever," he said. "This place is cleaner without it."

BELL'S NEXT STOP was Roxy Snipes's little house off Midnight's Main Street. He owed Roxy more thanks, but on his long drive home, something Dr. Hudson had said kept flitting through his mind.

Before Bell could knock on Roxy's door, the old bookkeeper invited him in. The heat was turned up, and he was halfway through a grueling game of Klondike Solitaire. He couldn't waste time answering the door.

"Hey, Rox. I just came over to say ..."

"Shhh," he said, completely focused on the cards arrayed across his old Tandy's screen. "Casual players can only win about one of every thirty games, and a perfect player should theoretically win every game. I am winning about one in every fifteen. Thus, statistically, I'm poised precisely between luck and skill. So, I try to think one step ahead. Quiet helps."

Bell lowered his voice, as if it weren't quiet enough.

"I wanted to tell ..."

"Shut up, Woodrow! The whole game might come down to this."

Roxy flipped a card.

"Well, crap," he grumbled. Then he added his latest statistics on a legal pad already full of numbers, dates, and notes. "I shoulda seen that coming five moves back."

"I'm sure if I wasn't here, you'd have caught it," Bell said.

"You're probably right. But now that you're here, what can I do for you?"

Bell pulled off his gloves and extended his hand to Roxy.

"I wanted to thank you for what you said to Jessie today," he said. "She's going to be a big help because of you. We might even find the key that cracks this case. So, thank you."

Roxy's delicate right hand vanished in Bell's bearpaw.

"You're welcome, Woodrow," he said. "I meant it all. Maybe the odds are against you, but you play this game better than anybody."

"Well, that's what I wanted to talk to you about, Rox," he said. "I have another favor to ask."

"Oh?"

Bell leaned closer. "You said a few weeks ago that Solitaire is about seeing patterns that help you count down to one."

"And patience," Roxy said. "And luck."

"Yeah, all that," Bell said. "But I'm interested in the patterns that help you narrow everything down to one. Am I making sense here?"

"No. I'm sure it made sense when I said it, but not when you say it."

"Yeah, well, here's what I should have said: Would you take a look at these"—Bell handed him Jazz's manila envelope—"and tell me what patterns you see? It's about counting down to one, you know?"

Roxy peeked inside.

"These are police things," he said nervously. "Oh, I don't know, Woodrow ..."

"They're missing girls. Nobody knows what happened to them. But it's just like your cards, Rox. There are patterns I can't see. But you see patterns other people don't. Would you just take a look and see what you see? Maybe there's nothing, but maybe there's something. Please?"

Roxy mulled over the proposition for what Bell considered an uncomfortably long time.

"What exactly are you looking for?" Roxy asked.

"I don't know yet," Bell replied. "Like you said, we're balanced precisely between luck and skill. If there's a pattern, I think you'll find it. Whether it's lucky or brilliant doesn't matter to me ... or to them."

Even before Bell left, Roxy Snipes was clearing his computer and virtual cards off the table to make room for a new kind of game.

ONE LAST STOP.
Dinner always came out at four p.m. in the Old Miners Home, so the whole place smelled like meatloaf and disinfectant when Bell signed in. Aides cleared trays from a half-dozen round tables as they magically converted a dining hall back to a day room for the third time today.

George Tomer slumped motionless in his wheelchair, pushed off to one side with all the empty dinner chairs near the alley window. But Bell knew he was inside himself someplace, so he dodged a janitor's broad dust mop and crossed the messy tiled floor to where George was parked.

He hated this place and came as infrequently as he could. It didn't matter that this was his unfortunate friend's last home, he hated it. The smell, the light, the silence ... they knotted up something in Bell's gut. He hated coming inside, but he also regretted leaving friends behind when he went back outside. Friends were what kept him coming back, no matter how much he hated it. Nobody could see him fidgeting with a black stone that he'd carried in his coat pocket since the last time he visited.

"Hi there, you old goat," Bell said, patting George's emaciated shoulder and pulling up a chair beside his friend. "Every time I see you, I swear you get better lookin'."

George Tomer's finger twitched. Bell interpreted it as a laugh. Or maybe he was flipping the bird. Hard to know.

"The boys miss you. Your stories. You remember the one about the three-legged dog? That might have been your funniest one ever."

George's finger trembled. Something that looked indistinctly like his big ol' smile floated across his lips like a cloud passing across the moon.

For a half hour, Bell reported the latest Deaf Row news. He told George some stories that were mostly true. He asked if Father Bert had come around lately, even though Bell knew he was there every day. And Bell showed him the lucky rock in his pocket.

George kept up his end of the conversation. His finger quivered the whole time.

"Well, it was good to see you, my friend," Bell said as the gathering blizzard turned the day gray-white. "I'm keeping a beer on ice for you. Take care of yourself."

Now, two fingers twitched madly. "Take care" or "Don't be a stranger"? Bell couldn't know.

Bell said his goodbyes, then walked across the newly clean floor toward the door. Halfway there, he stopped an aide and asked about Luther Nelson. She pointed down the hallway toward the patients' rooms. Bell peeked in every one until he found Luther sitting on his bed seriously mulling a sock.

"Hello, Nellie," he said softly.

Luther Nelson looked up. "Are you a doctor? You look like a doctor."

"No," Bell replied. "Just a friend from a long time ago. I wanted to say hi to you."

Nellie's sunken, cloudy eyes brightened.

"I remember you! You came yesterday to tell my mother about my brother ... um ... um," Nellie rubbed his onion-skin scalp, all tangled up in the snarl of his own memories. "I can't recall his name now. It'll come to me. But you told my mother he died in the war. She's crying right now, but she still has me and I love her. Somebody else brought my dinner."

Bell let him believe all of it. If Nellie believed his mother was alive, his ghosts made him happier than Bell's truth.

"I'm sure she loves you back, Nellie. Very much."

"Are you a doctor?"

"No," Bell said, "but do you need a doctor?"

"Daisy tells me all the time that I never get sick. She's making orange juice right now. It keeps me healthy. Cherish doesn't drink it, but it's true about the orange juice, you know?"

"Do you ever see Cherish," Bell asked Nellie.

"Who?"

"Cherish. Your daughter."

"Have you seen her? She went away."

Bell pulled gently at Luther's memory.

"Where did she go, Nellie?"

The old man shrugged his bony shoulders.

"Is she coming back?" he asked Bell.

The old detective didn't know what to say exactly, Again, some delusions were best not dispelled. But one thing was crystal clear: Cherish's ghost was fading away. He felt a pang of urgency to find answers before she vanished forever from her father's memory.

"I'll watch out for her, Nellie," Bell said. "I promise."

FATHER BERT CLANCY knocked on Bell's door long past dark. The driving snow numbed his face.

He'd come directly from the Old Miners Home, where he often helped the nurses put the residents to bed and prayed with them. But tonight, something had been different. He was as priestly pissed as Bell had ever seen him. Not furious but visibly peeved.

Bell invited him in and offered him a whiskey, although Bell guessed the priest wasn't there for spirits or one of their deep conversations. His cheeks were pink and frosted, but he didn't even sit by Bell's robust fire to warm himself.

"What did you say to George Tomer?" he asked. His question was uncharacteristically sharp.

"And how was your day, dear?"

"I was just over at the Home," Father Bert said, "and Lou, the night nurse, said you were the only one who visited George today. When you left—before you even walked out the door—she says he became extremely agitated. What did you say to him, Woodrow?"

"Not a damn thing," Bell said, summarizing that afternoon. "I talked about the fellas, told a couple jokes, told him we missed him. Nothing big. He wiggled his finger like usual the whole time. I said goodbye and looked in on Luther Nelson. That's it. I wasn't there very long."

Father Bert breathed deeply and calmed down a little. He considered it his holy obligation to protect the vulnerable patients at the Old Miners Home. In fact, he considered himself blessed by them. They were part of his flock, too.

"When I got there tonight, he was still distressed. He grunted like the words were clogged inside him. He even dragged his arm off the bed. George's body is too weak for that kind of upheaval. I swear to God, I've never seen him that disturbed. He was trying to tell us something. It's connected to you."

Bell shook his head as he struggled to recall every insignificant detail.

"I touched his shoulder. He tried to smile a couple times. I showed him the black rock he gave me last time. Just as I was leaving, George moved two fingers. I never saw that before, but I figured it was an involuntary spasm or something. Nothing else out of the ordinary. No grunting or arm-dragging. He was just normal George when I left."

"Yeah, well, what's normal for the spider is apocalypse for the fly," Father Bert said. Then he squinted at the far wall like he was doing painful math in his head.

"Tomorrow let's go over there together," the priest said after a bit. "I don't know what it was, but you said or did something. Sleep on it."

Bell didn't have time to decline the invitation before Father Bert yanked the front door shut behind him and disappeared into the storm.

Can priests get pissed off? he wondered.

THE NEXT DAY, the storm worsened.

The rest of the boys of Deaf Row hadn't ventured out on this intolerable morning, but Bell met Father Bert at Tommyknockers, where they warmed themselves with hot coffee. Main Street hadn't yet been plowed, but together they crossed the drifts to see George Tomer.

The Old Miners Home was warmer than usual. They hung their coats on hooks in the foyer and stomped their snow boots. Sideways snow blocked the sunlight through the big alley window, so the dining room was gray and quiet

"How is George this morning?" the priest asked Linda, the thirtysomething floor nurse who happened to be one of Ollie Fuhrman's nieces.

"He slept off and on most of the night," she said, "His breathing got hard. He wouldn't eat this morning. He's not himself. He'll be happy to see you, though. He's over there with his best buddy Nellie, as usual."

George Tomer and Luther Nelson sat together by the window where, today anyway, they could see nothing but white.

"Do they sit together a lot?" Bell asked the nurse.

"Pretty much every morning these days," she said. "At first, George could still talk and Nellie was less confused. Now, one can't say anything and the other ... well, you know. It's sad."

Bell's cop curiosity took over.

"What did they talk about?"

"They got very close and talked about everything, sometimes twice," she smiled. "You know, old times. George had his memories but couldn't always talk about them, and

Nellie was losing his memories and never stopped talking. On good days, they talked about their regrets, their families, memories. They laughed a lot, but they'd cry, too. Like old men do."

Bell persisted.

"But anything specific you remember?"

"No offense, but old-guy stuff," the nurse said, counting off her fingers until she had no more fingers to count. "Barbecue, trucks, guns, women, plain M&Ms, dogs, snow-shoveling, time passing, the damn wind, the old room above the store ... about ten billion other things. I'd never remember them all. But they were grand discussions."

"Did Nellie ever talk about his girl, Cherish?" Bell asked. Father Bert shuffled uneasily.

"All the time," Linda said. "Poor girl. That's when they'd cry."

Bell dug in his coat pocket.

"George gave me this rock," he said, showing it to her. "Did they ever talk about Profanity Peak?"

"Not that I recall," she said. "I wasn't always on the morning shift, and sometimes they put their heads real close, but I never heard them say anything about Profanity Peak. I woulda perked up."

"Why's that?"

"When I was a little girl, my uncle Ollie taught me how to fish up there. So it's a special place for me."

Nurse Linda apologized. She couldn't remember anything more. She excused herself to tend to her patients.

Bell turned to Father Bert and whispered as softly as a big man could but loud enough for his hard-of-hearing friend to hear.

"This Lou Gehrig's Disease," he said. "Is George's mind still working in there?"

"That's what they say," the priest whispered back. "Think about him like a computer with a faulty processor that ..."

The tech-challenged Bell already looked confused.

"Okay, think about him like your Crown Vic if it had a new engine but a bad transmission," Father Bert explained. "It runs just fine ... it just can't move."

"Except his finger."

"Yes, his finger. For now." Father Bert crossed himself.

"Go talk to him," Bell said, suddenly urgent. "I'll be back in a sec."

The big man left quickly and returned quicker. He'd gone back to his house for a large, detailed topographic map of the mountains, lakes, roads, and landmarks within a ten-mile circle around Midnight—including Mount Misery, Wisdom Gulch, and Profanity Peak. Once used as a guide for Bell's hunts for solitude, he'd forgotten all about it until this moment.

"Woodrow, what's this all about?" Father Bert asked as Bell unfolded his topo map across one of the Home's dining tables.

"Padre," he said, "we're gonna make George Tomer talk."

"But he can't walk," Father Bert said.

"*Talk*," Bell said a bit louder than he should. "Make him *talk*."

Bell sat down beside George and Nellie.

"George, I need your help."

Nellie piped up.

"Are you a doctor? You look like a doctor."

"No, Nellie, I'm not a doctor," Bell said. "But I want to help you. I think George can help you, too."

George Tomer's finger twitched noticeably, albeit weakly.

Bell rolled the wheelchair to the big table. Father Bert helped Nellie into a chair nearby where he could see everything, then sat beside George.

Bell didn't talk like an old detective, but a gentle friend.

"George, we're going to play a game. If you understand, wiggle your finger."

George's mottled finger twitched.

"Very good," Bell said. "Now I'm going to ask you a question. If your answer is 'no,' can you wiggle two fingers, like you did yesterday?"

Father Bert's eyes widened when George moved two fingers.

"That's really, really good," Bell praised. "Is it okay for me to lift your arm onto the table?"

One finger.

With Father Bert's help, Bell gently raised George's rigid right arm and laid it on the map, positioning his two moving fingers on the little crosshatch that was Midnight. His eyes moved so subtly across the map that Bell would have missed it if he hadn't been watching closely for any sign of recognition.

"Can you see the map?"

One finger.

"Are you touching Midnight?"

One finger.

"Or is it Denver?"

Two fingers.

"You once hunted rocks all over these places on the map, didn't you?"

One finger.

"You've never been here, correct?"

Two fingers.

Father Bert interrupted. "You know very well that it's not Denver and he's familiar with this area."

Bell nodded. "Control questions, like a lie detector. I'm making sure our system works."

He turned back to George's interview.

"In fact, you know this area very well, don't you?"

One finger.

"Oh, that's terrific, George," Bell said. "Do you want to continue?"

One finger.

"Great. Now I'm going to move the map a little bit."

Bell nudged it so Profanity Peak was under George's fingers.

"Is this Profanity Peak?"

One finger.

"Is this where you found the rock you gave me?"

One finger.

"Was it just a gift to be nice?"

Two fingers.

"Does the rock mean something important?"

One finger.

"Something good?"

Two fingers.

Bell glanced up at Father Bert.

"Something bad?"

One finger.

"You're doing great, George," Bell said. "Now, tell me: Does this have anything to do with Nellie?"

Nothing. Not yes or no. Bell thought for a moment.

"Does that mean you don't know?"

One finger.

"Something that *might* have to do with Nellie?"

One finger. George's answers came slower now.

"Maybe about his daughter Cherish?"

There was no movement for several seconds, then one finger. Bell interpreted not as a reluctance to answer, but as uncertainty.

"Okay, was this something you heard about? Something somebody told you?"

Two fingers.

"Something you saw?"

One finger.

Father Bert spoke up. "Ask him when he saw whatever he saw."

Bell pondered how he might get a mute man to tell him a date.

"George," he asked, "was this in the 1960s?"

Every successive decade, two fingers—until the 2000s.

"Before 2005?"

One finger.

"Do you know exactly when you saw this thing before 2005?"

Two fingers.

"Good enough, George," Bell said. "Did you see it on Profanity Peak itself?"

Two fingers.

"Was it *near* Profanity Peak?"

One finger.

Bell stood up and splayed both of his meaty hands across the map's margins.

"George, I'm going to move the map around slowly," he said. "Don't move your finger until the right place is directly under it. Do you understand?"

One finger.

Father Bert stood for a better overhead view. Bell guided the map beneath George Tomer's finger, moving out from the perfect circle that marked the pinnacle of Profanity Peak. He saw no reflection of familiarity at all in his friend's eyes. None.

The map continued to move slowly in silent circles under George's pale, gnarled finger, which never budged.

"George, do you know where exactly this place is?" Bell asked.

One finger.

"Are we getting close?"

One weak finger.

"Keep going," Father Bert said. "Go slower."

Bell returned to his gradual rotation in widening rings around Profanity Peak. Still nothing. He worried that he'd overloaded George, whose hidden mind might have simply shut down. Even Father Bert seemed to have lost faith.

Then his finger twitched. Bell fixed the map in place with both hands, while Father Bert gently raised George's finger to see what lay beneath.

In fact, the tip of his finger covered more than two square miles, way southwest of Profanity Peak. George's spot was bounded by the high-mountain Whitehorse Lake, the south fork of Beaver Creek, Pilot Knob, and a cluster of tiny dots just below the tree line representing man-made structures. The words were so small, Father Bert fished his reading glasses from his breast pocket.

He bent over close, then gazed up at Bell.

"Schattenland Asylum."

Bell was taken aback, but he couldn't be sure if George Tomer had merely seen the same haunting derelict as he had, or if he saw something more.

"George, are you saying it was the old asylum?" he asked.

Two fingers. George was faltering.

"Not the asylum, okay," Bell said, leaning close to the spot George had identified. One by one, he asked George about every label he saw—the lake, the creek, the knob, even a nearby trailhead—and every time, two fingers.

Bell looked closer. He couldn't read the words in the dim light, and he didn't carry a pair of reading glasses.

"Padre, what does this say?" he asked.

Father Bert leaned so close that he might fall face-first onto the table.

"It's just an abandoned mine," he said.

George's finger stiffened and tapped once.

Bell and Father Bert exchanged astonished glances.

"George, it's the abandoned mine?" the old detective asked.

One finger.

"You're absolutely sure? Not maybe?"

One finger.

Bell checked the mileage scale with his fingernail and measured the distance between the old asylum and the abandoned mine. The mine was roughly a half mile northwest of Schattenland, give or take a hundred yards.

"That's the cave," Bell announced.

"What cave?" Father Bert asked.

"The 'cave' where they found Erskine Midwinter when he escaped from the asylum as a kid. It wasn't really a cave. It was an old mine. While he was rock-hunting, George saw something there between 2000 and 2005 that might or might not be related to Cherish Nelson. Something bad."

Bell had another question.

"George, what you saw in the mine," he asked, "would it still be there?"

Nothing moved. He didn't know.

Now it was Father Bert who couldn't speak his words.

"But he ... back then ... why wouldn't he tell someone if it was so bad?"

Bell knew small towns had long memories.

"George," he asked, "were you afraid nobody would believe you?"

Just one finger trembled, then rose from the table. Yes.

The dim light in George's eyes had gone out. He was done.

ALL NIGHT, THE wind rattled Bell's bedroom window. The snow—really sleet blasting like sand against the glass—woke him up a couple times, so he stoked the fire downstairs and hoped the heat would rise, but the cold overwhelmed it.

He also hoped Charlie wasn't out driving in this storm, even in her sixteen-ton garbage truck. She should be under the covers with him, just waking up. He probably never told her that nights were warmer, even in summer, when she was in his bed. Maybe next time.

By morning, deep drifts and travel advisories smothered much of Flatiron County. This was the kind of storm that weathermen should name. Midnight was a frozen island.

Bell rolled out of bed. The floor was cold, even through his socks. He rummaged in a drawer for his long johns, then dressed quickly and warmly. Bundled like a Yukon prospector, he opened his frosted storm door only enough to prevent an indoor drift, and braved the furor all the way to Tommyknockers.

The diner was open. Bell took a seat alone at Deaf Row's usual table, the only customer in the whole place. Fancy was already there, and this week's cook—probably another ski bum caught halfway between the city and the slopes—had already fired up the griddle. Any other midweek morning, the place would be humming, but sub-zero wind chills tended to make homemade breakfasts taste better.

Bell ordered his usual—steak and eggs, over medium— and watched the tempest outside through a fogged-up window. The diner's lights flickered a couple times, and he knew that power lines up the mountain were already sagging with ice and being whipped around by hurricane-force winds.

Despite the howling gray gloom, most Main Street businesses were still open. Flags thrashed madly over the First National Bank. The town's lone snowplow driver cut a furrow down the street, moving the drifts from one side of the street to the other—then turned around to do it again. The lights had stayed on all night at the *Midnight Sun* because it was deadline day, and a mere blizzard was a trivial reason to delay the weekly newspaper. It had once published while a fire burned the building next door to the ground.

Bell saw a kid in a ski mask and long scarf push Wendell's Market front door against a sidewalk drift and come out with two paper sacks. Despite high winds and the burden of his load, he made a game of scaling an eight-foot pile of snow on Main Street before he hustled home with Mom's emergency groceries. Around here, snow days were celebrations for some.

Actually, Bell thought, a small town is a pretty good place to ride out a blizzard. The blustery snow and cold might have felt wicked to some, but folks in Midnight accepted a storm as the price they paid for the privilege of living in the mountains. To them, it was merely a nuisance, and it would pass.

But to Bell, it was a brick wall.

He itched to find a way to get up to that abandoned mine under at least six feet of snow on Mount Misery. Four-wheel-drive, helicopter, tank ... whatever it took. George Tomer saw something there, and Bell needed to know if it had survived almost twenty winters, whatever it was. Predators, human scavengers, and the high-country's harsh climate might have all destroyed his crime scene.

Crime scene? Bell didn't know that. He hoped it was a crime scene because that's where he knew exactly what to do. But he was entangled in George's silent story. He didn't know what was there or why it rattled George. *What* and *why* weren't yes or no questions that a finger wiggle could answer. A game of twenty questions—or forty or four hundred—might have killed the poor guy.

Whatever George saw wasn't necessarily criminal, much less related to Cherish Nelson. Eyewitnesses were the worst kind of evidence because they didn't always see what they think they saw. George himself wasn't sure what he saw. The mine's proximity to the Schattenland Asylum intrigued Bell, and the old detective didn't ignore coincidence. But in a leap that might have been too ambitious, Bell's brain connected the rock from Profanity Peak to a slaughtered girl. Maybe those terrible dots were only connected in George's mind.

Bell needed to see for himself ... but this goddamn blizzard stood between him and Mount Misery. It might be days, maybe months, before he could get up there. In the mountains, there was a million square miles of bare earth that might not be seen again until July. Ten months, fergawdsakes. Patience wasn't Bell's strong suit, or so he'd been told.

"More coffee, Woodrow?" Fancy asked, interrupting Bell's thoughts.

"Sure. Bad day for tips, eh?"

Fancy shrugged as she delivered his breakfast and poured him a fresh cup.

"It's winter in Midnight," she said, smiling. "It happens every year on exactly the same day."

"A snowstorm?"

"No," she replied. "Winter."

She had him there. On a day like this, Bell needed her sunshine.

"Yeah, well, if Father Bert was here," he said, "we'd damn sure pray for a whole day of global warming. Preferably tomorrow."

Fancy turned philosophical.

"Life isn't about waiting for the storm to pass," she said. "It's about learning how to dance in the snow."

Bell liked that.

"That's nice," he said. "You're a damn poet."

"Oh, I didn't make it up."

"Who did?"

"Facebook."

All Bell really knew about Facebook came from a cynical cop buddy. He said Facebook was like prison: People sit around all day, have a mug shot, write on walls, and get poked by guys they don't know. It probably would have been funnier, Bell thought at the time, if he knew what Facebook was. He still didn't.

Bell glanced at his wristwatch. Ten a.m.

"Got someplace else to be?" Fancy asked him.

"You might say that, but I'm not going there today."

Fancy had a sixth sense about these things. She'd been hanging around the guys in Deaf Row long enough to know how they thought before they thought it.

"Does this have something to do with Luther Nelson and his girl?"

The question surprised Bell, but he knew he hadn't been especially secretive about the case.

"Maybe," he said. "I need to actually look at something before I know if it's related to Luther's mess or if it's just another damn wild goose chase. But it's high up near Profanity Peak, and this blizzard ... it might be spring before I can get up there."

Fancy knew about storms.

"Hell, Woodrow, blizzards don't last forever," she said. "The best thing you can do when it snows is to let it snow."

"Facebook?"

"Nope. That cook we had last winter who thought he was a poet. The jackass quit after the first snow and ran screaming back to Florida."

Fancy pivoted back toward the kitchen with Bell's empty plate. Without turning around, she offered Bell a last bit of unpoetic advice.

"When the sun comes out, you might ask Ollie about his ancient excavator on tank tracks that musta belonged to Moses. He helped the Forest Service make trails up there and cleared boulders off the O'MyGawd Road with it in wintertime. Just sayin'."

BELL LET IT snow all night. And the next day. And the next night. His impatience morphed into abject hostility toward the Weather Service.

Icy sidewalks terrify old men. Broken hips never turn out well. So Bell didn't see any of the Deaf Row guys—

including Ollie Fuhrman—for a few days. They didn't know he now had a phone, he didn't know anybody's number, and nobody at the phone company knew what an operator was. And when Tommyknockers Diner closed on the third day, he even lost contact with his personal phone book: Fancy.

He was snowed in. Charlie was snowed in. Deaf Row was snowed in, every last one. The whole town was snowed in.

Bell wandered his cold house. He opened the refrigerator a hundred times and saw nothing new ... a hundred times. He took six naps in three afternoons. He ranked his future outpatient procedures by inconvenience. And he wondered almost constantly if he'd finally smashed head-on into the brick wall of a fifty-year-old murder case, a stubborn ex-partner, his preference to be doing anything else, no phone, and a crime lab that consisted mostly of old codgers just like him.

On the fourth day, the weatherman said "Let there be light" and it was good. The sky cleared. The temperatures teetered above freezing. In the few spots where the snowplow had scraped close enough, packed snow was melting, and black asphalt steamed under the sunlight.

Bell bundled himself up and shoveled two feet of snow from his walks, thankful for the diversion. Just like the dozens of old men who died of snow shoveling-induced heart attacks every year.

And then the weatherman created ... Roxy Snipes.

Just standing there.

"Goddammit, Rox, you scared the shit out of me! What the hell ...?"

Bell instantly calculated how many old men died of snow shoveling-induced heart attacks caused by the sudden appearance of an unexpected somebody.

"You should get a phone," Roxy said.

"I have a phone."

"Then you should get a number to go with it."

Bell had a number. He just didn't know what it was.

"I'll call Information as soon as I'm done here," he said. "Did you find anything in those cases I gave you?"

Roxy fumbled around in his big parka for Jazz's manila envelope. In his precise, almost robotic handwriting, he'd printed on the back, columns of numbers, rows of notations.

"You have fifty-two missing girls here. Forty-four different law enforcement agencies in six states. Twenty-four years in two non-consecutive subsets in two different centuries. Thirty possible datapoints per case. Significant unknowns in sixty-six percent of them. One-point-six typos per page."

"That's cops," Bell said, excusing a whole profession from proper spelling and grammar. "Anything they all share?"

Roxy continued.

"Five different ages between thirteen and seventeen. Distribution is weighted toward the upper end, with more than half being sixteen or seventeen. Thirty-six were blond, sixteen had darker hair. Most Caucasian, but seven black, four Hispanic, and one Indian. Their heights are mathematically random. Predominant eye color was brown, but blue, green, and hazel eyes appear in substantial numbers. Forty-nine percent had long hair—not unusual in the '70s—thirty-seven percent had medium, and fourteen percent had short hair. Three-quarters were last seen in slacks or jeans, the rest wore shorts or skirts."

Any computer could have calculated those details, but Bell only had this fussy, small-town bookkeeper obsessed with numbers. A human spreadsheet.

"Damn, Rox," he said. "That's excellent."

"I'm not done. Most went missing in summer, followed by October and April—prime times for runaways who don't want to be homeless in the winter. Overall, thirty-one percent went missing within a half-mile of a school, and most of those between three and six p.m. on school days."

With that, Roxy Snipes seemed to have exhausted his math. Bell waited a couple beats to be sure he wasn't interrupting again.

"Okay," Bell said, "what did all this tell you? When you looked at all these patterns, what did they say to you about all these girls? Anything?"

Roxy shrugged.

"Not a damn thing, Woodrow. It didn't take a math genius to see they aren't *all* related. In three different cases, one girl went missing on the same day as another girl who was six hundred to a thousand miles away. Couldn't be the same guy.

"And it's about logic, too. What is the likelihood that *all* of fifty-two teenage girls reported missing over twenty-one non-consecutive years in six states were abducted by a psycho stranger?"

"I don't know," Bell said. He knew, though, the chances were zero to zip.

"Well, I know. I looked it up," Roxy replied. "Overwhelmingly most children reported missing merely run away, get lost, have car trouble, help a buddy, miss the bus, ditch school, or just sleep where they shouldn't. A bunch of them run away voluntarily from institutional care or are kidnapped by estranged parents. Almost all of them come home alive or are located by cops or their families. Only a tiny, tiny number—just a fraction of one percent— are victims of foul play. So the data suggests most of these fifty-two girls simply walked off by choice."

Bell was disappointed by Roxy's math. Might Cherish Nelson have been a random one-off, the first and the last? What had looked to him like an experienced killer's handiwork might have been an illusion, a lucky kill. Bell's personal math from thirty years in Homicide told him there was no way in hell this was a first-timer, but if this psycho had other victims, they weren't crying bloody murder from their graves. Cherish was all he had.

"Well, thank you, Rox," he said, a little defeat in his voice. "I'd hoped there was something you'd see in that envelope, but it's just not there."

"Not so fast, Woodrow."

Bell held his breath.

"I didn't say *none* of these cases were similar," Roxy said. "In fact, six are too similar to be coincidental."

"In what way?"

"Remember that each report contains thirty datapoints? For a subset of any six cases, five specific matches—in other words, they all share the same exact five characteristics—would be pure luck. Nine would be more than coincidental but less than absolute. Twenty would be irrefutable uniformity."

"In this case?" Bell asked.

"Twenty-seven."

Bell's overgrown eyebrows popped up.

"These six girls' cases matched in exactly twenty-seven ways? Not just petty stuff like female, teenager, blah, blah, blah?"

"No, Woodrow. *Seven* girls matched in twenty-seven specific and significant ways."

"You said six," Bell said. "Who's Number Seven?"

"Cherish Nelson."

"She's not one of those girls in the envelope. How do you know?"

"I had a hunch, so I called Coogan," Roxy admitted. "He gave me all her details so I could compare them."

Bell shook his head in disbelief, even though he'd always put as much stock in coincidence as in dreams.

"So, these twenty-seven things," Bell asked, "like what?"

"All were sixteen or seventeen. All taller than average. All had medium-length blond hair. All in Colorado. All disappeared within two hours after school and within a half-mile of that school. All wearing jeans. All wearing sweaters of some kind. All described as good students without behavior issues. All on their way home or to meet friends. All in small towns. All walking along a side-street with minimal traffic. No witnesses in any of their cases ... and these are only the girls you know about."

Bell pursed his lips.

"Okay, Rox, but those aren't really odd behaviors for teenage girls."

The bookkeeper turned forensic analyst smiled.

"Let me cut to the important part, Woodrow," he said. "Cherish Nelson disappeared December 9 in 1969, right? That was a Tuesday."

Bell now suspected his friend might be seeing significance in irrelevant details.

"So what?"

"The other girls disappeared, let's see..." Roxy ran his finger down his hand-drawn graph on the back of the envelope. "December 1, 1970 ... February 15, 1972 ... April 3, 1973 ... September 13, 1977 ... April 1, 2003 ... February 28, 2006 ..."

"Sorry, but those dates mean nothing to me. What's the headline, Rox?"

"All Tuesdays."

Bell went silent. That wasn't irrelevant or coincidental. It meant something. His mind revved up. Of five school days every week, why would the abductor always pick this one? Unlikely the same day off from work over more than thirty years, but maybe an anniversary of some kind? Symbolic?

"And that's not the most interesting similarity, Woodrow," Roxy Snipes said. He puffed up taller than he really was.

"All those seven dates? Moonless nights. If those girls were all abducted by some freak, whatever he did to them, those first nights were completely black."

CHAPTER 8

CHERISH NELSON'S CASE was no longer an old man's pet project.

Six other extraordinarily similar girls missing under extraordinarily similar circumstances to one murdered girl weren't accidental. That those six girls were still missing made Bell uneasy. That it was looking more and more like a serial killer at work made him sweat.

Inside, Bell arranged his reports on the breakfast table by date. The fastidious Roxy Snipes had paper-clipped his six special NCIC hits together, and that's where Bell focused.

The six girls had vanished from tiny mountain towns scattered across the Colorado Rockies: Ouray, Idaho Springs, Crested Butte, Pagosa, Creede, and Leadville ... plus Midnight.

In some ways, the towns were odd choices, Bell reasoned. Outsiders would be recognized quickly and attract a lot of curious eyes. The pool of potential victims was smaller, especially if the stranger hunted a specific type of girl. And his escape route was typically one road in and out, and it was likely narrow, long, and often icy, anything but quick.

In other, depressing ways, these dinky towns were prime hunting grounds for a smart predator. They wouldn't be expecting deviance that, to them, only happened in big cities. Kids were more trusting, less street smart. And local law enforcement was commonly undermanned and undertrained. Bell knew that by the time small-town cops got their act together, they'd have squandered those crucial first forty-eight hours. Their UnSub and his girl could be a thousand miles and two very dark nights away.

Bell had never trusted criminal profilers and their voodoo, but he could draw certain conclusions. The predator blended in, maybe driving a muddy truck, Colorado plates, or a casual wave to passing cars as if he knew them. He didn't look or act like a sideshow geek who'd attract attention. A cop might drive past and think nothing. The bad guy didn't snatch random girls but stalked a very explicit kind of girl, so he had to wait somewhere and watch ... patient and observant, like a hunter. His blind rage erupted later.

And he was probably a Colorado guy who understood mountain driving. The seven presumed victims were all from Colorado, with no evidence—yet—that he worked elsewhere. Four went missing in the dead of a high-country winter, when roads were treacherous on more days than not. And somehow he kept his panic-stricken victims under control while he drove on dicey two-lanes back to whatever god-forsaken torture chamber he used.

If these seven girls were snatched by Erskine Midwinter—a dot that still wasn't connected—then he was fifteen when he butchered Cherish Nelson in 1969 and fifty-two when the last girl vanished in 2006. Today, he'd be in his late sixties. Chances were good that there were unknown others, maybe still piling up. The killer, Midwinter or whoever he was, would only have improved at snatching, slaughtering, and dumping his victims.

All the cop logic in the world didn't matter now. It was out of Bell's big hands. This was a Colorado Bureau of Investigation case, maybe even FBI. He punched some wrong buttons on his cellphone, then a few more wrong buttons, until he stumbled across the right ones.

"Hello, Big Man," Jazz answered.

"Goddammit ..."

"Yeah, it's Vulcan mind-magic. Be afraid. What's up?"

"Buckle up, Dr. Spock," Bell said. "This is gonna blow you away."

"Just Spock. Dr. Spock is the baby guy. Just Spock."

"Stick with me here, Spock. You might wanna take notes."

Bell laid it out as best he could without Roxy Snipes's unfathomable arithmetic. The fifty-two girls, thirty datapoints, probabilities, school days, the significant six, the twenty-seven-point match, small towns, Tuesdays, and new moons.

Jazz said nothing for a moment.

"This isn't just Big Man BS, is it?"

"Not this time."

"None of these are Denver metro cases. It's out of our—my—jurisdiction," she said. "You gotta take it to CBI."

The Colorado Bureau of Investigation was the big dog, with vastly more resources, fewer hoops to jump through, and a longer reach that any local law enforcement agency, including the Denver PD.

"I don't know anybody over there anymore, and they always want stuff to go through the proper channels," Bell said. "Would you mind?"

"Oh no," Jazz pushed back. "If you're wrong about all this, no way I'm gonna take the fall and look stupid. Unh-unh."

"Or get all the glory? C'mon, partner, help me out. This isn't about me or us or the regs anymore. It's bigger than us now. We might have at least seven dead girls and a serial killer. God knows how many others are out there. We don't have the resources or the authority to take it further. Just pick up the phone and call CBI. Tell 'em they can call me."

"You sonofabitch!" Jazz flared up. "This isn't about knowing anybody or getting credit or proper channels or any of that shit! You can't dial your goddamned phone!"

"That's harsh. I'm figuring it out."

"Goddammit!"

"So you'll do it?"

"I was kidding before when I said I would shoot you," she seethed. "Now I'm not kidding."

"I knew I could count on you. Just let me know when they'll call so I can practice answering the phone. I get all excited and I never know which buttons to push. Is it the red one or the number sign?"

"I'm tired of being your partner," she said. "You piss me off."

"Technically, we're not partners anymore ..."

"I still want a transfer."

"You're Denver's finest, Jazz. If I was still your partner, I'd never-ever ask for a transfer. You've always got my six and you shoot kinda good. You're better than a wife and almost as good as a girlfriend. So can you do this little favor for me?"

It surprised him when she didn't curse his mother.

"I gotta go," is all she said. "If I get some time today, I'll call a guy I know at CBI. A few hours won't matter after fifty years. You should thank your lucky stars that this might be a serial killer. Otherwise, I'd shoot you. Twice."

Bell appreciated Jazz more than he ever said or she ever knew.

"Thanks, Jazz," he said. "One more thing: Could you wait and call him next week? Like you said, it's waited fifty years and a few more days won't hurt. I need a little time for, you know, practicing on my phone and stuff."

Jazz clicked off without saying anything, but Bell knew what she was thinking.

BELL SAT THERE in his quiet kitchen, the phone still in his hand.

He looked at those smiling faces arrayed across the table and remembered Sarah at seventeen. In his memory, she always smiled, too. She'd always been more mature for her age, but at the time she was on the verge of adulthood for real. She had boyfriends, but none serious. She was more pensive than moody. She earned good grades and made him proud. She only got in serious trouble once, when she went skinny-dipping with her friends one night at the public pool where she'd learned to swim. That was around the time things turned nasty between Bell and her mother, who soon separated then divorced. Sarah stopped smiling.

Bell missed a lot after that. In fact, maybe he missed a lot *before* that. He had his share of regrets, and that was a big one.

Now he sensed some urgency to make things right, or at least better. He thought about calling Sarah, but she might be at one of her long lunches. Besides, she hadn't returned any of his earlier messages. He was starting to feel like a desperate freshman boy who wanted a prom date so badly that he chased girl after girl who told him no after no. Bell didn't want to be that needy or foolish.

So he put the phone down. Maybe tomorrow.

Friday meant date night, so Charlie brought pizza and a gallon of cheap red wine.

While they sipped from two coffee mugs that advertised an auto-parts shop, they ate pepperoni on the sofa, watching the fire. The fireplace never fully heated Bell's drafty old Victorian, but it warmed them to watch it together.

"I hate green peppers," he said. He hadn't eaten all day, but he was never hungry enough to eat green peppers. He plucked "that crap" off his slices and plopped it on Charlie's.

"You're too old to be so picky," she said. "There are children starving in India."

"So box up that crap and mail it to India. Those starving kids probably won't eat it either."

Charlie liked, maybe loved, a lot of things about him. For one, he could be funny. Occasionally. When he wasn't being ... Woodrow. At the moment, he was being Woodrow.

"I hear Roxy Snipes cracked your case," she said.

"Who told you that?"

"Roxy."

Bell huffed like a diffident black bear. He wasn't surprised.

"Rox did great. He didn't crack the case, but he cracked the code," Bell said. "I only see names and faces. They give me a reason to find answers. He saw patterns and numbers as the answers to the reason. When he was done, I had six more names and faces. He did better than a lot of cops I've known."

"So now what?" Charlie asked.

Bell sipped his wine, counting all the balls in the air.

"A lot of things that could go sideways," he said. "I gotta get up to that abandoned mine on Mount Misery somehow. I'm waiting on a DNA report from the toilet seat. And I have to scrape open some old wounds for six families. And after all that, I gotta find a lot of other shit that could go sideways, which will lead me to other shit that could go sideways. And I only have one week."

"One week?"

"Then I have to call in the real cops," Bell replied. It chafed him to admit he was no longer a "real" cop, but that's what he wasn't. "Out of nowhere, this case is above my pay grade. It isn't my little history hobby anymore. We might have seven dead girls and a serial killer out there. I can't arrest anybody. I can't radio for backup. I've got a gun, but I probably can't take him out. And all I have is a pissy ex-partner who wants to shoot me, and seven old farts with nothing better to do."

"And me."

Bell paused. "How do you mean?"

"How can I help you?" Charlie asked. She was stone-cold serious.

Bell floundered. He had never considered dragging her into his darkness, other than listening and providing clarity. And bringing pizza. But she was tough and hauled other people's garbage every day. She knew how things, even people, can be casually tossed aside.

And she knew this case.

Maybe it was the fire or the wine or the green peppers, but Bell instantly warmed to the idea. He loved who she was right now.

"Where do you think you could make a difference?" he asked her.

Charlie stared into the fire for a long time. She didn't know what she could do, but she wanted to do something.

"I drive a big truck. I'm still cute. I am insanely attracted to older men. I like green peppers. I once saw Bruce Willis at Tommyknockers. I'm writing a novel for teenage girls ..."

"That's it!" Bell interrupted.

"You really think Bruce Willis can help?"

"The novel, dammit."

"It's not done."

"No, not the novel," Bell said. "The computer. I don't know why I didn't think of this earlier. Are you on the hi-fi?"

"Wi-fi." Charlie shook her head. "But, yes, I have Wi-fi and Internet. What are you thinking?"

Bell fetched the six missing-persons reports from the breakfast table and handed them to Charlie.

"These," he said. "Maybe you can find any family still around. Preferably parents if they're still alive. Brothers and sisters. The closest relatives. I need phone numbers or addresses."

"Why?"

"Sometimes the cases aren't ever updated in the computer, so I just need to be sure the girls haven't been found," Bell explained. "Sometimes people remember something later that never got into the computer at all. And four of these cases happened before most small-town cop shops had computers. A lot of stuff can fall off the desk, if you know what I mean."

Charlie grabbed her coat and headed toward the front door.

"Whoa there. Aren't you going to stay tonight?" Bell asked. There was a little hope in his voice. "We've still got wine and green peppers."

Charlie smiled and flipped her leather coat's collar up.

"You've only got seven days, Woodrow," she said. "Why waste one whole night?"

AS THE DAYS grew shorter, nights grew longer.

Bell wished for shorter nights. On this one, he slept almost not at all. Whenever he drifted off, he startled back to the waking side of sleep. Too many loose ends, too many things that might never be explained ... too many ways for him to screw it up. Baby Grace floated through his dark room, asking if he knew who'd last spoken her given name. George Tomer was there, too, frozen in the corner, just watching Bell toss. Erskine Midwinter, whom he'd never seen and couldn't see now, loomed over it all.

But Luther Nelson never came up. He wasn't there anymore. Every day, he disappeared a little more. Bell wanted to believe that what Nellie loved about Cherish was still in there, if only as a shadow.

When dawn seeped around his blackout drapes, Bell got out of bed. *Why waste one whole morning?* he said to himself. He dressed and slogged through crusty drifts to Tommyknockers Diner.

The boys of Deaf Row didn't gather on Sundays, but it didn't matter. Bell only needed one of them: Ollie Fuhrman. He lived in a manufactured home behind his equipment yard up County Road 13, toward Mount Pisgah. It wasn't too far in miles but was probably too deep under snow for a casual visit. It might be a day before Ollie got to town ... and he owned bulldozers.

But there was an easier way.

"Do you have Ollie Fuhrman's phone number?" he asked Fancy as he poured his first cup of the morning.

"Who's asking?"

"The fuzz."

"Oh, okay," she said. "A girl can't be too careful these days."

She poked around in her apron for her cell phone. With one thumb, she ticka-ticka-ticked and handed Bell the phone.

After a couple rings, Ollie answered. "Hey there, Fancy girl."

"How the hell ...?" Bell couldn't figure out how everybody knew who was calling.

It wasn't the voice Ollie expected but it was familiar.

"Woodrow? Are you on Fancy's phone again?"

"Yeah, she didn't want to risk that I'd launch missiles in Russia trying to dial my own damn phone."

Ollie snorted.

"What moron sold you a phone?"

"Mountain Bell," he replied. "Hey, Ollie, I got a favor to ask."

"Shoot."

"I need to get up to an abandoned mine on Mount Misery, maybe a half-mile up the slope from the old asylum. I know this isn't the best time of year for a walk in the woods. There's probably six feet of snow up there. But Fancy tells me you did a lot of the trails up there with some badass snowbeast piece of equipment you have ..."

"A little excavator," Ollie said.

" ... with tank tracks."

"Yessirree. Three tons and she'll damn near go straight up the side of Mile High Stadium," Ollie boasted. "But I did that Forest Service work in summer. I don't know how she'd do in snow taller than a man at, what, ten thousand feet? I don't know if there are any old logging roads up there, and just getting the trailer close enough might kill us. Top speed in those conditions is gonna be about one mile an hour. There's gonna be a huge field of rock debris that the miners took out of their hole, and those rocks will roll around like marbles under the machine. And landslides might have covered up the mouth of the mine completely. Then there's avalanches, and an old guy in the cab ... maybe climbing Mile High would be easier.igh would be easierHigh would be easierH"

"*Two* old guys," Bell interjected.

"Oh no," Ollie protested. "I ain't sitting on your lap."

"Then I'll sit on yours. C'mon, what could go wrong? It sounds like fun."

Joking aside, Ollie needed more than the promise of a wild ride up the side of a snowy mountain—and maybe back down in a freefall.

"What's this all about, Woodrow?"

Bell explained how George Tomer had pinpointed the deserted mine, and how it might or might not be related to Cherish Nelson's murder. George didn't know what he saw, and Bell didn't know what to expect. But he had to look, and he couldn't wait til spring.

"Damn, Woodrow," Ollie said. "George ain't exactly the most trustworthy guy. I ain't sayin' he's a liar, but ... well, he tells stories."

"That was a long damn time ago," Bell said, peeved by Ollie's unfairly long memory. "Besides, you want to be a county commissioner, and that sort of requires you to be a liar most of the time. Look, I just have a gut feeling about this, Ollie. And I don't have many options right now. If I promise to vote for you, will you do it?"

The line went silent, too long for Bell.

"Ollie, you there?"

"Dammit, Woodrow, I thought there'd be more baby-kissin'. Nobody told me I'd be rollin' down a mountain screamin' like a little girl for one lousy vote."

Bell didn't wait for that image to burn itself into Ollie's brain.

"How about tomorrow?"

"Monday?"

"Can you think of a better day to plunge to your death?"

"Fuck you, old man."

"Okay, as long as I'm on top and there's no kissing," Bell poked back. "Maybe we can sleep late and I'll make a romantic breakfast before we hit the road. Seven a.m. too early?"

ON SUNDAY AT seven a.m. sharp, Ollie Fuhrman pulled up in front of the Bar F restaurant in the most monstrous Dodge Ram dually Bell had ever seen up close. It was towing a twenty-foot, three-axle flatbed trailer and a hulking piece of earth-moving equipment bigger than Bell expected. Bell readily admitted he didn't know the finer points of heavy metal, but he wasn't expecting the stinger-like boom with a bucket the size of a love seat.

Suddenly, the prospect of falling off a steep, frozen mountainside was real.

"How the hell ..." Bell stammered.

"... are we gonna get this up there?" Ollie replied as he climbed down from the cab like the stiff old guy he was. "I don't have the first clue, Woodrow. This might be the dumbest-ass thing you ever come up with. We might both be going to meet our Maker today, but I got a good map."

Ollie spread his big topographic map of the Mount Misery district against his rumbling fender. He pulled off one leather glove and traced a fine, serpentine line from the main road toward the derelict Schattenland Asylum and the mine beyond.

"The old dirt road from the blacktop to the old funny farm really doesn't exist anymore, but it's all we got," Ollie said. "We'll go as far as we can, then take the excavator the rest of the way, maybe a mile. If I recall, there's a narrow mine road that hangs off the mountain right here"—he bent closer and drew his finger along a barely visible contour—"and that's where you might need to get out and guide me."

"Jesus," was all Bell could say.

"And when we're done, we only gotta back-up this big-ass trailer down a road that doesn't exist. In the snow. Maybe in the dark. I might need you to guide me there, too."

"How long is this all gonna take?" Bell asked, not really wanting to hear the answer.

"It shouldn't take long." Ollie continued. "Two hours over there. One hour up the asylum road. At least an hour up to the mine from there. However long you need in the mine. An hour back to the truck. Two hours to back down to the blacktop. Then two hours home. What's that, eleven or twelve hours? If we don't die in a fiery bellyflop off a cliff, we'll be home by New Year's Eve. Maybe."

Bell turtled into his big leather coat. All of a sudden, the coffee and four sandwiches he brought for them sounded like a light snack.

"I don't suppose you could have explained all this yesterday," he grumbled to Ollie.

"Maybe I was too subtle about the fiery catastrophe of plunging off a cliff and dying in three tons of mangled steel. My mistake."

Bell's impatience sometimes got ahead of his sanity. But here stood Ollie, his big four-wheel-drive truck, and his iron snowbeast. *Why waste a whole day?*

"Let's get going," Bell said. "We're burning daylight and we all gotta die somehow."

RANDOM PATCHES OF slick black ice spread across the paved road all the way up to the gap in the trees that marked the asylum turn-off. Going off-road in the deep snow was risky enough ... the specter of backing that long trailer downhill in its own tracks in the frozen dark spooked Bell even more. Then, sliding back down a mountain road on the way home would be a whole different thrill ride.

Maybe it was best to take one way to die at a time, Bell concluded.

This was the first. The invisible road, such as it was, ended a half-mile short of Schattenland's remains and a mile short of the mine. They couldn't go farther in the big truck and trailer. Ollie stopped his Ram and stepped down into knee-deep snow.

"Not as deep as I expected," he said. "Let's eat lunch, then get this machine off the trailer."

After they wolfed two quick sandwiches, Ollie backed the excavator off the flatbed while Bell pretended to direct him. A half-hour later the machine was warm and pointed up the narrowing, uphill slot toward the asylum and the mine beyond.

Ollie hadn't been kidding about the excavator's forward speed. Its tracks crept along with grueling slowness. Its progress—maybe not the right word, Bell decided—up the hill was best measured not in miles per hour, but in hours per mile.

The excavator's heated cab wasn't big enough for both of them, so Bell tagged along behind in the tracks' packed snow, wondering how many old men died hiking up mountains through snow behind earth-moving equipment. Probably not as many as snow-shoveling, he bet.

It took most of an hour to arrive at the old asylum grounds. The deep snow around the building made it look smaller but no less unearthly. To Bell, it simply didn't belong here.

Ollie studied his topo map. The mine lay another half mile north and west, and the closer they got, the steeper the grade. He grappled with his coat sleeve to find his wristwatch. Just past noon, with at least an hour up to Bell's spot above the trees, and an hour back. He wasn't even sure they could get close enough to slog in against biting wind and blowing snow.

Foot by foot, they scrabbled along. Ollie occasionally stopped to let Bell warm up and catch his breath in the cab, but the big guy's legs were burning out. His windblown face ached from squinting his eyes to keep his eyeballs from freezing. And his lungs filled with noxious diesel fumes.

When the slope turned decidedly steeper and the trail narrower, the excavator growled deeper as its powerful engine labored over snowdrifts and the boulders hidden below. At times, the tracks slipped a little. At other times, they seemed to freeze up altogether.

Worse, above the tree line, the mountainside slanted at an increasingly precipitous angle. The excavator tilted toward the canyon. Even as its tracks inched closer and closer to the drop-off, Ollie couldn't steer her any closer to the safer side.

When Bell couldn't feel his feet anymore, that's when he gave up on this whole foolish idea and turned his little remaining energy to simple survival.

Then the excavator stopped.

Its engine geared down from a furious whine to a painful moan. Bell considered that it had finally run out of fuel, busted a belt or some other crisis. Through the diesel smoke and fogged glass of the cab, he could see Ollie studying his map again.

Fergawdsakes, we're fucking lost, Bell stewed. He was more angry than panicked, but not much more.

Bell spread his arms in the international sign for "What the hell?"

Ollie stuck his arm out the cab's side window and pointed up the slope.

The mine.

But Bell saw nothing but a smooth blanket of snow covering all but sporadic boulders. Not the unnatural shape of a talus pile, no gaping holes in the mountainside, not even a telltale depression. Just blinding, blowing white.

Bell rapped on Ollie's glass.

"What are you seeing?" he asked. "I don't see a damn thing."

Ollie pressed the map against the cab window.

"This cliff is right here and the face turns hard south at that rock outcropping," he hollered over the growling engine and wind. "If this mine was located on the map accurately and the contours are true, then it should be about twenty feet straight up that slope, give or take forty, fifty feet to either side. Or maybe not. Sorry."

Bell squinted and studied the slope again, twenty feet up and a hundred feet across. Nothing.

Ollie yelled again.

"This is a springtime job, Woodrow. Even if you find the mine mouth, it might be blocked by snow or rocks or both. It's a house of cards: Move anything and you could cause an avalanche. They'd never find our corpses down there, even if the damn global warming was real."

Bell peered over the edge of the bottomless canyon, then back down their tracks. Staying here much longer risked a cataclysm; turning around gave them a chance at a few more years and a natural death. Staying didn't guarantee they'd find anything; leaving guaranteed they'd find nothing.

Even though it wasn't a hard choice, Bell pondered a little too long.

"Is there any way you could use that bucket to pack the snow down a little for me to climb up there?"

"Are you fucking crazy?" an astonished Ollie gusted a cloud of frozen breath. "This boom won't reach twenty feet and you'd be crazy to climb around up there. If you busted a leg, I'd leave you for wolf meat."

"Okay, maybe you could lift me most of the way in the bucket. Real gentle."

Ollie huffed and shook his head.

"You ever seen a wolf tear apart an elk? Seems like it'd hurt."

"I'd stay close. I saw a shovel strapped to the back of your cab," Bell shouted. "I can use it to poke around."

"Charlie's gonna be pissed if all I bring back is wolf turds."

"I'll risk it," Bell said. "Just give me ten minutes to prod around in the snow for a hole. Only ten minutes, I swear, then we head home."

Ollie swore under his breath. He set his stabilizers, unfolded the boom to the mountain side and began ever-so-delicately to tamp the snow with the bottom of his bucket. If the snow-shelf gave way, he'd be swept off the mountain into an icy oblivion ... so he patted it firmly enough to walk on, and as softly as a three-ton earth-mover can to avoid an avalanche.

When he finished, Ollie had packed a semi-solid snow-slab the size of three side-by-side parking spaces. Then he lowered his bucket. Bell sat uncomfortably in it with his shovel until the boom swung to deposit him on the man-made slope.

When he climbed out, Bell's boots sunk a little but using the shovel like a walking stick, he could move around well enough. He poked as much as three feet down with the handle then moved sideways a few feet, poking again, over and over, always hitting rocks below. He covered his space methodically, racing against Ollie's clock to discover a void where a void shouldn't be.

"Five minutes!" Ollie shouted up to him. Bell held up a gloved hand to acknowledge his limit and kept stabbing his shovel handle into the snow, hitting rocks.

Then ... nothing. The handle sunk its entire length, up to the blade. Bell moved a couple feet to one side and plunged the shovel into ... nothing. Another few feet. Nothing. Finally, ten feet from his original hole, he hit solid rock again.

Bell stepped to the other side of the first hole and punched one more hole until he hit rock.

He stood directly over a void, not quite twenty feet up the mountain from Ollie's excavator, suddenly aware that his tenuous bridge might collapse at any moment. He moved hastily to the side where he'd hit solid rock.

"There's some kind of hole here," he called down to Ollie.

"Stand back!" Ollie yelled.

The excavator's bucket swung back over the spot. He sunk its teeth gingerly into the snow where Bell had punched through, then pressed.

A three-foot crust of hardened snow promptly caved into a yawning black hole. He watched the snow above it and listened for any sound of an impending avalanche. He motioned to Ollie to scoop enough snow away for him to get a closer look. Again, Ollie maneuvered the bucket with the precision of a brain surgeon until he'd exposed a cave half-blocked by snow and fallen stones from the slope above.

Bell knew it was the abandoned mine, almost exactly where Ollie said it would be. He scraped a few shovels full of snow away to see what he could see.

Beyond the first few feet was blackness. Weathered, sagging timbers supported the opening but before long—maybe today—they'd collapse. The mountain would take its hole back.

In an all-out effort to prove his insanity, Bell decided to go in.

"Flashlight?" he hollered to Ollie. Ollie responded by pounding on his wristwatch and making the international sign for "Go to hell." But after a moment's thought, he removed his gloves and rooted around in his coat pockets until he found his truck keys—and a quarter-sized light only big enough to illuminate his door lock at night.

Ollie removed it from his keyring then got out of the cab. He tossed the little flashlight in his bucket. He clambered back in the cab and pivoted the boom toward Bell, who snatched it out and tucked it safely in his pants pocket.

Bell waved at Ollie, then scrambled over to the mine mouth for a closer look before climbing in.

Inside, the subterranean air was dead, unmoving. Other than the distant hum of the excavator and the wind outside, there was no sound. Beyond the snow and rubble at first, Bell could almost stand upright, but the hole closed in the deeper he went.

When his eyes adjusted to the dark, Bell edged deeper into the mine. He focused on the uneven floor. He wasn't especially claustrophobic but at his age, stumbling around in the dark on a treacherous floor could be fatal. One wrong step and this mine would become his crypt.

Many other things were less certain. He couldn't know how deep it went, nor how many passages might branch off of this main tunnel. There might be a labyrinth of dark shafts, recesses, and crawlspaces, or it might open up into a hollowed-out chamber that doubled as a vagabond miner's only shelter. It was a hard life.

It could simply be one of thousands of played-out mines in these mountains. George Tomer's memory might have exaggerated its depravity. It might not even be the hole he remembered.

Or it might have been a secret hiding place for an insane little boy who grew up knowing where he could literally hole up with his unexorcised demons.

Maybe worse.

Bell baby-stepped his way through the darkness. The passage would have been less confining for a smaller man. But even hunched over, Bell's bulk filled the shaft. His right hand skimmed against one wall to guide him, his left shoulder touching the other.

The gray light from the mine mouth had faded to black. He took off his glove and wriggled his big hand into his pocket for the tiny light. He pinched it, and it threw a beam only about three feet in front of him. Not much but enough to see where he should step.

Barely thirty paces in, the narrow tunnel opened into a den where the walls had been gouged a little deeper into the mountain and supported by more timbers. Two smaller passages branched off but were mostly blocked by fallen rocks. The enlarged space wasn't much bigger than his bathroom, but it must have seemed like a suite to a poor prospector who spent his days clawing at solid rock, seldom seeing sunlight and always expecting his roof to kill him.

Bell shined his puny light down at the gravel floor, which was blanketed with a thin layer of dirt and millennial dust. Larger rocks had been cleared, and Bell could see a few small animal bones scattered around, probably left by hungry predators. A pile of decaying lumber and wire on one side was likely a small bed, and a couple of rusty cans lay nearby. Food and sleep. No trace of other human comforts survived.

But through the fog of his frosty breath, Bell saw something in the dust that he didn't expect: boot prints. Maybe modern hunters, hikers, or weekend prospectors, but certainly not hundred-year-old tracks. Other humans— possibly even a young Erskine Midwinter in the 1960s—

had been here more recently, and some left evidence that they'd passed through here.

And the faint odor, barely a wisp floating unmistakably in the cold, dead air. It wasn't sweat, filth, decay, or death, but perhaps a little of each. Maybe it was all that remained from those hungry predators, which might still be lurking in the black catacombs beyond. Maybe it was a rock-hunter's garbage rotting in one of the side passages. Maybe a sleeping bear back there someplace.

Bell had reached a dead end. The prospect of waking a sleeping bear and the fading light outside made any further exploration unwise. Ollie would be pissed that he'd been sucked into a fool's errand. Maybe in spring he could come back under better conditions to exhume \ the cave's mysteries, but not today. Time might have erased whatever George Tomer allegedly saw, or he saw it in a different cave, or he dreamed it up like he had once dreamed up a true love. But whether ghost, misremembered place, or fantasy ... nothing real existed right here.

For a big man in full winter gear, turning around in this darkened, pinched space was an awkward sequence of stoop, shuffle, and slow spin. As he rotated, Bell scraped his elbows and his butt against the craggy walls. When his head bumped a protruding edge, he bolted up slightly and his woolen cap snagged something on the ceiling.

In a split-second, thousands of bats, all disturbed from their winter hibernation, wheeled through Bell's imagination, and he covered his face. But no swarm was unleashed. Instead, he reached up to feel that a root or something had become entangled in the yarn of his cap.

A root doesn't make sense down here, Bell thought, *maybe a wood sliver from one of the old beams.*

But when he tugged the hat from his head and shined his little light on it, he flinched.

It was a little girl's baby doll, naked and limp. The doll's blond hair was thin and matted, its plastic body soiled. And when Bell turned it over, it mewled like a sick kitten. It was the kind that closed its eyes when laid in its toy crib.

But this baby's eyes neither opened nor closed.

They were sewn shut.

The stitching was crude, more figurative than literal. The ends of the black thread were unknotted and hung loose across the doll's cheeks like inky tears in the faint circle of Bell's light. And those eyes alone would have shocked the unshockable old detective, who saw something else even more horrifying.

A ten-penny nail had been driven into the baby's right ear, completely through its plastic head.

Bell caught his breath. Cherish Nelson's psycho killer had been here, standing in this precise spot. His mind ran amok: Was this his symbolic souvenir of Cherish's murder? Had it hung here since 1969? Is this what shook up the mild-mannered rock-hunter George Tomer?

Bell breathed deeply and deliberately. He needed focus, quick. He stuffed the doll inside his coat and took a final look around.

He shined his little flashlight at the floor around his feet, squinting to find any sign of the killer's presence, the doll's clothing, a wayward nail, even a footprint. Nothing.

Then he simultaneously turned his light and his face to the ceiling, less than a foot above. Even before his eyes could focus, he recoiled. His heart tumbled, and his light spontaneously flashed away, but what Bell saw instantly burned itself in his brain.

Dead babies.

Hanging by their feet.

Naked.

Frozen.

Too many to count ...

When he could fix his light on the horror again, he could see it wasn't a horde of dead babies, but more baby dolls. All had been stripped of their dainty dresses and dangled upside-down from rusty hooks pounded into cracks between the rocks. All were blond. All their eyes were sutured with black cord. And all had a nail driven through their toy skulls.

All twenty-two of them.

BELL SQUEEZED OUT of the old mine much faster than he'd come in.

The footing was no less precarious, but he could literally see the light at the end of that ghastly tunnel. He clambered over the snowbank and escaped into living air. The blowing snow hurt his face, but Bell half-scrambled, half-rolled like a man half his age down the slope toward Ollie's excavator.

Of course, Ollie didn't know what held Bell up, only that he was late, as usual.

"What the hell, Woodrow?" he hollered. "You said ten minutes. It's colder'n a Yukon well-digger's ass out here. Now we're an hour behind, dammit. I'm burning fuel here!"

Now Bell was in a bigger hurry than his driver to get off this haunted mountain.

"Let's go, go, go!" he said, already tromping back in their tracks. Ollie swiveled his cab around and revved his engine for their half-mile return to the truck, another hour in brutal weather that was socking in.

Bell led the whole way, sometimes so far ahead that he lost sight of the excavator. By the time he took shelter in the relative warmth of the truck, Ollie was still twenty minutes behind. The fuel gauge pointed squarely at a half tank. Rather than risk burning too much gas running the heater before the long trip home, in gloaming and dark, he huddled deeper in his uneasiness. His heavy breathing frosted the windows.

Eventually, Ollie arrived. He started the truck and turned up the heater full-blast so they could melt snow to drink from their empty coffee-to-go cups. After a considerable struggle against snow, cold, and gravity, they chained the excavator on the trailer just as the winter sun vanished. Because there was no room to turn the truck and long trailer around, Ollie had no choice but to back a half-mile down the way they came—and Bell was his guide.

They hit the blacktop more than an hour later, after five. As they turned back down Mount Misery toward Midnight, Ollie's headlights caught the earliest flurries of a new storm that would slow them down even more. At first, the snow fell light, then harder. Bell knew that sliding down a frozen mountain with three tons of rolling steel behind you is far trickier than going up.

In the greenish glow of the dashboard, the old men ate their last two, half-thawed sandwiches, which had frozen solid while they were up at the mine. Bell had barely spoken twenty words since they came down.

"What did you see up there, Woodrow?" Ollie asked out of nowhere.

Bell wasn't sure how to answer. He now understood why George Tomer didn't say anything for twenty years. It was all so incomprehensible, and not just to ordinary people who hadn't spent their lives mired in unnatural death. Bell was still processing it, too.

Ollie persevered. "You either seen something or you seen nothing. Either way, it's not like you to go all radio silent."

Bell fumbled around under his coat and laid something on the seat between them.

Ollie squinched his eyes in the darkened cab and glanced at it. When he realized what lay there, he leapt back and jerked the steering wheel in shock. The truck and trailer shimmied on the ice.

"Goddamn you to Hell, Woodrow," he blurted out. "That ain't right. That just ain't right. Jesus God, that ain't right."

Ollie's weathered hands trembled on the wheel.

"There's more," Bell said, staring into the snow swarming past the headlights.

"Jesus God. I thought it was real. I mean it's just ... Jesus God."

They said nothing for a long time, then Bell spoke.

"I thought they were real for a second, too. Twenty-two of them in there."

Ollie's voice wobbled.

"Twenty-two?" he asked. "I ain't goin' back, no fuckin' way."

Bell wasn't sure he'd go back either. He had only wanted to tell Luther Nelson what really happened. But then one question became a hundred, then a thousand. This miserable one-man crusade went sideways when Roxy Snipes found six more girls. Now it had crashed into the ditch. Bell hated like hell to give this case up, but that doll—those dolls— were somebody else's babies now.

Like Baby Grace.

"What the hell does it mean, Woodrow?" Ollie asked after a long time. "Why would some freak do that ...?"

Bell didn't answer. Normal people always made the mistake of assuming abnormal people were logical. They would ask "why?" but the answers always disappointed them because psychopaths' reasons don't make sense to normal people.

So Bell didn't know "why" some freaks became freaks. He couldn't fathom "why" a freak would kidnap young women, sew their eyes shut, and pound a stake through their brains. He didn't even know "why" the freak would do it to twenty-two toy dolls, much less living, breathing girls.

But in the bottommost depths of his gut, he knew "who."

THE TRIP HOME from Mount Misery took longer than they ever imagined, partly because they both stopped talking. Around eight o'clock, Ollie dropped Bell at his house and drove away, still shaken.

As Bell mounted his porch, he paused at the front door. He didn't want to take the doll inside to put it on his chair, his breakfast table, or kitchen counter, as if it would spread sickness. He didn't even want it on his dirty workbench. It was pestilent. But it was also evidence, and he couldn't leave it outside all night where it might be dragged off by a stray cat.

Instead, he stuffed the doll in a big garbage bag, then into an old cardboard box. He locked the box in his unheated mud room for the night. He didn't want to think about it anymore right now, although he suspected he'd think a lot about it all night.

Bell was hungry and thirsty, but first he soaped his hands longer than usual in the hallway bathroom. Then he popped open a beer and drank it straight down, then popped open another. He ate a slice of cold pepperoni pizza standing in front of the open fridge door.

When he closed it, he noticed a sticky note Charlie had pasted at eye level. She wrote "Call me."

And just beneath that was another sticky note in Father Bert's handwriting. No number. It said only, "Then call me."

Bell's phone was exactly where he'd left it that morning. He just didn't know where that was. And he wasn't sure he wanted to find it tonight. But while the priest might wait until tomorrow, not Charlie.

He tossed the sofa cushions, lifted the lids on all his kitchen canisters, checked the refrigerator, frisked the carpet under the bed, double-checked the refrigerator, riffled through a month of *Midnight Suns*, even examined the toilet tank closer than he had in nine years. He finally found his phone on the fireplace mantel, precisely where he had put it so he wouldn't forget.

He joggled the frustrating little buttons until "Best Girlfriend" appeared, just as Charlie had programmed it for him.

"Hey there, sweetie," she said. From the languor in her voice, he knew she'd been sleeping.

"Hey," he replied, as usual. Terms of endearment weren't in his vocabulary.

"How was your day on the mountain? Did you murder Ollie?"

"No," Bell said. "In fact, I think I promised to vote for him. Anyway, it was ... quite a day, to say the least. Can you come over?"

"Can you come over here instead?" Charlie replied. "I've got something you want."

"It's been a long day ..."

Charlie exhaled in that way women do when men are dense. She probably rolled her eyes, too.

"Not that, dumbass," she said. "Those families you wanted me to find? Well, I did."

"I'll be right over."

She lived too close to drive in summer, too far to walk in winter. Bell grabbed his coat and fired up the Crown Vic. While it resisted warming up, impatience took over. The trip would be, after all, only three minutes.

Charlie met Bell at the door with a hug that lasted a little longer than usual.

"C'mon in," she said. "I've got a fire going and you know where I keep the bourbon."

He shook the snow and cold off his coat, poured himself a stiff one and sank into Charlie's late father's favorite bearskin recliner. She never sat there because she imagined—although intellectually she knew otherwise—it had fleas. Bell had no such absurd fears, except clowns. If malevolence had a face, it'd be smiling and painted in brilliant colors ... which made it all the more disquieting that Charlie believed clowns were the universal explanation for everything.

But it was her father's favorite chair so she couldn't sell it, give it away, or dump it. She was stuck with her imaginary fleas.

Now, she sat cross-legged on the rug in front of the fire, safely distant from the chair.

"So what did you learn?" he asked.

Bell intended it to be a simple question, but Charlie had a more complicated answer.

"Grief is something that never heals," she said. "It just scabs over."

Bell knew all too well.

"Some people have open wounds for the rest of their lives," he said, staring down into his glass. "They pick off the scabs and the bleeding never stops."

"I talked to some of those today," Charlie confessed.

It took a moment for Bell to comprehend what she said.

"You were only supposed to get numbers and addresses for close relatives. You called some of them?"

"All of them."

"Some brothers and sisters who didn't remember too much," she said, "but the mothers remembered everything."

"For all six girls?"

"No. Four mothers, a brother and sister," she said somberly, "and one had nobody left but a cousin."

"I only needed numbers and addresses. Why did you call them? You're not a cop."

"Neither are you," she said. "I thought maybe they'd talk to a woman more than a man. Besides, I told them you'd call if you needed to talk to them."

Bell wanted to be annoyed and surprised, but he was neither. He knew this about Charlie, and maybe he loved her for it, too.

"Maybe I will."

"I wanted to know what you know about loss," she said. "I thought maybe they would teach me something that I need to know about you. But when I talked to those mothers

... my god. It's been fifty years for some of them, twenty years for another, but they remembered it like some terrible movie looping in their brains. None of these families knew what happened to their daughters and sisters and cousins, but they thought the worst. They just *knew*."

"When you don't know the reality, you wonder," Bell said. "Then you wonder until it becomes the reality."

"One mom, the one in Idaho Springs, still lives in the same house and has the same phone number because she wants to be where her lost daughter would look for her. Forty-eight years, Woodrow."

Charlie, who never cried in front of Bell, welled up.

"Did anyone say anything that might help us?" he asked her, trying to sidetrack the prevailing sadness of it all.

"Nothing," she said. "Just happy memories, then unhappy memories, then the melancholy, in that order."

Then came the ticklish question about any witness interview.

"Did you tell them what we are thinking?" Bell asked her, careful to not sound critical.

"No," Charlie said. "Only that we were following up on some old cases to see if there was anything new. Nobody had anything. In fact, most of them resented being reminded."

"They had to move on emotionally a long time ago, even if they didn't move away physically," Bell said. "I understand why you did it, and you did good. We had to shake that bush, but nothing ran out. Dead end. That's what happens most of the time."

"Yeah, well, I wish ..." she started then caught herself before she started really crying, "... nevermind. How about you? Did you have fun today out in the ice latitudes?"

Bell thought about those grisly dolls, and decided tonight was not the night to tell Charlie.

THE NEXT MORNING, the Crown Vic was frozen solid.

When Bell turned the key, the starter only clicked. Charlie was already gone when he woke up, so no jump. He decided to walk. Worst-case scenario, the Crown Vic might sit there 'til spring. Next to-worst-case scenario, freezing to death in a snowbank is said to be peaceful.

Bell didn't clomp home, but to Tommyknockers, where Deaf Row was already well on its way to a third round of joe. Elroy Richter, who should have known better, celebrated some happy news.

"When I read in the *Post* that some asteroid was gonna miss Earth and the Apocalypse wasn't going to happen," he said, "I went to McDonald's and ordered their biggest hamburger with extra fries."

That admission was a gift to Cotton Minahan.

"Are you sure it wasn't an ATM?" he needled. "Coogan's still waiting on his Happy Meal, but the teller couldn't stuff it into that little tube."

Everybody laughed but Dan Coogan.

"Hey, Minahan, don't worry about me," Coogan shot back. "Worry about those scary hairs in your ears."

Father Bert saw the perfect opening.

"Shall we bless this mess?" he asked. Everybody pretended to be devout by bowing their bald heads and brushing donut crumbs off their sweaters.

"Lord, give us the strength to forgive our enemies," Father Bert prayed, "or at least to outlive them. Through Christ our Lord. Amen."

Ollie Fuhrman wasn't there. Nobody had seen or heard from him. None of them knew about his Mount Misery escapade. Besides, all of them missed some mornings for benign reasons or sometimes no reasons at all. But the guys on Deaf Row always got low-grade willies that the missing man might have died in the night and was still lying in his bed. They never talked about it, but everybody knew it had occurred to everybody else.

Or maybe Ollie had simply wandered off. He really had no place to go, but these guys all had friends who'd fallen by the wayside. Not necessarily died, just wandered off. Or maybe the guys on Deaf Row had wandered off. At their age, there had been so much coming and going, so many ends had been forgotten, it was hard to know exactly who had wandered off.

Bell knew why Ollie wasn't there. Bumping up against genuine madness—not the abstract notion, but the real stuff you could actually touch—unnerved sane people.

While the boys continued their playful squabbling, Father Bert leaned close.

"The mountain," he whispered. "Want to talk about it later?"

The question caught Bell off-guard.

"How did you know about that?"

"Ollie came over late last night," the priest said.

"Why?"

Father Bert measured his answer carefully.

"Some I can tell you," he said. "Some I can't."

"What can you tell me?"

"Not here," Father Bert said, cocking his head toward the door.

They said their goodbyes to the guys and walked out together into the sunny cold, toward the priest's austere rectory next door to St. Barnabas. They talked as they trudged.

"Ollie dropped you off and came straight over," Father Bert said. "He didn't even go home first."

"God stuff?"

"He was pretty shaken up. He needed to talk."

"But Ollie's not Catholic," Bell pointed out, as if Father Bert might not know.

"Neither are you, but you tell me things."

"That's different."

The priest glanced quizzically at Bell. "Is that your final answer?"

Bell moved on quickly.

"About Ollie, what did he tell you?"

"The doll. It scared him. And he said it seemed to scare you, too."

Bell deflected that last part.

"Spooked maybe, not scared. But Ollie hasn't seen this kind of thing before."

"Have you?"

The old cop couldn't honestly say he had.

"But back in the day I saw other things that spooked me," he said. "A long time ago, I stopped being surprised about being surprised."

The rectory was warm, small thanks to a cantankerous basement heater that pre-dated Sputnik. Father Bert put on a fresh pot of coffee, and they sat in the priest's "study"—in reality, a never-used spare bedroom with a bookshelf, a writing desk, a laptop computer, and two well-worn leather chairs donated by a parishioner who was redecorating.

Bell's mind snagged on something.

"When I got home, I saw your note on the fridge," he said. "But you hadn't talked to Ollie yet. This isn't about Ollie at all, is it?"

"No. It didn't start there," Father Bert said, "but it ends there."

So Bell opened the door. "Where does it start?"

"A toilet in Purgatory."

"How the fff ... freak do you know about that?"

"Roxy told me," Father Bert said. "Anything new?"

"Nothing yet."

"Is the left-hand thing important?"

Bell scowled. "Who told you?"

"Doc Ely," Father Bert said.

"Left hand, right hand," Bell shrugged. "Too soon to know if it's significant."

"What about those six missing girls?"

"What the hell?" Bell's voice rose slightly. "How ...?"

"Charlie."

"Are you waterboarding these people?"

"Charlie's worried about you."

"How so?" Bell asked.

"That maybe you have invested more in Cherish Nelson's case than you can afford to lose. That maybe you don't believe you've lived with meaning and purpose. That mortality is making you more impatient than usual. That maybe you'll never see Sarah again. Trivial stuff like that."

Bell leaned forward in his scritchy chair, scowling at the floor.

"She worries too much. I'm fine."

Father Bert saw Bell's dark side more clearly than he did.

"That's what I told her. You're just getting old."

Bell stiffened.

"Getting old sucks—always has, always will. Being surrounded by smartasses doesn't help."

"Don't get all pissy with me about growing older," the priest said. "It's a privilege not everybody enjoys, you know."

"Can a priest say 'pissy'?"

Father Bert inhaled one deep breath and let it out in a long, nettled huff.

"Woodrow, I've known you a long time. You're just one of those people who act on their nightmares, not their daydreams, but when you act, it's truly amazing. You're just not that lovable."

"Old farts aren't very likable, much less lovable," Bell asserted. "But we're not here to plan my funeral. You called this meeting, padre. What's on your agenda?"

Sighing, Father Bert disengaged. He sat down at his little writing desk and opened his laptop. He clicked vigorously.

"Ollie told me how you found the mine and the twenty-two dolls," he said. "I was curious. So after he left, I got on the Internet. I found a website where you can see close-up pictures of any place on Earth from space."

"You're shitting me. From space? Like Buck Rogers?"

The priest turned his laptop around for Bell to see.

"That's your house. You can even see your Crown Victoria sitting in the alley. This image was shot by a satellite, let's see ... last June."

"You can focus on *anything*?"

"Only places, not sun-bathers," Father Bert said. "So after Ollie left, I looked for the mine on this website. Here's what I found."

Father Bert moved his mouse across his oak desktop and clicked. Bell watched as the mysterious satellite thingie spiraled down to a different spot. It was the abandoned mine on Mount Misery from above, without all the snow. Just a hole in the ground.

"That's George Tomer's mine last July," Father Bert said. "That's what you and Ollie found yesterday. Now look at this."

Father Bert zoomed out and moved the image with his mouse until he found a cluster of nearby buildings. As he zoomed back in, Bell recognized it.

"Schattenland," he said.

"Right. Also taken by a satellite last July. There are a lot of trees, but you can see the grounds pretty distinctly." The priest pointed out various features with his cursor's little arrow. "Here's the old road ... the main asylum building ... the caretaker's shed ... the cemetery."

"Jesus Chr ... I mean criminy. This is amazing."

Bert honed in a little closer.

"You can even see the outlines of some older burials in the cemetery," he said. "See these white patches where they just piled rocks over shallow graves?"

"Yeah, those were the mounds we saw in the back, under the snow."

"Right. Count them."

Bell got close to the screen and touched each one with his index finger.

"Okay. What's your point?"

"Twenty-one, right?"

Bell didn't believe in coincidence, but he believed in flukes.

"These go back to, what, the 1930s?" Bell said. "They couldn't have buried anybody there after the place closed in 1969. And twenty-one isn't twenty-two. Nothing to see here. It's just a mathematical accident."

"That's what I thought, too," the priest said, jumping his mouse to a little button on the screen. "Now look at this. You can see the same spot in satellite images taken every few years, going back twenty-five years. Here's 1996, the earliest shot we have."

The photo on the screen went from vivid, detailed color to blurry black and white, but it was precisely the same spot.

"Now, count those graves."

Again, Bell touched each fuzzy white blotch with his big finger. He looked up at Father Bert, stunned.

"Six."

The priest clicked to a new image. "This is 2001."

Bell counted.

"Ten."

Another click, another shot, this one from 2005.

"Twelve."

Again. This one 2012.

"Eighteen."

"And last summer, twenty-one," Father Bert added. "It's not a coincidence, Woodrow."

Bell was startled but not speechless. Assuming each grave contained a human body—and that wasn't a sure thing—somebody had been burying people in the abandoned

Schattenland cemetery for decades, up to a few months ago. How perversely brilliant, he surmised, if a killer hid his victims in the last place anybody would look—a cemetery?

But he dismissed that phantasm. The reality was bad enough: He didn't know what was buried up there.

"It could be kids playing a prank, or these Colorado tree-huggers burying dead squirrels," Bell said. "There are other explanations."

"And they just happened to create as many fake graves as dolls?"

Bell brushed him off.

"No, your holy math is wrong. There were twenty-two dolls, not twenty-one. Dumb luck."

Father Bert shook his head.

"Think about it: He didn't have twenty-two people to bury. Only twenty-one."

"The strain of pushing up against those saints is getting to you, padre," Bell scoffed. "But humor me with your calculations."

Father Bert patted Bell's arm with a weathered hand.

"He lost one and you know exactly where she is," he said, in all earnestness. "Cherish Nelson."

CHAPTER 9

WOODROW BELL NEVER left his phone where he thought he left it. Or maybe he always left it where he didn't think he left it. But it was lost. Again.

And again he left no couch cushion unturned, no coat pocket unfrisked, and no refrigerator door unopened. It wasn't on the mantel either. As he stormed toward the basement, cussing the phone for losing itself, the doorbell rang.

It was Roxy Snipes.

"Hey, Rox," Bell said as he opened the door. "Look, I'm sorry but I'm right in the middle of something ..."

"Looking for your phone?"

Bell stared back blankly.

"How the hell ...?" he replied. "You know where it is?"

"Nope," Roxy said. "My granddaughter called me a few minutes ago and said she'd been calling you all morning, but you didn't answer and she couldn't leave a message. You need to get voicemail, Woodrow."

"I promise to sign up at the Post Office if I ever find the damn thing," Bell said. "But for now, can I use yours?"

Without hesitating, Roxy Snipes held out his smartphone.

"Thanks, Rox. Hey, would you mind dialing up your granddaughter for me? Since you already know the number and all."

He punched a couple buttons and handed the phone to Bell. After a couple buzzy rings, Dr. Jessie Hudson answered, sounding urgent.

"Hi, Pops. Any luck finding Woodrow?"

"This is Woodrow. Sorry I missed your calls. My phone and I are going through a trial separation."

The professor relaxed.

"I hope it works out for both of you," she said. "I was calling to say we have something for you on that sample you brought me."

"Something is better than nothing," Bell said.

"The real work was done by one of my grad students and he should explain it to you. I'm going to transfer you to him. His name is Gordon Ross. He's going to be a superlative geneticist, probably in forensics, but he's a little weird. You'll see what I mean. Hang on."

A couple more buzzy rings and a young man picked up.

"Ross," is all he said.

"Gordon, is it?" Bell responded. "This is Woodrow Bell. Dr. Hudson said you ran the tests on a DNA sample I gave her ..."

"You're the toilet paper guy," the young scientist said. "Yeah, I'm the one who analyzed your TP sample and compared it to the DPD's partial profile from the hair in the locket. Dr. Hudson said you caught a murder case?"

"Maybe."

"Copy that," Ross said. "That's a cop thing, right? 'Copy that.' Like on TV?"

"10-4." Bell needled the kid. He wasn't even sure real cops talked like that anymore, but the kid loved it.

"Cool. Okay, detective, we can do this the easy way or the hard way. I can go all centimorgans, alleles, and homozygous on your ass, or I can speak English. You just have to ask yourself if you feel lucky. Well, do ya, punk?"

"Funny."

"I always wanted to say that to a cop," the kid snickered. "That's from an old movie called 'Dirty Harry.'"

"No kidding?" Bell cracked. "I'll ask for it at Blockbuster."

"What's Blockbuster?"

Dr. Hudson was right. This kid was as weird as Bell was impatient.

"About the DNA ..."

"Oh yeah. Scientific-speak or something a cop would understand?"

"Go ahead, make my day."

"Good one!" Ross was giddy. "Okay, your sample was a mélange of ..."

This wasn't starting well.

"A *muh*-what?"

"You didn't make the ... wait for it ... French connection?"

"Gordon ... "

"It's a mish-mash, a hodge-podge, a tossed salad of DNA," Ross said, surprisingly without a hint of Hollywood cop-talk. "In fact, there are six distinctive donors in this delightfully mixed sample."

"It was a freakin' outhouse."

"Copy that, detective" the kid said. "And if your prime suspect is a marmot, a squirrel, a coyote, or a pika, you've got your perp. Slap the bracelets on him and take him downtown! He's gonna be new meat in the joint!"

"Animals?"

"Mammals breaking bad. Probably licking or sniffing around the seat. Maybe just sleeping in there during the winter. Either way, they left their DNA right where you found it."

"You said you had six samples," Bell pointed out.

Ross rustled some pages.

"Two were human," he said. "A female and a male. Mother and son. The markers fit together like a good cop and a bad cop."

Bell couldn't contain his astonishment.

"A son? You're sure?"

Ross sounded confident.

"Surprisingly, your privy samples were pretty good, especially when you consider how you got them," he said. "For sure, it's a mother and son. You want me to get into centimorgans and stuff?"

"How long would this DNA have been viable? Weeks, months, years?"

Ross paused only a brief moment.

"In an open outhouse, exposed to the air, heat, micro-organisms, and elements, not more than six or eight weeks, max."

In that moment, Bell knew Rosemary Midwinter had lied. Her son Erskine, an increasingly likely serial killer, had been in Purgatory, in her foul outhouse, and probably in her house in the past month or so. And she knew it.

"One more thing," Ross chimed in. "The DPD's partial sample from the locket wasn't as good, and we didn't have too many markers available to us. Getting more granularity might take weeks of sequencing, so I just skimmed those few markers. They matched up closely with the son's toilet-seat sample."

Bell had no more time for French or Dirty Harry or Joe Friday. He desperately wanted a yes-or-no answer, quick.

"Are they absolutely positively from the same guy?"

The kid couldn't oblige.

"Our magical mathematics don't add up to a sure thing and you'd have a tough time in court—you know, 'Objection! You're all out of order! You can't handle the truth!'"

"Gordon ..."

"Sorry, I get sorta excited," he said. "Yeah, your outhouse guy is probably your locket guy."

Ross CLICKED OFF and Bell handed the cellphone back to Roxy.

"I don't know how to hang up or turn it off or whatever the hell you do," he said.

Roxy rolled his eyes and pushed one button.

"Okay," Bell said, "now turn it back on. I need you to call somebody else. Detective Jasmine Jackson, Denver Homicide."

Roxy waited. And waited.

"Are you gonna give me her number?"

Bell scowled.

"Goddammit. How can those things know who's calling you, but they don't know who you're calling? Can't you just tell the operator inside who you want?"

"That's not how it works."

Bell mumbled something, probably profane, as he grubbed around in his wallet for Jazz's card. He handed it to Roxy, who dialed with his arthritic index finger and handed the phone back to Bell.

"Detective Jackson," she said. "Who's this?"

"It's me again. Woodrow. Big Man."

"You come up as Wyatt E. Snipes."

Bell smirked in Roxy's general direction.

"Wyatt, huh?" he said. "He goes by the alias Roxy. Check him out."

Wyatt Eure Snipes, who never knew what his mother was thinking, flushed.

"What's up now, Big Man?" Jazz asked. "You need me to run the plates on a car double-parked at your nursing home? Did somebody steal a hearing aid?"

"Change of plans," Bell said. "I need you to call your guy at CBI right away."

"What's the rush?"

"This cold-case thing blew up overnight, literally," Bell said. "Maybe twenty-two girls. Maybe more. Maybe most of them buried up at the old asylum. Maybe we got a real psycho serial killer. And maybe Erskine Midwinter is our guy."

"That's a lot of maybe, Big Man," Jazz said. Her tone was somber and rare.

"I know," he said, "but this isn't a guess wrapped in a hunch. I found strong evidence in an old mine where Midwinter can be placed. There's a creepy connection to the Cherish Nelson murder. New graves have been dug at the asylum cemetery during the past twenty years when nobody has lived or died there for fifty years. Midwinter's mother said he disappeared decades ago but he left fresh DNA at her place in Purgatory."

"And now you need backup," Jazz said. "Manpower, forensics, databases. The whole enchilada."

"I can't go exhuming graves for shits and giggles," he said. "Somebody's gotta take a look in that cave and cemetery, asap. We need diggers, CSI, DNA, autopsy, cold-case guys, profilers ... every damn thing. And somebody needs to find Midwinter. I'm telling you, this might be bigger than Bundy."

Ted Bundy was long dead, but he still cast his warped shadow over Colorado cops. Four Colorado women were among at least thirty victims he admitted. Twice, they jailed him, twice he escaped, and twice they missed their chance to abort a serial killer's frenzy. It was an embarrassing fiasco that nobody had forgotten. For forty years, every cop in the state craved a second chance to set things right. Just mentioning "Bundy" was a dare. A double-dog dare.

"How can I help?" Jazz asked.

No sarcasm, no phony rivalry, no squad-room burlesque.

"This is Code Three, Jazz," Bell said. "Tell your contact at CBI to call me an hour ago. I've got everything they need to know. This son of a bitch might still be active."

"What can I do from here?"

"Thanks, Jazz, but I don't want to jam you up," he said. "This isn't a little cop favor. I know the regs."

"Fuck the regs," Jazz said. "You're my partner, Big Man."

It touched Bell, who wasn't easily touched.

"And you're too old for this shit," she added. Ah, the old Jazz was back. It wasn't in her nature—any more than Bell's—to expose too much of her soft stuff.

"Find Midwinter," he said. "Everything leads back to him. We need to talk to him. If he's not our guy, he's the unluckiest bastard since Richard Jewell."

Jazz reminded Bell of one complication: Midwinter fell off the radar almost twenty years ago. He simply wasn't in the system.

"He must have left some kind of footprint," Bell said. "When I was up in Purgatory, there was a crappy old pickup on Rosemary Midwinter's road where it shouldn't be. It was dark and I couldn't get a plate without being obvious."

"An old pickup in a small Colorado town," Jazz said. "Gee, that narrows it down."

"But Purgatory has eyes. If you can get me Midwinter's last prison mugshot, I can show it around up there. Maybe the sheriff knows him. If he's hiding up there someplace, somebody knows. In the meantime, you check whether the feds have some super-secret ghost-finder weapon we can use."

"Copy that," Jazz acknowledged. "I can send the mug now. What's your email address?"

Silence.

"You there? Did I lose you?"

"I'm here," Bell said. "I don't have email. I don't have an answering machine. I don't have a computer. And at the moment, I don't have a phone."

Jazz sighed.

"Okay, here's what I'm going to do. I'm going to text the mugshot to this number and to your lost phone, too, just to be safe. Real cops show photos on their phones, but maybe you should find somebody to print it out on paper for you. The way you did it when you were a rookie back in the 1930s."

"Hey, it worked for my partner Eliot Ness."

Roxy's phone dinged.

"You've got it," Jazz said. "Check your texts."

"How the hell ...?"

"Oh, fergawdsakes, find a kindergartner to explain it," an exasperated Jazz said. "I gotta call the CBI and hunt for your ghost. Find your damn phone and keep it close."

Jazz hung up and Bell immediately deputized Roxy.

"We gotta find my phone," he said. "Fast."

Roxy glanced around. "Where's the last place you saw it?"

"That's the dumbest question ever," Bell said. "It was in my hand."

"Where was your hand?"

Bell scowled at Roxy.

"Right here at the end of my arm, where it often is," he replied, but he played along. "It was last night, right here, and I was talking to ..."

Bell grabbed his coat and hustled Roxy out the door.

"I need a ride," he said. "It's at Charlie's house in my own damn car."

AFTER A SPEEDY stop at Roxy's house to print Erskine Midwinter's prison mugshot from 2003, Bell lit out to Purgatory, only fifty miles but a couple hours away on the black-ice highway over the Divide.

Midwinter stared at him from the passenger seat. Bell had seen more than his share of such images. Every one of them depicted somebody who'd fallen through a crack somewhere.

To Bell, all of them looked like animals captured in their natural habitat. The evil-looking ones could be genuinely unfinished souls, but an innocent face might be a hallucination. Some were manifestly alluring, but most were conspicuously ugly.

Their "look" told him everything he needed to know. He didn't need to know their crimes, and he couldn't explain his presumptions. He understood *what* they were at a glance. It was in their eyes.

Erskine Midwinter's eyes—the left one anyway—was a deep, dark portal to an abyss, with no distinction between the black iris and the black pupil. The other was as dead as his would-be victims had reported: Necrotic, askew, soupy.

In 2003, he would have been forty-nine, but he looked much older. His long, stringy hair hung like a shredded drape around his bald scalp. His gray, grubby whiskers were a week old and without purpose. Primal furrows subdivided his cheekbones and forehead. His loathsome life story was written there.

But it was his eyes, dissimilar but both hideous, that chilled Bell. One of them was fury, the other death. They could have been the last things Cherish Nelson saw. That might have pleased him.

Erskine Midwinter watched Bell the whole way to Purgatory, unblinking.

They arrived in late afternoon. A kid at the two-pump gas station stared at the Crown Vic going past. An older woman outside the junk shop eyeballed Bell, more than a glance, less than a glare. A couple of old men at Burgatory's window table—the same guys as before—monitored his parking job. Small towns were funny that way. For an outsider, the town limit was really a fine line between curious and suspicious.

Burgatory's tinkling bell announced him. The place was empty, except for the two guys who probably never left. Maybe Don't Even Ask, aka Rosemary Midwinter, was in back, where Bell could hear the usual short-order rattling of griddles and deep-fryer baskets.

"Afternoon, guys," he said as he approached the window table. "My name's Woodrow Bell, and I'm looking for this guy. Have you seen him around town?"

He showed Erskine Midwinter's photo to them. Both shook their heads and said nothing. He wrote his phone number on the back and left it on the table.

"Call me if you think of something," Bell said. "Hey, is the waitress Rosemary around?"

Not a word. They merely shrugged. In a small town, when a stranger asks strange questions, he gets strange answers.

Just then, Bell heard the kitchen's swinging door squeal behind him.

"Can I help you, boss?" said a no-neck, banty-rooster of a guy wearing a crapped-up apron, full-sleeve tattoos, shaved head, and a face blighted with meth sores. His head was slightly lop-sided, maybe from a bad birth or a worse beating, but it probably didn't embarrass him as much as his shortness. He couldn't have stood more than five-foot-four, but he talked bigger and sported the over-ripped arms of a prison-yard weightlifter. Bell guessed he was the cook.

"I need you to quit bothering my customers, man," he snapped. "Move your ass down the street."

Bell knew this guy. Not this particular guy but guys like him. They went to great lengths to appear taller and tougher than they really were, especially around big men. Prison—and this fifty-something fry-cook certainly did time, judging by the Aryan Brotherhood's iron cross tattooed on the back of one hand and the customary solitary-confinement scorpion on the other—made them more belligerent. And big men, especially cops, got nowhere playing badge-heavy Goliaths.

"Just talkin' here, dawg." Bell purposely used prison slang for "friend" and held his arms out to his sides to show he wasn't armed. "Just looking for somebody. You know this guy?"

Bell held up another photocopy of Midwinter's mugshot, but the cook never took his venomous eyes off Bell.

"Take a hike, boss," he said. Standing squarely in front of the double doors into the kitchen. "We don't call the cops here."

That meant the cook was carrying, or had a gun in arm's reach. Yeah, a felony in Colorado, but who gave a damn in Purgatory?

It also meant Rosemary Midwinter was hiding in back somewhere. Bell couldn't tell if this malignant little cook was just protecting his waitress or jonesing for a free shot at a cop. Either way, if Bell wanted to talk to her, he'd have to plow through the guy who stood between them ... and it wasn't worth a bullet wound to hear more of her lies.

"I guess pancakes are out of the question?" he cracked, to lower the temperature.

"Don't give me another reason to kick your ass, old man," the cook snarled. He pointed his fully inked arm to the door. "Out, motherfucker."

Bell obliged. On the sidewalk outside, a sharp wind sliced down Main from the east, so he walked west toward the gas station.

The greasy mechanic behind the counter had never seen Midwinter. Nor had the ladies in the junk shop that was also a hair salon, the pathetic roughnecks in the coin-op laundry, the daytimers in Jake's Saloon—including Jake himself— or anybody else. If Erskine Midwinter spent any time in Purgatory, he was invisible, feared, or beloved.

Bell rolled up Rosemary Midwinter's dirt road, just in case. He saw no cars or trucks anywhere nearby, but he rapped several times on her front door anyway. No movement inside, no sounds, no answer.

The winter sun was setting, Bell was getting nowhere, and he still had an hour's drive ahead, so Bell pulled out of Purgatory. But on his way home to Midnight, Bell detoured to the county seat, where the Malvado County sheriff didn't recognize the face or the name but swore the Bar F's chicken-fried steak was the second best in Colorado.

Sliding back into the Crown Vic in the sheriff's parking lot, he glanced at his phone in the cup-holder, where he'd forgotten he left it. He'd missed a call, it told him. The caller left no message because Bell had no mailbox. After a few anxious pokes that started to sound more like right jabs, he accidentally found a list of his recent incoming calls. No more than ten minutes before, somebody from Denver had phoned. No name.

Rather than risk a hundred dead zones on the way home, Bell sat there behind the Malvado County SO with his heater on high and slowly dialed the number. A woman answered.

"Mr. Bell, thank you for calling back," she said. "I'm Special Agent Dani Silva with CBI and I'm the one who called."

Bell had stopped saying it out loud but *how the hell ...?*

"Glad to meet you, Agent Silva," he said instead. "I'm assuming Detective Jackson at DPD called you about this case I've been investigating?"

"You mean Jazz?" SA Silva asked. "Yeah, we go way back. We went through the Academy together. I worked in the Springs before CBI pulled me up. Lots of women in the force now, but me and Jazz are the old ladies and we've seen a lot, good and bad. So when she tells me you're a stand-up cop, I know you're the real thing."

Bell never knew how to accept praise. It was a character flaw. His mother drilled it into him: *A big man knows when to be little.* It became a chronic condition.

"Thanks," he said, "but she lies all the time."

Silva laughed.

"She said you'd say that. She's got you pegged. She also told me some things about your case. It sounds like it might be a big one. Tell me how I can help."

Bell spelled it all out, connecting all the grim dots from Cherish Nelson to the twenty-two dolls, the dark moon, the mine, and Schattenland's growing number of possible graves. His best suspect, Erskine Midwinter, was a ghost but his DNA turned up at both the 1969 crime scene and his mother's property within the last two months. When he'd exhausted every little thing he knew, he admitted the case had outgrown him.

"It's bigger than both of us, Detective Bell," Silva said. Nobody had called him "detective" in almost ten years, nor should they. But he let it slide.

"That's an understatement," he said. "If it's as big as I think, it'll need CBI's resources. If it's just an old man's pipe dream, you'll find out faster than I can."

Silva responded quickly.

"If it's a pipe dream, then we've all been smoking," she said. "Jazz told me a lot of those details. I already talked to the Director and he's aboard, big time. He made me the lead agent and he put all of CBI's resources at our disposal. Anything we need. And I've already got the FBI looking for our boy Erskine Midwinter."

Bell hated to let go but this case required the cavalry. CBI and the feds could do more in a day than he and the old codgers on Deaf Row could do in a month, even on caffeine.

"Jazz must have given you the hard sell," he told Silva. "She's a better cop than I ever told her, but maybe she's a better saleswoman, too."

"She wouldn't admit it but she trusted you with her life and she still would today," the state agent said. "And that speaks volumes about you."

"Yeah, well, that's nice, I guess. But you've got this case now. And I hope you'll keep me in the loop. I'd like to hear how this all turns out."

Not so fast, Silva told him.

"The Director has also started the paperwork to deputize you as a temporary CBI agent," she said. "When he was a rookie at DPD, everybody talked about Detective

'Mountain' Bell. You're a damn legend. He says if you get a hunch, we should listen."

"Legends are dead guys," Bell said, "and if I'm dead then I've definitely been doing this too long."

"But you gotta promise not to shoot anybody," she said, and Bell wasn't sure if she was serious. "I'm not kidding, I need your help. You literally know where the bodies are buried."

"I'm not sure I ..."

"Well, get sure. This is lights and sirens, Big Man," she said. "Big Man is what Jazz calls you, right? From now on, if it's okay with you, I'll just call you Agent Bell."

"Jazz'd shoot me if I said no, so okay," he said. "What's next?"

SA Silva already had a robust plan.

"Tomorrow, you're guiding a team of agents up to the mine and the cemetery," she instructed. "You'll split up. One group will collect the dolls and do whatever forensics they can in the mine. The other will take the cadaver dogs to the old cemetery to sniff those piles of rock. If the dogs alert, we'll go back and dismantle them stone by stone, probably by the end of the week. Our forensic pathologist is standing by.

"We're also pulling all your DNA samples back to the state crime lab for a closer look. We're assuming they're evidence in a murder case, even though we already have a chain-of-custody problem.

"I have assigned one agent to collect all the documentary evidence you and your friends have found so our analysts can process all of it, another to gather every piece of paper generated on your guy, and yet another who'll re-interview the families of potential victims as we identify them.

"And finally, we're gonna crawl up Erskine Midwinter's ass. It won't matter if he's hiding on the moon. CBI and the feebs have super-sniffing, nuclear-Google computers that'll find him."

Silva's full-scale offensive astonished Bell, whose interactions with the state Bureau of Investigations had always been disappointing. This was clearly a new regime, but something puzzled him.

"All this happens in a matter of three hours? I don't get it. Why does it feel like we're preparing for the invasion of Normandy?"

SA Daniella "Dani" Silva had only one word.

"Bundy."

Before he could even smile, Bell understood. This was The Chance.

"Anything else we need to know, Agent Bell?" Silva asked him before signing off.

He didn't hesitate.

"Yeah, we're gonna need a bigger truck."

EARLY THE NEXT morning, even before the sun rose over the mountain, Bell's coffee had long gone cold, and the Crown Vic's fickle heater was in one of its moods. So he huddled down in his big leather coat exactly where SA Silva told him to wait: the wide spot where the old asylum road forked from the two-lane pavement into the trees.

At first light, Bell saw headlights swing around the bend ...then an army of them. A half dozen imposing four-wheel-drive vehicles were followed by three trailered snowcats and snowmobiles. A CBI crime-scene van brought up the rear. *So the cavalry has a big budget*, Bell mused.

The lead vehicle—an unmarked black SUV—rumbled up beside the Crown Vic.

"Big enough?" the driver hollered. "Get in. It's warmer in here."

The guy behind the wheel, an ex-DEA agent named Pete Galligan, was in charge of this operation. Four other CBI agents made room for Bell, and Galligan briefed them all as he broke trail through the snow for his forensic caravan along Ollie Fuhrman's faint, two-day-old tracks.

"Two snowcats will take the search-and-rescue guys up to secure the area and inspect the mine before any agents or CSIs go in," Galligan said. "The other snowcat will shuttle the rest of us to the asylum area. Two agents have been assigned to look for evidence in the structures. Everybody else will clear snow around the rock graves so the K-9 team can do its work. If the dogs alert, we're not gonna wait: We start moving the stones as cautiously as possible to preserve evidence. We have four forensic anthropologists and a medical examiner standing by."

It was Bell's nature to anticipate complications.

"There's a lot of snow up there, and even more cold," he told Galligan. "What if you have to exhume twenty-one graves in these conditions?"

"Then we come back tomorrow," a smiling Galligan gibed, but he wasn't kidding. Normally, Bell didn't think much of the DEA's prima donnas, but this kid was his kind of unpretentious.

The convoy halted an uphill half-mile from the asylum, no closer than Ollie had gotten. The temperature was minus-ten, maybe colder up the mountain, but the staging area swarmed into action. State Highway Department drivers off-loaded the tracked snowcats. The mountain patrol guys hitched rescue toboggans to the snow machines, overloaded with equipment. The search-and-rescue team, in their orange jackets, erected temporary warming huts and put skis and ropes in order. Support staff set up tents for hot food and drinks. CBI agents strapped up in their winter gear, secured evidence lockers, fired up generators, and checked their communications. Even the cadaver dogs wore special vests. All of a sudden, Bell felt under-employed and under-dressed in his big leather coat and turn-of-the-century snow boots.

SA Galligan gathered the team leaders together for his last instructions. *Be careful, communicate often, no cowboys. Trust your training. We might have a serial killer here. We can't afford mistakes.*

"And don't freeze up," he added as the teams dispersed to their separate assignments.

An agent tossed a heavy scarf to Bell and ferried him on a snowmobile through deep powder to the cemetery. There, several agents were already shoveling, inches at a time, within a cordoned patch where their high-resolution satellite images showed stone piles.

It didn't take long.

"Over here," one of the agents called out.

"Got one here," another shouted.

"Another one."

Soon, diggers had exposed many more heaps of loose rocks, none too big for a man to carry. Somebody outside the cordon returned to a supply sled to fetch a batch of ordinary household brooms, a gentler way to whisk away snow without disturbing what lay beneath.

From his spot outside the cordon, Bell counted the uncovered piles.

Twenty.

He counted again.

"One's missing," he exclaimed. Galligan counted the piles. He plucked the pages of satellite images from his pocket and compared them to the long line of possible graves. He determined that one last, unfound pile lay just beyond the cleared area. He directed one of his agents to the spot, where he started shoveling. In less than a minute, his shovel hit solid rock. He carefully dug around, then brushed away some loose snow to reveal the twenty-first grave.

The discovery relieved Bell. After being lost for so long, he thought, it would have been a shame for this last girl to be missing until the next thaw. He knew he should keep an open mind. He shouldn't presume these were clandestine graves, but ...

"Got one more here."

It took a moment for Bell to process what he just heard. Stunned, he peered down the row to its opposite end, where a CBI agent swept away snow from *another* cluster of rocks.

Twenty-two.

Sometime in the past six months—sometime since a satellite snapped its last picture of this exact spot— somebody had added another secret grave. Bell's gut twisted. Were there others?

For Bell, the hunt for Erskine Midwinter became surreal theater.

THE CBI DIGGERS cleared the snow another ten feet beyond the cordoned area, to be sure there weren't more stone heaps nobody could see from space. They found nothing.

SA Galligan radioed for the two cadaver dogs Luke and Solo, a pair of German Shepherds being kept warm at the staging area. In a few minutes, snowmobiles delivered them and their handlers to the cemetery.

"Body dogs" truly astounded Bell. He'd seen them at work back in his day. They could find a decaying corpse or skeleton—even the slightest residue of remains that have been moved—up to fifteen feet down in the dirt and easily fifty years in the past. Some could alert on a single drop of old blood or a shard of bone. If those girls, or even pieces of them, were under those rocks, the dogs would find them.

Bell watched the handlers prepare the dogs for their awful work. Unlike homicide detectives who might be hollowed out by death, it was merely a game for cadaver dogs. They get praise and treats for smelling death and sitting down. Simple as that.

Here, the snow and cold wouldn't matter to them. It didn't matter if a corpse was frozen. But in a cemetery, the dogs wouldn't know the difference between proper burials and victims of foul play. So today, the dogs would be confined to the cordoned space, which appeared to be beyond the margins of Schattenland's main graveyard where many of the poor dead were no less victims than these.

Luke and Solo's handlers led them around the outermost edges. They didn't alert, but they grew more agitated the closer they came to the stone piles.

Then Solo paused over one pile and sniffed exuberantly up and down its length.

Then he sat.

At the same time, Luke lingered over a different heap.

Then he sat.

Again and again, sniff and sit, a routine for which they got warm praise and goodies, then went eagerly back to their game.

Twenty-two times.

Galligan hadn't waited. After Solo's first alert, he called the CBI's chief death investigator to alert his forensic anthropologists and all the proper authorities. He reported multiple victims in unknown condition, shallow graves, rugged terrain, inclement conditions, and possibly several days' on-site. With six hours of daylight remaining and hazardous road conditions, two CBI vehicles would meet them in Lakewood for a headlong race up the mountain, but he needed them on-site pronto.

"And one more thing," he said solemnly. "Bring lots of body bags."

THE BODY GUYS arrived with two hours of daylight left and plunged straight into their sordid task.

Before dark, they had already mapped the area with the help of Galligan's satellite images. While one measured the dimensions of each grave, another probed each rock pile with a special device to draw any decomposition scents to the surface. Then Bell watched as they carefully swept around each grave with a metal detector, looking for any metallic trace evidence—bullets, jewelry, weapons, etc.— that might or might not be there.

Before they had moved a single stone, the sun had gone down. It was too dark to do the meticulous, delicate work of pulling decayed corpses, piece by painstaking piece, out of the frozen earth. Tomorrow.

This science crap was all too finicky and slow for Bell. He got it. He understood how defense lawyers could slice and dice sloppy evidence. He also knew how the smallest fragments, the easiest ones to miss, could speak the loudest. But whoever lay under these rocks—probably twenty-two young women—had no voice until they were back in this world.

SA Galligan left two agents at the staging area for the night, guarding what was now a crime scene and the team's equipment. Bell volunteered to stay there, too, as the unofficial guard of those unknown dead.

The mountain crew and their snowcats had found the mine, where they built protective ramparts against snowslides that might trap agents inside. Plaster casts were made from the few shoeprints that could be found in dirt patches. An agent photographed everything. Then CSIs gathered the dolls and stored each in a numbered cardboard box. They also collected soil and rock samples in the main "room" and the various passages that branched away from it.

Finally, in the cold dark, a crime-scene tech sprayed luminol for invisible traces of blood and other bodily fluids. The cave lit up. The walls and floors had been so thoroughly splattered that the blue glow illuminated the pitch blackness. One agent photographed the glowing stains, another swabbed them to learn exactly what caused them. Until they were tested, they might be remnants of a predator's kills, urine, even feces, although the amount, the dispersal, and the patterns suggested something much more hideous.

So all the mine's frightful evidence was catalogued and hauled down the mountain to the CBI crime lab in Denver. Galligan and a fresh team planned to be back at dawn to start excavating the stone piles that the crew had begun to call "graves." The body dogs proved dead humans were there, and most were buried long after the asylum closed. They were graves, Bell now knew. It was a matter of learning who was down there.

"It's weird," Galligan told Bell before he left Mount Misery. "Part of me hates to think about what we might find under those rocks, and part of me hopes it'll be those poor girls."

Bell knew what Galligan meant. For both, it was two different things: What they might *see* tomorrow was different than what they might *learn*. And what they see might fan the flame already flickering inside them.

For dinner, Bell and the two CBI agents ate MREs from the food locker and drank whiskey in their hot chocolate. As the temperatures dropped, they curled up in one of the bureau's spacious SUVs, which idled all night to run the heater. The day had been long, and the agents fell asleep fast.

Bell stayed awake for a long time. The seat wasn't that comfy, and the green glow of the dash didn't help. Plus, different parts of him had been cold all day; when one got warm, another iced up.

But mostly Bell thought about those six girls whose faces he knew. He both feared and hoped that he'd somehow recognize them tomorrow. He felt simultaneous mourning and relief for the nameless, faceless others who might be up there in that profane place. He didn't know how this case was so different from a thousand before it, or why they were always the same. Bell never believed in a God that would allow this to happen to innocent girls, but now he hoped they didn't just dissolve into the sky.

The half-cynical, half-hopeful, completely conflicted detective patted a dozen pockets for his phone. They were empty.

But if he knew where it was ...

If it wasn't dead or frozen solid ...

If the mountain gods allowed a connection ...

If he unwittingly pushed the right buttons ...

And if his cop bunkmates couldn't hear him talk about what he felt right now ... then he might call Father Bert or Charlie or both.

They'd know what he should feel.

A NEW, BIGGER convoy of CBI vehicles rolled into camp before sunrise.

It brought a small army of forensic anthropologists from the university and their best grad students, state crime lab death investigators, and all their excavation gear. In an ordinary exhumation of a clandestine grave, there might only be one of each with a couple shovels, but this was no ordinary case. CBI clearly wasn't sparing any expense or taking any chances that another prolific serial killer— maybe even more lethal than Bundy—might slip through Colorado's fingers.

Unpredictable weather, investigators' impatience, and the possibility of an active serial killer made this excavation more urgent than most.

Bell helped carry their equipment to the asylum's cemetery, where the professors had roped off three distinct work areas. The outermost band was for a contingent of support staff, mostly younger students assigned to every fetch-and-carry task. The next contained agents and more experienced students under the supervision of an archaeologist to sift debris and catalogue anything that might be relevant.

And the innermost ground immediately surrounding the graves was the "hot zone." There, the forensic professionals and their teams did the dirtiest work of cautiously unearthing whatever remained under those rocks.

Five forensic anthropologists worked at the same time on five different burial sites. The layer of snow insulated the soil below, so the digging was easier than if it had been frozen solid.

SA Galligan assigned Bell to the second zone, where he'd be among several people sifting for smaller artifacts. For him, it was largely a ceremonial post that acknowledged his role in bringing this case to light. He'd be as close as any of them to the most meaningful digging. He'd see what the scientists uncovered almost as soon as they uncovered it.

It didn't take long.

Within a half hour, all of the excavators hit some remains a few inches down, mostly rib, arm and leg bones that suggested whole skeletons lay under and around them. It appeared to Bell that they'd all been buried in shallow depressions, shrouded with a thin layer of shoveled dirt, then covered with granite rocks collected from the forest and nearby talus slopes.

The whole scene grew more quiet, more somber, more frigid, Bell noticed. The agents were no longer joshing each other. Even the grad students, most in their overconfident twenties, turned serious.

While the grad students carefully exposed those remains, the anthropologists moved to the next spot until they found indications of a burial, then they moved again. Before noon, all twenty-two graves lay open, with both old skeletons and newer remains all or partially visible. To the death investigators and bone collectors, it was already clear the burials clearly spanned many years. They were arranged from oldest to newest. The killer or killers had simply hidden them side-by-side, one after the other, in a straight chronological line.

Except one.

That one was the newest grave but it lay next to the apparent oldest. In one, the corpse was mummified, with some dried skin, long bits of hair, cartilage, and only wearing fashionably ripped jeans around her lower legs. In the other, they found collapsed and disarticulated old bones, clothing long rotted away. The forensic anthropologists judged the newer remains to be only five to seven months old, compared to the adjacent ones, which were decades old.

All of the corpses, newer and older, shared something else besides being buried together in this ungodly place.

Each skull displayed obvious damage—"catastrophic trauma," the forensic guys called it—on both sides. Bell knew precisely what caused it and they knew, too: The jagged holes were caused by somebody plunging a spike clean through the girls' living brains. In many cases, spikes still protruded from their skulls.

Toward the end of the day, Bell stood nearby as Dr. Phil Saylor, CBI's chief death investigator, summarized his first-blush findings. The former deputy medical examiner in Denver told SA Galligan the corpses all appeared to be young women, probably in their late teens, judging by development of teeth, skulls, and bones. All were buried face up, with their hands crossed over their mutilated chests. All were consistently laid between forty-five and forty-eight inches apart. No coffins, probably no shrouds. The stones had protected them from predator and weather damage.

Some appeared to have been buried in clothing, others not, Saylor told them. None were dismembered, and he didn't see any obvious broken bones, except that every rib cage had been opened violently. His team saw some evidence of ligatures, but these victims were probably not murdered here, he said.

"However, given the inaccessibility of this particular site, I'm guessing they weren't carried here," he added. "They might have been alive and forced to walk to a spot nearby where they were killed."

As each grave was exhumed, Saylor reported, agents and excavators were finding sundry bits: a pocketknife blade, earrings, beads, buttons, a piece of what appears to be a large, broken needle, fragments of broken glass, and other curious scraps that ultimately might help to identify the remains.

The bad news was that the killer's biological material would have disappeared long ago, according to Saylor. Determining rape from a mummified body was futile, he warned, and from a skeleton it was impossible.

The better news, he told Galligan and Bell, is that every corpse's teeth were mostly intact. Burial under dirt and rocks almost certainly preserved DNA material in bones, teeth, and remnant hair—all good sources of DNA. If the crime lab can find dental records or DNA profiles for comparison, these twenty-two girls could be identified.

"Cause of death?" Bell asked before Galligan could.

"We can't know for sure until we take a closer look back at the crime lab," Saylor said. "You told us about the spike and the nails through the dolls' heads. That means something. If these girls were alive when their skulls were perforated, it would have killed them instantly. Back at the lab, we'll look very closely at those wounds, and we'll bring in a forensic psychologist who'll interpret this."

"How long until you know?"

"We'll have a preliminary report very quickly," he said. "State law says we have to alert the county coroner here, and he's also the town drunk. This is gonna blow up after his first whiskey sour, so we have to move faster than his bartender."

. Bell's investigative curiosity wasn't satisfied.

"What do you make of the split-open chests?"

"Not sure if they're pre- or post-mortem. Sorry."

"One more thing, doc," Bell said. "Any evidence of their eyes being sewn shut?"

The CBI guy finally nodded about something.

"The soft tissue was gone in all but one, and whatever thread he used would have also decayed after a while," he said. "But, yeah, that newest one ..."

Like the homicide detective he was, Bell prepared to ask something else, but CBI's veteran chief investigator answered the question before it was asked.

"Is this is all related to your girl in Midnight?" Saylor asked. His assessment was empirical: "What I've seen here is consistent with the facts in your 1969 case."

Then he corrected himself.

"No, in fact, let me put it a little differently, Agent Bell," the death investigator said, adding his own emphasis, which came more from the gut and spoke to something more. "*Nothing* I've seen here is *inconsistent* with your 1969 case."

As TWILIGHT APPROACHED, agents and anthropologists catalogued all the remains, then laid each in a special white plastic envelope to be bundled and transported back to the crime lab. There, the bones would be articulated in their proper order and every centimeter examined under the brilliant glare of their morgue lights. The accompanying artifacts—including the dolls—would go under the lab's microscopes. Testing might take weeks, but some conclusions would be immediately evident.

The long caravan came down from Mount Misery after dark. Other investigators would come back for several days, but the most important task was done.

SA Pete Galligan delivered Bell to his frosty Crown Vic and kindly waited to see if it started. It barely did. As Bell scraped his windshield for the long trip back to Midnight, Galligan rolled down his window.

"You done good, noob," he said, poking fun at the "newbie" Agent Bell, his seventy-something rookie. "We wouldn't be here if not for you. We'll find your guy, I promise, and we'll know a lot more about these girls in the next twenty-four hours, so stick close to your phone."

If he only knew, Bell mused.

On the long, cold, dark drive home, the radio only fuzzed, so Bell was left to his thoughts and to the occasional patches of tricky black ice.

These deaths were obscene. Yeah, he knew dying was never glamorous. It's messy and uncomfortable. Some deaths were worse than others, and he'd sure seen a lot of those. Long ago, it became difficult for him to tell the difference between the sacred and the obscene, and he didn't expect a divine metamorphosis before he himself died. But he had no question about the obscenity of Cherish Nelson's ending, nor these other twenty-two girls' endings.

Bell knew this, too: He had dodged this case too quickly. Charlie knew it, Father Bert knew it, but he didn't until now. He thought too much and acted too slow, except when he was acting too fast without thinking.

He'd wasted his time, maybe most of his life, looking back. He'd been a good cop, among the best. But certain qualities of a good homicide detective—incurable suspicion, a long memory, an intractable sense of right and wrong, no tolerance for melodrama—also made him a feeble father, husband, and friend. Back then, Bell's heart had been less than honest with him. Then mortality sneaked up on him. All of a sudden, it was as if he'd sprung a leak and must lie down before he toppled.

Then this case. So maybe Father Bert was right. He needed this mystery as much as it needed him.

But that was his heart talking trash. His head needed to weigh in.

Bell reconstructed his circumstantial case. Right now, CBI had enough to arrest Erskine Midwinter on suspicion of murder ... he just didn't have Erskine Midwinter. He had bodies and similarities in methods and materials, but he didn't have a weapon, a motive, a witness, or the killer's opportunity. *What drove Midwinter, and how did his path intersect with his victims?*

The forensics might produce some unexpected direct link between Midwinter and the girls, maybe even undeniable proof he did it. For now, though, it all rested on a single, imperfect, fifty-year-old hair. That wasn't enough. Any rookie public defender could inspire reasonable doubt in one juror.

A lot of dots remained unconnected.

The cold sky was clear. Bell could see stars overhead, but no moon. Because he drove over a backroad through the mountains on a winter night, he passed few other cars. The dark helped him think.

Galligan was only partially right. Bell brought the CBI and everybody else to the Schattenland cemetery, but it was Charlie, Jazz, Fancy, Father Bert, and the fellas on Deaf Row who pushed Bell to the real cops. With coffee, faith, Solitaire, awful handwriting, gifted granddaughters, dirty houses, the damn hi-fi, cheap burner phones, bulldozers, physics, threats of bodily harm, and entire lives that nobody else cared about anymore—they'd delivered a road map that led straight to Mount Misery.

Bell didn't know if the feds would locate Midwinter, even if they had the world's most sophisticated and scary technology. If they didn't find any trace of him, they'd assume he vanished into the thinnest air of the Rockies, and then they'd move on to the next folder on their desk.

Wherever the killer was, though, girls were still dying, as recently as six or seven months ago. He couldn't be far. He wasn't invisible. He wasn't a vapor. Somebody knew him.

It was late when Bell got back to Midnight. He wanted to tell Charlie or Father Bert about the ugliness he saw on Mount Misery, so he rolled past their houses. All the lights were out, and it would only wreck their dreams.

Bell drove home. He parked the Crown Vic in the alley and climbed the back steps into his dark house. He scarfed a few saltines and couldn't find his phone, so he just went to bed. His dreams might be wrecked, too, but it didn't matter. He didn't put much stock in dreams anyway.

MORNING DIDN'T BREAK early. Bell overslept.

He was late, as usual, when he got to Tommyknockers. Deaf Row had adjourned, except Cotton Minahan. He drew his energy from the other guys. Bell recognized Minahan's goading and goosing was just his way of expressing kinship, the way guys did instead of hugging, sharing secrets and recipes, or weeping together at Hallmark movies. He also seemed to know everybody in the county, and inhaled local news and gossip in equal measure, often blending the two. He might be irascible with the Deaf Row guys but everybody else liked him well enough to chat because most of his stories started with "somebody told me."

It was odd to see him sitting there alone.

"Hey, Woodrow," he said when Bell came through the door.

"Hey, Minahan," he said, nodding to Fancy. She knew his nods, and this one meant he sorely needed coffee and his usual breakfast. "I didn't expect to see you here this late. Did the guys kick you out?"

The old fire chief leaned back in his chair, his cowboy belly face-front.

"Waitin' for you, Woodrow," he said.

"Why's that?"

"Ollie told me what you guys did last weekend. He's pretty shook up. Then Razor Ledbetter got a snootful and told somebody who told me about those girls up on Mount Misery."

"You believe every thirdhand fairy tale that comes from a drunken coroner?" Bell asked, not shocked that rumor traveled faster than news up here.

Minahan brushed it off.

"Hell, the news is mostly fake," he said. "Anyhow, when you didn't show up here, I figured you were up there yesterday with all those real cops."

Fancy delivered Bell's coffee, hot and black, at just the right moment. His teeth were grinding.

"I need some advice, Woodrow," Minahan continued, "I was wondering if you thought I should tell those state cops something I heard. I knew you wouldn't be interested, being retired and all."

There it was. Minahan showing his affection. Sorta.

"They're pretty busy right now. They want facts, not your silly rumors that are gonna waste their time."

"You're probably right," Minahan conceded and pulled on his coat. "Hey, look at the time. I got a thing to do this morning. Will I see you tomorrow with the guys?"

Something was wrong. Minahan never surrendered so easily.

"Goddammit, sit down," Bell groused. "You're a wise ass who's getting to be a wiser ass."

"I'm not getting wiser," Minahan said. "I'm just running out of dumb shit I haven't already done."

Bell pressed.

"What's so important that you waited so long for me to show up? What if I skipped coffee today? Would you still be sitting here on your butt tomorrow?"

Minahan smirked as impishly as a wrinkled old man can, then sat back down.

"My granny always told me, 'Don't go in if you don't know the way out.'"

"I don't even know what the hell that means, you senile old fart," Bell said, perturbed. "But what's on your mind, granny?"

"Somebody told me this story a while back," he said. "He had a friend up in Georgetown whose neighbor girl ran away last spring sometime. Just run off. She was kind of a wild girl for that little town. You know, twixting with a lot of her high school boyfriends, and smokin' pot, and wearing racy stuff like contact lenses and blue eyeshadow and more piercings than Coogan's tackle box. Then one night she has a fight with her parents and the next day she doesn't come home from school. Nobody was surprised because she was always talkin' about getting out of Georgetown and heading to the big city."

"Did her parents go to the sheriff?"

"My friend says mom and dad figured she probably just run off," Minahan said. "The deputies told them not to worry, it happens all the time, and she'd probably come back. Nobody took it real serious."

He had Bell's attention.

"Did she come back?"

"No."

"So you think it might be related to this Mount Misery thing?"

Minahan shrugged.

"I don't know. Girls run away from small towns all the time. They got crazy dreams. I don't even know why I brought it up. Just a weird feeling, I guess."

Bell turned detective.

"Do you have any idea when this happened?"

"Just last spring. That's all they said."

"A name?"

"Dammit, Woodrow, I can't even tell you who told me. Don't you have people for that?"

Bell grabbed his coat and abruptly headed for the door.

"Where you going, Woodrow?" asked Minahan, craning his wattled neck. "You haven't eaten your breakfast."

Bell was halfway out and didn't even look back.

"My granny always said, 'Don't go in if you don't know the way out.'"

"CLEAR CREEK SHERIFF'S Office. Deputy Pepper."

"Hi there, Deputy Pepper. My name is Agent Woodrow Bell of the Colorado Bureau of Investigation."

Even over the phone, he could hear the kid's asshole snap shut. Even real cops considered CBI agents to be real-er cops, and technically Bell wasn't lying about being an CBI agent.

"Yes, sir," Deputy Pepper chattered. He must still be a rookie who was eager to please, Bell figured, and he must have known this wasn't going to be another barking-dog complaint. "The sheriff isn't here, sir ... or agent. Nobody's here. Well, I'm here, but nobody else. How may I help you? I mean, if you need help, sir. Do you need help, because I don't want you to think ... ?"

"Thank you, deputy," Bell said in a low, very serious voice. "I like your style. Perceptive and in control. Good at interrogation. You sound like a lawman who might someday make an excellent FBI agent. I have a good feeling about you. I could use some help from a top-notch peace officer like you. I'm working on a top-secret case that the governor personally asked me to investigate. I need a little information. Just me and you, cop to cop."

Okay, Bell was lying about the governor part.

"The governor? Oh yes, sir, I'd be honored to help. Whatever the governor wants," the kid chirped. "Um, what does the governor want exactly?"

"He is very interested in a missing-persons case there in Georgetown. A high school girl who disappeared last spring, probably ran off. You got anything on her?"

"Yes, sir," he said. "I mean, maybe we do, sir. Can you hold while I take a look at our computer?"

"Certainly." Deputy Pepper put the receiver on the desk. While he waited, Bell overheard a police scanner in the background. Somebody called in a 10-45, a dead animal carcass at the grade school. Kids were freaking out. Backup requested. Deputy Pepper came back on the line before Bell heard if they called SWAT.

"Yes, sir," the kid said. "We had a runaway on Tuesday, March 24. Connie Walsh. Seventeen. Five-foot-eight. Blond. Blue eyes. Reported by Father James Walsh next day. He runs the First Colorado Bank up here. Back then, he said she had an argument with her parents the night before about her grades. She was last seen walking toward home after school. No real distinguishing marks ..."

"No *real* marks?"

"No scars or birthmarks. Only typical teenage girl stuff: bright red nail polish, pierced ears, nose, and tongue. It's a secret that she had a tiny butterfly tattoo way up on her leg where nobody could see. Her dad was pissed about it."

"And why would she be walking toward home if she was running away?"

"Good question, sir," Deputy Pepper said.

"What was she wearing when last seen?" Bell asked.

"Let's see," Deputy Pepper scanned his print-out. "Dad says light black jacket, running shoes, blue jeans and a Broncos sweatshirt, sir."

"Any evidence that she might have taken any personal possessions or clothing? Did she tell any of her friends what she was doing? Get on the next bus? Use drugs? Have any emotional problems?"

"Nothing like that in this report, sir."

"Please tell me you have a photo," Bell said, half-expecting these Barneys never asked for one. He was wrong.

"Yes, sir," Deputy Pepper said. "Pretty girl. I can email or text it to you."

Suddenly, whether he knew it or not, the kid was smarter than the tech-muddled old detective.

"Yeah, my phone doesn't have that." Bell reckoned he was lying, but in truth he didn't know one way or the other. "Send it to my partner, Special Agent Pete Galligan, at CBI-dot-some crap. I'm sure you have the Yellow Pages or whatever. You can look it up."

"Yellow Pages, sir?"

"Maybe they changed the color," Bell said. "But I'm sure a first-class detective like yourself can get to the bottom of it."

"Copy that, sir," Deputy Pepper snapped to verbal attention. "Tell the governor I won't let him down."

BEFORE BELL COULD bumble into CBI Special Agent Dani Silva's number on his phone, she called him.

"Woodrow, Agent Silva here," she said. "We have some very preliminary results on the remains from the mountain. We brought in several forensic pathologists from the ME's office, and they've still got a lot of work to do, but I thought you might want to know what we know so far. Maybe you could give us some perspective."

"Absolutely," Bell said. "And I have something for you, too."

SA Silva went first.

"The good news is, we were able to get good DNA from all twenty-two sets of remains, all teenaged females. It's in the lab now," she said. "One died several months ago, and the rest range from a few years up to decades ago."

She had more.

"At this point, our best-guess on cause of death is catastrophic trauma through the skulls' right and left 'external acoustic meatus,' which is doc-speak for the ears. The edges of several skull wounds suggest a heavy object, probably rusted metal, with a square shaft—consistent with your account of a railroad or mining spike that was long enough to pass through the skull completely and come out the other side."

And more.

"All girls' sternums were all cut by a large, smooth blade, probably a hunting knife and not a meat saw, likely post-mortem. Almost all remains showed evidence of being bound at the wrists and ankles with chains, and the freshest one's eyes were sewn shut. The other remains were too degraded to know for sure, but some had small, irregular nicks around the eye sockets consistent with a metal object like a large needle. We're looking for a goddamned mutant, Woodrow."

"No shit," Bell said. "And the bad news?"

"Still nothing on Midwinter," Silva admitted. "We're also dealing with old remains, which is always a complication. The DNA might not match up with any of our known missing girls. It also looks like some were buried before anybody collected DNA samples from families. And we can't reach out to dentists until we have some idea of who we have on the table. And as expected, we haven't found any trace of the killer's DNA. Cross your fingers on the girls' DNA."

"Maybe we won't need luck," Bell said. "I might have caught a break."

"Jazz was right about you going rogue. What did you catch?"

"Have one of your MEs open the mouth of the newest girl we found, the one with the ripped jeans. Look for tongue jewelry," he said. "And have one of your computer geeks check out the moon phase on Tuesday, March 24 of this year. If there's a piercing and it's a moonless night, she's probably a girl named Connie Walsh who went missing in Georgetown last March. Then you can send an agent as fast as you can up there for a DNA sample from her dad James Walsh, the local bank manager."

"How the hell do you know all this?" Agent Silva asked Bell.

"A granny told me."

LAST WEEK'S SNOW had melted into a dirty, slushy mess. Passing cars sloshed the slop onto the sidewalks and anybody who happened to be walking there.

Bell took the back way to Father Bert's bungalow at St. Barnabas. He'd been thinking about those lost girls buried on the unconsecrated margin of the asylum cemetery. They weren't much different from the dead babies in the mass grave that Father Bert once sanctified in the same cemetery. How could there be any difference among discarded, hidden innocents?

Bell didn't know. He wasn't real big on religion or Heaven or God. That was Father Bert's country. At the very least, Bell reckoned those girls deserved a prayer, and his priest friend knew a lot about that.

That's part of what Bell wanted to talk about. The rest ... well, he didn't know what the rest was just yet.

Then his phone rang. Because his phone was lost even if he had it, he needed a few seconds to find the right pocket, and a few more seconds to find the Answer button.

"Bell."

"It's Jazz, Big Man. We gotta talk."

"We're talking."

"Where are you?" she asked.

"Midnight," he said. "Walking."

"Find a place to sit."

"I'm not walking that far or that fast, Jazz."

"I'm serious."

Bell had no intention of sitting anywhere in this cold sluice. He stopped in his tracks.

"Okay, I'm sitting," he lied.

"No, you're not, but I got no time to argue with you."

Bell knew that tone. Jazz wasn't in a mood.

"Okay, what's up?"

She spoke slowly and deliberately, as if she were notifying a victim's next of kin.

"Erskine Midwinter is dead."

CHAPTER 10

BELL NEEDED TO sit.

He wanted to bellow a blue string of the foulest words he knew.

He hoped the blood thrumming in his head wouldn't kill him.

But he didn't sit, scream, or bust a vein. He stood there dumbstruck.

"Big Man, you okay?" Jazz sounded worried when she heard nothing.

"What ...? I mean, how ...? When?"

"Breathe," she said in that "next-of-kin" voice. "I've got everything you want to know, and stuff you don't know you want to know. But if you have a stroke, I might feel like crap for a couple minutes. So just breathe."

Bell hated to be ordered around, but Jazz made some sense. He inhaled cold air real deep and let it out in a frosty cloud. His temples still throbbed.

"You okay now?"

"Yeah, yeah, I'm fine," he said, although he was still off-balance. "What the hell is going on?"

Jazz knew explicitly what this news meant to her old partner, but he wouldn't want to be spoon-fed like a wimp. She didn't soft-peddle it.

"Your guy Midwinter died in 2006. He's been dead for more than fifteen years. I nailed it down two minutes ago and called you first."

The pounding blood now vibrated in Bell's back teeth.

Fifteen years?

"It can't be him," Bell uttered. "Something's wrong here."

"Trust me, Big Man. It's him."

"I love you, partner, but there's no way. I'm telling you, he can't be dead!"

Right then and there, over the phone, Jazz morphed into Detective Sgt. Jasmine Jackson. All business. "8/21/06. Unidentified white male. Drowned. Fifty-plus years old. Five-foot-eight, 165 pounds. Long gray hair. Withered right eye. The X-rays showed multiple badly healed broken bones, repeatedly smashed fingers causing severe osteoarthritis, plus dozens of old laceration scars on head, torso, and limbs—somebody literally smashed this guy up when he was younger and he had to be in pain ever since. Fingerprints illegible. Self-inked scorpion tattoo on posterior aspect of right forearm. Blue jeans, blue jersey, gray 'Littleton Fun Run 2003' T-shirt."

Damn close ... but not enough, Bell thought.

"It could be somebody else," he asserted.

Please be somebody else, he prayed. If Midwinter was dead, he'd been wrong all along. This mystery would never be solved.

"It isn't somebody else," Jazz said. "Back in the '90s, the morgue started taking pictures of all their homeless Does, sort of a last-ditch hope that somebody might someday recognize them. Ten years ago, the ME posted them all on his website. That's where we found Midwinter's photo. I pulled the morgue's file for Number 06-0561, which also had his close-up autopsy photos. Everything matches what we already knew: Freaky eye. Self-tattoo on the right arm—which also tells us he was left-handed. Right age, height, weight. His dead face is a dead ringer for his prison mug. I didn't have to look very close. No question, it's him."

Bell could hear his own breathing from the inside. His veins still pulsed in his ears.

"He drowned? Where? How?"

"In an abandoned storm-sewage tunnel under Aurora," she said. "He was one of the Mole People, the homeless underground. There's a scary other world down there, Big Man. Drugs, insanity, death. I was down there on a homicide investigation a few years ago. I wanted to throw up. There are a lot of human predators and they feed on each other."

"You're kidding, right?" Bell asked. "How could I never know about this crazy shit?"

"Cops don't go down there but it's always been there," Jazz said. "It's a freak show within a nightmare. It's pitch-black. You can't tell if it's day or night. The place reeks with vomit, human shit, motor oil, dead cats, old paint that assholes pour down the storm drains, pesticides from rich people's lawns. At night, the Mole People come out to scavenge in dumpsters and trade sex for drugs, but back underground they'll eat rats, stray dogs, raccoons ... whatever."

"So how does a guy drown underground?"

"When it rains, the storm drains fill up and the flash floods flush everything out ... people, too. He just got sucked down. They found him a few days later, floating leisurely down a creek through the suburbs."

Bell had no more fight in him.

"Where is he now?"

"You already know where all our John Does go," she said. "He's nothing but Number 06-0561 in the potter's field at St. Simeon Cemetery."

"I wonder if they know they have a serial killer," Bell said.

"*Alleged* serial killer," Jazz corrected him. "I hate to say that—honest to God, Big Man, I do—but we have a lot of bodies with the same sick story after 2006. Who did those if he was dead?"

Bell's faculties trickled back.

"Copycat?"

"No media. There was nothing to copy," Jazz said. "Hell, us cops didn't even know what this was until, what, a couple months ago? Maybe not until yesterday."

"You know about yesterday?"

"Silva called me last night. She's over the moon. She thinks you're Sherlock Holmes, Magnum, and Batman all wrapped up in one. She said this is a grand-slam."

Bell didn't see it that way now.

"Yeah, except maybe our killer isn't our killer. That tends to be a problem for juries."

"I was just a poor black child when you told me something that I tell my rookies," Jazz said. "You said, 'Kid, everything is possible—until it isn't.'"

I said that? Really? Only old men recognized their own bullshit.

"Sounds like bad dialogue in a bad cop show. Forget I said it."

"Too late," Jazz said, possibly having second thoughts. "Maybe Midwinter isn't our guy, but I guess it's not impossible ... yet. Have you thought about a team?"

In truth, Bell hadn't. Nevertheless, if Midwinter was the psychopath Bell imagined he was, he trusted nobody, period. The only partner he'd ever consider would be younger, controllable, and equally psychopathic. From the monstrosity Bell had already seen, there could be nobody who exhibited Midwinter's unique perversity. A team? Not yet an impossible scenario, but not likely by a country mile.

But everything is possible—until it isn't, right?

The truth was that some things are so unlikely that possibility is a pipe dream.

If Midwinter died in 2006, as Jazz swore he did, then many things were truly impossible.

The man who left one hair in Cherish Nelson's locket couldn't possibly be the same man who peed on Rosemary Midwinter's outhouse seat.

A dead Erskine Midwinter couldn't possibly have killed anybody past 2006.

Whoever slaughtered Cherish Nelson in 1969 must be the same deranged sadist who slaughtered Connie Walsh last March, fifty years later—problem was, it couldn't be Midwinter.

Then there were the possibilities.

Was it possible that Bell was hunting some other ghost? Had Bell presumed Midwinter's connection to the Schattenland asylum meant something—when it was merely a genuine coincidence (which he didn't believe existed)? Did Roxy Snipes see real patterns, or did he see only what he wanted to see and imagined it was relevant?

Bell was back at Square One, where possible and impossible were all tangled up, where everything was definitely possible and possibly impossible at the same time.

FOR THE REST of the day, nothing made sense.

Bell roamed around Midnight, which should have taken less than an hour but instead exhausted the whole afternoon. He tried to make all the old pieces work together in his head, while trying to imagine where new pieces might be hidden. When he took stock of everything, that's all he had: Pieces that didn't fit together.

He sensed he'd experienced a gap in time that was fifty years wide. Most of what he thought he knew for sure was an illusion. Cherish Nelson and twenty-two other girls were slain in spectacularly ugly ways and ... after that it got fuzzy.

Everything he counted on turned out to be only half true. That's the problem with half-truths ... you might have gotten the bad half.

A bank of snow clouds in the west blocked the sunset, so night fell early. Frozen vapor in the air haloed around the streetlights, which left meteor trails across Bell's eyes. But lights hadn't yet come on in people's windows. He smelled snow coming. It was time to go home.

Charlie waited for him there.

"Been here long?" Bell asked as he came in. He didn't know how cold he'd gotten until the house's warmth hit him.

"Long enough to know I shouldn't have been here this long."

"You can be here as long as you want," he said. "You either help me think or keep me from thinking too much. Both good."

"What's your pleasure tonight, Woodrow?"

Sometimes when she pronounced his name she sounded curious, and sometimes she sounded like she already knew.

"Dinner and bourbon and rethinking everything I know," he said. "Not necessarily in that order."

Charlie was good at all those things.

"Maybe it's the weather," she said. "Things get crazy around here because of the weather, y'know?"

They held each other up as they slipped toward Tommyknockers for burgers. They took a table near the back where Bell sat with his back to the wall, an old cop habit that let him watch the door, everybody, and every movement in the place. It never really paid off, but old cop habits die hard.

"A day, huh?" Charlie asked.

"That obvious?"

She smiled. "Most days are days with you. Maybe that's why I stick around. You don't waste days. Plus, I saw you walking this afternoon and I honked. You were someplace else. So, what makes this a day?"

Bell toyed with his silverware, which he arranged in a perfectly senseless order. His mind was still adrift.

"Midwinter probably isn't my guy," he said. "He's been dead for a long time. Nobody made a mistake; I just didn't consider the possibility that I was wrong about everything."

"*Probably* isn't your guy?" Charlie asked. "It sounds like maybe you're not totally convinced."

"Everything adds up to zero," Bell said. "His hair in the locket, left-handed, a weird connection to the asylum, abductions of other girls, a psycho prone to frenzied violence ... all circumstantial but probable cause. Being dead while girls are being murdered? That's a pretty good alibi."

"Sounds like forty-five."

Bell squinted as if something was out there in the dark, but he couldn't see it.

"What the hell is forty-five?"

Charlie rolled her eyes.

"In every cop show, they identify a suspect at twenty minutes past the hour," she said. "They arrest him at thirty minutes past the hour. Then they realize the bad guy is somebody else at forty-five. Bad guy gets what's coming to him at fifty-five. Mushy ending. Everybody smiles. Fade to black."

Bell wasn't amused.

"That's Hollywood. That's imaginary crap."

"We're all imaginary, aren't we? Maybe somebody else is dreaming us up or maybe we're dreaming them up. We imagine fake worlds where things happen the way we want them to happen, but they never happen that way at all. Or maybe they happened exactly that way, and we were faked out. Or we faked out ourselves."

Charlie was doing it again: Taking another one of her hard lefts, hoping to jar something loose under the hood.

"You need a beer," Bell said.

Maybe, but Charlie continued.

"Back when you first asked me out, I told you no. You tried again, and I said no again. Then sort of a third time. And a lame fourth. I asked you if you knew the meaning of the word 'impossible.' Do you remember what you said to me?"

Bell's memory didn't go back that far.

"Something indisputable, I hope."

Charlie teased him back.

"Oh, dear boy," she said. "You said, 'Everything is possible—until it isn't.' That's when I fell in like with you."

"Oh, God. I need a new line."

"Yet here we are having burgers and beer, and *probably* going home together to make mad, monkey love," she said.

"Or maybe just heavy petting," Bell said. "It's been a day."

Charlie laced up all the frayed ends of her kooky banter that was never kooky in the end.

"Don't fake yourself out, sweetie. You're only at forty-five. Anything is still possible ... and clowns. Don't forget the clowns."

BEFORE SUN-UP THE next morning, Bell made waffles while Charlie showered.

After breakfast, Charlie left for her garbage rounds and Bell swept powdery overnight snow from the walks before trudging over to see the guys on Deaf Row.

As usual, he came in late, right as they started sharing all the white lies their families told each other.

"My dad told me that cats could talk but they wouldn't do it around me," Dan Coogan remembered. "I spent kindergarten to third grade trying to sneak up on our damn cat."

Bell could see that Cotton Minahan had a predictably off-color remark but bit his tongue because Fancy was pouring coffee at that moment.

"Hell, I told my little sister that the stork delivers dogs and that those dogs eventually grow into humans," Ollie Fuhrman admitted. "So that poor little girl prayed and prayed every night that our dog Trixie would do it quick so she wouldn't be the youngest child anymore!"

They all laughed, including Fancy, who told the next tall tale.

"My sister told me that the lumps in tapioca pudding were really frogs' eyes," she told them. "I still don't eat tapioca pudding."

Roxy Snipes went next.

"My grandfather told me that there's a big screw connecting your bellybutton and your asshole," he said. "So if you fiddled with your bellybutton your butt would fall off."

"That's nothing," Elroy Richter said. "When it came time for me to learn how to swim, my grandpa told me the bottom of the river smelled like strawberries. I practiced and practiced swimming so I could smell the bottom of the river. Before I got down there the current dragged me a half-mile downstream, dammit. But I haven't given up: I'm still trying to smell the bottom."

Again, Cotton Minahan had another off-color remark and again, uncharacteristically, he held it in.

"My mother told me that every blanket contained a different dream," Doc Ely recalled. "If I had a nightmare, all I had to do was pull up another blanket and I'd have a happy dream. Years and years later, I told Caroline that story and before she passed, she bought me a blanket. It's still on my bed, and she comes to me every night."

It took a moment, then Father Bert jumped in.

"I had an uncle who was a lapsed Catholic," the priest said, crossing himself. "He was still very moral, but he told me that every time I lied, an angel got diarrhea. Of all the reasons not to lie—the Ten Commandments included—angels with short squitters were the most powerful to me."

"Why's that?" Coogan asked.

Father Bert pointed heavenward.

"The angels were up there, and I was down here. Even a little kid could figure out those physics."

Everybody laughed, but more than one of them privately wondered if it wasn't at least a trifling sin for a priest to discuss diarrhea.

"What about you, Woodrow?" Minahan asked. "Or do you still think there's a Tooth Fairy?"

Bell thought for a moment.

"At least I still have all my teeth, Minahan," he poked back. "When I was about six or seven, my big brother told me there was a killer hiding in my closet. If I farted, he said, this killer would come out at night and kill us all. But then one night, I couldn't hold it in any longer and one little fart popped out."

"And what happened?" the gullible Roxy asked as if it were a real-life cliffhanger.

Bell leaned forward, his voice low and somber.

"I shot him," he said.

"The killer?"

"No. My brother."

A hush fell over Deaf Row and the rest of Tommyknockers' breakfast crowd.

"Okay, it was only a rubber-band gun, but he deserved it," Bell said, relieving only some of the suspense. "And that's the exact moment I knew I wanted to be a cop."

The old guys guffawed. Even Minahan couldn't top that one.

"You can pick your nose," he laughed, "but you can't pick your family!"

While Fancy poured them another round of coffee, nobody saw Bell slip out the door.

BELL FOUND HIS phone exactly where he didn't remember setting it down while he'd made waffles that morning: on the windowsill over the sink. Of only four numbers programmed into it, he found SA Dani Silva's last—on his third try.

"Good morning, Agent Bell," she answered.

Someday he'd ask how she and everybody else knew, but a bigger question occupied him at the moment.

"Has your lab found anything new on the suspect DNA from the locket and the outhouse?"

"Negative," Silva said. "They've got their hands full with profiling the remains. You made their job a little easier late last night, though."

"How'd I do that?" Bell asked, settling in at his breakfast table for whatever came next.

"Those six girls you identified as possible victims? You nailed it. All six were buried up there on that mountain. You gave us all their survivors' names and addresses, so we scrambled agents to collect their families' DNA. The comparisons are extremely preliminary but pretty strong. I'm sorry for their families, but those girls were found because of you. Maybe that's one good thing that comes from all this. Good work."

"That wasn't my list," he said. "Two top-notch investigators did that."

Silva had another bit of news from the morgue.

"You were probably right about Connie Walsh, too," Silva reported. "She still had her silver tongue ring and jeans, like you said."

"I had a reliable informant on that," Bell interjected.

"Yeah? Well, anyway, both are on their way back up to Georgetown to be identified by her parents. Galligan also got the photo from Clear Creek County, and we took swabs from the father yesterday, so DNA tests and facial reconstruction are running right now. A lot of damage to the left side of her skull where the spike went in, but the bone doctor doesn't think it'll be a stumbling block."

"The date and the moon?"

"Just like you said. A Tuesday and no moon, just like the other six."

Two days after exhuming those graves on Mount Misery, seven girls had faces again. That was warp speed. The Colorado Bureau of Investigation had all hands on deck for this one. Bell wasn't surprised how fast the state could move when it wanted to, only that too many times in the past, it didn't want to.

"How much longer before you have DNA profiles on the others?" he asked Silva.

"Not long. Less than forty-eight hours. The older, more degraded samples might need to be sequenced to amplify what's there, but we should be able to do all that in the next seven days."

Bell remembered when it took weeks, even months, to process simple DNA, all at a prohibitive cost most small police departments couldn't afford. Now, forensic genetic tests were faster, cheaper, and more reliable—and too many cops put too much faith in them. DNA testing was a swell tool, but merely a tool.

"While you're at it, would you ask your team to take a closer look at Erskine and Rosemary Midwinter's DNA, too?" Bell asked.

"Why? Jazz tells me Midwinter might be off our list of suspects," Silva said. "Death is the ultimate 'get out of jail free' card."

"Word travels fast. Yeah, I know he probably isn't our guy, but anything is possible ..."

Silva finished his sentence.

"... until it isn't. Jazz told me that a long time ago," she said. "So, what are you thinking?"

"Just connecting dots," he said. "With Midwinter, there's always been a lot of 'possible' and not enough 'positive.' Now we need to be sure. I figure you guys have bigger, badder machines, that's all."

Silva didn't disagree, but she had too few DNA analysts and too many other priorities right now.

"We'll get to it as soon as we can," she promised. "But my guys are assholes-over-elbows in dead girls. The sooner we identify them, the sooner families know, and the sooner we can build our case. If our prime suspect has been dead for fifteen years but girls are still dying, we sorta need a new prime suspect."

Bell wasn't easily deflected.

"And the sooner we know who we're looking for, the sooner he meets Bundy in Hell."

A few seconds of silence followed before SA Dani Silva spoke again.

"Well played, Big Man."

They left it at that, with a promise to keep each other in the loop. If Silva was anything like Jazz—and he reckoned she was—Bell knew she'd do everything in her power. Not for politics, but for those girls.

There at his breakfast table, still cluttered with the morning dishes, Bell lost himself in tumbling thoughts about old bones, new hopes, dark moons, and dead killers. He was tired. He wanted to sleep, but it was still morning. His coffee with Charlie came too early, and the coffee at Deaf Row had never kicked in. His mug sat there on the table, half-empty, cold, and waiting to be dumped. Even worse, its handle faced left.

Bell wasn't superstitious or nitpicky about such nonsense, but it seemed to him that a coffee cup's handle should always be on the side most convenient to the drinker. On the right if he was right-handed, on the left if he wasn't. Otherwise, it was an omen that the day ahead would suck.

And that's how he knew he was too tired: He gave a damn about the handles on coffee mugs.

But before he could turn it right, time stopped and restarted. His brain reset.

Bell picked up his phone. While he futzed with the tiny keypad, he miraculously discovered a button labeled "Redial."

"Agent Bell," Dani Silva answered. "Long time, no hear. It seems like we just talked, oh what, three minutes ago? Is this a butt dial?"

Bell didn't even know what a butt dial was, but it didn't matter at the moment.

"You said the spike went into the left side of Connie Walsh's skull."

Silva checked the girl's folder.

"Correct," she said, ruffling some papers. "Let's see, our examiner said the entry wound was a sharp force injury by an object with a shank 3.8 centimeters square and sixteen centimeters long—consistent with an inch-and-a-half square spike that's about six inches long, slightly more than the width of the average adult female skull—penetrated the left temporal region, driving bone fragments into the skull. It likely pierced the brain stem, then punctured a small hole in the opposite side of the skull, propelling bone shards outward. So, it passed left to right."

"Oh God."

"What?"

"Tell your forensic paths to look at the skull damage on every girl and document which side the entry wound is on," Bell said. He couldn't speak fast enough. "And as best they can, put the girls in order."

"In order of what?"

"Dying."

"Are you going to explain this to me?" Silva asked.

Bell skipped past her question.

"We need to know if all the girls' wounds are the same or different, and if anything changed around 2006," he said. "I don't know how you guys can do it without identifying them. Use your magic machines or carbon dating or some damn thing. But it's more urgent than urgent."

Silva was as persistent and stern as Bell.

"Agent Bell," she said, emphasizing the "agent" part, "I want to know what you're thinking. That's an order."

Bell hated orders but at this moment, they needed each other.

"We might have two different killers," he said. "Maybe Midwinter and somebody else who picked up where Midwinter left off when he died. Same methods and materials, with a tiny difference: Midwinter was left-handed, but the next guy could be a rightie. So, if all the girls before 2006 had entry wounds on the right, and all the girls after 2006 had it on the left, it's probably two different killers."

"Any idea who could that be?" Silva asked. "Even remotely?"

Who would a loner psychopath trust that much? Why team up at all? A predator teacher with a predator student? Why would a pathologically selfish psycho share his deviant thrills with anybody else? What made them the same kind of sick? How did they find each other?

Bell had more questions than answers. In fact, he had no answers at all. He wasn't even sure he had all the questions.

But he had a theory.

"Rosemary Midwinter," he said to Silva.

"The mother?" Silva sounded dubious. "Didn't you say she's elderly and slight? She couldn't possibly ..."

"Tell that to Baby Jane."

"Who?"

Bell hated it when his good ol' days were years behind everybody else's good ol' days.

"Nevermind," he said. "My point is, she's hiding something. Maybe it's something she saw. Maybe it's Erskine himself. Maybe she taught him. Or maybe she was—or is—the prick's partner. I don't know, but she's in the middle of all this."

Silva capitulated so quickly that Bell wondered why.

"Rather than kicking my own ass for letting you outfox me, let's skip to the chase," she said. "What miracle do you need from me this time?"

"Not much," Bell said. "Just unleash your magic computer to dive deeper into Rosemary Midwinter's life. And put a rush on identifying the first girl where the M.O. changed. And go all gnat's-ass on the Midwinters' DNA samples."

Silva was brusque.

"Not much, eh?" she asked. "No problem. I'll put Agents Earp and Ness on it right away."

"Oh, and dig up No. 06-0561 at St. Simeon Cemetery in Aurora."

"I knew I shouldn't have made you an agent," Silva said, not entirely joking. "Is there anything else, Mr. Director, sir?"

Yes, there was one little thing.

"Can you do it all today?" Bell wondered.

"Good talk," she said. And then Special Agent, Dani Silva of the Colorado Bureau of Investigation not-so-politely hung up.

FOR A SECOND day, Midnight thawed in a winter heat wave. That is to say, the temperature peaked slightly above freezing.

Bell found Father Bert shoveling slush off the St. Barnabas sidewalk.

"More old farts die with a snow shovel in their hand than their wives," he hollered at the old priest from the street.

"That's a fascinating fact, Woodrow," Father Bert said, leaning on his shovel. "But more men shovel snow than their wives, so it stands to reason."

It took Bell a second, then he reminded himself he was talking to a smart-ass priest.

"No, I mean ... nevermind," he said. "Clearing a path to Heaven, are you?"

Father Bert hoped for the best but planned for the worst.

"If it helps bring sinners to God, then it's God's work," he said. "But if it keeps parishioners from slipping on their butts and suing the Vatican, then it's State Farm's work."

"Can a priest say 'butt'?"

Father Bert propped his holy shovel against his holy porch.

"It's not your funeral and I don't owe you money, so what brings Extra Special Agent Woodrow Bell within a block of a church on this sunny day? Communion? Confession?"

"Lunch," Bell said. "Want some?"

"Grilled cheese and tomato soup in the rectory?" Father Bert asked. "Or heart attack-on-a-plate at the Bar F?"

"Tough choice. Grilled cheese."

Father Bert had a way with grilled cheese, so while he prepared his specialty, Bell warmed a cup of cold coffee in the priest's antique microwave.

"We missed you at Deaf Row this morning," he said.

"Emergency confession," Father Bert replied. "A weekend game of spin-the-bottle gone wrong."

"Teenagers?"

"No," said the priest. "Old Miners Home."

Bell pictured the old folks sitting in a horny little circle.

"Good for them," is all he said.

Father Bert changed the subject to *avoid* picturing it.

"Seriously, Woodrow, what brings you?"

"I can't just drop in for cold coffee and grilled cheese? Why would you think I need some kind of secret motive to visit a friend?"

Father Bert smiled.

"It's what I do," he said. "And I know about digging up Mount Misery. I know you're troubled by what you saw and what you're thinking."

"Yeah?" Bell scoffed more than asked. "How?"

"Because I know you and because Charlie told me. So what's bugging you, Dirty Harry?"

For starters, it bugged the Dirty Harry in Woodrow "Mountain" Bell to be *known*—by his priest friend, his lover, his old partner, anybody—but it also connected him to them in a way that comforted him. So it bugged him that it bugged him.

"If you know me so well," Bell said, "why am I here?"

Father Bert stirred their soup.

"I think you don't know why you're here. I think you want prayers for those girls—maybe yourself—but you don't know how to ask. I think you've seen a lot but nothing like what you saw up there. I think you know too many people die before their time and you can't believe in any God who'd allow that. I think you don't want to risk that you're completely wrong about Heaven or Hell. And I think you like my grilled cheese."

Bell didn't look up, only wheeled his cup in little circles and said nothing.

"If I'd been with you and the boys at Deaf Row today," a more serious Father Bert said, "my blessing might have asked God for small graces in the small things, so we might understand the big things."

"And clowns."

"What?"

"Long story," Bell said. "Look, those girls would probably appreciate you putting in a good word for them, and I pray all the time that there's a Hell for all the motherfff...freaks I've busted and at least one I haven't, and your grilled cheese is okay but your coffee sucks. But that's not why I'm here."

Bell was lying, and he figured Father Bert knew it. All those things, and maybe others, were exactly why he was there. He simply lost his nerve.

"Okay," the priest rolled his eyes and played along. "Why are you here, my son?"

"I just wanted to give you a heads up, padre," Bell said. "If you know anybody at St. Simeon's graveyard down in Aurora, you might warn them that somebody's coming to dig up Erskine Midwinter."

BELL DIDN'T YET know it, but that afternoon a judge granted the Colorado Bureau of Investigation's emergency request to exhume Number 06-0561 from the pauper's field at St. Simeon Catholic Cemetery. The next morning, the gravedigger's backhoe hoisted a concrete grave liner, a kind of shell that protected a casket from water and the weight of dirt above. This one, though, that looked like a busted septic tank, and exposed what was left of Erskine Midwinter—or whoever he was.

There wasn't a lot. Unknown transients didn't get lavish send-offs. He'd been buried in one of the cheap pine boxes reserved for nameless indigents, unembalmed. Six inmates from the county jail had acted as pallbearers, lowered the coffin into the wet hole and left. The on-call priest said a quick prayer and left, which was more than most homeless corpses got. Nobody cared that much.

Lifting the rotted wooden coffin without spilling the decaying remains inside was impossible, so it was photographed in the gelid, muddy mess. Then a CBI anthropologist in a hazmat respirator clambered down in the grave. He dismantled the collapsed coffin and collected the mostly skeletonized body piece by grim piece, which he placed carefully in a plain cardboard box.

Back at the morgue the next morning, the medical examiner reassembled this morbid puzzle on his stainless-steel autopsy table for a close-up examination.

Only twenty-three pounds of him remained. Most soft tissue was gone. Some patches of hair and mummified skin clung to his skull, which was full of mud. Only a few teeth remained. Swatches of Number 06-0561's thrift-store burial suit stuck to his long bones and rib cage. He wore no jewelry, no belt, no shoes.

But the M.E. saw something else: No bone was unbroken. The fractures were all healed, some quite poorly, but every part of Number 06-0561 had been splintered, snapped, or smashed. Many showed the telltale signs of being childhood injuries, some had been broken more than once, and some had clearly been caused by blunt objects. He hadn't fallen out of a tree or crashed his bike as a kid ... he'd been deliberately pulverized over a long period of time.

As an older man, Number 06-0561 developed debilitating arthritis in his hands and feet. His finger and toe bones—all crushed at some time in his past—had slowly eroded where they touched. At the time of his death, X-rays revealed his digits were achingly gnarled and deformed.

The M.E. knew the simple act of eating a sandwich would have been clumsy and painful. Snatching and killing a teenage girl would have been virtually impossible for the last five to ten years of his life.

One more thing he couldn't explain, except as a peculiar artifact of an aberrant life's trajectory: Number 06-0561's bones contained a faint trace of an unknown radioactive substance. It was curious but hadn't been life-threatening nor consequential enough to justify a deeper examination.

In the end, the man—or rather, the bones—on his table had suffered excruciating agony in his past, but the forensic pathologist found no evidence to overturn the cause of death as drowning. He extracted DNA from Number 06-0561's femur and quickly summarized his findings in a succinct, two-page report, which he then personally handed to CBI SA Pete Galligan, who'd watched it all.

BELL FOUND HIS phone exactly where he'd lost it, in the pocket of yesterday's workpants.

All day, he'd tinkered with a clock that hadn't worked in years, organized the tools in his frigid shed, mucked around in his dusty basement workshop, and waited for a call from Dani Silva that didn't come.

Today—because the clock still didn't work, his tools would never be truly organized, the basement got dusty again overnight, and because patience wasn't his strong suit—he called her.

"Agent Big Man," SA Silva answered. "Long time no hear. What's it been, forty-eight hours?"

"Forty-nine hours and thirty-four minutes."

"Time flies when you have unreasonable expectations," she needled.

"Yeah, well, you have an unreasonable expectation that I'll repair that particular character flaw," Bell needled back. "You got anything on my Family of the Year?"

Silva was ready.

"There's good news that's bad, bad news that's bad, and keep-your-damn-shirt-on news. What do you want first?"

"Tell me the bad news that's good," Bell said.

She ignored him.

"Okay, here's the good news that's bad," "We found some really sickening stuff on Mommie Dearest."

"Where? Jazz couldn't find anything."

"I think Jazz told you: When Rosemary was an inmate, she sued the state for guard brutality," Silva reported. "In case there was a trial, the Attorney General's Office asked CBI to crawl up her ass to find dirt. We found some obscure old records and talked to a lot of people who knew her, junkie friends, cellmates, pimps. The whole file was hiding in plain sight right here in our basement."

"And ...?"

"Short version: She's an angry freak."

Bell already knew that much. Silva continued.

"Rosemary was born off-the-grid in Bitter Creek on December 9, 1942. In the 1920s, her father Lot Midwinter worked as a three buck-a-day powder monkey in Leadville's Matchless silver mine, according to the state archives. During the Depression, he and an unnamed working girl literally ran off with a second-hand circus. He was a barker and she danced as a 'hootchie-kootchie' girl by the stage name of Fifi—basically a stripper. Both had monkeys on their backs. He was a violent drunk and she was a morphine addict, according to some old jail bookings along the two-bit sideshow's circuit."

So, the Midwinters' dysfunction went back at least a generation, Bell thought. They didn't know anything different. Still, it was a leap of Biblical proportions from carnival hophead to psycho serial killer.

"Fast-forward to World War II," Silva went on. "In 1942, the FBI lists Lot Midwinter as a draft evader but he's in the wind. Later they find out he's been hiding since Pearl Harbor in the mountains around Bitter Creek with Fifi, who's still on morphine but now pregnant, presumably with Rosemary."

"How did they find out?"

Silva's voice softened.

"An unidentified man claiming to be the father delivered the newborn to a doctor in Bitter Creek, then vanished. The baby was very small and sick. Her placenta was still attached, for God's sake. Symptoms were consistent with morphine withdrawal. The anonymous father never came back. And coincidentally, from that point forward, we still can't find any record of our so-called Fifi, like she never existed. It's likely she died in childbirth."

Bell tried to reconcile the bitter, crude, misanthropic Don't Even Ask with an innocent baby nobody wanted.

Silva pressed forward with her sad story.

"This poor doctor didn't know what to do. He nursed this unnamed orphan and called the sheriff, who took a report and called the local priest. When she was reasonably healthy, the church took the baby girl and arranged for the doctor and his wife to adopt her. That's when she got her name: Rosemary."

Bell already knew this story didn't have a happy ending.

"But something happened ..."

"Yeah," Silva said. "In 1950, when she was eight, Rosemary suddenly went missing on her way home from school. The sheriff's reports strongly suggested the mystery man—who we later learned was probably Lot Midwinter himself—had taken her back. We don't know where they went, how, or why, but there's no blue sky here."

Little pieces began to fall into place for Bell.

"But she shows up again."

"Right," Silva said. "Four years later, twelve-year-old Rosemary magically shows up on the doctor's doorstep, dirty, malnourished, barely able to talk ... and pregnant. She's now using the name Midwinter. The doc takes her in and, again, calls the sheriff. She refuses to talk and the whole thing is dropped. Baby boy is born July 31, 1954, and Rosemary runs away that night with her new baby. That's your guy."

"Where'd she go?" Bell asked.

"Every place and no place," Silva said. "When they weren't squatting in empty cabins and vacant buildings, they were homeless. In 1959, game wardens reported chasing her out of an abandoned powderhouse up near you, in Wisdom Gulch."

Bell himself finished Rosemary Midwinter's dreadful story.

"I think Lot Midwinter raped his daughter," he said gravely. "She didn't say outright that it was her father, but it was definitely not a stranger. That freak didn't snatch her out of fatherly love. Check your magic computer. If he died in the early 1960s, it's him."

"Way ahead of you," she said. "In 1962, Lot Midwinter's decomposing corpse was found by hunters in a mountain shack above Bitter Creek, and the doctor swore he was the mystery man. He was stabbed in the groin, and his junk was stuffed in his mouth. The knife was never found. Maybe Rosemary didn't do it, but this was a rage killing ... and she had good reason to be enraged."

Bell added up the grimness.

"So, Erskine Midwinter's grandma is a drug-fiend and sideshow stripper who's also his aunt. His incestuous, child-raping grandfather is also his father. His mutilator mother is his sister. And he himself is a psycho serial killer. PTA meetings must have been a riot."

Silva wasn't shocked at all, but she dropped another shoe.

"Well," she said, "here's the bad news that's bad."

"Oh shit. What?"

"It's gonna take months, maybe years, before we can identify the specific girl where the killing method changed. The forensic anthropologist noticed a big gap—maybe twenty or thirty years—between the seven earliest victims and the fifteen newer ones. We have three sets of remains that could be the girl where the method changed, but even when we have DNA profiles, we won't know who they are, how or when they were abducted, or where."

"How long?"

"Impossible to know," Silva said apologetically. "We'll identify all of them someday, I promise, but not this year. Sorry, Woodrow."

"Goddammit to hell. We can't wait that long. Our killer is active right now."

"The hits keep coming, Big Man," Silva said. "The medical examiner said Midwinter's arthritis was so bad that he couldn't possibly have grabbed those girls or killed them so spectacularly in the last few years of his life. And he was in prison for twenty-six years before that. Do the math: Our guy didn't have the opportunity or the dexterity to kill a female cockroach with his bare hands after 1977."

In one breath, Silva had wiped the slate clean. Now, Bell knew nothing ... except that somebody killed those girls, that Erskine Midwinter was there when Cherish Nelson died, and that the freak's demons were real.

"Then we've got to get off our asses and find out how he's involved," he said, "because he *is* involved. And I'm telling you one more time: Rosemary Midwinter is in the middle of all this mess."

"And that's the third thing," Silva stressed. "We getting close to a DNA comparison of our homeless guy, the locket hair, and your outhouse schmutz. It's going to tell us more, but we have to wait for it. I know you're in a stormy relationship with patience, but you need to kiss and make up. For the kids."

"Our differences are irreconcilable," he said. "How long must I pretend?"

Silva refused to be pinned down. Instead, she ordered Bell to relax.

"I don't know," she said. "A day, maybe two. It's our top priority. Just hunker down, do a puzzle, learn how to text, and wait for me to call. Just don't go all Dirty Harry on me. Got it, Agent Bell?"

"Copy that," he confirmed.

He lied.

BEFORE SUN-UP THE next morning, Bell packed a small bag. Not a change of clothes and a toothbrush, but the fifty-caliber Magnum and his old Marine Corps .45. Just in case.

Overnight, snowmelt had re-frozen on the highway to Purgatory. The Crown Vic's traction trumped Bell's impatience to track down Rosemary Midwinter, so he had plenty of time to think about how it would go down. It might go sideways down a dozen rabbit trails.

She wasn't likely to run, but she might try to hide again. She could be at her broken-down trailer, or she could be in the wind. She probably wouldn't answer his questions, but that didn't mean she'd say nothing. Handcuffs might not be necessary, but she'd be unlikely to go quietly. Bell had never shot an old lady, but he wouldn't hesitate to shoot an old serial killer. And he didn't expect her to confess, but she ... might.

Bell kept his eyes on the slippery road, but his mind was a thousand miles away. Killing her rapist—even if he was her father—the old detective could understand, but what made Rosemary Midwinter's lifelong psychosis so powerful? Why didn't it end? She spawned a serial killer from a waking nightmare, but why join his freak show with such ferocity? What compelled their slaughter? How could a woman—a mother, no less—kill and butcher teenage girls who might have been her granddaughters in a different life?

At this altitude, the morning sun glanced off the roadside snow, causing Bell to squint. He saw only the snow-covered road in front of the Crown Vic, but no farther down the highway. By noon, the asphalt would warm up, the glaze would thaw, and the blacktop would show through, but for now, the reflected brightness obscured everything underneath. He plowed ahead toward Purgatory.

Bell's strategy wasn't as simple as it should be. Cruising around town to get the lay of the land was out of the question. Too many eyes watched. He couldn't just park across Main Street and wait until he knew Rosemary was in the diner. Nor could he walk up without spoiling the surprise. And what if Rosemary's feisty little bouncer blocked his way again?

A mile outside of Purgatory, Bell pulled off the road and got out. He pulled off his big leather coat and strapped the Magnum's brawny holster across his chest. He also tucked the old .45 into his coat pocket. Just in case.

Before he could get back on the road, Bell's phone rang somewhere under his arsenal. By the time he rooted it out, it stopped. For once, he had this: He pressed Redial.

"Hey, Woodrow," SA Dani Silva answered. "Are you home?"

It was better for both of them if she didn't know.

"Yeah," he said. "What's up?"

"I have the DNA report and there's a problem."

Bell didn't like the sound of that. He'd expected science to confirm what he already presumed, not add unforeseen complications. Answers, not questions.

"Problems?"

Silva didn't bury the lede.

"Rosemary Midwinter has another son."

"What the hell?"

"Our dead guy was unquestionably Erskine, and he definitely left a hair in your murdered girl's locket. The university people got that right. But they were both right and wrong about the outhouse DNA."

"I'm confused."

Silva explained the best she could.

"They said your tissue contained a mother and son's DNA, and they were right about that," she said. "But the son wasn't Erskine Midwinter. It was a different male sibling. And that brother's mother is Erskine's sister."

"So he has another sister *and* a brother we never knew about?"

"Yes and no," she replied. "And that's where it gets weird."

Isn't it already weird enough? Bell thought. Silva went on.

"I couldn't explain all the complicated DNA shit if I wanted to," she said, "but we already suspected Erskine Midwinter's mom—probably Rosemary—was also his sister. The shocker is that this unknown brother is also Erskine's son."

Bell was wrong. Silva definitely buried the lede.

"Oh my God," he said. "Erskine screwed his own mother, who is also his sister, and they had a child?"

"Yes."

"This is so fucking tangled up ... how could that university guy get it so wrong?"

"Don't be too hard on him," she said. "You were in too big of a hurry, as usual. They rushed it. At a glance, they didn't catch the tiny differences between all your DNA samples. Your locket hair wasn't a great sample. Then our lab sequenced them, and the markers told a slightly different story. It changes the whole narrative."

Bell's mind shifted back into cop mode.

"Who's the brother or the son or whatever?" he asked. "Where is he now?"

"We only have his DNA, not his name. He might or might not be Eddie Midwinter, who did hard time up in Wyoming in the '90s. We're still running it down because Wyoming's Internet apparently stops at the Nebraska border. But if our UnSub—maybe Eddie—peed on Rosemary's toilet seat within the past month, then there's a chance he's still up in Purgatory, whoever he is. I'd bet Rosemary knows exactly where he is. I'm sending Pete Galligan up there ASAP to question her. Stay by your phone."

Bell didn't want to come clean, but he did.

"Don't bother. I'm already here."

Silva paused, then exploded.

"I told you to stand down. You disobeyed a direct order, goddammit!"

Bell hated direct orders.

"Then I quit," he said calmly. "Besides, your retirement benefits suck."

"Have it your way, smart ass," Silva barked. "Now you're a civilian and you're interfering with a police investigation. Step off immediately or you'll be arrested. Are we clear?"

"Good talk," he replied. And then ex-Special Agent Woodrow "Mountain" Bell of the Colorado Bureau of Investigation not-so-politely hung up.

NOBODY EVER SNEAKED into Purgatory.

Bell drove through town, neither too fast nor too slow. As he passed Burgatory, where the unhurried townsfolk should be well into breakfast, he saw a carelessly scrawled sign on the door: *Closed.*

He continued to Packer Road, beyond the farthest edge of town. It hadn't been plowed since the last snow a couple days before, and he saw fresher tire tracks coming from and going to Rosemary Midwinter's shabby trailer. Maybe an old lady's friendly lift to and from the diner. Maybe a lost traveler. Maybe Rosemary's secret son. Maybe something, maybe not.

Again, Bell parked out front and watched for signs of life. Nothing moved, inside or out. No steam from the propane heater vents. No lights. No sound. If not for the fresh trail of boot prints back and forth from her unshoveled porch, the place looked abandoned.

Bell left the Crown Vic running and followed the footsteps to the front door. He had no special man-tracking skills, but even flatlanders could see somebody had been there since the last snow. The work boots' treads were sharp and their backward Galt imprint clear. They were no more than a day or two old, some newer. And they were left by a man who wore bigger, heavier boots.

What he saw intrigued him. What he *didn't* see disturbed him: No smaller prints. Unless the mystery man had carried her back and forth, Rosemary Midwinter hadn't come or gone for at least two days.

Bell pounded on the door frame. Not the polite knock of a Girl Scout cookie-seller or a deliveryman behind schedule, but a cop's loud, intimidating thumps with the side of his fist, intended to be heard anywhere in the house. Subtle tapping was for rookies and doorbells were for death notifications.

"Rosemary," he bellowed, "it's Woodrow Bell. If you're in there, I just want to talk."

He heard no sound. If Rosemary Midwinter—or anyone else—was in there, they didn't twitch. Bell knew she wasn't throwing short-order breakfast plates on sticky tables at the diner. Maybe she stayed overnight with a friend, if she had one. Maybe she'd left town for a few days—or after his last visit, for good. Maybe she simply refused to answer his pounding.

None of it felt right. All those scenarios complicated matters. Whatever came next wouldn't be easy, but Bell wasn't sure what came next.

His cop instincts kicked in. If he'd had backup, his partner would wait out back in case anybody ran. But he had no backup. He reached discreetly under his coat and unsnapped the big holster across his chest. And he slipped the .45 from his pocket and clicked off the safety. Just in case.

The flimsy front door put up no fight. Bell rammed it so hard that it tore from its fragile hinges and crashed through the front room. He lurched inside, gun extended and ready.

The filthy trailer was darker, colder, and more lifeless than the winter outside. Icy air slithered through the open back door, which swung slack against its chain. Frost rimed the bleary windows. No pictures hung on the wall, no phone, no TV, but empty beer bottles lay everywhere.

Bell's breath puffed in tense, visible drafts as he quickly searched the cluttered bedrooms and kitchen. Two unmade beds, different sizes of clothes strewn everywhere, and two coffee mugs on opposite sides of the table told Bell that more than one person lived here; porn magazines on a cardboard-box nightstand convinced him that one of them was a man. Probably Rosemary's other son, the elusive "Maybe Eddie."

When Bell was sure he was alone, he thought about tearing the place apart for hidden evidence of murder. He knew that serial killers often kept grim souvenirs close, that some so enjoyed the risk of being discovered they often left clues in plain sight, that they all screwed up in unexpected ways—even Bundy.

Then out of the bone-chilling stillness, a humming sound. It wasn't close, and Bell felt it more than heard it, but it wasn't there before. He knew that sound carried farther in the cold so he held his breath and stood dead-still to pin down where and what it might be.

It was the sound of an idling engine—a rough one—and it came from Packer Road. Bell kept himself out of view and peeked around the front window's cold, metal casing.

A green Ford pickup sat in the middle of the road a hundred yards from the trailer, running and watching. Bell recognized it from the night he first visited Rosemary. Now, it was too far to identify a plate number or the two people in the cab, but it was too close for Bell to be careless.

These two probably weren't a silly California couple curb-shopping for a country estate where they could smoke legal pot in the Colorado foothills, Bell mused. Until he knew better, he thought it was wiser to consider the pickup a potential threat, possibly a rattled Rosemary and her mysterious son, "Maybe Eddie" Midwinter. Possibly armed.

They'd certainly seen the Crown Vic out front, Bell knew. They'd assume they'd been spotted—which they were. And they'd assume Bell was calling for backup—which he wasn't. He left his phone in the car. Maybe. He was never sure where he left it.

Whatever the pickup couple had planned, the plan changed when they realized Bell was there. Now they weighed their next move. They might graciously inquire why their front door was slightly askew, but Bell ranked that as the fourth of three possibilities: They could call the sheriff, run away fast, or lay siege to the trailer with guns and fire. The first was unlikely, the second unoriginal, and the last unhealthy for all of them.

But it was the last, Bell knew, that gave them any slim hope of eluding capture. Alive, Bell was too close. Dead, there was a chance nobody else knew. Worst case scenario, killing him would buy time. Best case, they'd disappear back into the shadows, nobody the wiser. He'd be just another body burned beyond recognition in a tragic trailer fire.

Bell unholstered the Magnum and weighed his options. He had thirteen rounds, that's all. If he needed a fourteenth, the firefight was over.

Bell cracked the sliding glass ever so slightly and pulled the ratty sofa against the wall under the front window, even though the foil-thin aluminum siding, wall, and couch all together weren't substantial enough to stop a bullet. He crept to the drafty back door and softly closed it, flipping a latch that wouldn't keep intruders out but might slow them down. He propped the broken front door against its bent jamb with a thrift-store recliner.

All at once, he heard his phone's muffled ringtone coming from the Crown Vic. It might be Pete Galligan, Jazz, Charlie, even Father Bert—although not likely the highly exercised Dani Silva—but at this moment he focused only on that damn pickup, which sat there, droning in its own menacing white fog.

After several rings, the phone went quiet.

He didn't have time to consider his next move. It happened without him.

The old pickup's engine raced. Its back wheels reeled nowhere for a couple seconds before it fishtailed across the snow toward the trailer, fast.

Bell braced the Magnum against the window frame and aimed squarely at the windshield. But before he could squeeze off one booming shot, the pickup skidded sideways on the snowfield and swiveled back toward the road. They were running.

Bell busted back through Rosemary Midwinter's wrecked front door and scrambled to the Crown Vic. Miraculously, its obstinate engine turned over on the first try, but its tires reeled. He threw it in reverse, then gunned it forward. The Crown Vic caught enough traction to pitch ahead.

By the time Bell had spun a slippery doughnut back toward town, the pickup was out of sight. When he hit the icy blacktop through Purgatory, he didn't have to guess which way the truck went. There was only one way out of town. Ten miles down the mountain, the driver would have a few more choices, but only one road ended in the perfect place to evaporate into thin air: Denver.

And that road ran through Midnight.

Bell's phone wasn't in the ashtray where he thought he'd left it so he wouldn't forget it. It was on the seat where he forgot he'd left it ... under him. After some awkward contortion, he liberated it and dialed with his beefy thumb.

SA Dani Silva answered immediately.

"This better be a social call, Bell," she said. "I'm still pissed and you're still a civilian."

"No time for small talk," he said. "I think our UnSub is heading toward Denver. Older model green Ford pickup. Colorado plates. Two occupants, likely an elderly woman and unknown male companion. Possibly armed. I'm in pursuit but they're way ahead of me."

"Are you shitting me? A civilian in a high-speed pursuit? You call this standing down?"

"Dani, I'm sure this is Rosemary Midwinter and her other son, possibly your guy Eddie," Bell told her. "If they get to the city, we'll never find them again."

"You have probable cause?"

"Road rage? Speeding? Failure to report tips? Surprise me. Anyway, that's your job. I'm only a civilian, remember?"

Silva shifted gears without a breath.

"Okay, Galligan is headed your way right now," she said. "Intercept or roadblock? Your call, Woodrow."

Bell already knew.

"Stationary roadblock at Midnight," he said. "They can't escape without driving straight up the side of a mountain. But you've got less than thirty minutes. Scramble the sheriff and the local PD, and call a guy named Ollie Fuhrman in Midnight about getting a big-ass bulldozer out there."

"Copy that," Silva responded, "I'll patch Galligan in on your phone. Conference call."

"Ain't gonna happen. Trust me," he grunted. "Just block the road."

They clicked off. Bell sped up a little, but the ice kept him realistic. He'd be irrelevant if he skidded off the road or crashed through a guardrail. But he was still so far behind the pickup that he couldn't see it on the twisting mountain road ahead.

He'd been watching for any signs that they'd hidden behind some trees on a secluded side road or among eighteen-wheelers in a chain-up area—or plunged off the mountainside themselves—but saw nothing. No, instinct told Bell that Rosemary Midwinter and Maybe Eddie were barreling off the mountain to slither down some Denver rat hole. He only hoped they'd never get past Midnight.

Then his phone rang. It was Silva again.

"While we were talking a few minutes ago," she said, "we confirmed that Eddie Midwinter is Rosemary's other son. White male, early fifties, DOB August 19, 1970. Busted in 1995 for the attempted abduction of a sixteen-year-old girl at knifepoint in Cheyenne. She escaped and he got eight years in the Wyoming pen. Paroled in '03. Last known address Purgatory, Colorado, where he apparently pissed on your toilet seat. It's a pretty good chance he's in that pickup."

It suddenly made sense. Father and son got out of prison at the same time, twenty-six years after dad's last killing. By then, dad's arthritis had crippled him, so his son took over the family business. Erskine introduced his demons to

Eddie like a father teaches his son how to catch a ball. Then daddy is suddenly gone, and son carries on his sick memory.

Two killers, one sadistic compulsion.

One left-handed, one right.

One then, one now.

But where does Rosemary fit? Bell couldn't answer that one. She'd given birth to two monsters and probably killed her own father, but what kept her close enough to Eddie to hide him in her own home? Motherly love?

"We'll sort this out after we grab Eddie," Bell said. "But first we have to grab Eddie. I gotta go."

"But ..."

Bell hung up before Silva could respond. He tossed his phone brusquely on the dashboard and accelerated. He didn't want or need the distraction as he skated across a dicey road in pursuit of a killer, maybe two.

He hadn't gone a half-mile when the phone rang again.

"Goddammit," he snapped. "What now?"

It wasn't Silva. It was a guy.

"Are you that big-ass cop?"

"Who's this?"

"I'm the guy who kicked your big ass out of the diner," the voice said. "Eddie Midwinter."

CHAPTER 11

BELL WAS DAZED.

"How'd you get this number?"

Eddie Midwinter sniggered.

"You gave it to me, dumbass. You wrote it on the back of my daddy's picture that you left on the table. Is your memory slipping there, gramps?"

"Nah, I remember you just fine," Bell said. "Little guy, big talker."

"Aw, c'mon," Eddie oozed. "I think if you got to know me, we could be friends. Maybe roommates."

"I don't think so, Eddie. I saw the way you kept house. You suck. But I gotta admit, the porn really matches your drapes."

"Yeah, I saw you sniffing around the trailer today," he said. "Sell it to you, cheap."

"No, thanks. I'm looking for a split-level with indoor plumbing. Why didn't you come in and say hi?"

"I called this number while you were in there, but you didn't answer. That wasn't friendly."

That was the call to the Crown Vic while he was in the trailer, Bell realized.

"I'm sorry I missed you, Eddie. But, hey, we've got time now. Why don't you pull over and we can chat? I'm only a couple minutes behind you. We can catch up."

That made Eddie snort.

"That'd be great, but Mom is about to wet the seat—if you know what I mean—and we're late for a big party. Maybe when you get down to Denver sometime, we can have dinner. What's your name again?"

"Woodrow Bell, Denver Homicide," he lied. "So, Eddie, is your mom there?"

"She can't talk right now, Woody. But don't worry, she's got something else in mind for you. A big surprise. So what do you want to talk about while I've got you on the phone?"

"Those girls. I went up to the asylum. I know what you did."

Eddie paused a long moment, but he didn't hang up.

"I can't take all the credit," he said. "My dad did some of them."

Bell flew past the abandoned Summit service station and roadside tourist stop at the top of the long, downhill grade into Midnight, now only twenty miles away. He doubted Galligan's roadblock would be ready, but he had to keep this killer on the line.

"Why did he do it, Eddie? Why did he kill those girls?"

"A bad childhood. Isn't it always a bad childhood?" Eddie jeered. "But in Dad's case, it was true. His mom—my grandma—made him do it. So Dad told me that he just wanted to see what it felt like to kill his mom."

"What did your grandma do to make him so crazy?"

"Oh, he wasn't crazy. He always said crazy wasn't enough," Eddie said, then turned somber, even angry. "She was raped and she got pregnant with my dad. The bitch hated him because he was devil spawn. She did things to him you wouldn't do to a rattlesnake She busted him up real bad. She did that fucked-up eye, you know. She hurt him every way she could without killing him so she could hurt him some more. Then she'd suck him and make him do her. She was a sick, sick bitch, way sicker than him."

"His own mother?"

"I didn't stutter, asshole," Eddie snarled. "My Nanna was a freaky pervert granny. Go figure. She fucked him up. Then she sent him off to that asylum and they fucked him up some more."

Bell's back tires hit a patch of ice and the Crown Vic slipped sideways, only enough to remind him to keep his eyes on the road while he navigated the dark labyrinths of Eddie Midwinter's back story.

"Think hard: Did you ever meet your grandmother face-to-face, Eddie?"

"Never did. Dad said she dumped him in the nuthouse and ran off with some guy a long time before I was born and disappeared for-fucking-ever. Then he met my mom and they lived happily ever after for a couple days. Just didn't work out. After he left, it was just me and her. You got a mom? Tell me about her. Tell me all the dirty stuff she did."

Bell couldn't completely ignore the taunt.

"Did Rosemary hurt you?"

"It was all my fault. Plus, she didn't know any different."

"How was it your fault, Eddie? What did you do that was so bad?"

"Mom said I was born with the devil in me," he said. "She'd been hoping I'd die since I was a child. I don't know why she didn't just drown me in the bathtub when she was giving me a bath because she hated me all her life. Hating things was her way."

"How did she hurt you? Physically? Mentally?"

"Everything. Maybe that's why I always had a desire to inflict pain on others and to have others inflict pain on me. I always seemed to enjoy everything that hurt."

"Then your father, Erskine, came back ..."

"After they let him out of prison, he rescued me," Eddie said. "I was a grown man in my thirties, but he showed me how to make it all better. That's when the fun started."

"How so?"

"He still wanted to kill granny, but she wasn't there, so he hunted other girls before they could hurt their little boys, like his mom did to him and my mom did to me. Like father, like son: I've hated humans for a long time. So I asked him to show me how to do it. He watched."

"But why these particular girls?"

"Do you like girls, Woody? My dad's demons wanted girls. Sugar and spice and everything nice," Eddie said. "We didn't want to hurt them, we only wanted to kill them."

"Why?"

"All of my victims—all of *our* victims—were criminals. They were only going to make more little boys so they could hurt them. You and me are the same, Woody. We kill criminals."

"We're not the same, Eddie," Bell insisted. "You need help."

"Okay, maybe I carried it too far," he said. "Maybe I chose the wrong career, killing girls. I should have gone to college and gone into real estate and got myself an aquarium, that's what I should have done."

"Why didn't you?"

"I loved the hunt, the challenge of what the thing was. I was good at it. The killing for me was secondary. I got no rise out of it ... well, for the most part. But the figuring it out, the challenge — the stalking and doing it right, successfully—that excited me a lot. The greater the odds against me, the more juice I got out of it."

"I don't get how a human can do that stuff. I've seen a lot, but nothing like you did."

"Thank you, dawg, that's very kind of you to say," Eddie said. "It's not hard. You learn what you need to kill and take care of the details. It's like changing a tire. The first time you're careful. By the thirtieth time, you can't remember where you left the lug wrench. I killed so many women I have a hard time keeping them straight."

"Thirty? Jesus, how many are there, Eddie?"

"After the first five, a gentleman doesn't count," Eddie said. "I will tell you that once I engaged, I was engaged. It was like a videogame. It was like I was trapped inside of me. Hell, you've been there, Woody, you know what I am talking about."

"You're a psychopath, Eddie. That's what I know."

"Not fair, dawg! Us psychopaths have feelings, too."

"That's bullshit and you know it," Bell growled. "You're empty."

"Okay, just kidding. But it wasn't all as dark and scary as it sounds. I had a lot of fun… killing somebody's a fun experience. It's like Disneyland without the crowds."

"What you did wasn't playing around in Disneyland."

"For fuck's sake, Woody, I don't play with bodies. This isn't 'Criminal Minds.' Me and Dad couldn't kill our real mothers—that's just sick, right?—but we could fantasize about it. I was carrying out fantasies with those girls, but we weren't playing with them."

"No, they never had a chance," Bell said, trying to keep his tone flat although he boiled inside and wanted to scream. "You assassinated them."

"Assassin? That sounds so exotic. I was just a murderer."

"You are so casual about slaughtering these poor girls. I just can't wrap my head around that, Eddie."

"Think of it this way: When you see a pretty girl walking down the street, what goes through your head? Do you get a little stiffie?" Eddie asked. "When I see a pretty girl walking down the street, I think two things: one part of me wants to take her home, be real nice and treat her right. The other part wonders what her head would look like on a stick."

The county road at Mile Marker 195 meandered ever-upward to the trailhead at Quandary Peak, one of Colorado's soaring "Fourteeners." Bell knew the main exit to Midnight was at Mile Marker 183—only twelve miles ahead. Galligan—no, all of them—had only ten more minutes at best.

"Tell me about the sadistic shit. Why did you do those things, Eddie?"

"Dear ol' Dad taught me everything I know," Eddie said.

"The cleanser?"

"He scrubbed them clean because they were dirty girls, like granny scrubbed him raw with bleach and steel wool."

"Their eyes?"

"He sewed their eyes shut because granny said she couldn't look at him because he was a monster who made her puke."

"Those spike in the brain? Jesus Christ ..."

"Daddy hammered spikes in their ears because granny refused to listen to him scream."

Bell still couldn't wrap his mind around the Midwinters' madness.

"But why butcher them, Eddie? Why open them up and take ..."

"The heart? Well, every man wants to steal a girl's heart, am I right?"

"For Christ's sake, you did it while they were alive!"

"That was the best part," Eddie said. "You feel the last bit of breath leaving their body. I was ... God."

"Why did you always snatch them on a Tuesday?"

"Dad told me that Tuesday was the day in the nuthouse when they lined up all the loonies for electroshock," Eddie said. "So Tuesdays just became one of those heartwarming family traditions."

"And why before nights when there'd be no moon?"

"We could be invisible, and they couldn't run away. Maybe you don't know, but Dad and me both went to prison because of girls who ran away. So we fixed that. Like Dad always said, 'Live and learn!'"

"So why did you call me, Eddie? Why are you telling me all this?"

"Because I like you, Woody. And because people need to know how good I am. I'm tired of working so hard and not getting credit. You know I never got my name in the papers? Now maybe I will. Dad would be proud that I made something of myself."

"The reporters will want proof. How do I know you're telling me the truth?"

"I have a box right here with me," he said. "It has ... mementoes. I'll let you see it someday. But you can tell the papers that last hottie, Connie, had a sweet little butterfly near her cootchie. They can check."

Bell already knew he had the right guy. Now everybody else could be sure, too.

"This is all so fascinating, Eddie, and I have so many questions. What do you say we pull over and just talk?"

"Nah, I got places to go, and girls to do. You call the papers and tell 'em all about your buddy Eddie Midwinter. Tell 'em I'm smarter and badder than that pussy Bundy. Anyway, I shouldn't be driving and talking on the phone to a cop who's driving and talking on the phone to a serial killer. You gonna give us both a ticket, Woody?"

"Oh, I forgot to tell you something, Eddie."

"Yeah?"

"Your dad fucked his own mom," Bell said. "And you popped out."

"What the ...? Nanna?"

"No. Your Nanna died before she ever knew Erskine or Rosemary. She had no part of this. This is where it gets unnatural, Eddie: Your grandpa raped Rosemary—his own daughter, for God's sake—and Erskine popped out. Then Erskine got out of the asylum and he screwed Rosemary, too, and you popped out. So your dad is really your brother and your uncle, and everybody screwed your mom. Your damn family tree is a telephone pole, buddy. No branches. You're an inbred mutant. That's what I'll tell the papers."

"You're a lying asshole. Cops lie."

"I'm not lying," Bell said. "But your dad did. Yes, his mom beat the holy shit out of him like your mom beat the shit out of you, too. He never told you they were the same person. So here's the truth: You both had the same mom. You both hated the same woman. Every time you killed one of those girls, you were both killing Rosemary."

A long silence.

"I know what you're doing. You're trying to mess with my head."

"Why would I do that, Eddie? You've already told me everything, right?"

"You cop maggots make me sick," he said. "The devil is inside us all. You, too. You act like you've got angels in you but really you've just got your own devils."

The road sign said "Midnight, 6 miles." Bell tried again, maybe his last chance.

"You're absolutely right. I've got demons, you've got demons, we've all got demons. We can get those demons out of you. I know just the guy. So let's end this. Just pull over. You and Rosemary can walk away alive. But you need to pull off the road before somebody dies."

"Big deal. Death comes with the territory," Eddie said. "See you in Disneyland."

And just like that, they were done talking.

Eddie Midwinter hung up less than two minutes from Midnight.

BELL COULD SEE the flashing lights of Galligan's CBI roadblock from a mile away, long before he saw Eddie's pickup anywhere ahead of him. He'd expected a few cruisers to raise a blockade that looked more formidable than it really was, like propping corpses in the parapets. But this one easily spanned two lanes of traffic, barrow pit to barrow pit, in a high-intensity, super-bright fusillade of red, blue, white, and yellow.

Yellow? That wasn't right. Bell knew cop cars didn't have yellow lights.

As he drew closer, Bell saw only empty highway, no sign of Eddie. He couldn't have dodged the roadblock, he couldn't possibly have gotten around Bell, who saw no sign of him leaving the highway, and he certainly didn't evaporate into nothingness. Not forward, not back, not sideways, not into the sky.

Bell pounded his steering wheel in frustration and anger. This freak of nature had eluded notice for almost twenty years. Nobody even knew he existed. Now that Bell and Galligan had him bottled up ... he slipped away again, like a shadow into another shadow. Like Bundy.

Then the veil of Bell's rage fell away as he neared the roadblock. For a second he wasn't sure what he saw.

Not Eddie's pickup, but the wall of vehicles barring the way. A few police cruisers, their lights flaring, stared him down. But smack on the center line sat one of Ollie Fuhrman's fifty-ton bulldozers, its yellow warning lights rotating steadfastly. On either side, impeding nearly the whole strip of asphalt, were Midnight's lone snowplow and one of Charlie's garbage trucks. The rest of the roadway was dammed up by a school bus (and its driver's polite red "Stop" sign), the MFD's antique fire engine, and a half dozen other civilian cars Bell recognized immediately: All of Deaf Row had joined the blockade in their personal vehicles, from Roxy Snipes's twenty-year-old Toyota to Father Bert's godless Bronco—and all were flickering their bright beams off and on grandly.

And Special Agent Pete Galligan stood resolutely in front of them, but not to intercept Eddie Midwinter. He looked straight at Bell and pointed across the median, into the muddy barrow pit, through the Highway Department's delicate fence, into Midnight. Eddie had skirted the whole motley obstruction by going off-road.

Eddie and Rosemary couldn't hide in Midnight, not with the decade's biggest commotion—since Midnight last had a winning football team—happening on the highway.

They couldn't double back to the highway in either direction. There was only one escape: Straight up the side of a mountain.

O'MyGawd Road.

Bell's prey drive exceeded his survival instinct. He wheeled hard left and gunned the Crown Vic across the median. Down one steep side of the ditch and up the other, the undercarriage scraped so forcefully across the rocks that Bell was sure he'd mortally wounded his car, but he couldn't stop now.

O'MyGawd Road started off placidly enough at the far edge of town. The two-lane pavement ended at the edge of town and became a wide, graveled roadway up a gentle slope through some trees. But around the first bend, it turned mean.

Bell saw Eddie's tire tracks in the snow because nobody else was stupid enough to defy O'MyGawd in winter. The Crown Vic's back tires spun a little as Bell pushed her up the first rise, and he hoped she could stay on the road long enough to catch Eddie Midwinter. Bell cinched his seatbelt tighter, although it probably wouldn't save him. If the Crown Vic couldn't hold the road, there was a good chance he'd plunge down a glacial canyon and die in a spectacular mess. On the other hand, if Eddie survived, he'd warm up in Bitter Creek and disappear, maybe forever.

Bell caught a glimpse of Eddie's truck on the switchbacks a quarter-mile above, but he seemed to be moving faster than Bell, who couldn't make the Crown Vic go any faster. The grade grew steeper, and every time Bell cursed it, the car struggled more and more.

As snow began to fall, he pushed the accelerator harder. The engine pushed back. The defiant heater conked. The sharp fumes of burning oil flooded the car, but he browbeat her relentlessly higher.

Then, almost the same moment Bell smelled the engine heating up, the needle on his oil-pressure gauge dropped through the floorboards. The Crown Vic was bleeding out. Bell knew he must have peeled off the oil pan when he bounced across the median ditch.

But he couldn't stop. His hemorrhaging car wouldn't run much longer. When its life blood all leaked away, the Crown Vic would simply seize up. Bell feared being stranded on an icy mountain track where mountain goats wouldn't willingly go, but he'd chase Eddie Midwinter til the end, on foot if he had to.

And he'd have to.

The Crown Vic death-rattled, coughed once, then lapsed into a coma in the middle of the O'MyGawd Road. There wasn't time to mourn. Bell had lost sight of Eddie's pickup.

Cold, gray clouds shrouded the surrounding peaks and were lowering. The sun had vanished yesterday, and snow came down harder now. It wouldn't be long, at this elevation, before wind, snow, and clouds turned everything so painful and white that Bell wouldn't be able to stand without wobbling nor open his eyes without wincing. This place would be a colorless Hell in the frozen sky. In the coming white-out, Bell would go numb. His breath would freeze solid, and he'd fall asleep forever as a human-shaped block of ice, even if he stayed inside his coffin-cold Crown Vic.

Bell had one chance for a warmer death: Call for help. He reached for his phone on the passenger seat, but it wasn't there. He shoved his big hand between the seats. Not there. He searched the floormats. Not there either. It wasn't on the dash, in the armrest or ashtray, between his legs, or in any of his dozen coat pockets. He got out of the car and walked around to the other side of the car, where he found his phone lodged between the seat and the door. In his mind, he asked himself *why does finding phones have to be so hard?* Out loud, he just said "Shit."

He shook off his woolen gloves so he could punch those impossibly dinky keys with a shivering finger. But before he could dial, the phone rang.

"This is Bell," he answered.

"Gee, I thought we were friends," Eddie said. "Do you think you could have mentioned your friends were waiting to kill me?"

"Maybe you're right, Eddie," he said. "I'm getting forgetful. My bad."

"I didn't expect to run into you up here in Disneyland, Woody. I guess it's a small world after all."

"I wouldn't miss a chance for some quality time with you, Eddie."

"Having car trouble, dawg? I saw some pretty gnarly black smoke back there."

"Nah. Just stretching my legs. We've been driving a lot today, without any stops. Maybe Rosemary needs a break. You oughta pull over and let her pee."

Eddie was having none of that.

"Oh, she's fine," he said. "We had a little problem back there on the highway and she got my seats all wet. But we're all good now, right, Mom? Thanks for caring, Woody. No matter what they say about you, you're a good guy when you're not being a cop."

"I'm always gonna be a cop, Eddie, and you're always gonna be a bad guy. So I'm always gonna be chasing you."

The wind blasted snow against Bell's face. He opened his door to seek shelter in his car when Eddie's disembodied voice stopped him.

"Hey, Woody," he said. "Look up."

Half snow-blind with no place to hide, Bell squinted through the veil of gusting snow, up the slowly drifting O'MyGawd Road, to a sharp turn in the road fifty yards up the mountain. There sat Eddie Midwinter's old green Ford pickup, pointed back downhill. Toward Bell.

"Good to see you," Bell said. "What do we do now?"

Eddie turned deadly serious.

"You're stuck, old man. Can't go up, can't go down. Your crappy fucking car is dead ..."

"Bullshit, Eddie," Bell bluffed.

"Then why no exhaust, boss? What idiot shuts off his car up here in the middle of the road during a goddamned snowstorm? Your car is dead, and you're dead. And none of your buddies has the balls to come up here and find your fat ass til next summer."

"Are you sure about that?"

"I'm sure about this: Mom's a good shot. One stupid move and you're dead. Take your gun out and show it to me. Now!"

Bell pulled the old .45 out of his coat pocket and held it up.

"Throw it over the cliff," Eddie commanded.

Bell heaved the pistol into the cold abyss but never took his eye off Eddie's truck.

"Now walk towards me, you fat fuck. Keep that one hand where I can see it."

The wind-chill deadened both of Bell's ungloved hands, one holding the phone and one out to his side as he shuffled through the falling snow. It was deep enough that he couldn't clearly see where the road ended, and a long fall began.

"I'm freezing, Eddie," he said. "Can I button my coat?"

"What's the point, boss? You're gonna be dead and cold soon enough anyway."

"You don't want me to die of hypothermia before you can kill me, do you? Don't you want to feel the last bit of breath leaving my body? Don't you want to look into my eyes and be God?"

Bell knew he'd pushed the right button when Eddie paused ever so slightly.

"That's an offer I can't refuse, Woody. Button up, sweetie pie, or you'll catch a cold."

While Eddie laughed at his own dark wit, Bell stopped. He pretended to fuss with his buttons while he slipped his hand under his coat to unsnap the Magnum's holster. He raised the phone back to his ear.

"Okay, Eddie, how's this gonna go?"

"Just shut up and keep walking," the killer said. "Mom wants to say goodbye."

Bell slogged up the grade toward Eddie's pickup. The falling snow and the truck's wipers made it hard to see inside, but there were obviously two people watching him. By the time he came close enough to smell the truck's exhaust and make out their faces, Eddie ordered him to stop.

"What now, Eddie?"

Eddie reached across Rosemary and opened her door.

"Say goodbye to Mom," he said.

Eddie shoved Rosemary Midwinter's gaunt, naked body out. She flopped into the snow like a pile of pale kindling, not moving. She was dead. Not just dead, but violated in awful and all-too-familiar ways. A hunting knife protruded from her skull and her torso was hacked open. Bell couldn't see anything but blackened gore on her face—and everywhere else—but he presumed without seeing that her eyelids were sewn shut, too.

"My God, Eddie."

"Please don't judge me, Woody," he said. "Our relationship was ... complicated."

"You're sicker than I thought. Why did this happen?"

Eddie explained as if it all made perfect sense.

"The last thing I wanted to do was hurt Mom, but it was always on my list," he said. "When I was a kid and I couldn't fight back, she damaged me. So when she was old and couldn't fight back, it just seemed like the right thing to do to repay her for all her love and devotion. I just couldn't find a Hallmark card that said everything I felt."

"Why now?"

"You. Life was good until you came snooping around, boss. Then she was the weak link. She woulda spoiled everything if I wasn't just inside the door that day you came to the trailer. So I put her down. The day you came back to the diner? She was hanging in the cooler til I could fix her up real nice for her funeral up there at the nuthouse, but you screwed that up, too. So it's all your fault, Woody."

"Not my fault at all, Eddie. This is all on you."

"Let's agree to disagree," the killer said. "Back there on the road? When you told me about my dad and my mom— or my brother or whatever the fuck—I gotta admit it pissed me off. So I kinda killed her again, just to clear my head. Or clear *her* head."

Eddie laughed like the madman he was.

"If you and your demons wanted to keep your secrets," Bell asked, "why are you telling me all this shit now?"

"Oh, Woody. I told you everything *you* know, but I didn't tell you everything *I* know. That's some other cop's problem now, because you're gonna be dead in a—"

The phone died first.

"Eddie, you there? You there?" Bell repeated, looking straight at the killer's shadow through the pickup's windshield. The silhouette shrugged.

Eddie Midwinter stepped out of his truck and leveled a revolver at Bell. Not big and not this particular serial killer's weapon of choice, but any veteran cop knew it'd do the job. At the same time, Bell dropped his useless phone in the snow and hunkered deeper for warmth before dying. Eddie couldn't have seen that under his coat, Bell wrapped one hand around the Magnum's grip and cocked the hammer.

"If you're gonna shoot me, Eddie, don't miss. It hurts like hell to linger."

"Shut up," he said. "That's the mistake the movie bad guys make every time: They talk too much before they kill the good guy. So ..."

Eddie raised his pistol just as Bell hauled out the Magnum. He fired at Eddie as he was trained to do, dead-center.

But he missed.

Eddie had a clear shot at a big target, but he wasn't fast enough. His head literally exploded when Bell's stray bullet hit him in the face. His mostly headless body dropped straight to the ground and pumped a few gushers of blood out of his wrecked neck into the snow before Bell's cannon-like shot had stopped echoing.

EDDIE MIDWINTER WAS dead.

Rosemary was dead.

Worse, the Crown Vic was dead.

Bell was stuck alone, shivering, with a dead phone in a snowstorm on a perilous road halfway up a godforsaken mountain ... with two unhelpful corpses he couldn't simply leave for the coyotes.

He briefly considered hijacking Eddie's still-running pickup, but the Crown Vic completely blocked the precarious O'MyGawd Road going down; snow and ice blocked it going up. The gory Ford might provide temporary shelter, but it wouldn't keep him alive until spring made the O'MyGawd passable again.

Dead Eddie, slaughterer of untold numbers of teenage girls and a pitiless mother-butcher, came to Bell's rescue. He had left his blood-spattered cellphone on the driver's seat.

"I owe you one, Eddie," Bell mumbled as he wiped the phone across his pantleg.

But under the best conditions, the fumbled-fingered old cop wasn't good with his own phone. Bitter cold and a stranger's phone upped the degree of difficulty. He remembered nobody's number, but he remembered where he kept one. He fished a business card from his wallet and dialed a Denver number, 303-555-8799.

"Jackson."

"It's me, Jazz, It's Woodrow."

"This isn't your number. You're lucky I picked up. Hey, I hear you got fired."

"Fake news," Bell said. "But right now I need backup, big time."

In one long, run-on burst, he explained his predicament and begged Jazz to send help. But even before she could scramble the cavalry, Bell saw a single circling yellow light plowing sluggishly up O'MyGawd.

It was Ollie Fuhrman's damned bulldozer, speeding along at a mile an hour. A half-dozen snowmobiles followed, and a familiar old Bronco brought up the rear.

Standing there in the cold, it wasn't the rescue party that made him smile, nor even the pleasant thought of holding Charlie close again. It wasn't that this desperate case was finally closed. It wasn't his urge to call Sarah to tell her he loved her very much. And it wasn't that he now had at least one more night of dreaming, even though he didn't put much stock in dreams. Yes, those things were all better than good.

But at the moment he smiled because his closest friend was coming for him, and he knew the priest always hid a pint of Jameson, a good Irish Catholic whiskey, under his front seat.

CHAPTER 12

EPILOGUE

WOODROW BELL CHECKED his watch, although he had no place to be. Nursing homes always made him feel time was racing.

The big man paused at the front door to the Old Miners Home. Most days, this place haunted him, but today wasn't one of those days. The Sunday morning sun was rising above the mountains, warming everything. He knew he might soon come to stay at the Home much longer, although on this morning of all mornings, it no longer felt imminent.

Charlie stayed with him that night. In the dark, they talked for a long time about a vague future and how time was growing short and about how they needed each other. The word "love" never came up, but it felt to Bell that Charlie had something important to tell him. All night he reached out to touch her, to be sure she was still there, or maybe to make sure *he* was still *here*. If he dreamed, it was mostly about her always being there.

But he'd definitely dreamed little fragments about this particular morning for a long time. Not simple dreams, really, but he put no special stock in dreams anyway.

Luther Nelson sat, as he did on most mornings, snow or shine, at the big window that looked down on Sunrise Street, the narrow alley that ran past the east end of the two-story brick building. His Alzheimer's transported him to a past that was too painful but stopped short of a present that made sense. Bell knew at least one incomplete memory survived inside Luther someplace, and that's why he came.

Beside him was George Tomer, who was sometimes an old friend and sometimes new. Only Luther knew which, and George never said otherwise because as long as he was a friend, new or old, Luther had one. Life was good.

"Good morning, you old farts," Bell said as he drew up a folding chair beside them. "Beautiful day, huh?"

Luther smiled big. George wiggled one finger.

"You need to stay out of the sun," Luther advised Bell. "You're not aging well."

"Copy that," is all he said.

"I was telling the mayor about all the excitement yesterday," Luther then announced loud enough for all to hear. "It was something."

Bell wasn't surprised the news about the incident on O'MyGawd Road had traveled so fast. Midnight was still a small town.

"Do tell," Bell said.

"I broke my leg off, but it grew back, thank God. Are you a doctor? I don't know you. I'm Luther Nelson, but you can call me Luther Nelson."

Bell held out his hand.

"Happy to meet you, Luther Nelson. Hey, I have something to tell you. Can we go to your room?"

"No funny business," he warned.

"No funny business," Bell promised.

He helped Luther from his chair and held the old man's elbow all the way back to the long hallway where he lived. He was even more fragile than the last time. Bell's timing wasn't perfect, but it was none too soon. It wouldn't be long before it didn't matter anymore.

Bell closed the door behind them. They talked for a long time about Luther's late wife Daisy and their daughter Cherish. They reminisced about her music, her eyes, and the way she laughed, until Luther pictured her alive again. And when Bell believed Luther was safely back in those days, he described—in the gentlest way he could—how Cherish had gone away, why it happened, and who did it.

In the end, Luther Nelson finally knew what happened to his sweet girl.

Bell wished only one more thing: That in the next moment, Luther would forget it all.

FATHER BERT WAITED on the sidewalk outside the Old Miner's Home. Not for Bell, but for some whisper from God. The old priest, by virtue of his retirement and devotion to the home's purpose, conducted Sunday morning services for the patients. He didn't always know what he'd say, but he always knew how he felt.

"Good morning, padre," Bell greeted him, with more exuberance than his usual grunt.

Father Bert stepped up and hugged Bell tighter than he ever had. Actually, he never had. For a priest, he wasn't much of a hugger, and neither was Bell.

"Are you doing okay?"

"Maybe a little frostbite, and I'm probably gonna need a new car," he said. "But the sun came up and my obituary wasn't in the paper, so it's all good."

"You know, they teach you in priest school to accept that every morning is a gift from God," he said. "But after yesterday, I'm a believer. It only took fifty years. Don't tell the Archbishop."

"Our secret."

"Did you tell Nellie about everything?"

Bell nodded solemnly.

"And ...?"

"I spoke the words and he seemed to hear. I don't know if it meant anything today, or if it will matter tomorrow. But I spoke the words."

"It mattered to you because it mattered to me because it mattered to him," Father Bert said. "We count."

"I called Joe Harper last night," Bell said. "His daughter didn't want to wake him, but she said she'd tell him this morning. He'll be happy. It was always his case."

"Well, he can close the case now," Father Bert said. "He had a good partner, Woodrow."

"Yeah, well ... maybe me and Lucille will go up to Bitter Creek when the snow melts," Bell said. "Maybe I'll just sit with him a while."

"Bless you," Father Bert said. He knew what it would mean to both his friend and to the haunted old detective.

"Somebody should tell George, too," Bell continued. "Somebody like you."

"I did. Last night. He wept. It's heartbreaking that his ruined body will allow him to cry, but it won't allow him to laugh. Once, before he lost the ability to talk, he told me that he loved to sleep, because in his sleep, he could dance again. So last night, after I told him how he'd helped you, I sat with him until he went to sleep. I'm sure he danced."

"I'm sure he did."

"I'm thinking I should bring him to Deaf Row tomorrow. It'd be good for him to get out. Maybe he'd like to see the guys ..."

"That'd be good for all of us."

They said nothing for a moment, then Bell spoke.

"About yesterday ... "

"Hey, don't," Father Bert said. "You would have done the same for me."

"What?" Bell acted befuddled.

"What?"

"About yesterday," he said, "I think I left my gloves in your car. Did you find them?"

The priest clenched his jaw.

"You can be a prick, you know?"

Bell just smiled.

"Can a priest say 'prick'?"

ON MONDAY MORNING, Bell arrived late at Deaf Row, as usual.

The old guys' eyes brightened as he stomped through the door, knocking the snow off his boots. Father Bert angled George Tomer's wheelchair into a space between Roxy Snipes and Elroy Richter, who was telling a stupid story about a dyslexic man who walked into a bra. And Fancy circled with a full pot, touching them all as she passed.

"Hey there, Bullitt," Cotton Minahan hooted at Bell. "Me and the boys got you a little something for your next joyride."

Amid an eruption of laughter, he slid a quart of Pennzoil across the table.

Even Bell laughed, but he secretly warned himself to not make a habit of it.

And the morning began, as it did most days, with a blessing. After he'd settled into his usual chair beside Bell, Father Bert crossed himself and bowed his head:

"God, thank you for reminding us that everything good gets old. Amen."

—

AUTHOR'S NOTE

*"No one can tell what goes on in between the
person you were and the person you become.
There are no maps of the change. You just…
come out on the other side. Or you don't."*
—**Stephen King**

I**VAN** D**OIG,** **A** late novelist I greatly admire, once told me
that characters such as these "have lived only in the world of
this book." He's right, of course, but they are made real by
people who live in this world. The fellas of Deaf Row came
to life in the blink of an eye when my friend, writer Gordon
Ross, first told me about his coffee club, a handful of old
men who met most mornings in a small-town diner to solve
the problems of the world. That little remark blossomed
into the story you hold right now. Others helped me breathe
life into these characters: Gary Berchenbreiter, Kenyon
Blower, Rowena Carenen, Don Carlson, Dr. Vincent Di
Maio, Shari Freyer, my secret curator Leigh Hanlon, Gary
Hazen, Kimberley Howe, Linda Konner, Patricia Law, Clair
McFarland, David Mittelman, Steve Woodson, and Rev.
Father Stephen Ziton. And forever and always, I am deeply
grateful to my wife Mary, who believes.

And finally, I'd like to thank all the homicidal maniacs
out there who generously contributed to this story. They not
only shared pieces of themselves with the unholy Midwinter
family, but they loaned me their words, too. The Chapter
11 on-the-road dialogue between Woodrow Bell and Eddie

Midwinter largely incorporates verbatim lines from real remarks and writings of modern American serial killers.

Monsters are real.

—**Ron Franscell**
Placitas, New Mexico

ABOUT THE AUTHOR

RON FRANSCELL IS a lifelong journalist and the acclaimed author of 19 fiction and nonfiction books. His most recent is "ShadowMan: An Elusive Psycho Killer and the Birth of FBI Profiling" (2022, Berkley). His atmospheric true-crime "The Darkest Night" is a bestselling account of a crime against two childhood friends that rocked his small hometown. The *San Francisco Chronicle* listed his literary fiction "Angel Fire" among its 100 Best Novels of the 20th Century West. His two earlier mysteries, "The Deadline" and "The Obituary" are WildBlue Press titles. He and his wife live in Placitas, New Mexico.

See more at *www.ronfranscell.com*

OTHER BOOKS BY RON FRANSCELL

Nonfiction

SHADOWMAN: *AN ELUSIVE PSYCHO KILLER
AND THE BIRTH OF FBI PROFILING* (2022)
ALICE & GERALD: *A HOMICIDAL LOVE STORY* (2019)
MORGUE: *A LIFE IN DEATH* (with
Dr. Vincent Di Maio in 2016)
NIGHTMARE AT NOON (2015)
EVIL AT THE FRONT DOOR (2014)
THE SOURTOE COCKTAIL CLUB (2012)
DELIVERED FROM EVIL (2011)
THE DARKEST NIGHT (2008)

Fiction

THE OBITUARY (2003)
THE DEADLINE (1999)
ANGEL FIRE (1998)

Crime Buff's Guides

Crime Buff's Guide to Outlaw Los Angeles (2017)
Crime Buff's Guide to the Outlaw Southwest (2015)
Crime Buff's Guide to Outlaw New Mexico (2015)
Crime Buff's Guide to Outlaw Arizona (2015)
Crime Buff's Guide to Outlaw Pennsylvania (2013)
Crime Buff's Guide to Outlaw Washington DC (2012)
Crime Buff's Guide to the Outlaw Rockies (2011)
Crime Buff's Guide to Outlaw Texas (2010)

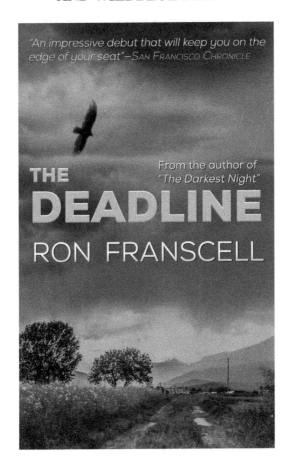

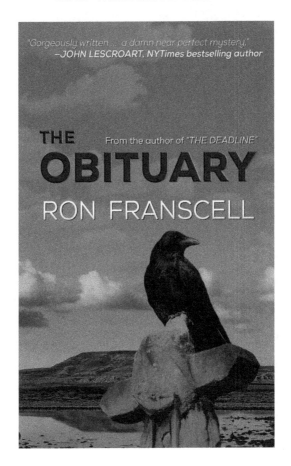

CPSIA information can be obtained
at www.ICGtesting.com
Printed in the USA
LVHW081248250123
737859LV00005B/135